Praise for Fi

'A gorgeous book about seco
from the darkness and back
with love and overflowing
Milly Joh

'A poignant and emotional story about loss, grief,
and the beautiful dawn of a second chance of love,
life and happiness. Bittersweet but full of hope'
Judy Finnigan

'A poignant and uplifting read about loss, love and learning to
put yourself back together again after facing the unimaginable'
Sophie Cousens

'A poignant but hopeful journey through grief and the
struggle to let go of those we have loved and lost'
Sunday Post

'A beautiful story'
Bella

'A beautiful story about learning to live and love again. Took me
from heartache to hope, and left me smiling through my tears'
Zara Stoneley

'A beautifully written story of love, loss and hope. I adored it'
Emma Cooper

'Full of heart and tenderness, Anna and Brody
carried me with them every step of their journey
– a truly outstanding book to lift you up'
Jane Linfoot

'Beautifully told and full of hope, this love
story will touch your heart'
Helen Rolfe

Fiona Lucas is an award-winning author of contemporary women's fiction. She has written heart-warming love stories and feel-good women's fiction as Fiona Harper for more than a decade. During her career, she's won numerous awards, including a Romantic Novel Award in 2018, and chalked up a no. 1 Kindle bestseller. Fiona lives in London with her husband and two daughters.

Writing as Fiona Lucas:
The Last Goodbye

Writing as Fiona Harper:
The Memory Collector
The Other Us
The Summer We Danced
The Doris Day Vintage Film Club
The Little Shops of Hopes and Dreams
Make My Wish Come True
Kiss Me Under the Mistletoe

Never Forget You

FIONA LUCAS

ONE PLACE. MANY STORIES

HQ
An imprint of HarperCollins*Publishers* Ltd
1 London Bridge Street
London SE1 9GF

www.harpercollins.co.uk

HarperCollinsPublishers
Macken House, 39/40 Mayor Street Upper,
Dublin1, D01 C9W8, Ireland

This edition 2023

1
First published in Great Britain by
HQ, an imprint of HarperCollins*Publishers* Ltd 2022

Copyright © Fiona Lucas 2022

Fiona Lucas asserts the moral right to be
identified as the author of this work.
A catalogue record for this book is
available from the British Library.

ISBN: 978-0-00-857012-5

MIX
Paper from
responsible sources
FSC™ C007454

This book is produced from independently certified FSC™ paper
to ensure responsible forest management.

For more information visit: www.harpercollins.co.uk/green

This book is set in 10.8/15.5 pt. Sabon

Printed and Bound in the UK using 100% Renewable Electricity at
CPI Group (UK) Ltd, Croydon, CR0 4YY

For Norina Coupar
(1947–2019)

PART I

5 years ago . . .

CHAPTER ONE

YOU CAN'T RUN away from your problems, Lili . . .

The voice of reason, which sounded suspiciously like my sister's, echoed in my head as I walked briskly down a quiet London street. *I'm not running away,* I replied silently and very reasonably. *I'm taking time to think. It's a healthy, productive thing to do.*

And, given the circumstances of my life, a very sensible one. I had a big decision to make, one that might change the course my life had been on since the age of eight. I hadn't been able to think properly inside the house – too many eyes, too many expectations – so I'd come to the one place in the city where I knew I would find not only solitude but clarity.

Office buildings of different ages towered over me as I hurried down a narrow cobbled street. I passed the silent doorways, shut against the heat, and ducked through a wrought-iron gate into the grounds of what had once been a church.

The tower remained, as did three of the walls, but the roof and any stained glass had been lost generations earlier, thanks to a bomb blast in the Blitz. Where rubble and dust had once been was now a beautiful garden. Ivy wound around the delicate tracery at the tops of the empty windows. Fragrant shrubs perfumed the air.

It was mid-July and, thanks to a week-long heatwave, unbearably hot in the city centre. Even though it was only mid-morning, the pavements were beginning to bake and the air shimmered with exhaust fumes. But here . . . Here it was cool and shady, the noise of the traffic muffled. It was like slipping into another world. And, in this world, I could let everything slide away and be myself, no one looking, no one judging. That, in itself, was more delicious than the gentle breeze playing with the hem of my summer dress.

I followed the path through a small porch into what would have been the nave of the church. Benches were arranged around a fountain made from a large, flat stone set into the paving stones. I slipped one sandal off and extended my foot, relishing the shock of the cold water as it hit my skin and trickled down over my toes.

I kicked my other sandal off and walked a short way to sink both feet into the soft, springy grass near one of the high, arching windows. There were flowers up there amongst the ivy, possibly clematis or jasmine, but they were hidden too well by the vigorous climbers to tell which. I stepped a foot onto a warm patch of earth at the edge of the flower bed in an attempt to get a better view and reached for the branch of a nearby shrub to steady myself. However, before my fingers even locked around it, my hand jumped back, an almost electrical pain shooting up my finger and along my arm. 'Ow!' I said loudly and stumbled back onto the grass, clutching my throbbing finger.

'Are you okay?'

I almost jumped out of my skin for the second time, as I turned to see a rather tall man running towards me. 'Um . . .' was all my adrenaline-riddled brain would allow me to say, then I waved my hand in his general direction. 'Bee . . .'

His gaze was momentarily caught by the rather large black-and-yellow insect zig-zagging away from the bush I'd been reaching into. 'You've been stung?' he asked in a curling Scottish accent.

I nodded.

'Don't worry,' he said. 'I've got you.'

For a moment, I thought he was going to go all Indiana Jones and suck the poison out of my finger. I was almost disappointed when he dashed off across the grass to where a fancy-looking tripod and camera stood, rummaged in his backpack, and returned with a small plastic case.

'It only works if you get to it quickly,' he said, nodding at me to hold my hand out while he unpacked the contents and assembled what looked like a fat syringe with a little clear plastic cup on the end instead of a needle. He took my hand, placed the device over where I indicated the sting was, and pulled the plunger. The suction caused the skin to balloon into a little dome and, magically, a little bead of what I assumed to be venom appeared on the surface. I watched wide-eyed as he released the device and wiped the evidence of the bee attack away with an antiseptic wipe. 'There . . . It might still throb a bit, but it won't be nearly as bad as if it had stayed in there.'

'Th-thank you.'

'You're welcome.' He smiled at me, and I had another pulse-spiking adrenaline surge.

'Do you think it's going to die?'

He stopped smiling and looked confused.

'Bees die after they sting something, don't they?' Now it had occurred to me, I was quite upset about that. After all, it had hardly been the bee's fault I'd lumbered into its nectar-gathering session.

He glanced in the direction of where we'd last seen it. 'I'm pretty sure it was a wasp, so I think you're okay on that front. No bee murdering going on today.' There was a lovely roll of the 'r' when he said 'murder'. His expression grew more serious. 'But what about you? You're not allergic to bees . . . I mean, wasps . . . are you?'

He began turning my hand around to view my finger from different angles, checking for swelling, and oxygen no longer seemed to be reaching the bottom of my lungs as efficiently as it had done a few minutes earlier. Maybe I *was* allergic?

'I don't know,' I said, managing to string a coherent sentence together, despite the soft brush of his skin against mine. 'I don't think so. But people develop weird allergies out of the blue sometimes, don't they? My aunt ate shellfish with no trouble her whole life until she turned twenty-nine, and then – *Bam!* – one butterfly king prawn and they had to call an ambulance. She's needed to carry an EpiPen ever since.'

Why was I telling him this? And why wasn't he letting go of my hand?

'Are you okay?' he asked again, leaning in and looking into my eyes.

He was much taller than me, even though I was a pretty average height, but not burly – the sort of boy who would have been a rangy youth but had filled out a bit now he was a man. I guessed he was maybe a year or two older than me, and he had slightly shaggy dark hair with just a hint of red where the sun hit it, and the most ridiculously thick lashes. He wasn't what some people would consider traditionally good-looking, but there was a strength to his features and a warmth in his brown eyes that was very appealing.

'Yes . . . I think I'm okay,' I said.

His smile widened and he loosened his grip on my hand, let it fall and started packing his syringe thingy away.

'What exactly is that?' I asked.

'Oh, just a useful bit of kit I like to carry with me, I travel a lot – and sometimes to places with much scarier bugs than a common-garden English wasp.'

I nodded. This was probably not the time to tell him the closest time I'd got to being anywhere abroad was a hen night in Dublin with my cousin. Expensive foreign holidays weren't a feature of my upbringing. Not that nobody hadn't wanted to travel; it's just that other things . . . other priorities . . . had made it impossible.

'I didn't mean to scare you when I came running over,' he said. 'I was just taking a few shots of the garden.'

I laughed softly, closing my sore finger in my other hand. 'You did make me jump. I thought I was alone. Not many people know this place exists. Not even Londoners.'

'I stumbled upon it on a previous visit, but it was dark then, and I always promised myself I'd come back during the daytime. I'm about to go travelling and I have a connecting flight tonight from Heathrow, so it seemed a shame not to take the opportunity while I was in London.' He stared up at the golden light filtering through the ivy. 'This place is just so . . .'

'Magical,' we both said at the same time, breaking into matching smiles. And for a couple of seconds that was all that mattered.

'Why here? Why not one of the bigger tourist spots?'

'I love exploring new places, finding those hidden, unusual parts of a city that add to its personality . . . its identity. London is so much more than the Thames and Big Ben, Buckingham Palace, and Nelson's Column. It's also *this* . . .' He spread his arm to indicate the garden in which we were both standing.

'Yes,' I said, my voice dropping to a whisper. It occurred to me how unusual it was to find a man who wasn't just interested in how things seemed, who liked to peel back the surface and find out the truth they held.

'It'll be our secret, then,' he said and smiled at me again. However, this time it was more intimate. It felt as if he was inviting me to join a club where we were the only two members. I was ready to sign up on the spot, no fourteen-day cooling-off period required.

The conversation had reached a natural pause, a place where it would have been easy to walk away, continue my tour of the garden, but I didn't make a move towards my sandals, still sitting by the edge of the fountain.

I searched my brain frantically for words – any words – that might prevent this moment from coming to an end. My gaze latched on to his camera. 'Can I see what you've taken?'

Great. Now he knows the barefoot, bee-sting girl is nosey as well as weird and a little bit accident-prone.

He looked uncomfortable for a moment, then said, 'Sure.' I followed him over to his tripod, where he hit a lever to release the camera. He held it out so I could see the screen on the back but kept his hands on it so he could operate the various buttons.

The first pictures were gorgeous. He'd captured the light slanting through the elaborate windows, lighting up the leaves of the trailing climbers from behind so they glowed with colour.

'Oh . . . !' I said as he moved the images on again. Amidst the sun-drenched foliage, there was now a figure . . . Me. The sun was above and behind me, lighting my long, mousey-but-wavy hair up at the edges into a golden halo. I twisted my head and shot him a questioning look.

His mouth grimaced but his eyes kept smiling. 'You walked into the shot as I pressed the shutter. I was so absorbed in what I was doing, I didn't realise you were there until I saw you through the viewfinder. And then you screamed—'

'I didn't scream,' I quickly corrected him, hoping I was right.

The humour in his eyes told me just how loudly I had proved myself wrong. I twisted my mouth to hide a smile as he scrolled through the next few images. 'Just the one shot . . . ?' I couldn't help but notice two or three more.

'I always fire off a few at a time. Complete habit. But I'll delete them if you want?'

I looked down at the display and exhaled. I'm a pretty self-contained and private kind of person. It should have been an automatic 'yes', but, in this picture, I didn't look like a little girl lost, no idea which direction her life should take.

I looked like a young woman who was exactly where she was supposed to be. I almost looked beautiful.

'No,' I said, twisting my head to meet his eyes. 'Don't delete them. It would be a shame.'

I suddenly became aware of just how close we were standing to each other. I found myself staring at his lips, and when I tore my gaze away and met his, he was looking at me with a strange intensity. 'Can I take your photograph?'

'I thought you already did that,' I said quietly, unsure why his question had sent a quiver through me.

'I'd like to take one of you looking at the camera, looking at me the way you are just now.'

Oh. Like that.

Like I wanted to kiss him.

I swallowed. Did he know that? Could he tell? My pulse began to trot. Maybe I did need an EpiPen after all. 'W-why?'

'You're part of my journey now, part of my memories of London. And I like to capture my memories on my travels, as many as possible: countries, places . . . people.'

I felt oddly flattered I might be part of that gallery. 'Okay,' I said slowly.

He got me to stand in the archway of the porch and asked me to rest a hand against the soft, pale stone. Moments before, he'd been smiling, full of easy bravado, but now he looked at me with a single-minded focus that made my heart stutter. Yet I didn't go rigid, as I often did when someone yelled 'cheese!' in my direction. I felt completely at ease.

When he finished, he showed them to me. Who was this woman staring into the lens with such confidence? She was practically glowing. It made me wonder if that was what he had seen too when he'd pressed the shutter.

He began to collect his belongings, stuffing the camera into a padded bag full of lenses and other mysterious equipment. 'That's me done here now,' he said. 'I'm away to the next location.'

He was going? 'Next location?' I asked, keeping my tone light and airy, as if I wasn't already considering turning into a stalker and 'accidentally on purpose' bumping into him there.

'Yup,' he said, as he collapsed the legs of his tripod. 'I'm doing a series of photos around the theme "Secret London". I've got a couple of ideas of places to go to, but after that I'm just going to wing it, see what I can find.'

His kit was now all stowed away, but he made no move to leave.

'I . . . I might be able to help with that,' I said, surprising myself with my boldness.

'Funny you should mention that,' he said, his expression becoming suddenly serious. 'I was thinking it's probably not wise for you to be alone just now.'

My eyes widened. 'It isn't?'

He shook his head. 'There could be a delayed reaction to that sting. I think someone should probably keep an eye on you for . . . oh, at least an hour or so. And it just so happens there's a great little café tucked away—'

'Just around the corner,' I finished for him, a smile breaking out on my face. '*Déjà Vu*. They do the best iced lattes this side of the river.'

9

He slung his camera bag over his shoulder and made a wide gesture with the other arm. 'Please . . . lead the way.'

But, Lili . . . the little voice in my head warned. *You haven't—*

Yes, I know, I whispered silently back as we made our way out of the garden. *But the whole disaster of my life will still be there in an hour, won't it? I'll make a decision then.*

CHAPTER TWO

THE DAY WAS certainly not going the way I'd expected it to when I'd left the house that morning, ready to mope around London in an attempt to decide whether to chase my dreams or tell destiny to take a hike. But it seemed destiny had a trick up her sleeve, and it had come in the form of a rather tall Scottish man with a camera.

His name was Ben, and he was a travel photographer. We'd gone for a coffee, where he'd told me all about the few ideas he had for unusual places to visit in London, and I'd thrown a few suggestions into the mix. He'd told me his first stop was the Mithraeum, an underground Roman temple where they were supposed to have sacrificed bulls and all sorts of unmentionable stuff. I said I'd never been. He'd joked that if it was really creepy, he might need someone to hold his hand. I had volunteered. And that had been that.

And at some point during our perusal of the carefully lit ancient artefacts, we'd decided to spend the rest of the day together. Not by spoken agreement, just . . .

To be honest, I didn't know how we'd done it. It was merely that we seemed to be in tune with one another, like we could communicate on a secret wavelength the rest of the world couldn't tune into.

What was I doing? I wasn't this girl – impulsive, impetuous, prone to dropping everything and just heading off somewhere at the drop of a hat. But, as I strolled the streets of London, my hand still joined with Ben the Photographer's, I'd started to wonder if destiny knew what she was doing.

It wasn't quite three, yet we'd been all over the city. After the temple, we'd gone to Leadenhall Market, where Ben had been entranced by the colourful Victorian cast iron and glass structure. Then he'd taken one of my suggestions, and we'd headed off to the conservatory at the Barbican. He'd snapped away when we got there, completely in his element, muttering between shots about the juxtaposition of delicate and exotic plants with the stark concrete of the Brutalist architecture. Then it had been the hidden tunnels of Piccadilly underground station, and now we were wandering through the narrow streets of Soho, still hand in hand, scouting for hidden sculptures on buildings.

Someone Ben had got chatting to while we'd toured the tunnels under Piccadilly had mentioned that an artist had placed stone noses all over the city in protest at the rise in use of CCTV cameras. While most had been removed, seven were still tucked away on various buildings in Soho and Covent Garden. It was a bit of a cult thing to try and find them all, apparently.

We'd already found numbers one to six, the last couple found in Dean Street, and then we turned into Meard Street in search of the final one. 'There it is!' Ben exclaimed almost immediately, pointing to a white plaster nose high up on the red-brick wall of a Georgian townhouse. He let go of my hand and pulled his camera out of his bag, then spent a good five minutes experimenting with different angles, crouching down low, looking at where the light was coming from and then working both with it and against it to see what produced the most interesting shot. I could have watched him work all day. When it came to creativity, he was unfettered, limitless.

During our conversations, I'd also revealed I was a creative sort of person, although music was my thing, not the visual arts. I didn't know if that made it different. I couldn't just create something in a perfectly captured moment and then email it to someone. For me to 'create' I had to be present, along with my violin. I always found it terrifying.

Besides, while Ben chose what to photograph, used his imagination to see things the way no one else saw them, I just played the notes someone else had written. It was hardly in the same league, even if one teacher had called me 'prodigiously good'. That's how I'd ended up spending the previous year at one of the most respected music schools in the country.

And it had been a year of utter hell.

But spending the day with Ben was making me see things in a different light. I wondered if I could learn from him, absorb some of his bravery, and if I could, maybe my second year at the London Conservatory could be different. If I decided to turn up for it, of course. I was still on the fence about that one, despite the deadline I'd imposed on myself that morning to stop avoiding the issue and choose one way or the other.

'How do you know what angles to take the photographs from?' I asked. 'Can anyone learn?'

Ben turned and walked back to me. 'It's partly picking up

the basics – lighting, composition, that sort of thing so, yes, I could teach you some of that, but the rest is just experimentation. You never know what's going to work until you try it. And sometimes the picture is good, and sometimes it's awful, but even if it is, I've learned something in the process.'

'You're not afraid to fail,' I said, and it was more an observation than a question.

'Not really. Like I said, sometimes I learn more through failing than getting things right.' He let his camera drop and came and stood close to me. 'Get your phone out, and I'll give you some tips.'

When we finished our lesson, he took a few more shots of the nose on the wall then stowed his camera back in his rucksack. 'That's the last of them . . . ' He checked his watch. 'Still time to fit a couple more things in before I have to head off to the airport. Something different.'

We listed off the things we'd already done that day. 'No more gardens,' he said thoughtfully. 'Got two of those already. Unless you can think of somewhere nearby with a maze. People love mazes, and they're so interesting to photograph – all those clean shapes and lines.'

I shook my head. 'Wish I did. There are a couple on the fringes of the city – a big one in Crystal Palace Park, but it's hardly a secret, and another one in Bexleyheath, but both are a bit of a trek.'

'Pity . . . ' We began to stroll in the direction of Covent Garden Market and Ben threaded his fingers through mine again, making my breath catch. He did it as if he almost hadn't thought about it, as if it was the most natural thing in the world. 'Did you know there's a secret to solving a maze?'

'What? A particular maze?' I asked.

'Any maze.'

I gave him what I hoped was my best 'don't bullshit me' look. 'If you say so . . . '

He laughed. 'No, really! Look, I'll prove it to you.'

And that was how I found myself standing in front of the famous yew hedge maze at Hampton Court Palace about an hour later. 'Go on, then, genius,' I said, nodding to the wooden gate that marked the entrance. 'How do we do this?'

He just grinned again. 'Left or right? Pick one.' I raised my eyebrows, not quite able to hide my smile. He was being *so* cocky. 'Pick,' he said, giving me a faux stern look that turned my insides to custard.

'Okay . . . Right.'

'Fine. I'll take left. All we have to do is keep one hand – you right, me left – on the maze wall and follow it until we get to the centre.'

I laughed. 'You're kidding. It can't be that easy.'

'Wanna bet?'

'Okay.' I knew I was going to do it, and I knew I didn't even care if I won the stupid bet or not. When had I last had fun like this? Pointless, purposeless wonderful fun? 'What do I get if you're wrong and I'm right?'

He grinned. 'Loser buys the ice creams.'

CHAPTER THREE

MY RIGHT HAND hovered lightly over the prickly, blunt-cut yew hedge as I jogged through the dirt paths of Hampton Court's maze. It had seemed like a fun idea to have a race when Ben had suggested it, but then he'd shot off like a greyhound at the races, and I'd been left standing there on my own.

It couldn't be as easy to find the centre as he'd said it would be. I'd be stuck in this stupid maze for hours, and where was the fun in that? We only had a short time until he needed to head off to the airport, and I didn't want to spend those precious minutes apart.

I couldn't believe I'd met someone like him. And by chance, too. Just because I'd had a random urge to escape the house to mope about my problems instead of doing it in my bedroom.

My first year at music school had been a disaster. I'd felt like a fish out of water from day one. What was a council house girl from Penge doing in a place like that? I thought I'd arrived at a place where talent was the only thing that mattered, that I'd finally be able to mix with 'my people', who understood and shared my love of music instead of bullying me for being 'weird' and 'up myself' because I loved to play the violin, but instead of reverse snobbery, I'd found actual snobbery. There had also been jealousy.

Like me, Charlie Banister, one my classmates, was from a less-than-privileged background, but instead of seeing this as a reason to support each other, he'd decided I was his direct competition and he'd taken every chance to cut me down, which only made my nerves worse. It was a horrible, vicious cycle, and my self-appointed nemesis was the eye of the hurricane. I'd barely made it through the end-of-term performance, and I'd been having nightmares about sitting in the violin section in a concert hall all summer.

Why couldn't I be more like my sister? Tough, sensible, letting nothing faze her? She would have told Charlie Banister in no uncertain terms where he could insert his violin bow, and then wouldn't have thought twice about him again.

I'd just about come to the decision that I was going to pull the plug, tell my parents the extra jobs they'd taken on since I was little to pay for my music education had been for nothing, but then Ben Robertson, Travel Photographer, had crashed into my life and turned everything upside down.

I had a crush on him as big as the London Eye. It really was quite sad. I ought to give myself a stern talking to. Because that's what it was, right? A crush? It couldn't be anything else. Not if he was jetting off this evening and didn't even know when he might be back in the UK.

Just as I thought I would go round and round in the stupid maze forever, one green hedge blurring into the next, the space opened out in front of me, and I realised I was standing in the centre. It had worked! It really had worked.

And there was Ben, waiting for me, wearing a pleased-with-himself grin that should have been annoying but was actually just delicious. I wanted to kiss that smile away, I decided, and if I didn't do it now, maybe I'd never get another chance, which would result in me kicking myself for all of eternity.

Time to take charge of your life, Lili, instead of cowering in the shadows. Time to leap on the opportunity of the moment.

'I won. You're buying the—' he started to say, but I strode right up to him, slid my hands up his chest and into the hair at the back of his head, pulling him closer, and then stopped when I was half a millimetre away, giving him the opportunity to back out, but his arms came around my waist, pulling me closer.

At first, the kiss was light and soft, a 'hello' kiss, a 'getting to know you' kiss, feather-light touches that set nerve endings zinging, but then it changed gear, deepened, and the hunger became not just for his mouth on mine but for all of him. Not just the muscular arms that were clamped around me or the firm chest I was pressed up against, but him. Everything he was, inside and out.

When he finally dragged his lips from mine, we rested our foreheads together, eyes closed, our breathing shallow. 'Wow,' he whispered. 'I'd been imagining doing that all day, but I must have a pretty poor imagination for things like that because . . . just . . . wow.'

I smiled gently, buoyed up by the fact I could make someone, make *him*, feel that way. 'I think your imagination is just fine. It's not that it's . . . it's . . . ' I hesitated, scared to let the words out. What if I was reading too much into this?

But Ben pulled back so he could see my whole face, one

hand still cradling my neck, and finished my sentence for me. 'It's us.'

I nodded. 'It is.'

We just stared at each other for a long moment, saying nothing but, at the same time, I felt as if I was spilling myself out before him, all the secret things no one knew about me, all the talent and potential and hope, but all the flaws too, all the things I never wanted *anyone* to see.

I lowered my lashes and looked away, afraid of what I was feeling. 'Do you do this every time you visit a new city? Fly in, charm a local girl, then fly away again?'

For a few seconds, there was nothing but silence. 'No,' he said, sounding emphatic but also maybe a little offended.

I flicked a glance at him.

'Don't do that,' he said. 'Don't pretend you don't know this is different.'

I swallowed. There wasn't really anything I could say in my defence. That was *exactly* what I'd been doing – ducking out, retreating to a place of safety before this feeling completely overwhelmed me and took my heart on the tidal wave that came with it.

'Lili?'

I loved hearing him say my name. Well, my nickname. My younger sister hadn't been able to say my full name when she was little, and that had been her best attempt. My parents had thought it was cute, and somehow it had stuck.

I slowly raised my eyes to meet his.

'No, I don't pick up random girls in foreign cities and spend the day with them. You're the first, the only . . . ' He brushed my cheek with his thumb. 'Don't you know that?'

'Yes . . . ' I whispered back in between kisses. Even though it made sense to me that this charming man would have a woman in every port, I believed him. My heart was so full, I almost couldn't bear it, but there was also a little rip down in one corner, one that was threatening to tear further as the minutes ticked past.

'I'll never forget today,' I said softly. 'I wish it didn't have to end.'

His chest rose and fell heavily. 'Me too.'

I pulled him to me and hugged him hard, attempting to hide the fact I felt perilously close to crying. I didn't want to do that in front of him. However, when I spoke, I suspected the rasp in my tone gave me away. 'When's your flight?'

He checked the functional-looking chunky watch he wore on his wrist. 'I ought to get going, well . . . *now*.'

But he didn't go anywhere. Instead, he kissed me again. We wasted at least another ten minutes before making our way back to the exit, making only a few dead-end turns along the way.

When we got to the entrance, we found the gate padlocked. Thankfully, it only came up to my waist, so it was no obstacle for Ben's long legs, and he clambered over first and held his arms out for me. Unfortunately, the hem of my dress got stuck on one of the pointed wooden struts, and I almost face-planted onto the tarmac on the other side of the gate, which resulted in us both giggling as Ben lifted me up and over and then placed me carefully on the ground.

'I wish the gate had been bigger,' I said, sighing. 'Then we would have been locked in and you'd have no choice but to stay a little bit longer.' I pulled a face, realising how selfish

I was being. 'Sorry . . . That would have meant you'd miss your flight, and I wouldn't want that.'

Ben stared at me. 'I would,' he said, and then he dug into his jeans pocket, pulled out his phone and tapped away on it with fierce concentration.

'Ben?'

'I'm cancelling my flight,' he said.

'What? No!' I reached out to try and pull his hand away from his phone screen, but he captured my fingers in his. 'You said earlier that you've been planning this trip for a year! You can't miss going to all those places, especially New Zealand, for me! It's been your dream since . . . forever!'

'I won't miss out,' he said. 'Trust me.' When he'd finished messing around on his phone, he grinned at me. 'Where do you want to go next? Wanna grab some dinner? Or do you want to try one of those "secret" bars you told me about? The one you get to by going through a door disguised as a vintage fridge sounds fun, or the one that looks like a detective agency.'

'Ben!'

'It's okay,' he said, grabbing me by the hand and leading me towards the palace. 'I had a flight from London to Amsterdam tonight, and I was going to spend a day taking pictures of canals before catching another flight from there to Singapore tomorrow evening. I can still make my connection if I fly tomorrow afternoon.'

I walked beside him, dazed for a few moments. 'Really? You really did that? Just to be with me?'

He stopped and turned, waited for me to look at him. 'I really did.'

CHAPTER FOUR

MY LEFT SHOULDER was stiff, and I stretched to ease it. The movement brought me from the shallows of sleep into consciousness. I blinked and found Ben looking down at me.

Oh, yes. I'd gone to sleep lying on his lap, and by the looks of his groggy expression, he'd also dozed off, feet propped up on a low table, back resting against a padded bench in the darkened lounge area of the hostel he was staying at.

I hadn't realised that when he'd cancelled his flight to Amsterdam that it had been non-refundable. He'd said it hadn't cost him much to find one the next day, but he'd only had his hotel booked for one night, so he'd had to pull in a favour from a travelling acquaintance who worked in a hostel in Southwark because that was all his carefully rationed funds would allow.

However, it meant we didn't really have anywhere private to go. He'd managed to find a space in a room with four sets of bunk beds, two of which were currently occupied by sleeping men, so we'd hung out in the lounge area on the ground floor, full of funky and easily cleanable cheap furniture. I stretched again, yawned, and pushed myself to a sitting position. 'What time is it?' I said, rubbing my eyes with the heel of my hand.

Ben checked his phone. 'Ten past four.' His voice sounded lovely all sleep-roughened. I leaned in and gave him a kiss.

Although I felt bad about costing him money he couldn't afford before his big year-long trip around the world, I couldn't regret the fact he'd stayed. Last night had been amazing. After sorting out the hostel, we'd gone to somewhere near Kings Cross that did stupendous curries for a couple of pounds a bowl, then he'd managed to blag us seats at a 'floating cinema' in what looked like a mini Canary Wharf somewhere in West London by promising he'd take a few free shots as publicity. Well, when I say 'seats', I mean a tiny boat for two that bobbed up and down on the water as we'd watched *Jaws*.

After the film, we'd just walked and talked through the streets, which had started out full of noise and colour, populated by drunk people either looking for a club or the wrong night bus, but had grown gradually quieter as the night had deepened. In the end, it had almost seemed as if we were the only two people left in the city. We'd arrived back at the hostel at about two and had talked some more before eventually nodding off.

'Hungry?' he asked and walked over to the brightly lit vending machine on the other side of the room. I nodded, so he fed it some coins and returned with a couple of packets of Hula Hoops and a Twix to share. 'Sorry. You have to learn to forage and eat what's available when you're travelling on a budget.'

I popped open my packet of crisps and tucked one leg underneath myself. 'It's just what I wanted,' I said, throwing a couple of Hula Hoops into my mouth. 'If you'd taken me to the Savoy for breakfast, this is what I'd have ordered.'

He laughed, and I smiled back at him. I loved that I could make him laugh. 'I'm not sure they serve Hula Hoops at the Savoy.'

'Well, they should,' I said, mumbling through the crunchy potato rings as I stuffed another handful into my mouth. All that walking earlier had obviously given me an appetite. As I chewed, I wondered what inhabited the vending machines in some of the far-flung places he must have visited. 'What made you want to travel for a living?' I asked when I'd finished my mouthful. 'How did it all start?'

Ben leaned back against the padded bench and sighed. 'Right from when I was little, I remember being obsessed with atlases. I was always getting the one my father owned out of the bookshelf and turning the pages, wondering what it would be like to live on those little dots of colour in the middle of distant oceans or up on the mountain ranges that ran like spines through countries and continents. I suppose, in some ways, I'd been planning to leave Invergarrig since I was old enough to read.'

'What's it like, your hometown?' I asked.

'It's nice enough . . . I mean, it sits on the edge of a loch, and there are mountains, even a castle.'

'Sounds like the sort of place people would choose to visit, not leave at the first opportunity.'

Ben looked down, breaking eye contact. 'I never really felt at home there.' I shuffled close and snuggled up against him, my back pressed against his side, and his arm came down over my shoulder. 'I always felt like I didn't belong, like an outsider. Is that weird?'

I shook my head. 'No . . . I get it completely. Not many

kids where I grew up play the violin. It made me different.'
I sighed heavily. 'And now I'm not even sure I want to do it
any more.' I put my bag of crisps down and turned around so
I could see his face. 'What made you feel that way?'

'My dad,' he said, without emotion. 'He made it clear I was
a disappointment to him.'

I frowned. 'Why would he think that? You're carving out
a niche for yourself, doing a career you love. Isn't that what
everyone wants?' In contrast, my parents had supported me
every step of the way to pursue my dreams. That was why
thinking about dropping out had been so hard.

He exhaled. 'It's not a "proper" job, apparently. He wanted
me to follow in his footsteps, go into insurance . . . '

I pulled a face.

Ben laughed softly. 'Exactly! And the fact I didn't want to
do that caused a big issue.' He fell silent for a moment. 'But,
to be honest, that wasn't the start of it. He's always been like
that – picking away at my sister and me. Nothing we did was
ever good enough, and it got even worse after my mum died.
She used to go to bat for us, even though I now realise she
might have been scared of him too. So, I suppose the question
should be: why *wouldn't* I want to leave Invergarrig as soon
as I got the chance?'

'Your mum died? Oh, I'm so sorry, Ben.'

'It's okay. It happened a year after I'd left home, and my
sister bore the brunt of living with him alone – she's two
years younger than me, so she was only seventeen when it
happened. I didn't realise it at the time, but I think he got
even worse after Mum passed. I think that's when Cat really
started to struggle.' He stared into the darkness on the other

side of the room for a few seconds. 'At first, she acted out. You know, basic teenage rebellion, but now . . . ' He turned to look at me, and there was a bleakness in his expression. 'I'm worried about her.'

'Do you get on?'

He grimaced. 'Occasionally. I think she can only see me as the annoying big brother who likes to boss her around. It threatened to cause a real rift between us, but she cleaned up her act recently, and I hope to God it's going to stick . . . She's pregnant, you see. She just told me this last weekend.' His expression grew even more hollow. 'I might not even be back in the country when she has the baby, but I'm going to see what I can work out. She needs me, even if she can't see that at the moment.'

I rubbed his arm and laid my head against his shoulder, and for a few seconds, we just stayed like that. I sensed it was time to talk about something else. 'Okay . . . so we've got eleven hours before you need to be going through security at Heathrow. What do you want to do today?'

'I really don't care,' he said, turning to kiss me softly, 'as long as I can spend it with you.'

*

I rode the Tube with Ben all the way to the airport when the time came. I couldn't bear to say goodbye to him until the absolute very last second.

We'd watched the sun rise over the Thames, eaten bacon rolls with huge polystyrene cups of tea from a kiosk in Borough Market, then visited a café full of arcade games, which we'd played for nearly an hour. I was a pinball wizard, apparently. Who knew? After that, I'd persuaded him to go to Nunhead Cemetery with me – not as famous as Highgate, but just as striking – and then we'd headed back into the centre of town, browsed a few markets, including one tucked into a courtyard outside a church along Piccadilly.

But eventually, we'd ended up at Terminal Three, dragging those last few minutes together out as much as possible. 'When will I see you again?' I asked him.

He held on to me tightly, pressed an emphatic kiss into the top of my head. 'I don't know . . . I won't be back in Europe for at least six months, and even then, not the UK, but I'm supposed to be in Bulgaria in February. I know . . . Come to Sofia and meet me!'

I stared back at him. If he'd asked me that question even twelve hours ago, I'd have jumped at the chance, but early this morning, while we'd been studying the elaborate headstones at Nunhead Cemetery, I'd come to a realisation. Life was too short, wasn't it? I couldn't give up on my dreams. I had to be brave and adventurous, like Ben was. 'I can't . . . ' I replied mournfully. 'I have music school. It's not the sort of place where you can just take a few days off and disappear.'

He thought for a moment. 'Then I'll cancel Bulgaria and Croatia and come back to the UK early.'

'No! You've been planning this trip for years!'

He gave me a look that made my insides melt into a gooey puddle. 'If there's anyone who makes me want to stay in one place, it's you.'

I shook my head. 'You can't abandon your dreams for me, Ben, just like I shouldn't let my go of mine because of you.

We'd always regret it later.' I sighed, searching the hard angles and painted steel of the airport terminal for an answer, but I came up empty. 'We'll just have to be patient. When can you get back *without* compromising your plans?'

He was quiet for a few moments, and I could tell he was flicking through calendars and travel schedules in his head. 'June. Maybe . . . Part of my plan was to do extra work in certain places to fund the next leg, and it really depends on how quickly I find jobs and how much they pay.'

'A year, then?'

'Realistically. I couldn't promise any earlier for certain.' He turned away momentarily, obviously frustrated. 'But I don't like leaving things so open-ended. It's not fair to you . . . And I don't much like the idea, either.'

'Then let's make it a specific day. What date was it yesterday?'

'The twelfth of July,' he replied, his eyes full of curiosity.

'Then we'll meet one year from the day we met. Here . . . '

'In Heathrow Airport? That's hardly very romantic!'

I punched him lightly on the arm. 'No, you melon. In London . . . I know! In the garden at the church . . . at St Dunstan-in-the-East.'

He smiled at me. 'It's perfect. And it's a date. Nothing will stop me being there.' He sounded so serious I almost laughed, a nervous reflex, maybe, because I didn't want to cry instead. He must have seen my lips twitch because he said, 'I mean it. Don't you believe me?'

'Of course I do. If I know anything about you by now, it's that you don't dive into something unless you're fully committed. That's just who you are.' And it was why I suspected

I could easily fall for him, even after a day and a half, even though it made no sense at all, and I didn't believe in things like fate or love at first sight.

'You'll be there? You won't forget?'

He looked so uncharacteristically vulnerable that I couldn't resist pulling his face towards mine and kissing him. 'I won't forget,' I whispered as we rested our foreheads against each other. 'Besides, I'm getting your number . . . We'll be in contact the whole time, even if we can't see each other in person. There's no way we're just disappearing from each other's lives for twelve months and then turning up at St Dunstan's hoping for the best. That would be daft.'

I pulled my phone from my bag. It seemed weird we hadn't exchanged numbers before now, but since we'd been right next to each other for the last day and a half, it hadn't really been necessary. 'Oh, crap,' I said as I tried to wake it up. 'It's completely dead.' I'd had about fifty per cent battery when I'd left the house the day before. At the time, I'd thought it would be plenty.

'It's okay,' Ben said. 'I'm really low, but I've got enough juice to put your number in my phone, then when I get to Schiphol I'll charge it and send you a message so you've got mine.' He handed me his phone, and I tapped my number in and gave it back to him.

'I'll be waiting,' I said, already knowing that even though it would only be a few hours, it would feel like a lifetime.

Ben glanced at the departures board and frowned. 'I've waited far too long. I'd better get a move on, but before I go . . . ' He pulled a small paper bag from his pocket and handed it to me.

I unfolded the top and peered inside. 'Oh, Ben . . . You didn't have to buy me anything!' I knew he didn't have the money. Inside was a fine silver chain with a tiny silver bee pendant. I made a hiccupping sound that I wasn't sure signalled laughter or tears. It was possibly both.

He gave me a wonky, slightly self-conscious smile. 'I tried to find a wasp, but no one does wasps, apparently, so it was this or nothing.'

'I love it!' I said, clutching it tightly as I kissed him again. 'When did you manage to buy it without me seeing?'

'Remember when you were browsing the stall full of semi-precious stones at the market, and I went to grab us some cold drinks? I may have found this then.'

He took the necklace from me and made me turn round so he could hang it around my neck and fasten the catch. I turned back to face him. 'Do you know,' he said, 'that bees travel miles and miles away from their homes, but they always find their way back?' He leaned in and kissed me softly. 'It means you'll find your way back to me, Lili.'

'Actually, that's just what my family call me. I'm actually called . . . '

But I realised he was only half listening. His gaze had been snagged by the departures board. 'My gate number has just popped up. I'm going to have to run!' He kissed me quickly.

'But—'

'Send me a message once your phone's charged! Tell me then!' He jogged away and disappeared into the security hall before I could argue.

I stared at the empty space between the doors where I'd last seen him, and I stayed there until the departures board showed his flight had departed, then I turned – my body suddenly heavy and complaining about the lack of sleep – and headed towards home. However, I knew I wouldn't sleep until the message he'd promised had arrived.

PART II

CHAPTER FIVE

Now.

SHE WASN'T SURE if she'd roused from slumber or if her surroundings had come slowly into focus. Her eyes might have been closed, lids having just fluttered open, or they could have been open already. She really couldn't say for certain. All she knew was that it felt as if she'd been wandering around in a dense, pearly fog, and now the sky had cleared.

This place was beautiful. A gauzy mist hovered above the unruffled surface of a lake surrounded by low mountains, their weathered tops rising above the treeline. The curving beach was covered with dark stones of different sizes, some just pebbles, some full-grown rocks, slick with seaweed. Beyond the arc of the shoreline, there was a hump-backed bridge made of ancient stone, and, behind that, the turrets of a castle poked above a row of evergreens. It was as if she'd been dumped down in the middle of a fairy tale.

A noise penetrated the thick blanket of her thoughts. Seagulls. She could hear seagulls. Usually, she found their cries irritating – a horrible, greedy nagging – but as they echoed through the cold morning air, they sounded exquisitely forlorn.

Other sounds began to filter in: the lap of the gentle waves against the rocky beach, the rumble of a car pulling away and getting quieter as it climbed over the hump of the bridge and disappeared from view.

She seemed to be on the edge of a small town, but like no town she'd ever visited before. It was a couple of centuries old at least. The main street was probably only a hundred metres long, flanked on both sides with uniform, white-rendered buildings, all with contrasting black window and door frames.

She stood up, eager to explore, then paused to look down at her legs and feet. She'd been sitting down. On a bench. Beside a bus stop. For some reason, that seemed like new information.

How long? How long had she been sitting here on this bench? Furrows appeared above her eyebrows as she tried to concentrate but it was no good. She had no idea how long she'd been sitting there or even how she'd ended up in this place.

Something in the back of her brain, something sensible and machine-like, rubber-stamped this revelation as important, but for the life of her she couldn't work out why. It hurt to think about it, actually. Really hurt, like a band tightening around her temples, so she let the thought go, let it soar up into the sky with the seagulls, and then she turned and walked up a slight incline towards the large Georgian church standing guard at the top end of the High Street.

The smell of frying bacon hit her nostrils as she passed the open door to a bed and breakfast with a café on the ground floor. She gravitated towards it, crossing the threshold. There was an empty table just inside the door, and she eased herself into a chair and soothed her grumbling belly with a rub of her palm.

A guy in an apron appeared beside her. He nodded at the menu propped up between the salt and pepper pots in the centre of the table. 'What'll you have?' he asked in a soft Scottish accent, finishing his question off with a smile.

'Tea,' she said hoarsely, even though she had made no such decision in her conscious brain. 'And bacon.'

The guy was still smiling at her. She was starting to find it unnerving. 'Roll or buttie?'

'Roll,' she replied, marvelling at the sound of her own voice, familiar and strange all at once. And not Scottish, she noticed. Her accent was crisper, less rolling. Definitely English.

She pondered the significance of this as the guy in the apron vanished again and, what seemed like only seconds later, a lovely soft roll with thick bacon poking out the sides appeared in front of her. She ate every last scrap, punctuating bites with gulps of hot tea. When she finished, she sighed, letting the sights, sounds and smells of this quaint little town wash over her.

A short while later, she blinked. The plate from her bacon roll was gone. She took a sip from her half-finished mug of tea and shuddered. Stone cold. She placed it back on the table and stood up, heading for the open door onto the street.

'Hey!'

She stopped in her tracks and turned to find the man in the apron with his hands on his hips. 'That'll be five pounds fifty, please.' He wasn't smiling any more.

'Oh. Sorry.' She patted the pockets of the thin jacket she was wearing. The only problem was that they seemed to be empty. Where was her handbag? Her purse? Her phone?

Her heart began to race uncomfortably under her ribcage,

and her head, which had been blissfully empty of clutter up until that point, was suddenly jam-packed with thoughts and sensory information, all clamouring for her attention. She looked up again to find the man scowling at her. 'I . . . I . . . ' she stammered. The grease from the bacon began to congeal in her stomach.

'Who are you?' he asked, stepping in front of her and blocking her exit. 'Are you staying here? I can't see any solo guests on the bed and breakfast list.'

She shivered, and the alarm in her head began to sound again, this time screaming its lungs out. Suddenly, this perfect little town, this lovely fairy-tale place, didn't seem so welcoming.

She stared at him helplessly, her head pounding, a gale rushing in her ears. Her throat felt as if someone had threaded a drawstring around it and pulled it tight. The room began to swim around her and she shot out a hand and gripped onto the edge of a table to stop herself from falling.

She couldn't answer his question, she realised, as she began to shake from head to toe. Because she didn't know what her name was. She just didn't know.

CHAPTER SIX

Now.

BEN FINISHED THE last bite of his full Scottish breakfast and pushed his knife and fork together. He was stuffed but, with any luck, he wouldn't need to eat again until early evening, which meant he'd be able to power through lunch. The burst pipe in one of the cottages last week meant renovations had fallen behind, and he needed to get a move on if he had any hope of finishing them on schedule. Come tourist season, he was aiming to not only have a new home but three shiny and updated lochside cottages as holiday rentals as well.

He pushed his chair back and stood up, picked up his plate and headed for the dishwasher.

'You'll not have another potato scone?' his Aunt Norina asked, glancing over her shoulder from where she was cooking enough to feed an army. On the other side of the kitchen, the current guests of her bed and breakfast were sitting around the long pine table, hungry and expectant.

Ben shook his head.

'Coffee, then? You like a good cup of coffee.'

He walked over to his aunt and kissed her on the top of her head as she flipped bacon over in the large frying pan.

He had to bend a little to do it, seeing as he was six foot four and she was only four foot eleven, and then he headed out of the kitchen and across the hall.

He walked up the short, dead-end street where the B&B sat, past the Invergarrig Inn to the centre of the town, enjoying the comparative silence of the outdoors. He'd been back in his hometown for almost a year now. It seemed like an age. And while he was grateful to his Aunt Norina for giving up one of her rentable rooms so he could have a permanent residence, he'd been counting down the days until the renovations on his cottage would be finished and he could move in. Privacy . . . Breakfast without an audience. Sounded like bliss.

And now the day was almost here. There were a few more jobs to do, but some of those could be done after the move. If it were up to him, he'd have camped out while the work carried on – sleeping bag on the floor, propane stove for cooking until the electrics were done, but that wasn't an option this time. He had Willow to think about.

First things first. Before he got started on fixing the new plug sockets to the wall in the second bedroom, he was going to have a *proper* coffee. The stuff his aunt ran through her filter machine was disgusting. His plan was to get a takeaway Americano and head down to the pier so he could drink it listening to the waves, watching the shifting reflections of the mountains on the loch.

He lifted his hand to brush his thick hair out of his eyes and realised that he still had pale-pink nail polish on one hand. If Rick, the local builder, saw this on his fingers when they met up for a quick pint at lunchtime to discuss a plastering quote, he'd never let him live it down. But Willow had wanted to give him a 'glow up' last night, and he found it hard to resist his five-year-old niece anything.

Just as he did every morning, he passed the newsagents, the whisky shop and three gift shops on his way down the High Street. He could recite the shop names in order, and who owned them, when he was lying in his bed at night, dreaming about sun-kissed beaches and lush rainforests. He supposed some people found comfort in this kind of monotony, and he was going to have to try, even if it nearly killed him.

He was a couple of doors down from The Thistle Café when he realised a commotion was taking place on the pavement outside. Rob, the owner's son, was arguing with a woman. 'You can't leave,' he was saying. 'You've not paid!'

The woman, who wasn't even wearing a decent coat, despite the chilly wind blowing off the loch, just stared back at Rob, her breath coming in short gasps. She looked like she was going to bolt down the street at any second.

Ben drew closer. He knew the tell-tale signs of a panic attack when he saw one. 'What's going on?'

Rob gestured towards the woman, pink in the face. 'She's trying to skip out on her breakfast!'

'Is that right?' Ben asked, and the woman turned to look at him, blinking, her mouth half-open, as if she wanted to say something but couldn't find the words.

For a moment, the world stood still. 'Lili . . . ?' Ben sputtered, his brain rapidly trying to process what his eyes were telling him.

Was it? Was it her?

And if it was, what was she doing here? In this place, in this town?

41

Rob's eyes widened. 'You know her?' He turned to the woman. 'You know him?'

She flicked a glance in his direction and shook her head, but she was still caught in the grip of the panic. Her own mother could have been standing there, and she'd probably have declared her a stranger. There was no way Rob was going to get any sense – or any money – out of her while she was in a state like this.

Ben pulled a ten-pound note from his pocket and handed it to Rob. 'This should cover it.'

Rob didn't look pleased, but he could hardly complain in front of a queue of waiting customers, so he disappeared back inside, shoving the money in the pocket of his apron. Ben put a gentle hand on the woman's arm and steered her down the High Street towards the loch. When they reached the well-kept green just before the shore, he turned left towards the small stone pier.

When they were safely away from prying eyes, he talked to her in a low, calm voice, the same way he'd done for his sister more times than he could count. It was a struggle, but eventually, she began to regulate her breathing, seemed as if she was gaining a little control. 'Th—thank you,' she said hoarsely.

'No problem,' he replied, unable to stop himself staring at her.

It was her. It had to be.

He'd thought about her a million times since that hot summer's day more than five years ago. Kicked himself about how it had ended a million times more.

'Lili?' he said, less of a question, more of a softly spoken wish. 'It's me . . . Ben.'

She continued to look at him blankly.

Right. Ouch.

Either he was completely wrong, and this wasn't the woman he'd met in London, or he obviously hadn't been as memorable to her as she had to him. He studied her face carefully. The bone structure was, well . . . she and Lili could have been sisters. But her hair was different – a short blonde bob, completely different in colour, cut and style from Lili's tousled waves. And her voice wasn't the London accent he'd expected; it was much more polished, like a newsreader on the television.

Okay . . . Now he was really taking her in, he was starting to second-guess the gut instinct that had forced a name from his lips.

It had happened frequently in the first couple of years after they'd first met. He'd catch a glimpse of someone – in Nepal, or Sydney or Ushuaia – and be sure it was her. It never had been. Just his imagination conjuring up what he wanted to be true. Weird how his brain had played the same trick on him after all this time, when he'd just about managed to forget her.

'Where're you staying?' he asked as they reached the railing at the edge of the small car park right in front of the pier.

'Staying?' She looked genuinely surprised.

'Well, you're not a local.'

'How do you know?'

'It's a small town,' he explained. 'I know most people by sight, if not by reputation, and I'm pretty sure I haven't seen you here before.' He was certain he'd have remembered someone who looked so much like Lili.

Anyway, that didn't really matter at the moment. He just needed to work out how to get her back to her hotel or whatever, and then he could be on his way, back to building a life in this town, back to where his focus should be at the moment: on Willow. This was just a distraction, his brain's way of pranking him – tormenting him – with images of the life he'd walked away from. 'How did you get here?'

'I think I caught the bus,' she replied quietly.

'You *think* you did?'

She nodded. 'I remember sitting over there—' she pointed to the bench just beside the bus stop '—before I walked up the street to the café.'

'Where had you been heading – Glasgow or Campbelltown?' There was only one bus service that ran through the town a handful of times each day, so it might help to work out which direction she'd been travelling.

'I . . . I don't know.'

Ben stopped leaning on the railing and stood up. 'You don't know?'

She stared back at him helplessly. 'I'm sure I know . . . It's just that I can't quite seem to pull that information out of my brain at the moment.'

Ben frowned. It was likely the panic attack had left her feeling disoriented, but to forget how you arrived somewhere? That was odd. 'I think we need to contact someone for you. Are you travelling with family? I don't think you should be on your own just now.'

'Yes . . . Yes, I'd like that.'

'Where's your phone?' He was counting on the fact she might have listed someone as an emergency contact.

The woman shoved her hands in her coat pockets and rummaged around, then tried the back pockets of her jeans.

Eventually, she looked back at Ben, confused. 'I must have lost it.'

'You don't have a bag?' he asked, then realised it was a stupid question. It was obvious she wasn't carrying one. She must have put it down somewhere in the confusion. 'Do you know where you left it?'

Her lips began to wobble, but she pressed them into a firm line as her head moved side to side.

'Wait there for a moment . . . ' He quickly pulled his own phone out of his pocket and rang Rob back at The Thistle Café and asked whether anything had been handed in or if he'd found a bag left by her table, but no joy.

He looked out over the loch as his brain searched for the next logical course of action. 'Listen . . . I think maybe the best thing to do at the moment is call the police, see if they can help you.'

The town police station was gone now, replaced by a bigger one in nearby Lochgilphead, covering the whole area. Depending on where the patrolling officers were, it could be up to an hour before they arrived here, but he couldn't think of anything else to do. Maybe she'd hit her head, needed medication? Whatever it was, something wasn't right. 'Can you tell me what your name is?' he asked as he woke his phone up and prepared to dial in the non-emergency number for the local police.

Her face went pale, and a look of horror passed over her features, as if she'd just received some devastating news. 'I . . . I don't know,' she stammered. 'I don't know what my name is.'

Ben stared back at her. How was that possible? He was tempted to laugh, sure she was playing some kind of joke on

45

him, but the desolation in her eyes caused him to swallow hard instead.

'The first memory I have – not just today but *ever* – is sitting at that bus stop,' she continued shakily. It was as if hearing herself say the words out loud caused her brain to finally catch up with the ramifications of what she was telling him.

Her legs buckled, and she clutched onto his sweater to steady herself, then pulled herself closer so her forehead was almost touching his chest. On reflex, Ben's arms closed around her. He wasn't sure she had a steady grip, and it looked as if she might crumple in a heap at any second.

And as she clung onto him, taking great juddering breaths, Ben looked over the top of her head at the empty bus stop. It occurred to him that if this *was* Lili, there might be a really good reason why she had no idea who he was.

CHAPTER SEVEN

One year before the wedding.

I SAT ON the Tube, my violin case clutched to my chest, desperately trying to stop myself from shaking. The scruffy man sitting opposite me gave me a weird look. I dipped my head, so I didn't have to meet his eyes.

This was a bad idea. I should get off at Westminster and head straight back to Victoria, where I could get a train home. I'd be drinking tea in my parents' kitchen within the hour.

But when the doors huffed open, I closed my eyes, clenched my jaw, and willed myself to stay sitting. They eventually slid closed again, and the Underground train rumbled along to its next stop. My stop. The hammering inside my ribcage intensified.

I avoided going into central London these days if at all possible, preferring to stick to my sad little life in the suburbs. There were too many reminders of what could have been in the city centre. The whole place was ruined for me now, thanks to *him* – Ben the bloody Photographer.

Like a complete mug, I'd waited for a phone call or a message, even a pathetic lone emoji to arrive, after we'd parted at the airport. And I'd waited, and I'd waited.

At first, I made excuses: he'd got delayed. He hadn't reached his hotel, so he hadn't been able to charge his phone. And then I'd got scared. What if something had happened to him? What if he'd had an accident travelling alone? Or maybe he'd been kidnapped? As the days went on, the scenarios I'd invented had become more and more outlandish. At one point, I'd even convinced myself that he'd had something planted in his luggage and was now languishing in a Dutch prison, falsely accused of being a drugs mule. But as the hours had turned into days and the days had turned into weeks, I'd had to get real.

It had been pure fantasy, hadn't it? The whole thing. He'd never intended on calling me at all. I'd just been a diversion, an amusement, like the other sights and sounds of the city, a way to pass the time until the next flight. Yet I'd fallen for his patter hook, line, and sinker. Like I said . . . a complete mug.

But at least I hadn't turned up the next summer to meet him in the garden, all hopeful and dewy-eyed, thinking I'd met 'The One' and that he'd be there waiting for me. I wasn't that stupid.

I'd gone back to the London Conservatory demoralised, my self-esteem nastily dented, and that had been a mistake too. I'd dropped out two months later. Not the quiet non-appearance at the start of term I'd planned, but a shameful fall from grace that had made it impossible to return.

That had been some time ago, and now I worked in the fried chicken shop down the end of Penge High Street. Some glorious new career that was. Eventually, I'd become so sick of myself moping around and whining I'd decided I had to do something about it. Which was why I was *making* myself head into the city centre now with my violin clutched to my chest.

I hadn't told anyone what I was doing. Because what if I failed? What if I messed up and embarrassed myself again? It would just be more proof that I was empty of all the potential everyone had seen in me.

It was my parents I felt the worst about. I'd seen the disappointment on their faces when I'd told them I was dropping music school. I'd sensed the emotional landslide inside of them as they'd kept their faces neutral, all their hopes and expectations for me slithering to the ground.

I darted off the Tube at Embankment and headed up Villiers Street towards The Strand. The day had been crisp and bright when I'd left the house, the sky cloudless behind the winter sun, and I hadn't bothered with a coat. The tightness of the sleeves around my armpits always seemed to impede the movement of my bow arm, so I'd chosen a thick, baggy jumper. Not very attractive, but it was warm and allowed for freedom of movement.

However, while I'd been underground, the clouds had gathered, and the wind was icy, finding its way between the looping, open knit of my sweater. I shivered as I crossed the road and hurried up one of the many narrow streets that lead to Covent Garden.

I didn't know if I was allowed to busk here without a permit, and I hadn't checked. Maybe because I was hoping someone would shout at me and tell me to move on, and then I could let myself off the hook and go home, no damage done.

Stage fright.

People think of it as the jangle of nerves before you step into the spotlight. They believe the adrenaline coursing through your system ultimately helps you hit even greater heights of brilliance. That was never my experience. For me, it was pounding, churning, dizzying terror. I couldn't think, couldn't move. Sometimes my vision narrowed and I couldn't even see properly. I certainly couldn't play. On the few times I'd been forced to try, it had sounded like someone torturing next door's parakeet.

The thought of standing in a concert hall still made me go weak at the knees, but I had to do *something*. I couldn't just stay at my parents' house, stagnating. So maybe I could do this. Maybe I could play for strangers rushing past as they hurried to the office or the next tourist hotspot. All they would hear was a few snatched seconds. It wouldn't be the same. I couldn't *let* it.

I didn't head for the main busking spot in front of the church that flanked Covent Garden Market, its huge columns and porch creating the impression of a grand stage. A juggling team had set up there, pulling in a crowd of fifty or more, and I could hear the 'oohs' and 'ahs' of appreciation as I scurried past, looking for a little nook or street corner I could position myself on.

I found a spot up James Street, not far from Covent Garden Tube station. I took a deep breath, placed my violin case at my feet and unclasped it. Octavia was a fine-looking violin, beautiful to hold. She wasn't centuries old or eye-wateringly rare, but she was precious to me all the same. Mum and Dad had gone without a couple of holidays to pay for her. In fact, they'd gone without a lot of things over the years to allow me to chase my dream of being a professional musician, something that weighed on my mind every day.

I brought Octavia up to my shoulder, rested her under my

chin and raised my bow, taking a few practice strokes, just to get my nerve up. A few heads turned at the unexpected noise. My stomach churned harder. I ignored it and began to play 'Spring' from Vivaldi's 'The Four Seasons', a sure crowd-pleaser, but it felt as if my whole body had gone rusty, that my muscles had forgotten how to move to make a suitable noise.

It must have been bad because I played for ten minutes before someone chucked a coin in the direction of the open case. I kept going, almost as scared to stop as I had been to begin. It was easier not to watch people walking by, so I closed my eyes, feeling the weight and elegance of the instrument in my hands, and dived into some other familiar pieces.

As I played, the music seemed to swirl inside me, oiling my rusty joints, bringing grace and fluidity to my movements. Next, I picked a faster piece, one that was full of joy and soaring sounds. A small smile curved my lips, and I began to tap one foot.

Clink, clink, clink. The coins started to arrive more frequently. I still wasn't brave enough to open my eyes and look at anyone, so I just kept playing, one melody merging into the next.

I ended up playing my favourite piece, one I thought I'd never play again, after the mess I made of it the last time I'd tried in public. It wasn't very well-known if you weren't a violin player, but it was both difficult and gorgeously haunting at the same time. When I finished, I felt as if something had been released from inside of me, something hard and heavy that had been weighing me down for months.

I opened my eyes to put Octavia down and discovered, much to my surprise, that a crowd of more than twenty people were standing around me, all looking expectant. I almost left my case sitting on the pavement and bolted right there and then, but instead I swallowed, nodded my gratitude as they began a soft round of applause.

'Play it again, love,' one older man in a high-vis vest and work boots said. 'That was lovely.'

I smiled weakly back at him and, instead of taking the break I'd planned, I launched back into the piece. This time, I kept my eyes open.

I was halfway through when the heavens opened. The first drop of rain hit like a tiny cannon ball, splashing onto my scalp and running through my hair. It was followed by another and yet another, and soon the crowd was scattering, running this way and that as the temperamental February rain sought them out with its tiny missiles. All except one guy . . .

He'd been standing at the edge of the crowd, and I hadn't really noticed him until that point. He was lean but not skinny, with the kind of face that could have put him anywhere from early thirties to early forties. He wore a wool coat and smart leather shoes. I just knew that if I ever got close enough to catch a scent of his aftershave, it would be the expensive kind, not the stuff my mum gets in Superdrug to put in my dad's Christmas stocking. I faltered, my bow slowing.

'Don't stop,' he said, looking into my eyes with an intensity that made me feel both uncomfortable and exhilarated. 'Your playing is exquisite.' And then he stepped forward, unfurling a large black umbrella with a curved wooden handle, and held it over me.

He nodded in encouragement, and I began to play again as he stood outside the safety of the umbrella, shielding me and my violin from the thundering raindrops.

He *did* smell good, I realised, and it almost put me off my stride during a particularly difficult section of the piece. When I finished, I cradled my instrument to my torso to protect her from the rain. 'Thank you,' I whispered.

'Do you know Pachelbel's "Canon in D Major"?' he asked. 'I'd love to hear you play that.'

'But you're getting wet.'

'I don't care.' He held my gaze as I lifted my violin and began the piece he'd mentioned. The rain was still falling, but it had used up its stamina, and had shifted down a few gears to a drizzle.

Still, he held the umbrella over me. Still, he looked right at me, smile gone but the echo of it hovering around his mouth. I met his eyes, surprising myself with my boldness, given that he was older, definitely wealthier, and way, *way* out of my league. I probably would have looked away if I hadn't been able to see in his face that the music affected him the same way it affected me.

By the time my strings vibrated with the last notes, I was praying it would rain for the rest of the afternoon.

CHAPTER EIGHT

Now.

WHEN BEN ENTERED the kitchen back at the B&B, he found his aunt rinsing some crockery off before putting it in the dishwasher. 'Shona was on the phone again just now,' she said as she scrubbed vigorously at a plate. 'Now they're doing weddings at the castle, she's keen for someone local to do the photos so they can offer it as part of the package to prospective couples. You know, someone who knows the area, who can get the best shots . . . '

Ben sighed. He'd already told his aunt where he stood on this. 'One, I've retired, and, two, travel photography is very different from wedding photography. But I've got something I—'

'Och, it can't be *that* different! I mean, there's a mountain right behind the castle, for goodness' sake! All you've got to do is frame it up and then shove a few people in front of it. How different can it be?'

'It just is,' he said, 'and besides, I have the cottages to focus on. We need the money they're going to bring in. Maybe next year . . . ' Norina didn't look pleased, but she dropped the subject. Ben was glad because he really didn't want to delve into further reasons why his camera was gathering dust at the bottom of his wardrobe. 'Anyway, the reason I came looking for you is that I have a . . . um . . . situation.'

He launched into the whole story about the woman he'd met outside the café. 'It was starting to rain, and she was still looking pretty shaky . . . I couldn't abandon her, could I? So I brought her back here and put her in the sitting room since it's empty of guests for the moment. I hope you don't mind.'

'No,' Norina said, looking thoughtful. 'You couldn't have left her alone out there without a proper coat or a phone. You did the right thing, Ben.'

He'd kept thinking about his sister – another person he'd let down – and how, if it was her in that state, he'd have wanted someone to help her. Whether this woman was Lili or not really didn't matter at that present moment. She needed help. That's all there was to it.

'I'm just trying to work out what to do next. I was going to call the police but . . . '

Norina sighed and glanced in the direction of the sitting room. 'The police can wait. The first thing you need to do is get that young woman to a doctor.'

*

Who am I?

The words circuited her head over and over as the tall man drove her down the side of the loch in his aunt's car. However, her brain didn't seem at all inclined to share the answer to that question, which seemed most unfair.

55

Who . . . ? Who . . . ? Who . . . ?

The question drummed against her temples, pulling them taut, causing her forehead to ache. She closed her eyes and laid her head back.

'Are you okay?' The tall man . . . Ben . . . sounded tense.

She opened her eyes, then realised he was probably worried she'd slipped into unconsciousness, but it was a far more mundane reason than that: even though it wasn't noon yet, she was utterly exhausted. 'Yes . . . Yes, I'm fine . . . Or as fine as I think as I can be, given the situation.'

He nodded and turned his attention back to the road.

She'd tried to tell him she'd get the bus to the hospital, but he wouldn't have it. Anyway, he'd very correctly pointed out that she had no money, which had kind of decided things for her. And that she'd already been on a bus that morning and had got all . . . confused. *What if it happened again?* he'd asked. The thought made her head ache even more than it already did.

She looked out the window, finding the colours and the light soothing. Bracken and heather painted the hills with swathes of rust, ochre, and olive, beneath a sky created from a palette of greys. 'Thank you . . . for doing this.'

'You don't have to keep saying that, you know.'

She flushed. 'I just feel bad about taking you away from your family, or whatever plans you had for today. I don't expect a trip to the community hospital was top of your list.'

He made a huff that could have been a grudging laugh. 'Nope.'

'Tell me about yourself,' she said, and when he didn't answer, she glanced across at him. He was giving her a really strange look. 'Well, someone's got to make conversation. And the fact I can't tell you about my life is the reason we're heading to the hospital in the first place.'

'Good point,' he said, staring straight ahead again. For a moment or two, she thought he was going to ignore her request, but eventually he said, 'I live with my aunt at the B&B, along with my niece, Willow. We've just bought some holiday cottages from someone retiring from the business, but they need a bit of updating and repairing. That's where I would have been going today, to do some odd jobs.'

'Sorry . . . '

'You've said that almost as many times as you've said "thank you".'

'I just—'

'I know . . . You feel bad. But it's nothing I can't catch up on tomorrow. Besides, if our situations were reversed, wouldn't you help someone in your shoes?'

'I would. At least I *hope* I would.' She had nothing to go on, obviously. Maybe she was a right cow and wouldn't have lifted a finger . . . but if she stilled her mind, concentrated on what was *inside* herself, that was the truth she found there.

'There you go.'

They arrived at the small hospital in Lochgilphead about half an hour later, where she was seen by a triage nurse, had some bloods taken, and then was put through a dizzying round of tests – blood pressure, temperature, EEG, reflexes, a CT scan – and *so* many questions. Finally, almost four hours into the ordeal, she was actually ready to see a doctor.

He led her into a consulting room and invited her to sit down. 'Good afternoon. I'm the duty psychologist here, Dr

Manzar.' He glanced towards the door. 'Would you like your partner in here with you?'

'Oh!' The thought anyone might assume she and Ben were together hadn't even crossed her mind. 'He's not my partner . . . ' she said, aware of a flare of warmth in her belly as the suggestion burrowed itself into her consciousness, 'but he is my friend.'

Some might quibble that label, possibly even Ben himself, but he'd been by her side almost constantly since the incident at the café. There was something oddly steadying and familiar about his presence, and – for the moment, at least – he was the only person she knew in the world. Not only could she do with some moral support, but a second pair of ears to digest and remember what the doctor had to say would also be useful.

The doctor got up, opened the door, and motioned for Ben to come inside.

'Dr Manzar?' he said as he came in, his eyebrows lifting in mild surprise.

'Yes?'

'I'm Ben Robertson,' he said, holding out his hand. 'Catriona Robertson was my sister. I came along to a couple of appointments with her – oh, about six years ago.'

The doctor stopped looking perplexed, and he smiled broadly at Ben. 'Oh, yes! I remember now. That means Norina must also be your aunt. Whenever I have family visiting, I always recommend Fernpoint B&B. Invergarrig is the perfect place from which to explore this area.'

Ben smiled and shrugged as he sat down on the empty plastic chair. 'I've been roped into helping her out there.'

The doctor nodded. 'Well, it's nice to see you again.' He grew more serious. 'And I was so sorry to hear about Catriona.'

Something had happened to his sister? She glanced across at Ben. A shadow had fallen across his expression.

'Well . . . You're a most unusual case,' Dr Manzar said to her. 'The reason for all the tests was to rule out any underlying medical condition that might be causing your memory loss, but I'm pleased to say everything has come back negative. There's no indication of a head injury, infection, or seizure.'

She nodded, knowing she *should* feel better there was nothing physically wrong with her, but in some ways, a positive result would have been a relief, because until she had an explanation for what was going on inside her head, she doubted finding a solution was possible. 'Do you know what's wrong with me?' Her voice sounded small and quiet to her own ears.

Dr Manzar crossed one leg over the other and balanced his clipboard on his thigh. 'I suspect you have a form of dissociative amnesia.'

'Suspect?' Ben said. 'You don't know for sure?'

'It's what best fits the symptoms and circumstances, but diagnosis of this kind of amnesia can be tricky, but since there's no physical cause, this is the most likely scenario.'

None of this was making her feel any more hopeful, but she nodded mutely, more to signal she'd heard and understood than anything else.

'Normally, people with this condition might lose all or some memories of a particular time period, or maybe only memories associated with a particular place or person. It's much more unusual to have generalised amnesia – no knowledge at all about your own identity. I've only come across one other case in my twenty years as a psychologist, and never one of this particular nature.'

She swallowed. This information, although hardly unexpected, was making her head pound again, and she was dangerously close to bursting into tears. She wished she *could* slip into unconsciousness and let them run their tests and find out what was wrong with her while she lay peacefully in a hospital bed. That way, she wouldn't have to deal with any of it.

Come on, a voice said inside her head. *You can't run away from your problems.*

She didn't know whose voice it was – maybe it was her own – but it was making a very good point. Even though she felt like limply collapsing to the floor and sobbing, she forced herself to slow her breathing, to pay attention to what the doctor was telling her. She needed to understand. 'Checking out' wasn't an option.

He gave her a sympathetic look. So much for faking it 'til she made it. 'I know this is hard . . . Do you want to take a break?'

'No. I'll be okay, honestly. Carry on.'

Dr Manzar nodded. 'Dissociative amnesia is nearly always a result of some kind of psychological trauma. It's the brain's way of protecting itself. The mind shuts down, if you like, rather than dealing with the painful situation. Sometimes that combines with the "fight or flight" response, and people will not just distance themselves psychologically, but they might also put *literal* distance between themselves and the situation, taking unplanned and unexpected travel, and may only realise they've lost their memory when someone asks them for some pertinent personal information.'

She nodded, her teeth clenching together. That was *exactly* what had happened when the guy at the café had asked for her name. 'Will I . . . Will I get my memory back?'

Dr Manzar nodded. 'Most people suffering from this type of amnesia do eventually recover their memories, although there's no set timescale for that to happen.'

She began to tremble inwardly. This news made her feel hopeful and scared at the same time. 'It might be a few more days, then?'

'Maybe. But it could be weeks or even months.'

'Years?' she asked hoarsely, hoping against hope she was wrong.

'Well, that would be more unusual, but it can't be ruled out. I'm sorry.'

Ben shifted in his chair. 'What about treatment?'

'In such cases, psychotherapy is usually very effective.'

Her heart sank. 'There's nothing you can do today, no procedure, no pill, that might hurry things along?'

The doctor shook his head. 'I'm sorry. Treatment will involve uncovering the memories responsible for the dissociation and then dealing with those. Often there's an attempt to integrate the two sets of memories, but I also want to prepare you for the fact that regaining your memories may not be a gradual process. They may all come flooding in at once, and if this happens before the two sets of memories have been integrated, it's possible you won't remember anything that happened while you've been in this dissociative "fugue" state. Just like you did this morning, you might find yourself somewhere you didn't expect to be, wondering how you got there.'

More memory loss? Her inward trembling amplified to the point where her legs began to shake, and her breathing became fast and shallow. She was going to have another meltdown, right here in this tiny, sterile consulting room, wasn't she? Heaving in a couple of ragged breaths, she looked at Ben in panic.

He looked almost as pained as she did to hear this diagnosis. When he saw her looking at him, he reached out and held her hand. There was something about the warmth, the pure reality of him, that helped her feel a little more grounded. She wanted to hug him, she realised, to just bury her face into that fleece-clad shoulder and cling to his solid bulk once more. Hanging onto him by the pier had been the only time her universe had felt steady that day.

Dr Manzar looked sympathetically at her. 'I know this must all be very distressing for you, but there is hope. Please remember that. I'm going to refer you to a specialist memory loss unit in Glasgow.'

'I can't talk to *you*?'

Dr Manzar shook his head. 'While we do have a mental health unit attached to the hospital here, it deals mainly with community cases. You need someone who has more experience with this condition than we can offer.'

That was the moment she chose to burst into tears. She leant over, and began to make large, gulping sobs until she was sure there was no more breath left in her body. When she looked up, Dr Manzar was holding a box of tissues. He offered her one, not looking fazed in the slightest.

'It's completely understandable, and – dare I say it – completely normal for you to feel the way you do. But it is very likely you will get your memories back. It just might take some time. You'll be in good hands with the memory unit . . . ' He turned away and tapped something on the computer on the desk behind him. 'You'll probably get a referral letter in a couple of weeks.'

She sat up straighter. 'A couple of weeks? What do I do until then? Where do I go?'

Dr Manzar looked confused. 'You go home, of course.' He looked at her hand, still joined with Ben's. 'Since you're friends, I assumed you lived nearby.'

She shook her head, slid her fingers from Ben's firm grip and brought her hand to sit in her lap with the other one. 'We only met this morning. Ben's been . . . well, he's been very kind.'

'Oh.' Dr Manzar's forehead folded, creating two deep horizontal lines. 'I wasn't . . . In that case, I'm going to have to inform social services.'

'Social services?' Ben didn't look hugely pleased with that idea.

'I'm afraid so,' Dr Manzar said. 'If you can't go home because you don't know where it is or have any kind of support from friends or family, that means you'll be classed as a vulnerable person. We need to make arrangements, for you to get all the support you need.'

She swallowed, holding back a fresh round of tears. *Vulnerable*. She hated that expression. Mostly because it described exactly how she felt at that moment. Without any shell of memories or knowledge about the world and her place in it to protect her, she felt as if every nerve ending was raw and vigilant, exposed. And, somewhere in the depths of her subconscious, she knew she'd felt this way before, and it was a dangerous, dangerous place to be.

CHAPTER NINE

Almost a year before the wedding.

IT WAS A few weeks before I saw the man with the umbrella again. Most days, I lugged Octavia up to London and picked exactly the same busking spot at exactly the same time, and one bright winter morning, I was playing an Irish folk song that had the crowd of twenty or so clapping along when I saw a flash of camel-coloured wool at the back of the crowd. I knew it was him, even before I fully registered his face.

He wasn't smiling or tapping his foot like the other onlookers, but I knew his gaze was locked on me. Despite the cheery sunshine up above, I sorely wished it would rain. *Don't wander off*, I prayed. *Don't leave without saying a word*.

And after the next song, I took an unscheduled break. The audience scurried away, back to their sightseeing or their office jobs, but he stayed. 'Hi,' I said, resisting the urge to look at my feet. I had a feeling this man never needed to take refuge in the tops of his shoes.

'I came back to check if you really were as good as I thought you were.'

And . . . ? I asked silently, looking at him from under my lashes, too much of a coward to say the word out loud.

He answered me anyway, smiling that smile again. 'It was much better. You're growing, improving . . . I think you have a lot of potential.'

I swallowed. 'Thank you.'

He glanced around at the dirty street, the crowds of unimpressed tourists and passers-by. 'This really isn't the right venue for a talent like yours. You ought to be performing in concert halls, grand theatres.'

I couldn't help myself. I burst out laughing, partly from the irony of his words and partly because of the sheer stupidity of his suggestion. Yes, I had the talent – I knew that – but I lacked the ability to do any of the things he'd suggested, which *was* stupid. And pointless. And sad. Even so, hearing him compliment me that way applied balm to my battered creative soul.

'That's very nice of you to say that, but I honestly think I'm better off here.' He didn't know my story, and I wasn't about to tell him. I'd rather he went on thinking I was wasting my potential than knowing the truth.

'My name is Justin De la Hay. I'm a choreographer of contemporary dance – think edgy modern ballet, and you're on the right track.'

If you'd asked me to guess his career, that's not what I'd have come up with. He looked like a financier or a lawyer. I hadn't expected him to be an artist too.

'Anyway,' he continued, 'I know you think you belong on a street corner, but I don't, and I might be able to introduce you to people who could help you reach your true potential – if you're interested?'

I hugged Octavia to myself and chewed his words over. As

much as I thought it was impossible to hope for that, I found myself nodding.

'Would you like to go somewhere to chat about it? I promise I won't take up much of your time.'

The sensible girl from Penge inside me hesitated. He might be gorgeous. He might be sophisticated. But he was still a stranger. I didn't know him.

He seemed to sense my disquiet because then he added, 'We can go to the café over there . . . ' He nodded in the direction of one of the restaurants that lined the square, with wooden tables and big red umbrellas. 'We'll sit outside. You'll be perfectly safe.'

He smiled again, and this time I smiled along with him. 'Yes,' I answered quietly. 'I think I would really like that.'

*

I was standing on the landing, checking my thousandth outfit choice for the evening ahead in the only full-length mirror in our house, when my sister's highlighted head appeared at her bedroom door. She took in my floaty maxi skirt and ankle boots. 'Where you going?'

'Who says I'm going anywhere?'

'Come on . . . You've hardly worn anything but leggings for what seems like years and suddenly you're putting on make-up and leaving the house, practically bouncing down the path.'

Lo was right. My wardrobe had changed a bit in the two weeks since Justin had taken me for coffee, but I just smiled and changed the subject. 'Do you think this is a bit . . . you know . . . ?' My younger sister was always making fun of my eclectic dress sense, calling me 'hippy' and 'flower child', and

67

I usually responded by letting her know that, most days, she dressed like a middle-aged bank manager.

'I don't know. Where are you going?'

'Papillon.'

She frowned. 'Where's that?'

'Covent Garden.'

'Oh, *that* Papillon! Wow . . . I thought you were talking about somewhere around here.'

That made me smile. Penge had its charms, but it wasn't the most likely destination for upmarket French cuisine.

'He really likes you then, this guy?'

'Who said there's a guy?'

'No leggings . . . Bouncing down the path . . . Come on, Lil. I *know* there's a guy.'

'Oh, Lo . . . '

She rolled her eyes at my use of her childhood nickname. Since she got her entry-level job at a management consulting firm, she'd been trying to make us all call her by her full name, but old habits die hard. I'd decided that if my two-year-old sister was going to call me 'Lili', which only bore a passing resemblance to my name, then I was going to call her 'Lolo', which bore even less to hers. To four-year-old me, it had made complete sense. Over the years, our nicknames had eroded into 'Lil' and 'Lo'. Hardly anyone in our wider family used our full names any more. I suspected a few of them didn't even remember what they were.

I dragged Lo into my bedroom so we could chat without being overheard from downstairs. 'His name is Justin, and he's amazing. He's artistic and clever, really good-looking, sophisticated . . . '

Lo squealed and pulled me into a hug before pushing me away again and holding me at arm's-length. 'Oh, my god! I'm so happy for you! It's about time you bounced back after what Photographer Guy did to you.'

'It's not really like that,' I said, easing myself from Lo's arms and brushing off any mention of Ben. I didn't want to spoil this moment by thinking about him. 'Justin's out of my league. And it's more like a business meeting. He says he knows people who can help me with my music. We're just getting together to discuss that.'

Lo raised an eyebrow. 'At Papillon? On a Saturday night? Sounds like a date to me.'

I nodded sadly. 'I'm too young for him. Too . . . '

Lo gave me a stern look. 'Don't do that, Lil. Don't you put yourself down. Why *wouldn't* he want to be with you? You're sweet and loyal and clever and so, so talented. He'd be lucky to have you!'

And this was why I loved my sister to bits. I knew it hadn't been easy for her over the years, always seeing Mum and Dad shower me with praise and attention, always bragging about me to friends and family because of my music, but she'd never been jealous, had never decided to compete for our parents' attention, as some of my friends and their sisters did. If there was one person I could count on in the world, it was Lo.

'Well, you know that, and I know that,' I said, 'but he hasn't quite woken up to the fact yet. Which is probably okay, because I don't want to get into anything serious with anyone right now. But I still get to go out to a fancy restaurant with a charming older man. That's better than staying at home and watching *Casualty* with Mum and Dad.'

'Ouch,' Lo said. 'Rub it in for your single sister, why don't you?' But she laughed and pulled me towards her again, hugging me tightly. 'Even if he can't see what a catch he's got, he's given you something precious. I haven't seen you light up like this in a long time.'

'I know,' I said. At first, I'd been relieved to leave the Conservatory, but as time had gone by I'd mourned the future I'd abandoned.

Lo patted me on the back, and we disentangled ourselves. As I pulled away, I caught my reflection in the mirror, and I instantly saw why my sister made fun of me. I looked hopelessly young and air-headed in my flowing skirts, layered necklaces, and silver bangles. I held my breath and turned to her, a thought suddenly occurring to me. 'Can I borrow something of yours?'

CHAPTER TEN

Now.

THE EXAM ROOM door closed. Ben looked at the woman who might be Lili, and she looked back at him. 'So, it's definitely amnesia,' she said, more for something to say, Ben guessed, rather than because it needed saying.

'Yes.' He'd been hoping that the visit to the hospital would provide some answers, set a chain of action in motion that would help her in some way, but all they'd accomplished was pin a label to her, and it was one they'd both suspected all along.

'I need to use the ladies',' she said quietly.

He nodded, and she gave him a backwards glance as she headed down the corridor to where a set of patient toilets were clearly signposted. He exhaled as she disappeared inside and turned a full circle, running both hands through his hair. What was he going to do about her?

Was she Lili? Or was his memory of her, now five years old, being overwritten by the face of the woman he'd met today? Was he merging the two similar but separate faces into one? He just couldn't tell.

And if it *was* her, why had she come to Invergarrig? Was

this some weird, wouldn't-believe-it-if-you-paid-me coincidence? Or had she meant to come here because some part of her remembered his connection to this place? And if she had, what did that mean?

He was pacing up and down the waiting area when he spotted Dr Manzar heading out of the treatment room, and he waved to catch his attention.

'Everything okay?' the doctor said.

Ben walked towards him. 'I just want to know what happens next . . . What do we do about reuniting her with her family? Where does she go in the meantime?'

'Well, social services will try to find her somewhere to stay. It'll probably be emergency accommodation, which is limited in a rural area like this. It might mean sending her on to Glasgow since that's where she'll be receiving treatment. She can discuss all of this with the on-call social worker when they arrive. But it could be a while. Sorry . . . I know you've been here a long time already.'

Ben frowned. 'Okay.'

'Well,' Dr Manzar said, 'if that's all . . . ?'

'Actually, there is something else I wanted to ask you . . . '

The doctor's eyebrows lifted slightly. 'Yes?'

'I'm really not sure about this, but there is a possibility that she and I have met before.'

'A possibility?'

Ben sighed. 'She resembles someone I met very briefly a few years ago, but there are also differences that don't add up, so I really can't be sure. And even if I'm right, I'm not sure I know much that will help. We only spent just over a day in each other's company. All I knew was that she lived somewhere within easy travelling distance of London, and her first name. Do you think I should tell her?'

Dr Manzar pursed his lips together. 'I would prefer to let the specialists at the memory unit advise you on that. Like I said, she's in a vulnerable position at the moment, not just physically but emotionally and psychologically. She's desperately searching for a sense of identity, and if you're wrong, it could be really upsetting for her.'

'Okay,' Ben said, but the frown he'd been wearing deepened. He didn't like the idea of keeping it from her, but what Dr Manzar was saying made sense.

'However, I'd definitely mention it to the police when you speak to them.'

'That was going to be my next move.'

'Social services will almost certainly contact them after speaking to her. Tell them what you know, and they can check it out with any reports of missing persons from that area. Then you'll have proof – or not – to back up your suspicions.'

Ben nodded, feeling a little more relieved. That sounded like a sensible plan, but it meant that, very soon, he'd leave the hospital and she'd disappear into the night with an anonymous social worker, untraceable, uncontactable. He glanced in the direction of the ladies' loos before looking back at Dr Manzar. 'What if I could offer her somewhere safe to stay tonight rather than a hostel somewhere far away? Would that be allowed?'

'What do you mean?'

'My aunt and I might be able to offer her accommodation.'

Dr Manzar looked thoughtful. 'I wouldn't normally suggest something like that, but seeing as I've known your family for at least a decade . . . and I know you and Norina must have had all the usual safeguarding checks in order for Willow to stay with you, I suppose I could tell the on-call social worker to visit you in Invergarrig rather than you both having to wait around here for another couple of hours.'

'That would be perfect.'

'The final decision will be up to social services.'

'I know. Thank you.'

Moments later, the subject of their conversation emerged from the ladies'. She looked as if she'd splashed water on her face and had freshened herself up a bit. She went to slump into one of the plastic chairs, but Ben shook his head. 'Change of plans. The doc says you can come back to Invergarrig with me – as long as you're okay with that?'

*

She waited behind Ben as he approached the first cottage in a row of four and opened the sturdy wooden door, its black paint stark against the white render. The social worker who'd turned up to chat with her had also been Willow's social worker, and he'd signed off on Ben's suggestion to let her stay at his cottage temporarily. No need to be shipped off to a hostel or wherever 'vulnerable people' ended up, thank goodness.

Before following Ben through the open door, she took one last look at the mist gathering at the other side of the loch, ghostly grey in the moonlight. Did she know this place? Had she been here before? Was that why she'd come to this town?

She was still finding it difficult to come to grips with being a blank sheet of paper, an anonymous person with no existence, no past, no future, other than today. In one part of her brain, she understood it perfectly, but in another . . . well, that part shrank away from prodding, scared of what it might find.

They stepped into the front room of the cottage, decorated in neutral tones with splashes of colour here and there – a checked blanket in the same hues as the heathery hills outside, cushions in earthy tones. 'This is it,' Ben said, leading her into a small kitchen with a dining table at the back of the cottage. 'You can't use the downstairs toilet just now, and there's a few bits of tiling to be done here and there, but other than that, everything is functional. I'll leave the heating on low all day. That way, you won't have to bother messing around with the controls.'

He showed her how the oven worked and where the light switches were, and then they toured the upstairs, which had two good-sized bedrooms with a bathroom sandwiched in between. 'You're probably better off in the front room,' he said. 'Bigger bed.'

She nodded. She'd noticed the back bedroom had only a single. The lilac walls and the small wardrobe and desk suggested it was intended for his niece. She would have chosen the front bedroom anyway, even if she'd had to sleep on the floor, for its view over the loch through a large sash window. Thankfully it had a king-sized bed, currently bare of anything but a mattress.

This would be his room, she realised. It suited him. There were some stunning black-and-white landscape photographs on one wall, and above the bed was a large print of what seemed to be a ruined church, ivy winding around the tall, elegant buttresses of a glassless Gothic window. She was about to ask where it had been taken when there was a noise downstairs, and a husky female voice called out Ben's name.

'Up here!' he yelled back, and a moment later, a rather short and rather round woman with sandy wavy hair and a no-nonsense expression appeared in the doorway, carrying what looked like a rolled-up duvet in a bag. She was joined by a rather breathless little girl with long, dark pigtails and large round glasses. 'I carried the pillowcases and sheets all the way here!' she announced proudly to Ben, then she spotted their guest. 'Hiya!' she said brightly. 'You must be the lady who's staying in our cottage for a wee bit.'

'Yes . . . and thank you. I'm guessing you must be Willow.'

The girl beamed at her. Shyness was definitely not a problem for this one. 'Have you seen my room? You can stay in that one if you like.' She lowered her voice and leaned forward as if imparting serious information that the two other adults in the room wouldn't understand. 'It's purple. You know, for *girls*.'

She stifled a smile. 'I saw it. It's lovely.'

'This bed will do fine enough,' the woman said as she dumped the bag onto the bed and held out a hand. 'I'm Norina – Ben's aunt. Don't you worry, pet. We'll make sure you're okay until everything gets sorted out. Oh, and I thought you could do with this . . . ' Norina handed her an older-looking smartphone. 'Just in case you need anything. The B&B is just around the corner, and we can be here in a jiffy.'

'Th-thank you.' She took the phone and clutched it to her chest. They were all being so kind it made her eyes fill, and she had to take in a breath before she could talk again. 'I just

76

wish I could do something to repay you. Can I help you with the B&B tomorrow? There must be something I can do there.'

Norina regarded her carefully. 'I could do with an extra pair of hands at breakfast, and there's always a heap of washing to be done. Do you think you're up to it?'

She nodded, smiling, and hoped desperately she was being truthful, because for the first time that day, she didn't feel completely useless.

'What's your name?' Willow asked.

She felt a slight tremor, similar to the feeling she'd experienced outside the café, but maybe she was getting used to coming up blank when someone asked that question because it was only that – a tremor. An aftershock. She blinked at the little girl. How did she answer this? 'Um . . . I don't have one at the moment.'

'Everybody has a name!'

'I know . . . And I do too. It's just . . . '

Before she could find the right words, Ben knelt down and explained the situation to his niece quickly and simply in a way that made sense to a child her age. Willow nodded when he'd finished, accepting what he'd told her without doubt, but it obviously had set her thinking because, after a few moments, she said, 'I sometimes have pretend names when I'm playing warrior princess games with my friends. Perhaps you could have one of those? You know, just 'til you remember yours?'

'A warrior princess name?' Ben asked, looking perplexed.

Willow laughed, snorting and covering her mouth with her hand as she giggled. It was adorable. 'A *pretend* name. One you use for a bit 'til you go back to your real one.'

'It makes sense,' Ben said, and both he and his aunt looked enquiringly at their guest.

She nodded her agreement. 'I suppose it does. I can't just be called "Oi, you!" for the next—' she swallowed as she realised she had no idea how long it might be '—the next couple of weeks.'

Willow bounced up and down. 'Can I help? I always come up with the best names, don't I, Uncle Ben? I know . . . Moana!'

Ben gave her a weary look. 'We are not naming her after someone from a Disney film. Besides, you named your hamster Moana, and it would be confusing to have two of them.'

'Elsa, then!' Willow said, equally hopeful.

Ben rolled his eyes and shook his head.

Willow concentrated with the kind of fierceness only a five-year-old could muster. Finally, she looked up and said, 'How about "Alice"? Like the book we're reading at bedtime?'

'*Alice in Wonderland*?' Ben asked.

Willow nodded earnestly. 'Because Alice is lost in a place she doesn't know too.'

The look of hope on the little girl's face was too much for her to bear. 'Okay,' she said. 'I'll be Alice.' She might as well. It was as good a name as any.

CHAPTER ELEVEN

Eleven months before the wedding.

I STOOD OUTSIDE the fancy French brasserie in Covent Garden, tugging at the worn ends of my coat sleeves repeatedly. It was chilly, so I pulled it closer around my body. The rich blue sky was studded with stars, meaning there was no cloud cover, and while the shift dress I'd borrowed from Lo was a decent thickness, it was also sleeveless.

Just as my toes were starting to freeze inside a pair of Lo's heels, Justin arrived. He was wearing a beautiful suit, as always, with his smart shoes and his camel-coloured coat. His sandy-blond hair was perfectly combed, with just a little bit of rakish floppiness at the fringe. When he smiled at me, the jittery sensation that had plagued me all afternoon intensified.

'You look lovely,' he said and leaned in to kiss me on the cheek.

I closed my eyes before he pulled away, inhaling his crisp aftershave, then reminded myself I shouldn't read anything into a peck on the cheek. He probably greeted everyone that way.

The next couple of minutes were a blur. He ushered me inside, greeting the maître d' by name, and we were led through the elegant restaurant, full of thick white linen and sparkling crystal, to our table. I was slightly confused as Justin pulled out a chair for me because I'd been picturing a cosy little table for two, but this one was set for four.

A waiter appeared. 'Would you like to order a drink, sir?'

'Not just at the moment,' Justin said, handing the wine menu back to him. 'We'll wait until the rest of the party arrive.'

I stopped admiring the gilt and crystal of the restaurant's decor and whipped my head round to look at him. 'Rest of the party?'

Justin beamed back at me from across the table. His smile was one of the most beautiful things about him. 'I should have told you, I know, but I wanted it to be a surprise.' He'd only just finished saying the words when he looked towards the door. 'Oh, look. Here they are now . . .'

I followed his gaze to where two immaculately dressed men were standing. One was tall and stocky, with the face of an East End gangster, but when he arrived at our table and introduced himself as Felix Lambert, and his partner as Haru Morishita, instead of having the voice to match his appearance, he sounded more like Sir Patrick Stewart.

'Felix and Haru are two of my oldest friends,' Justin said and then returned the favour with the introduction. They both gave me a kiss on each cheek, and then we all took our seats. 'I've asked them along this evening, not only because they're a terrifically fun couple, but because Felix here is a composer, and we have something we'd like to discuss with you.'

My smile was plastic as I looked back at Justin. I knew I'd told my sister this wasn't a date, but I realised that up until that moment, I'd been hoping it was, that maybe he saw me as more than a project to work on.

Justin explained that Felix was composing a piece of music for a dance he was choreographing and that Haru was going to be the soloist performing it. It would be the opening number in an evening of contemporary dance that Justin's company was working on which would ultimately run at Sadler's Wells.

'Justin told me you are very talented,' Felix said. 'Of course, we would need to audition you properly, hear you playing the actual piece, but I think you might be just the right person to bring the freshness and dynamism we're looking for.'

My mouth went dry. This was amazing. All I'd ever wanted was to play professionally, but just as soon as the elation flushed through me, terror arrived hot on its heels. 'I . . . I really don't think I'm—'

Justin swatted my objection away, grabbing my hand and looking into my eyes. 'Of course you're good enough!'

I swallowed. That wasn't what I'd been about to say. He smiled at me, as if that alone would solve any and all problems the universe held. As I looked at him, I was tempted to believe him, but I knew I wasn't that lucky. 'This would mean playing . . . in front of people?'

Justin's smile held, but confusion clouded his eyes. 'Who else would you play for?'

'And there'd be a fee, of course,' Felix added, as if he wasn't really listening to our part of the conversation. 'And I assume you've been in a recording studio before?'

I brightened. 'A studio?'

'It seems like the best idea,' Justin said. 'Live music for dance performances can be so tricky. Sorry . . . I've told Felix how great you are with a crowd around you, but I think if the audition turns out okay, it might be for the best. Especially for a – how shall we put it? – a less *seasoned* performer.'

I didn't bother telling him he'd got the wrong end of the stick, that I wasn't disappointed in the slightest about not performing live. 'I'm just so grateful you'd think of me,' I said, smiling so hard my cheeks ached. Maybe there was a way forward for me after all? A career I could carve out for myself that didn't involve stuffy chamber orchestras and stifling solos?

I relaxed as the meal continued. Justin spoke the most, dominating the conversation, and I couldn't help but marvel at him. He was so together, so confident. I tried not to stare at him too much, sure Felix had clocked me adoring him from afar, but my eyes were drawn to him when I wasn't consciously making them rest on something else.

It's enough that he thinks I'm talented, I told myself, *that he thinks I'm worth something.* I hadn't felt that way in a long time.

Even so, as the bill was paid and Felix and Haru began to shift in their chairs, readying themselves to go home, my heart sank. It had been one of the most magical nights of my life. When would I ever get a chance to eat somewhere like this again? Or to feel as if I was in the middle of something, doing something important with important people, rather than always looking on from the fringes?

They all air-kissed me and each other goodbye, and after Felix and Haru left, Justin helped me into my coat, and we walked outside into the brisk March night. I expected him to say his farewells to me too, but he said, 'Why don't I walk you to the station?'

I blinked at him. 'It's okay. I'm used to getting the train on my own.'

Why? Why did I say that?

He glanced towards the narrow roads leading back towards The Strand. 'I don't like to think of you walking out there by yourself.' He paused to look at me intently. 'Not when you look like you do in that dress.'

I was glad it was dark because he couldn't see how furiously I was blushing. 'If it's not too much trouble.'

He smiled again then, but this one was different. It wasn't the dazzling one he'd blessed us with many times over dinner, like a floodlight, illuminating everything. This one was a spotlight trained solely on me. 'It would be my pleasure.'

CHAPTER TWELVE

Now.

ALICE SAT ON the edge of the bed, the duvet wrapped around her shoulders. She was wearing brushed cotton pyjamas from a bag of clothes that one of Norina's friends had been going to give to the charity shop but had given to her instead. Not everything had fitted, but there was enough basic clothing – jeans, jumpers, and tops. She'd also discovered a new pack of underwear in the bag, along with some basic toiletries, which she'd suspected Norina had bought from somewhere in town while she and Ben had been at the hospital.

The blind was up, and Alice stared out of the window into the night. She'd tried to sleep but, despite her exhaustion, she'd only managed a few fitful hours before opening her eyes, feeling fully awake again.

A security light illuminated the narrow drive that ran between the row of cottages and the iron railings overlooking the loch, throwing bright rippling reflections onto the water, but beyond that . . . Nothing. Here, at the beginning of the Highlands, there was little light pollution, so the night was complete. Even the hills on the other side of the water had been swallowed by the darkness. Sometimes she thought she could discern their shapes, but then the blackness shifted, and she wasn't sure if it was just her mind playing tricks on her.

She glanced across at where her jeans, jumper and under-wear sat neatly folded on the chair in the corner. This was what her life was now . . . a few sparse details, the rest of the picture lost. All she had was a small pile of clothes and a borrowed name.

Alice. She rolled the word around her mind. It was as if it was almost right but not quite, like a pair of shoes, no matter how comfortable, that belonged to someone else.

She turned her attention back to something more concrete, the clothes she'd been wearing that day. She'd examined them carefully when she'd got undressed. They were good quality. She'd recognised the designer brands instantly. How? She shook her head, still wondering why she remembered those names when her own was lost to her.

Who am I?

This was the question that had not only roused her from her sleep but prevented her from sinking back into it. It was as if, now the shock of the day had worn off, she was starting to come to grips with the implication of what was happening to her.

She was so grateful to Ben – her rescuer – and Norina for jumping to the aid of a stranger so quickly, even to little Willow for brightening her evening, but when she thought of them, they seemed so solid, so certain of their identities and their places in the world. Whereas she felt . . . unconnected. Set adrift. In her more outlandish mental wanderings, she wondered if she might simply evaporate. After all, there was nothing much to anchor her to reality.

Willow's serious face as she'd talked about the purple bedroom being for girls came into her mind, and at first, her mood lifted, but then there was a sudden drop, like a roller coaster pitching downwards after a slow and suspenseful climb.

Do I have children? Are they missing me, wondering where I was when it was time to tuck them into bed this evening? Is there a husband or a partner frantically searching for me?

When she'd had a shower earlier that evening, she'd checked her abdomen, looking for any tell-tale scars. There hadn't been any evidence of a C-section, but of course that didn't rule children out.

She looked down at her finger. It was too dark to see properly, so she reached over and turned on the bedside light. There was a faint silvery mark at the base of her left ring finger, and when she touched the spot, it was smoother than the surrounding skin. The more she examined the mark, the more certain she became it had been left by a wedding band or possibly an engagement ring.

Had it been stolen or lost, as her bag and phone had been? There might have been a deeper dent in her flesh if it had recently been removed, but how long would it take for something like that to fade? Only minutes, she suspected. Hours at the most. Which didn't help her much. She could have been married five years ago or engaged yesterday, and there was no way to tell which.

The only other piece of jewellery she wore was a silver pendant – a small silver bee on a chain that she'd discovered during the dizzying rounds of hospital tests. She touched it gently. It was pretty but somehow seemed out of step with her other belongings.

However, she was too tired to ponder that, so she turned the light off and went back to staring at the loch. At first, it was utter darkness, but as she sat and patiently waited, the small details she'd noticed earlier came slowly back into focus, shades of grey against the blackness of the night.

Now that the truth of her situation was finally hitting her, she'd expected she'd feel more emotional, but she was oddly calm. How could you grieve for a life you never even remembered you'd had? She just knew it was missing, felt the gaping hole inside of her. But it didn't ache. It was just . . . empty. The only thing that niggled was one word the doctor had said at the hospital.

Trauma.

She lay down on the bed, spread the duvet out over herself and stared at the ceiling, making a show of enticing her body into sleep, even though she doubted it would cooperate. If there was anything keeping her awake more than the million and one questions circuiting her head, it was the answers to those questions – answers she wasn't sure she wanted to know.

CHAPTER THIRTEEN

Now.

'AH, THERE YOU are,' Norina said to Ben as he walked into the kitchen at the B&B for his breakfast. 'Can you look at the sink in room eight this morning? It's not draining again.'

He sighed. Having plunged it the previous weekend, he'd hoped it would have been sorted. 'Will do.'

The guests occupying that room didn't leave until after eleven. When Ben got around to checking the sink, he found Alice in the room, making swift work of changing the sheets and pillowcases. 'Hi,' he said when he saw her. 'Just here to do a bit of light plumbing. I'm under orders.'

Alice smiled as she plumped a pillow and placed it back on the bed. 'She's a force to be reckoned with, your aunt, isn't she?'

He let out a gruff laugh. 'She is that.'

He did some preliminary checks on the sink – definitely blocked again – and was just about to get going when Willow burst through the door. 'There you are!' she said. 'Can we go on a fairy walk? Please?'

Alice shot him a quizzical look. 'A fairy walk?'

'Why don't you fill Alice in?' Ben said to Willow.

'It's something we do every Sunday,' the little girl said, lolling against the door jamb. 'We go up to the castle gardens and hunt for fairies, and pixies, and sprites! I never seem to be fast enough to spot them, but Uncle Ben does sometimes, don't you, Uncle Ben?'

Alice hid a smile. 'You do?'

'Only sometimes,' he replied seriously.

'I know!' Willow said. 'Why don't you come with us? Then you can see for yourself.'

'I'm not sure Alice will want to—'

'Why not? I've never seen a fairy before.' Alice shot a wink at Ben. 'And I'd like to see the castle up close.'

'Yay!' Willow said, practically bouncing up and down. 'It'll be nice to have another girl come along. Auntie Nee-nee's hips aren't up to fairy walks. I'll go and get my coat!'

'Hang on, wee miss! If you hadn't noticed, Alice and I have work to do. It'll have to wait until after lunch.'

Willow's face fell. 'That's going to be ages!'

'How about you do the homework you've got, and then we can have an extra-long walk?'

Willow's disgruntled expression didn't change, but she said 'fine!' in a way her mother would have been proud of and stomped off.

'She's a lovely little girl,' Alice said when Willow was out of earshot. 'Quite a character.'

'That she is,' Ben said, as he went back into the tiny en suite, knelt on the floor and put a bucket under the U-bend so he could undo it.

'What brought her to live here with you and Norina?'

Ben stopped what he was doing and stared at the plastic

joint he was unscrewing. When he'd got back to Invergarrig, the town grapevine had already been at work so everyone had known what had happened to Cat, which had saved him the chore of telling the story over and over, but it meant he wasn't used to saying these words out loud. He cleared his throat, continued removing the U-bend, and attempted to keep his tone neutral. 'My sister, Willow's mum, died almost a year ago.'

He'd been able to hear the rustle of sheets, pillows being punched and fluffed, but the noise stopped. A shadow fell across the open bathroom door. 'I'm so sorry. I shouldn't have asked, shouldn't have been so nosey . . .'

He turned to look at her, silhouetted against the bright morning light streaming through the tall windows on the other side of the room. She maintained eye contact, didn't look away, which was more than some of the townspeople had done when he'd returned home.

'That must have been awful,' she added softly.

He grunted. That was an understatement. 'Yeah, it was. But it was worse for Willow.'

He turned to fiddle with the plumbing again, finding it was easier to talk when he was looking at the underneath of a sink. 'Sometimes I wonder if she really gets it, if she isn't expecting her mum to walk through the door one day, sit down at the kitchen table and talk someone into making her a cup of tea, the way she always did.'

'Did your sister live in Invergarrig too?'

He shook his head. 'Glasgow.'

'That must have been a big change for Willow,' she said. 'To lose her mum and move here in all one go.'

He got up off the floor and met her enquiring gaze. 'Willow was already living here. Norina's had custody of her for the last three years. Cat had . . . issues. Addiction issues. She got clean while she was pregnant and stayed that way for a couple of years. I didn't ever doubt her love for Willow, but her lifestyle . . . ' He shook his head and looked away. 'Willow needed stability, a chance to have a proper education, not skip from place to place to avoid angry landlords. Or worse.' He sighed. 'I hoped we wouldn't need to rely on it, but I pushed Cat to draw up a will, and after she died we discovered she'd named me as Willow's guardian, not Norina, as we'd all assumed she would, so Willow is my responsibility now.'

Alice nodded, her eyes full of understanding. 'Well, she seems a very bright and confident little girl. You seem to be doing a terrific job.'

'We're . . . managing.' At least, he hoped they were.

'And you sure you don't mind if I come on this walk with you?'

He turned his attention back to the sink, a messy problem but a simple one compared to examining how he felt about Cat's death. 'I'd be glad of the company.'

CHAPTER FOURTEEN

Eleven months before the wedding.

JUSTIN AND I strolled along The Strand towards Charing Cross station. Even though it was only half past ten, it was still moderately busy. People milled on the pavement, either just having spilled out of a theatre after seeing a West End show, ready to eat or wend their way home. Others were fresh off the train, raring to start their night out in the bars and clubs of nearby Soho. Lights glittered, and buses and taxis rumbled past us intermittently, along with a few brave cyclists.

Justin jammed his hands in his coat pockets, his expression earnest. It made him look closer to my age. 'Can I ask you something?'

'If you like.'

'What made you leave the Conservatory?'

I gulped in a breath. Oh. He wanted to talk about that – the one thing I'd really rather not discuss. But I'd dug my own grave regarding this. When we'd gone for coffee, I'd been so desperate to make him like me that I'd mentioned where I'd studied music. It had only taken a little bit of burrowing on his part to get more out of me. However, as I mirrored him, hiding my clenched fists in my own pockets, I realised that maybe he was the one person who might understand.

'I got in on a scholarship. I knew I was really lucky, and I was so excited to go. Finally, I could be with people who loved music as much as I did. I thought it would be heaven.'

'But it wasn't?'

I sighed. 'No, it really wasn't.' And I went on to tell him about Charlie Bloody Banister and his campaign to make sure he shone, and I didn't.

'You didn't let him get to you, did you?'

I looked back at Justin, my expression heavy. 'I wish I could tell you I didn't. It started out as something so small . . . I was asked to play principal second violin in the Conservatory's concerto orchestra – quite a coup for someone only just starting their second year. Charlie got in, but only as fifth chair in my section. Every time we played, I could feel him watching me, judging me. Sometimes he'd scrape his chair or do terrible fake coughing to put me off. It didn't always work, but I began to get more and more nervous every time I performed, just in case it'd be one of the times it did. Things went from bad to worse after that.'

It hadn't helped that when I'd returned to the Conservatory for my second year, that I was feeling low and unmotivated. I had Ben the Photographer to thank for that, too – but I didn't tell Justin about that. It seemed too personal to reveal at that point.

'And then it just became a vicious cycle – the more nervous I got about performing, the more mistakes I made. Even the tutors and lecturers commented on it.' I looked down at my feet as I walked. 'I knew they all thought they'd made a mistake, that they should have given the scholarship to someone else. Eventually, it got too much, and I dropped out.'

'You couldn't have lasted it out?'

I laughed softly to myself. I was sure someone like Justin could have done, but I'd discovered I was just as pathetic as they all thought I was. Too weak. Not cut out for it. 'I was given one last chance, a solo.' I paused. My stomach chilled even at the thought of it. 'I made an absolute mess of it. Just forgot the music mid-flow . . . And then I sat there on the stage, frozen like a rabbit in the headlights until somebody started to slow clap. I'm sure it was him – Charlie. I ran off the stage, crying my eyes out, and promptly threw up in the nearest toilet. After that, I couldn't face going back. And even if I could, what good is a violinist who can't play in front of people?'

Justin stopped walking and turned to face me. He put a hand on either of my shoulders, making me look at him. 'But you know that what you've been doing, coming up to London to busk . . . That shows how incredibly brave you are. You proved to yourself that you *can* play in front of people.'

I gave him a watery smile. 'I know, I am pleased about that, but . . . '

'But?'

'It's not the same.'

'Why not?'

I broke eye contact. 'Because those people don't matter. They can't shape my future, give me the dreams I want for myself. They might enjoy a piece of pretty music as they stroll on by, but that's it.' While those had been the very reasons I'd started busking in the first place, they were now starting to chafe.

94

'I don't think you give yourself enough credit.' He waited for me to look at him again. 'I believe in you.'

I smiled, just a little, and saw the corners of his mouth curl up in return, but then he grew serious, let his hands drop from my shoulders, and we began walking again. 'If you want to survive in this business, you can't let other people define you.'

I made a small, scoffing laugh. 'That's easy for someone like you to say.'

His head turned sharply. 'There are always people out there who want to undermine you if you have real talent.' He fell silent for a moment. 'I don't normally share this with people, but I think you need to hear this . . .'

I held my breath, heart swelling that he might have singled me out in any way.

'I was married,' he said, his voice and expression bleak. 'She was a dancer . . . We built my company together, both as hungry for success as each other, and while we were still making our mark, it was okay. But once we'd reached a certain level, she became restless. I didn't see it at first – I loved her so much, you see. I put Paulina on a pedestal, and it blinded me to who she really was.'

'What did she do?' I asked breathlessly.

'She betrayed me.' He stared ahead as we neared Charing Cross and turned down the cobbled road that ran beside it towards Embankment Tube station. 'She deserted me on the opening night of one of our most important premieres. No word, no apology – just disappeared. Thankfully, we had an understudy. Later, I discovered she'd left me for another man who had connections to the Royal Ballet. I'm pretty sure something had been going on for months, if not years.'

I stared at Justin. I couldn't compute how anyone could consider him anything less than perfect.

His expression darkened. 'That bitch only married me for what I could do for her, and what she thought she could get out of me. She took everything I'd done for her and threw it back in my face.'

I felt a sudden flush of hatred for this anonymous woman, for how she'd hurt him, because it was clear the wound went deep, even now. Yet, I marvelled at how together he appeared, how confident. It gave me hope that one day I might bounce back too, that maybe I wasn't a lost cause after all.

We'd reached the outside of the station, and he stopped and turned to me. 'This is what I'm saying . . . You have to take what happened to you and let it make you stronger. It's the only way.'

I nodded mutely. I knew he was telling the truth; I just didn't know how to do that.

As if he was reading my mind, he said, 'And this job is your first step.'

'What if I can't do it? What if I freeze and can't play?'

'Didn't you say that it's when you play live you have an issue?'

'Yes.'

'I think you can do it – you've been busking in front of people for weeks.'

I wished I had his certainty. 'Thank you,' I said, 'for everything you've done.'

He stared back into my eyes. As the seconds ticked past, I began to flush, and just as I thought he was going to dip his head, that he was actually going to kiss me, he exhaled loudly and turned away. He waved his arm to attract one of the black cabs parked under the nearby bridge, then took my hand and led me towards one with its orange 'For Hire' sign lit up.

'What are you doing? I can't—'

'I don't like the thought of you travelling home alone on the Underground, and then the train,' he said. 'It's late, and you're a beautiful young woman . . . '

I forgot to argue with him because there was only one thought circuiting my head: *He called me beautiful.*

He opened the rear door and ushered me inside, and prepared to talk through the rolled-down passenger window to the driver. 'Where do you live?'

'Penge. But that's more than ten miles away.' I glanced at the driver and lowered my voice. 'It'll cost a fortune!'

He shrugged. 'I won't be happy unless you let me take care of you this way.'

I was tempted to argue. Not because I didn't want to take a cab – I really didn't like travelling on my own at night; sometimes there were some real weirdos on the stopping train to Orpington – but because it felt like too much.

Yet again, he read my mind. He looked at me seriously, but there was a playfulness behind his eyes. 'Let me do this for you.'

I stared back at him as he rested his hand on the roof of the cab, his face above mine and oh so close. I wished he would close the distance, but he'd given no indication that he saw me as anything but a talented youngster to help along the way. And that would have to be enough. It *was* enough. After our dinner tonight, and our talk as we'd walked back to the station, I no longer felt as if the world was ending.

He had a way of building me up so I could almost believe in myself again.

'Good night.' He closed the door and rapped a couple of times on the roof to signal the driver, but before it could pull away, he opened the door, jumped inside and grabbed my hand. 'I can't bear to say goodbye,' he said, looking deep into my eyes. 'You're the most astonishing creature I've ever met – an angel – and I haven't been able to stop thinking about you for weeks! I'm sorry, but I just have to do this . . .'

And he leaned in and kissed me the way I'd wanted him to all evening.

CHAPTER FIFTEEN

Now.

THE WINDING DRIVE that led to Invergarrig Castle was long, lined with grassy banks. There was a field on one side, a lichen-covered woodland on the other, shielding it from the main road that led out of town. Alice walked beside Ben in comfortable silence as Willow ran ahead, now and then scampering back to them with a guess at where the elusive fairies might be found.

It had been a long day. She'd been up since four, unable to sleep properly and knocking on the door of the B&B at six on the dot. However, she'd rather be on this 'fairy walk' with Ben and Willow, rather than sitting in that little cottage, only her thoughts for company.

Work at the B&B had been satisfying. Norina had put her in charge of bacon, mushrooms and toast. It had felt completely natural to stand at the large six-ring hob, pushing rashers around the pan, as if it was something she'd done a thousand times before. It had made her happy to think that something from her missing life had stuck, that she had at least one piece of information about herself – she could cook.

However, whether she could do anything more complicated than breakfast was still to be seen.

She glanced across at Ben, who had his hands in his pockets, his gaze far away. She'd been aware of him the very second he'd stepped into the kitchen that morning, even though she hadn't turned to look at him. She might have been imagining it, but she'd sensed him studying her. Not in a scrutinising way, but in a way that had made it hard to concentrate. One or two bits of bacon might've ended up a little darker than they should have been. She'd flipped them onto the other side and hoped Norina wouldn't notice.

They walked in silence for a while, watching Willow skipping ahead, listening to her singing just for the joy of it. 'Can I ask you about something the doctor said the other day?' Alice said.

'Of course.'

'I don't think I really took it in at first, but am I right in thinking he said that if my memories come back in a rush that I'll forget what happened while . . . Well, while I'm in this fugue state, or whatever it's called.'

'That sounds right. Why?'

Alice frowned. 'It wasn't nice, what happened the other morning . . . Realising I didn't know where I was or even who I was. I think I'd rather avoid that if I could, but I don't know if there's anything I can do to stop it.'

'I can understand why that would make you anxious.' Ben thought for a few moments, then added, 'I might not have a solution for that problem, but I can think of something that might help in a different way.'

'You can?'

Ben stopped walking and called for Willow to not get too far ahead. 'Have you got the phone Norina gave you?'

Alice nodded and pulled it from her pocket.

'If you do lose your memories again, you won't be able to remember where you've been, but that doesn't mean you can't keep a record to fill in the gaps in your knowledge.' He gestured for her to give him the phone, opened the camera and handed it back to her. 'Words and thoughts, maybe not, but pictures and images, yes. At least it would give you a clue.'

Alice stared intently at the phone screen, which was currently focused on the gravelly path and her boots. 'You mean, like a diary of sorts?'

'I was thinking more of a visual record of places you visit – road signs, landmarks, that kind of thing, but whatever floats your boat.'

Alice looked at him and smiled. 'That's a great idea. I mean, it won't stop me from forgetting anything, but at least I'll have some clue what has happened to me until that point, and I can also make a record that I've got a tentative diagnosis.'

'So what's first? The mountains? The castle?'

She looked around. It was a perfect winter's afternoon. Wispy clouds smeared the bright-blue sky and clung to the hills. 'The mountain. But I'd like to take a picture of the front of the castle later.' It was partly hidden from view by a tall hedge that surrounded the formal garden, and only the upper floors and turrets were visible.

She turned to the low mountain in the other direction, lifted the phone and pressed the red button just as Willow ran back towards them. 'Are you taking pictures? Take one of me! *Cheeeese!*' Alice laughed and did as she was told, catching the fearless glint in Willow's eyes and the missing tooth in the middle of her bottom gum. 'What do you think we'll see today, Uncle Ben? Pixies?'

'Possibly . . . We could take the bridge over the river to see if we can find *fuathan* . . .' He winked at Alice. 'Water sprites.' And then he and Willow spent a full five minutes discussing the best place to hunt mythical beings that day.

After half an hour, during which there had been a possible sighting of benevolent fairies called *seelie* in the woods, Willow grew bored and found a grassy clearing to spin around in. 'Come on, Uncle Ben!' she yelled. 'Let's see who can go fastest!' She threw her arms wide and her head back, giggling harder the faster she turned. 'Film me, Alice! Film me!'

Alice held her camera up and started her phone's video camera rolling. She'd expected Ben to fob his niece off, but he ran into the phone's viewfinder and started spinning right along with her. It wasn't long before the pair of them were laughing uncontrollably.

'Alice!' Willow called breathlessly as she stumbled out of a spin, tried to walk in a straight line, then tumbled onto the tufty grass. 'Take over from me! We can't let a boy win!'

Alice hesitated, unsure of what to do, but Ben was still spinning, a look of fierce concentration on his face. 'Um . . . I don't know . . .'

'It's easy,' Willow said, looking across at her. 'Just try. You can do it.'

Her words were so simple, yet so full of faith, that Alice tucked her camera back in her pocket, ran over to where Willow had been standing and began turning on the spot in her stead.

'Cheater!' Ben called, laughing as he lurched and then saved himself from going down. But it wasn't long before both she and Ben collapsed onto the grass a short distance away from Willow. Alice had no idea who'd lasted the longest. 'Are the trees supposed to spin like that?' she asked, the grass soft against her back.

'If they don't, you've been doing it wrong,' Ben replied, which made her laugh again, a welcome relief from the heaviness that had been weighing her down.

'Where did you learn all that stuff about fairies?' she asked, aware that if she tried to stand up, she was probably going to hurl, which wasn't an attractive option.

'My primary school teacher was very big on Scottish folklore,' Ben said, then lowered his voice, so Willow, a short distance away, couldn't hear. 'The rest I just make up.' He let out a groan, rolled over to place his palms on the grass, pushed himself onto all fours and stood up, swaying slightly. He held out a hand to her. 'Ready?'

Alice wasn't sure if she was, but she took the help he offered. Once upright, she held onto his muscular forearm with her other hand, using him for balance. His touch was familiar and oddly thrilling at the same time.

For a few seconds, they stayed like that, but then Willow came and tugged his other hand. 'Can we go and look at the garden near the castle now? I want to pretend I'm a princess.'

'Of course,' Ben said. 'And then we need to get home to do your spellings for tomorrow morning.'

They walked slowly back through the woods until they crossed a stone bridge with a grand balustrade, then joined the drive again, following the sweep that led round to the castle's front entrance and the formal gardens.

As they drew close, Alice heard voices. She expected to see a group of tourists but when she turned the corner of the hedge, she was confronted with a wedding party. There were bridesmaids in ivory taffeta with tartan sashes, men in morning suits, and a bride with a furry cape on top of her gown.

'The gardens are this way,' Ben said, skirting around the edge of the driveway so as not to intrude and pointing to a wrought-iron gate. Alice was vaguely aware of him and Willow disappearing through it. She knew she ought to just take a picture of the castle and follow them, but her feet seemed to have stopped working. One by one, the wedding party cast curious frowns in her direction, but Alice was unable to back away or even shrug an apology.

Some distance away from the group, she noticed a photographer, tripod set up, thumb poised on the shutter cable. The bride gave Alice one last quizzical look before turning and giving a dazzling smile as she clung onto her tall and handsome groom.

I can't be here, Alice thought. *I really can't be here.*

And she turned, the heels of her boots grinding into the gravel, and ran back down the drive as fast as she could go.

CHAPTER SIXTEEN

Now.

WILLOW RAN DOWN her favourite path in the castle's formal garden. In the spring, the arches of wisteria created a tunnel of dripping lilac flowers, but, in February, only the gnarled branches remained, twisting through the metal struts. Ben had an urge to capture the winter beauty of the plant, and even though he could have taken a snap on his phone, he pushed the thought away.

He looked over his shoulder to see where Alice had got to, but there was no sign of her. 'Willow!' he called out, keeping his eye on the gate. When, after another minute or so, Alice didn't appear, he grabbed his niece's hand and headed back out of the garden.

While she'd seemed far less confused today than she had yesterday, the idea of Alice wandering off spooked him. She could get on a bus, take a trail up into the hills, walk into the loch . . .

'But I haven't finished being a princess yet,' Willow complained as they marched out onto the gravel drive and headed back towards town.

'I know.' Ben scanned the area, trying not to communicate

his growing sense of panic to his niece. 'But I can't find Alice. Can you see her anywhere?'

'There!' Willow said a couple of seconds later. She pointed further down the drive, and Ben could see a sky-blue coat bobbing along before it disappeared around a curve in the drive, the exact same shade as the warm coat Norina had found for Alice. Frowning, he scooped Willow up and gave her a piggyback. Why had Alice run off? She'd seemed so relaxed and happy only moments before.

Once back in town, he headed for the B&B, checking with Norina if she'd seen their guest – which she hadn't – and asked her to mind Willow while he carried on searching. He was just coming out of the front door, taking the front steps two at a time, when he ran into Tamesha Wilson, one of the local police officers.

'I was just looking for you,' she said. 'Social services gave me a call.'

He nodded. 'They said they would. Otherwise, I'd have contacted you myself.'

'So . . . where is the young woman?'

Ben frowned and started in the direction of his cottage. 'I was just about to go to where she's staying. Care to join me?' He could only hope that Alice had run back there. Where else would she go?

'Sure,' she replied, her thin braids bobbing as she nodded her head.

As they walked down the narrow road that ran behind the Invergarrig Inn, he filled her in on what he knew of the story and his suspicion that he and Alice had met before. When they got to the cottage, he knocked on the door then, when he got no answer, tried the handle. It wasn't locked. 'Alice? Are you there?'

'Did she remember her name?' PC Wilson asked as they crossed the small living room.

Ben shook his head. 'Willow picked one out for her. It made sense at the time.'

The police officer shrugged and followed him through to the kitchen, where, much to his relief, he found Alice. She was standing completely still, staring at the kettle, as if she'd been meaning to put it on but had just zoned out. She jumped when he said her name softly.

'This is PC Wilson,' he said. 'One of our local officers based in Lochgilphead.'

'Oh, yes . . . Of course,' Alice said. 'Thank you for coming.'

'Why don't I make us a hot drink,' Ben said, 'while you go and talk in the living room?'

He joined them a few minutes later with three steaming mugs of tea.

'And you really don't remember anything?' PC Wilson was saying. 'Not even patchy details, before you found yourself at the bus stop?'

Alice shook her head. 'I don't even remember being on a bus, although I must have been.'

'Hmm,' Wilson said. 'I'll see what I can do. I can certainly look into missing persons in the Argyll area and I'll check hospital admissions to see if there are reports of anyone with a head injury skipping off without being discharged – although you said you've been to the hospital, and that's unlikely?'

Alice nodded. 'They couldn't see any signs of injury – I had a CT scan.'

Wilson sighed. 'Since you're unfortunately unable to provide any further information, the only thing we can do is work out if someone is looking for you, but I have to be honest, I'm not sure we're going to turn up anything locally.'

Alice's face fell. 'You don't?'

'You don't talk like you're from around here,' she said, shooting a knowing look Ben's way, and he was grateful she'd found a way to present this information to Alice without giving him away. 'Although, like me, you might have moved to Scotland. However, if I went with my gut, I'd say home is much further south . . . You actually sound like you're from my neck of the woods.'

'England?' Alice asked.

'I might even go as far as saying London, so I'm going to ask the Met and surrounding police forces for missing persons information as well.'

Alice nodded, looking a little lost.

'I'll be in touch,' Wilson said, smiling sympathetically and rising from her seat.

Once Ben had shown her out, he returned to the living room to find Alice sitting there, most forlorn. 'What now?' she said.

He shrugged. 'I suppose there is nothing we can do except wait.'

CHAPTER SEVENTEEN

Ten months before the wedding.

WHEN I'D FIRST started seeing Justin, I'd imagined him living in one of those big, white Georgian houses in Chelsea, surrounded by family heirlooms and antiques. The reality had been quite a surprise. His third-floor ultra-modern apartment overlooked Kensington Gardens. The whole building was elegant but stark, full of hard edges and diagonal lines, and Justin's flat was probably the most immaculate dwelling I'd ever been in.

I'd quickly become aware that most choreographers did not live in the kind of luxury he did. Even those who had critical acclaim did not earn pots of money. However, Justin had 'family money', as he called it, although he never talked much about his family or where that money had come from. I got the impression he hadn't had a happy childhood and that he was fairly distant from most of his relatives, including his parents, who lived in Singapore. It only made me more determined to give him the love he was so clearly lacking.

The furnishings were elegant but sparse, suiting the Art Deco influences in the twenty-first-century design. Since every piece of furniture, rug or lamp seemed in perfect harmony with the other objects around it, I'd assumed he'd hired an interior designer, but it turned out he'd chosen everything himself. I was in awe. He had such taste. Sometimes, I just wandered around the apartment, taking in the textures and colours – the pale, plush velvet of the sofas, the polished mahogany and brass accents, the blond wood herringbone floor, the thick, deep rugs with their geometric patterns.

The bedroom was my favourite room in the flat, all soft greys and lavenders. I lay on the bed, the sheets pulled up over half my naked body, allowing the Sunday morning light to slant across me and illuminate Justin, who was dozing beside me. I'd stayed over the night before after an outing to the opera. I checked my phone and realised it was already noon. I rolled over and slid a leg out of the bed, but a muscular hand reached out and grabbed my wrist.

'Where do you think you're going,' he said, his voice gravelly. I stared back down at him, at the golden hair flopping back over his forehead, the glint in his blue eyes as he looked at me.

'I'm getting up,' I explained, a playful smile on my lips. 'We've got plans today, remember?'

Justin grunted and tugged my arm. I'd been using it to prop myself in a sitting position, so I fell back on top of him and he threw his warm arms around me and kissed the top of my head. 'Let's just stay here all day.'

I chuckled. 'We've already spent all morning in bed. Besides, you promised me lunch at that brasserie on the other side of the park.' And before he could argue, I slid from his grasp and stood up. 'There's always later.'

His eyebrows puckered together in a high arch, making

him look like a particularly sad basset hound. 'You're staying at your parents' tonight.'

'I do still live there! Although, I think my parents might dispute that, seeing as I'm here more nights than I'm not.'

He rolled his eyes in lieu of a coherent objection.

'We've got time before we go to dinner this evening.'

The rest of my family had guessed there was a man on the scene. They'd started asking questions: who was he? Did he have a good job? Was he nice to me? Once those basic questions were dealt with, Mum told me to ask him to Sunday dinner, and today was the day. She was going to do her famous roast chicken, so I knew she was pulling out all the stops. Being late or failing to turn up because we were too loved up to leave the bedroom was not an option.

Half an hour later we were strolling through Kensington. I was wearing jeans and boots, things that had always been staples in my wardrobe, but I'd also added a seriously gorgeous silk blouse and leather jacket Justin had bought me, guarding my eyes from the bright April sun with a pair of sunglasses I'd stolen from him.

It was warm enough to sit outside at the brasserie, at a tiny round table with chairs that wouldn't have looked out of place in a chic Paris café. I dug into my smoked salmon and scrambled eggs and let the fantasy continue to play inside my head, and when I caught my reflection in the restaurant window, I realised I saw a woman who looked as if she was ready to get herself up, dust herself off, and start to take charge of her life. I had Justin to thank for that. For his support and unwavering belief in me. For seeing the 'me' I'd lost sight of.

I reached for his hand and tugged him to meet me over the top of the table so I could kiss him.

He smiled when I released him. 'What was that for?'

'For being too good to be true,' I replied.

*

We were supposed to be at Mum and Dad's at half five, but at quarter to six, we were still sitting in traffic the other side of Crystal Palace. I peered at the queue of cars ahead, straining to see if the temporary traffic light was any closer to turning green. I could imagine Mum flapping around the kitchen and making 'it'll be fine' noises that would eventually segue into a monologue about what she could do to prevent the chicken drying out and the roast potatoes from turning to ash.

She looked flustered and hot when we finally arrived, and she opened the door, wiping her hands on a tea towel. Justin presented her with a large bouquet as he declared how dreadfully sorry he was that we were late and how utterly delighted he was to meet her. Mum blinked back at him as if she'd just opened the door to Prince William and accepted the flowers with a flush in her cheeks. I was surprised she didn't curtsey.

I hugged Mum as Justin presented his gift to my father – a wooden box with a very nice bottle of Chablis inside. Dad slid up the lid to inspect the contents, then replaced it. 'Don't know much about wine,' he said gruffly, 'but that looks like an all right drop.'

Lo appeared at the top of the stairs, then skipped down them before elbowing me in the ribs and grinning. 'Not bad,' she muttered, so only I could hear. 'And look at you . . .

Nobody told me we were dressing up fancy.' She took in the expertly tailored charcoal dress I'd worn at Justin's suggestion, another prize from our shopping trip the day before.

Mum had gone all out with the roast dinner. The stuffing had sausage meat as well as the mix out of the packet, and she'd made the Yorkshires herself. (Aunt Bessie is not a woman who is allowed to darken our door.) Justin raised his eyebrows. 'Yorkshire puddings with chicken?' he said. 'What a wonderful idea!' I could tell he thought it a little odd, and I suppose it was, but I'd never really thought about it. Mum's yorkies are just so good, we always have them with every roast, even if it's not beef.

Justin went about making a good impression as we began to eat. He told them a little about his family, then moved swiftly on to his work, starting with a few funny, self-deprecating anecdotes about his early days as a choreographer that left Mum looking wide-eyed and Dad chuckling so hard he almost spat out his gravy.

Lo didn't say much, which was unusual for her. I could feel her beady eyes on me more often than I saw them on Justin. Eventually, she leaned into me and asked, 'What are you doing with your knife and fork?'

'Eating,' I replied, not looking up from my plate.

Lo snorted softly. 'I think you've been spending far too much time in fancypants restaurants.'

I kept cutting my meat, fork balanced perfectly in my left hand, and my knife held properly in my right. Lo wasn't wrong. I *had* been spending more time in 'fancypants' restaurants in the two months since I'd met Justin. On one occasion, he'd noticed my discomfort when I wasn't sure which fork to use or what to do when I needed to spit out a bone, so he'd been teaching me proper table manners and etiquette. If I aspired to be part of his world, these were skills I needed to learn.

As Mum brought out the apple crumble, complete with 'proper' custard, Dad leaned back in his chair, folded his arms over his chest and looked at Justin. 'So, how exactly did you two meet? Lil said she was up in London, but she's been a bit cagey about the details.'

My stomach clenched. I still hadn't told Mum and Dad about the busking, and I realised I probably should have broached the subject before now.

Justin shot me an encouraging look. 'I was walking through Covent Garden, minding my own business, and there she was – playing her violin in the middle of the street, sounding like an angel.'

Mum dropped her spoon in her bowl, and the handle sank below the surface of the custard. 'You were playing? In front of people?'

I tucked my bottom lip under my teeth and nodded.

'It was the most exquisite sound I've ever heard. Your daughter has a unique talent, you know. She really needs to make the most of it.'

Dad straightened in his seat, his eyes ablaze. 'That's exactly what we've been telling her!'

'Well, you're right,' Justin added. 'I don't think a gift like that should be wasted.'

My mum's face fell. I knew what she was thinking – I'd already flushed that chance down the toilet.

Justin, who I'd discovered was very good at reading people,

noticed her expression and turned to me. 'You have told them about the job, haven't you?'

'She said some bloke has offered her some money to play for him,' Dad said. 'Is that what you're talking about?'

I sighed inwardly. I'd explained about Felix and the dance show, but I didn't think they'd really understood. For some reason, if I wasn't sitting in the middle of an orchestra, they didn't see it as real performing.

'We've been searching high and low for the right musician – the right *artist* – to play this piece,' Justin said smoothly, squeezing my knee under the table. 'We needed somebody exceptional, and we think we've found her.'

He went on to explain just how big of a deal this was going to be, just how much it was going to put me in front of people who would appreciate me. Mum's expression softened as he talked, and Dad's went from bemused to completely enraptured. Justin had them eating out of his hand completely.

'Why didn't you tell us all this?' Dad asked.

My shoulders sagged. I could have told them they just hadn't listened when I'd said the same thing, but where would that get me? And, at that moment, my parents were looking at me like they believed I could be something again, and I wasn't about to do anything to spoil that.

Dad got that look on his face he always got when he had something important to get off his chest. 'Well, Justin, I have to say, I'm a man who doesn't mince my words, and I was a bit narked when you were late today, and I wasn't sure about you being a good bit older than our Lili, but I have to say I'm really happy she has you in her life. I want to thank you for everything you've done for her. We're really grateful, aren't we, Sandra?'

Justin beamed at them radiantly. 'Thank you. I do believe I have a knack for searching out young talent and helping it develop.'

It was lovely knowing they liked Justin and hearing them talk about me this way, but I couldn't help feeling that my parents were showering adoration on the wrong person, at least partially. Yes, I was also really grateful to Justin for everything he was doing for me and, of course, I thought he was amazing too, but what about me? I was the one who actually played the flipping violin.

CHAPTER EIGHTEEN

Now.

THE FOLLOWING AFTERNOON, Ben headed through a tongue-and-groove door in the corner of the kitchen and up a short and narrow winding staircase that led up to Norina's storage space.

The whole time he'd been grouting the bathroom in cottage number two, he'd been replaying the time he'd spent with Lili in London in his head, hoping to find some vital piece of information he could supply to PC Wilson, something that might make a positive ID possible. He'd come up blank.

It was so strange. He felt as if he'd known Lili inside and out, but it was only now he realised how little he'd known *about* her. At the time, things like surnames, addresses or what year they'd been born hadn't seemed important. Those were mundane details they'd get to later. It was like those precious hours together had been a down payment on the time they'd both expected to have with each other – because he knew for a fact neither of them had intended for things to end there. Not for the first time, he lectured himself about how he'd messed things up between them, how he'd robbed the pair of them of the chance to find out what their relationship could become.

However, as he'd pressed grout in between the tiles, he'd realised he might have *something* that would help. He'd put a few things in the small attic above the kitchen when he'd first started travelling a lot and even more since he'd come back, waiting for his cottage to be ready.

Behind a couple of cardboard boxes filled with lampshades and other odds and ends, he spotted a large black frame. He pulled it from its hiding place, rested it on an old office chair with only one arm and stepped back to look at it.

This print was the twin to the one currently in his bedroom – well, Alice's bedroom now. The arched Gothic windows were covered with climbing ivy, the sunlight dappling through the leaves of the trees beyond where stained-glass had once been, but down in the left-hand corner, staring into the sunlight, so it caught the edges of her hair and made it luminous, was a woman.

She was turned away from the camera, face mostly obscured. All that could be seen was the curve of her forehead and cheek, the jut of her chin. The similarity to the woman staying in his cottage was striking. It hadn't just been his imagination working overtime. But it also wasn't enough to know for sure.

He was just putting the framed print back in its resting place, when an alarm went off on his phone. Crap. Time to pick Willow up from school. He'd have to get back to that later.

*

Willow skipped across the school playground towards him, a book bag in one hand and a large piece of paper in the other. 'Look, Daddy! I did a drawing!' A couple of the other parents looked puzzled. Most paid no attention at all.

Ben scooped her up into his arms, and she planted a large wet kiss on his cheek as he strode across the playground, putting some distance between them and plentiful sets of listening ears. The grapevine in Invergarrig was always thriving, and its most fertile seedbed was right here at the school gates.

Willow jabbed a finger at her masterpiece. 'That's me and you and Auntie Nee-nee,' she said proudly, pointing to differently coloured crayon scribbles.

'So it is,' he replied, although he wasn't quite sure which scribble was him and which was his niece or aunt. Once they were out on the road, he set her down and let her walk beside him. Her warm little hand found his, making his heart clench.

'Willow?'

'Uh-huh?'

'Do you remember what we said about you calling me "Daddy"?'

She looked away. 'Not really . . . '

Hmm. He wasn't so sure he believed that. 'Willow?' He stopped walking and turned to face her, waiting until she looked at him, which she did by keeping her head turned but swivelling her eyes in his direction. That one small act of defiance couched in obedience reminded him so much of her mother, that it pulled him up short.

He'd been letting himself get distracted, hadn't he? He'd been so caught up with the appearance of Alice . . . Lili . . .

whoever she was . . . that he'd forgotten the very reason he'd come back to Invergarrig in the first place.

Even if the woman staying in his cottage did turn out to be 'the one that got away', it would no more be possible to disappear into the sunset and claim a happily ever after with her than it had been five years ago. He was too busy trying to build that here in Invergarrig. For Willow, not himself.

'Remember how we said I'm not your daddy, that I'm your Uncle Ben. But that doesn't mean that I don't love you?'

She sighed heavily, making her seem at least a decade older than she actually was, poor kid. 'But you're *kind* of like my daddy now Mummy isn't here. You look after me, and we're going to live in our cottage together . . . ' She looked back at him hopefully, and his heart developed a new crack to go with all the others she'd created in it. 'I know. And I'm very proud and happy that I get to look after you, but you already have a daddy.'

She frowned, and her bottom lip protruded, then tugged his hand to signal they should start walking again. 'But I don't remember him.'

'I know you don't, sweetie, but Auntie Nee-nee and I are trying to find him because we think he should know that you're living here.' That was only half the story. Ben knew the name of Willow's father, but there was no telling if the guy was alive or dead, or even if he knew of Willow's existence.

All the books he'd read on parenting, being a foster parent or guardian to a child, maintained the importance of allowing the child access to her biological parents, if safe. He didn't want to take that away from the guy – he had to give him a chance to step up when . . . if . . . they found him. Willow deserved that.

Willow chewed her lip. 'Okay,' she said, but Ben couldn't help but notice there was no skip in her step all the rest of the way home.

CHAPTER NINETEEN

Ten months before the wedding.

AFTER OUR FAMILY dinner, Mum batted away any offers of help in the clearing up from me, saying I should go and 'entertain' Justin in the living room while the rest of them did the washing-up and made a pot of tea. It felt strange, standing in my childhood home with him, a place he clearly didn't fit into, but then I caught a glimpse of myself in the mirror over the gas fireplace and I realised that, in my new dress, I looked more in keeping with him than I did my surroundings. I had a weird out-of-body sensation, as if I were straddling two worlds, fully part of neither, but ready to step from one into the other.

This is what finding yourself feels like, I told myself. *Embrace it.*

Justin walked over to the mantelpiece and inspected the photographs on top, and then a series of me and Lo in our school uniforms displayed on the wall. One photo on a side table seemed to catch his attention in particular. 'Where was this taken?' he asked, picking it up.

'Oh, that's Fran and Nigel and their family with ours – they used to live next door. Mum and Fran were so close they were practically like auntie and uncle to us. That was taken on a caravan holiday we all went on in Devon when I was . . . oh, about fifteen.'

'Those are their sons?'

'Yes. The one at the end is Wayne, their eldest, and the one next to me is Sam. They were a bit like the big brothers I never had.'

Justin put the frame back in its place, his expression unreadable.

The rest of the family returned, Mum carrying a tray with a teapot and mugs, and Dad a plate of biscuits. I was afraid we'd run out of things to say, but Justin continued to carry the conversation, telling stories and answering my parents' polite questions about his work. I saw Lo roll her eyes a few times and shot her a look that was part question, part *cut it out!* What was her problem anyway? Justin was being perfectly charming.

'Why don't you take me for a walk around the neighbourhood,' Justin said when there was a lull in the conversation and Mum had gone to make yet another pot of tea, 'and show me where you grew up?'

'Okay,' I said, eager to be on my own with him, even though I wasn't convinced Penge had enough sights to keep us out of the house for more than half an hour.

Once we were out of sight of the house, I thought Justin would take the opportunity to pull me into his arms and kiss me but he kept walking, unusually quiet after all his chattiness back at the house. I reached out to touch his coat sleeve, but he couldn't have felt it because he didn't respond.

'Justin? Is something wrong?'

'That man in the photograph, the one who had his arm around you . . . ?'

'Sam?'

He dipped his chin just once in acknowledgement.

I laughed nervously. 'We were just shuffling together for the photograph so the person taking it could get us all in. Like I said, he was like my big brother . . . '

'That's all?'

I swallowed. I had nothing to be ashamed of, and I didn't want to lie to him. 'Well . . . we did have a "thing" when we were a bit older. But his parents moved away once he and his brother left school. We hardly see them any more.'

'A *thing*?'

'Nothing serious. A summer fling after we'd both left school . . . '

Justin frowned and shoved his hands in his coat pockets. 'I know it's stupid, but when I think of you with anyone else, I can't stand it.'

I reached out and touched his arm. I knew exactly how he felt because I felt sick imagining all the beautiful, wonderful women Justin must have been involved with before me. 'He didn't get me the way you do,' I said softly. That's what I liked most about Justin, that he *saw* me. I didn't have to explain anything to him or try to be something I wasn't.

He pulled me towards him, fiercely circling his arm around my back, and pressed his face into the hollow of my neck, kissing me there. 'I know I'm acting like a jealous idiot, but that's what you do to me, my angel. You turn me upside down and inside out. I've never felt this way about anyone before.' He took a deep breath and looked into my eyes. 'I'm behaving this way because I'm falling in love with you, do you get that?'

I reached up and touched his face with my fingers and kissed him back. 'I think I might be too.'

He kissed me again, deeper, harder, even though we were standing in the middle of a residential street and the net curtains of the house we were in front of were twitching. 'This is crazy,' I said. 'It's all happening so fast.'

'When it's right, it's right,' he said, and I felt the certainty of it too, deep inside my chest.

'Come back to the flat with me tonight. I can't stand the thought of your side of the bed being empty.' He let his fingers slide down my arm and intertwined them with my own. I felt as if we'd knotted together, fused somehow.

'I said I'd stay here . . . '

'I know, but I want to be with you all the time. I don't want to have to come here and share you with your family. I don't want to share you with anyone.' He paused for a moment and looked into my eyes. 'Come for tonight, and then . . . stay.'

'What did you just say?'

'I said that I want you to come and live with me. It makes sense, practically speaking. Rehearsals are going to ramp up as you prepare to record your track with Felix, and there are more people I want to introduce you to. This is only the start.'

'Isn't it too soon? We've known each other for two months, have only been dating for one . . . '

'It makes sense, Angel . . . We belong together. You can feel that too, can't you?'

I nodded. I could.

'So, what do you say?'

125

For a moment, he looked so much like a lost little boy that I felt our ages were reversed, and I was engulfed by an overwhelming urge to make sure that nothing ever hurt him, that I would always take care of him. I kissed him on his forehead, and then his eyelids, and then his mouth. 'Okay . . . I'll come and live with you.'

CHAPTER TWENTY

Now.

ALICE APPROACHED THE sitting room at the B&B, her heart jumping as if it were on a trampoline. She'd been invited to have dinner with Ben's family each night, and she'd been laying the table when Norina had appeared and told her PC Wilson had returned, wanting to talk to her. When she stepped inside the room, Ben and Norina were already waiting.

'I think I should probably talk with Miss, er . . . Alice . . . alone,' PC Wilson said.

'It's okay. I don't mind them being here. And I'm a bit worried I might forget anything you tell me.' She still fretted about that constantly, even though she was far less foggy than she had been a couple of days ago.

'Okay,' PC Wilson said. 'It's up to you.'

'Have you found something?' Alice asked, unable to wait any longer. This woman might hold the answers to who she was, how she could get her life back.

PC Wilson nodded and launched into an explanation of how she'd checked local missing persons to no avail, and they'd also had no hits on a nationwide level in Scotland.

She was still waiting for information from the Metropolitan Police in London.

'But I also contacted the bus company and asked them to check their CCTV on any routes heading in and out of Invergarrig two days ago. Someone matching your description was seen boarding the bus to Campbelltown at Glasgow coach station early on Saturday morning and getting off here in Invergarrig. I saw the footage myself, and it certainly looks like you. The clothing you said you were wearing is identical. And there's something else . . . '

Alice's eyes widened, and her pulse began to skip. PC Wilson reached down beside the chair she was sitting in and held up a tan-coloured leather bag with a cross-body strap. 'You are clearly seen carrying this bag in the video, and it was found under a seat when the bus was cleaned. Do you recognise it?'

Alice stared at the bag. She willed her brain to do something – jolt awake, click into place, whatever it needed to do – but all she could hear inside her head was silence. It was horrible. She shook her head.

'Is there anything helpful inside?' Ben asked.

'No phone or purse or any kind of ID – not even a bus ticket. My guess is that if you weren't robbed *before* you got on the bus, someone found the bag after you got off and helped themselves. Sorry.'

Alice nodded sadly.

'But there are a few personal items inside. Why don't you take a look to see if anything jogs your memory?'

The only things left in the bag were a small packet of tissues, a lip balm, a silver keyring with three keys on it and a tube of hand cream. They could have belonged to anybody. 'Thank you,' Alice said quietly as she handed the bag back to the police officer.

'We've finished with this now,' PC Wilson said, smiling. 'You can hang on to it.' She then reached into her pocket and produced a small clear plastic bag with blue stripes and writing on it. Inside lay a birthday card or something similar. 'This was also inside. I wanted to see your reaction to the other contents before I showed you.' She handed over what Alice realised was an evidence bag.

'It's . . . It's an invitation – for a wedding this Saturday. In Kent.' Simple and classy, snowy white card with gold foil lettering. Alice read the front three times, but the names inscribed there meant nothing to her. She then turned it over to see what was on the back. 'There's no RSVP, no contact information . . . '

'There might have been a separate card and envelope for that,' PC Wilson said.

Alice nodded dumbly, warring against the disappointment threatening to lay on her chest like a lead weight. She reached for the silver bee necklace instinctively. It lay deeper than the neckline of her borrowed blouse, and she wasn't about to go rummaging, so she made do with feeling for the bump of metal under the fabric. Just that was enough to provide some comfort, a sense of anchoring herself, so she didn't get swept away on this tide of new information, none of which really told her what she wanted to know, and only added further questions to the queue inside her head.

PC Wilson gestured towards the invitation. 'There's some writing on the back. I don't suppose it means anything to you?'

Through the plastic, Alice managed to read a few scrawled words: *Rehearsal – 6.30 p.m. 24th Feb. Going?* Was this her handwriting? She had no idea if it was or if it wasn't.

'No . . . it doesn't mean anything to me,' she said sadly. It was as if the door to all other memories before this week was bolted shut as tight as a bank safe. 'Can I keep this?'

PC Wilson nodded and rose from her seat. 'And, of course, if anything does come back to you, let me know.'

'Yes, I will,' Alice replied. 'Thank you.'

While Ben showed the police officer to the door, Alice stared at the invitation. This was something, she had to remember that. It might not be a name or an address, but if this wedding invitation had been in her bag, it meant some people somewhere wanted her to share a special day in their life with her.

Now all she had to do was find them.

CHAPTER TWENTY-ONE

Nine months before the wedding.

I DIDN'T KNOW anything about contemporary dance, but I soon learned Justin was a big name in that world. He'd acquired funding a few years earlier to renovate an old fire station near Euston as a home for the company. The building held not only rehearsal studios but a small theatre, and The Fire Station, as it was now known, had become something of a creative hub.

Justin had decided to do an 'intimate' preview of the four-dance programme he'd been working on, a chance for both press and fellow artists to get a sneak peek at his new work and create a buzz about it a couple of weeks before a ten-day run at Sadler's Wells.

The only snag was that the performance was a month away and Haru was rehearsing to a rough piano track that Felix had recorded, which wasn't ideal, but I wasn't due to record the violin track for another week or so. However, since I was now living full time at Justin's flat, he heard me rehearsing the piece frequently, and it had only served to highlight to him the difference between the two versions. The violin had a different emotional tone, he'd explained, something that Haru would need to adjust to when he danced. As a result, he asked me to come and play at a rehearsal one Friday afternoon.

I arrived at The Fire Station clutching Octavia to me. The building had a beautiful red-brick Victorian frontage and had been extended at various times over the decades, resulting in a complicated layout. Justin led me up a flight of stairs and through a dizzying succession of corridors before opening the door to a large and airy rehearsal space. I took my shoes off to protect the sprung beechwood floor and nodded a greeting to Haru, who was warming up on the other side of the room.

'It's just the three of us going to be here,' Justin said, rubbing my back with the flat of his palm. 'You'll be fine.'

I nodded, hoping he was right, but my stomach quivered uncontrollably.

I started to play, but while I was hitting all the right notes and keeping tempo, it sounded scratchy and harsh. Justin must have heard the difference, too, because halfway through the second attempt, he held up his hand. Haru had just ended a spectacular turning jump by rolling on the floor, and he hauled himself up, breathing hard. I brought my violin down from my chin.

'Sorry,' I said quietly. 'I'm nervous.'

Justin merely smiled and walked over to me. He led me to the corner of the studio, put his hands on my shoulders and turned me to face the wall. 'Pretend we're not here,' he said, but then, as I began to play, he stayed close to me, keeping his hand on my back as a point of contact.

Standing facing the corner, feeling his warm palm through my blouse, the universe shrank down to just the two of us. I began the piece again, and this time I did it the way it was meant to be played, with soaring highs and lows, the notes woven together with emotion.

When I finished, Justin kissed me on the forehead. 'There. I told you that you could do it.'

On the final run-through, I managed to turn around and watch Haru. When it ended, Justin walked over and hugged me. 'That was astounding! The best time yet!'

'I couldn't have done it without you, without your encouragement.'

'That's because we're a great team,' he said, then lowered his voice so only I could hear. 'You and I were always meant to be.'

Once again, I was tempted to pinch myself. Had I slipped into an alternate reality, one where it was possible for someone like Justin to adore me this way?

'Now I've seen you on stage with Haru,' Justin said thoughtfully, 'I wonder . . . It added so much depth to the piece to have you there too. Do you think . . . ? Would you be able to . . . ?' He raised his eyebrows, and the quiver in my stomach returned. I had a horrible feeling I knew what he was about to ask. 'Do you think you'd be able to play it live?'

There it was. Exactly what I'd been dreading.

The worst thing was that I knew he was right. I'd sensed the energy flowing between Haru and me as we performed in unison. It *would* be better than playing a track.

'Six months ago, you wouldn't have believed you could play in front of a huge crowd in Covent Garden,' he reminded me gently. 'You're stronger than you think you are. It might be time to push yourself once again, the way you did that first morning when you headed up to London with your violin.'

'The day we met,' I replied quietly, the significance not lost on me.

'I know you're scared, but we have another month before the preview. I really think you can do this.'

I wanted to believe him. In fact, I did believe him – or at least, I believed that he had unwavering faith in me. The only problem was that I wasn't so sure I had it in myself. 'It took me half an hour before I could play properly in front of you and Haru. How am I going to play in front of a whole audience?'

'The theatre here only holds three hundred, max.'

Three hundred. A shiver shot through me. Even though that was tiny compared to some performance venues, it was as if I could suddenly sense the audience in the studio with us, row upon row of phantom bodies, all with piercing bright eyes.

'Justin . . . You know I would do anything for you, but . . . ' I swallowed and tried to still my stomach. 'Are you sure this is a good idea? What if I freeze? What if I vomit right there on stage? I'll ruin your big moment. I don't want to do that to you.'

Justin took my violin from me and laid it and the bow reverently on top of the upright piano in the corner of the room, then he returned and held my hands in his, looked deep into my eyes. 'This isn't just about me – it's about you. I think you owe it to yourself to try.'

There was such adoration in his eyes. I felt so loved, so special. My heart cracked a little. I squeezed his hands, hard. 'I want to. For you.'

Haru walked over to us, throwing a hoodie on over his dance clothes. 'Why not add in a safety net?'

Justin frowned. 'What do you mean?'

'Well, I've performed with live musicians before where there was also a track in the background. You could get Lili to play along with it.'

I saw Justin wince at the use of my nickname. He preferred my full name, said it was much more elegant, and always introduced me that way, but 'Lili' was what I'd called myself when I'd first met Haru and Felix, so that's what they continued to call me.

'It's not what I'd envisioned,' Justin said, rubbing his chin.

'It would take so much of the pressure off,' I replied. 'Can we try it, at least? I'd rather do that than back out and let you down completely.'

Justin thought for a minute or so, and then he said, 'Of course, my angel. I want to do whatever makes you happy, whatever is best for you.'

CHAPTER TWENTY-TWO

Now.

'IT'S A PITY people don't do their wedding invitations properly any more,' Norina grumbled to Alice as Ben showed PC Wilson to the door. 'In my day, the parents of the bride would have had their names at the top of the invitation. None of this "Together with their families, so-and-so and so-and-so invite you to their wedding". At least then we'd have surnames to put with the bride and groom's first names.'

Alice nodded. If there'd been more to the invitation, it had been lost. It would *have* to be enough. 'What's today's date?' she asked, her gaze flicking down to the crumpled piece of card in her hands.

'The twenty-first,' Norina answered as Ben walked back into the room.

A tiny flicker of hope ignited inside her. 'This says the wedding is on the twenty-sixth. In five days' time, people who might know me will be gathered together in a certain place at a certain time. It could be the answer to everything!'

'What's the name of the venue again? It was a stately home or something, wasn't it?' Ben asked.

Alice read the gold-leafed words out to him, even though

she was pretty sure she could have recited the invitation blindfolded at that point. 'Hadsborough Castle.'

He pulled his phone out of his jeans pocket and typed the name into Google. A couple of seconds later, he was on the website. He held his thumb above the phone number on the contact page. 'Shall I call them? They might be able to give us more information.'

She nodded, but when she heard the muffled ring tone, and he offered her the phone, she backed away. Her stomach had just rolled violently, and it was taking all her concentration to keep its contents in place. Ben frowned and held the phone up to his ear. Alice hardly heard what he said. She had to sit down in one of the armchairs near the fireplace and put her head close to her knees.

'Are you okay?' Norina asked.

Alice tried to nod without moving her head too much. A few deep breaths later, she was able to sit up again. She noticed Ben was off the phone, and her heart sank. A call that short couldn't be good news.

'Nothing,' he said, scowling.

'The wedding isn't taking place there?' Norina asked.

'No, it is. But they couldn't – wouldn't – tell me anything else because of data protection.'

'I think I need some fresh air,' Alice whispered, just about finding her voice again, and she rose and headed through the kitchen to the small walled garden that lay to the back of the house, causing the security light over the back door to come on. She stopped at the little pond near the edge of the lawn, its surface covered with swirling patterns of ice, and reached for the tiny charm at the end of her necklace, pulling it free from her blouse. Even though she didn't remember anything about how she'd come to own this pendant, as her fingers explored the bumps and protrusions of the bee's body and wings, it felt familiar. Comforting.

Ben came out and stood beside her. 'Sorry.'

She frowned and hugged one arm around her middle while her other hand closed around the pendant. 'Don't be. It's not your fault there are data protection laws. And thank you – for stepping in and talking to them. I don't know what came over me.'

Trauma. The word the doctor had said scooted through her head again. She batted it away. She didn't want to be that person.

She stared at the variations in the ice, white where it was thickest, darkest black where it was paper-thin. This was what trying to reconnect with her life felt like. There was a barrier preventing her from getting back to it. Sometimes it seemed dense and impenetrable, other times so flimsy she was sure she could make a hairline crack and spill herself back into it, but each time she tried, she discovered she was wrong.

She shivered, feeling the cold of the February evening right down to her core, but she didn't make a move to go back inside. It was cooling and calming her fractured thoughts, giving her a chance to sift through them, to actually turn the different possibilities over and examine them carefully. Finally, one certainty planted itself in the forefront of her consciousness.

'I have to go,' she said, looking up at Ben.

'Norina will understand if you'd rather miss out on a noisy family dinner after all this. We can get you something to take back to the cott—'

'No, I mean I have to go . . . to the wedding.'

Ben's mouth hung open. 'But that's . . . It must be five hundred miles away.'

'It's the only way. There's no data protection law that will stop me turning up in person. Somebody there must recognise me. I wouldn't have the invite otherwise!'

'It's too much of a risk! You could be heading off on a wild goose chase, no closer to home than you are at the moment, and what if you get confused again, lose your way . . . At least here you're safe.'

She dipped her head, aware he might be right. But still . . . She couldn't let this idea go. 'PC Wilson said she thought I was from London. The wedding's in Kent. That's right next door!'

A strange expression crossed his features, and he looked away. 'What about the memory clinic in Glasgow . . . The appointment letter might arrive any day now. Wouldn't it be better to wait and get an all-clear from the doctor before you go anywhere?'

Why was he arguing with her? Up until now, he'd been nothing but helpful. She didn't get it. 'But if I find my family, I can go to a hospital near them. There must be other units like that in the country, other doctors who can help with this. I have to try, Ben. It's my only hope. I have to find the bus times, see if I can get a train from Glasgow—'

'No.'

Alice stopped speaking. The word had come out of him hard and fast, a knee-jerk reaction. He seemed surprised at the force of his own conviction. 'No?' she echoed.

'I mean, I don't think you should. Let's get a hold of PC Wilson, tell her what we know and let her look into it. The wedding venue will give her information they won't reveal to us. And the London police might come up with a missing persons report, and then none of this will be necessary.'

'But what if she *can't* find anything in the next few days? What if there is no report? I'll have lost my chance.'

'Alice . . . Don't be stupid . . . Don't—'

She dropped her hands and glared at him. The expression on Ben's face changed, as if something she'd said or done had completely floored him, but her anger had gained momentum by that point, and not much was going to stop it.

'Don't you *dare* tell me that I'm being stupid! You have no idea what it's like to be in this situation. None! And don't you dare tell me what I can or can't do! It's none of your business.' She turned and strode in the direction of the house. 'And don't call me "Alice"!' she yelled over her shoulder. 'It's not my name.'

CHAPTER TWENTY-THREE

Eight months before the wedding.

WHEN I RECORDED Felix's sublime modern violin piece, he ushered me into a little booth and went to listen somewhere I couldn't see him, which helped. There was an engineer behind a big glass screen, but he was much more interested in the knobs and sliders on his sound desk than he was me. It took me a while to warm up and play properly, but we eventually laid the track down, and I was actually very proud of the piece we created together.

The plan for me to stand on stage while the track played remained, and I'd been practising playing along with it. I'd become much more confident performing in front of Haru and even Felix, but I knew it was a big jump to face an audience again. However, maybe Justin was right – I needed to believe him without question, he said, not sabotage myself with my own wayward thoughts.

On the night of the preview, I tucked my nerves aside, knowing that Justin must be feeling a hundred times more anxious than I was. He'd been quiet all day. Reviews of his previous show had been mixed, and I knew he was hoping this performance would silence the naysayers for good.

I emerged from the dressing room adjacent to our bedroom, putting on a pair of earrings whilst searching for my bag. He was standing by the window, hands in his suit pockets, looking blankly out across the road. He turned when he heard me come in. 'Hmm . . . ' His brows drew even more tightly together as he looked at my cocktail dress. 'I'm not sure about that one. How about the long one we got you the other week?'

I paused. 'Are you sure it won't be too formal?'

Justin shook his head, so a few minutes later, I emerged from the dressing room again.

'Much better,' he said, smiling. 'Now, what are we going to do about that hair?'

I reached up to touch the blunt ends. He'd suggested getting it cut about a fortnight earlier. My stomach had sunk at the time, but I'd known he'd been right. It was time I went for something more sophisticated. Even though I'd lost about fifteen centimetres, it was still hanging just below my shoulders, and I'd begun to straighten it religiously.

'Up would be better, don't you think?' Justin said, tipping his head to one side.

To be honest, I didn't really mind which way I wore my hair, but I could see his point. With the long dress, maybe something more formal would be appropriate. I headed over to the dressing table and began pulling my hair into a low twist. When I'd finished, Justin came to stand behind me, and he placed his hands on my shoulders, and we both looked at each other in the mirror. 'There. Perfect. You look wonderful.' He placed a soft kiss on my temple and then went off to find his cufflinks.

*

'Ready?' Justin said as we stepped from the car he'd ordered to take us to The Fire Station.

I nodded, clutching Octavia to me. 'I'm feeling good,' I said. 'Confident.' At least, that was what I was telling myself. Fake it 'til you make it, right?

'Enough to give it a go without the track?' he asked, smiling hopefully at me.

I considered his words carefully before I answered. 'I want to be. For you, I really do, but . . . '

'But?'

I shook my head and squeezed the violin case tighter. 'Sorry.'

He nodded, placed his hand on the small of my back, and ushered me inside.

The theatre at The Fire Station was small compared to most auditoriums, but it still seemed vast to me when I stepped into it an hour before the preview was about to start. The stage was at ground level, marked out by large sheets of specialised dance flooring and draping black wings. The seating bank was similar to ones I'd seen in schools or other community spaces and could be collapsed back against the wall when not in use, creating extra room for rehearsals.

It was a functional space, not a red curtain or a hint of gold leaf in sight. I was grateful for that as I stood behind one of the wings and the auditorium slowly filled. On the other side, Haru was ready in his costume, warming up. I kept my eyes on him, finding comfort in his slow and methodical move-ments, and attempted to convince myself I could emulate his

143

professionalism. It was a heartfelt piece, haunting and lyrical, and only ten minutes long. This was the only solo dance on the programme. After that, there were various group dances. By the time they got to the end of the evening, the audience would have forgotten about me and my violin playing. I just needed to get things into perspective.

At the appointed time, the house lights dimmed, and a hush fell. There was just enough of a residual glow to make out the front row from where I was standing, and I spotted Justin, sitting front and centre, his handsome face tense. I knew he couldn't see me, but I sensed he was looking in my direction. It gave me strength.

The stage manager gave me a nod. There was a small X in tape on the floor where I was to stand stage left, in the back corner. The lighting was low for this piece, with none near the backdrop, so Justin has assured me I would only be a silhouette.

The stage manager gave me a thumbs up, so I lifted Octavia to my shoulder, closed my eyes and listened carefully for the opening notes of the track above my thundering pulse.

I opened my eyes again. Why hadn't it started? I glanced towards the stage manager and found him frowning at me. He made an urgent, 'do something' kind of gesture, but it made no sense to me. I couldn't do anything without the track.

There had been silence in the auditorium at first, a sense of expectation and anticipation, but now the crowd began to whisper and fidget. I felt as if every eye was on me.

What was wrong? Was there a technical problem? I tried to send all these questions to the stage manager with my eyes, but his arm movements just grew more and more frantic.

I tore my eyes from him and looked at Justin instead. I'd adjusted to the darkness enough by that point to make out his features. He was staring back at me, looking distraught. 'Please,' he mouthed, his expression imploring.

I had no choice. I couldn't wait for them to sort out whatever was wrong with the music. I drew my bow across Octavia's strings, hitting the first long note.

Come on, I told myself, telling my body to relax, my fingers to grip the bow lightly. *Do this for Justin.*

And, somehow, my self-lecture worked. The first few bars weren't great, but they were audible, and as time went on, muscle memory took over, my fingers and arm moving as if they hardly belonged to me. I was doing it. I was playing.

It was as wonderful as Justin had said it would be. There was something special about playing live while I saw Haru bring out the emotion and rhythm of the piece with his body, and it kept me anchored, not thinking about where I was and how many people were watching.

At least, it did until someone in the audience coughed. It was loud and brash, not a polite little noise hidden beneath a hand, and while I knew it was unlikely my music-school bully could have tracked me down, but in that moment, Charlie Banister was right there, watching me, taunting me.

I was right in the middle of one of the trickiest sections of the piece, and while I didn't stop playing, I hesitated, losing the flow. Haru had to add an extra turn to compensate.

I glanced across at Justin. He was looking tense and unhappy on the front row, and all I could think about, despite his support during the last few weeks, was how my doom-and-gloom prophecy was coming true. I was letting him down.

I was ruining his big night. Why had I thought I could do this . . . ? I was rubbish. Useless.

Then, as a whole, the audience took a sharp intake of breath. I wondered what had happened. Had Haru tripped? A quick check to the far side of the stage reassured me he hadn't, and it took a couple more moments before I realised what was going on.

My arms were by my side, bow and violin hanging limply. I'd stopped playing.

But Haru . . . Haru was still moving, never missing a beat or a movement, his arms and legs sweeping in graceful arcs as he turned and leapt. And I . . . I was standing there, useless and broken, proving all my doubters right.

As I watched Haru, I realised that the audience hadn't begun to shuffle and whisper as I'd expected them to. They were transfixed by the beauty of his dancing. He moved in silence, the only noise his bare feet brushing against the floor. He was braver than I would ever be.

Maybe I was nothing. Maybe I was horribly broken. I couldn't pretend to be anything else after failing so spectacularly in front of all these people. But maybe I could carry on too, like this courageous dancer. Maybe, even broken, I could still play the violin.

As I watched him, I could hear the music playing inside my head, and it began to swell inside me. I lifted my arms and, keeping my eyes on Haru, I drew my bow across the strings.

The atmosphere in the room changed and the audience sat up straighter in their seats, surprised but also energised. Even Haru's dancing took on a greater intensity, as if he was inhabiting the movements more strongly. All of this spurred me on. I closed my eyes, and I played. I played for my life. And for Justin.

I lost all sense of time and space. All that existed was the music. I felt it soar and swoop within me, and with it came a sense of peace, a sense of *self* that had been missing for far too long.

CHAPTER TWENTY-FOUR

Now.

BEN WAS NAILING a stretch of skirting in the kitchen of cottage number two. He'd have to give the buildings proper names at some point, something Scottish sounding that the tourists would like, but he'd always been better with pictures than words, so for now, he just mentally referred to the rentals as one, two and three.

He really wasn't paying attention to what he was doing and had missed the tack more times than he'd hit it. Letting out a low huff, he dropped the hammer and sat back on his haunches. He'd slipped out of the B&B without having breakfast that morning, which meant he hadn't seen Alice since she'd stormed out of the garden the evening before. But he hadn't wanted an audience. He'd go and find her around lunchtime when she'd finished helping Norina. If she really was going to leave, he'd like to clear the air between them. He was hoping he could talk her into remaining in Invergarrig for at least a few more days, which would give PC Wilson a chance to come up with something concrete.

He stood up and scrubbed his face with his hand. How should he handle this? What should he do? Because when she'd shouted at him, she'd let go of the necklace she'd been fiddling with, and while he'd caught glimpses of a chain around her neck, he'd never laid eyes on the pendant at the end of it until that moment.

It was a bee. A tiny silver bee. He would have recognised it anywhere.

His heart had stuttered, leaving him speechless as she'd stalked away.

It *was* her.

Lili.

For some reason, he couldn't get his head around that. Which was totally ridiculous, seeing as he hadn't been able to stop thinking about it ever since he'd run into her outside the café. In his gut, he'd known it was her, but the reasonable part of his brain – the part that knew this was too much of a one-in-a-million coincidence to be true – had told him to shelve that idea, let the police and doctors solve the riddle. Maybe he'd *wanted* to leave the question of her identity unanswered and get on with the practical problem of helping her get home, because maybe it would have been easier all around if it wasn't Lili after all.

But now he had solid proof.

He swore under his breath and paced around the tiny kitchen. What was he going to do? About her . . . about everything?

He'd got no further to working that out when there was a knock at the door. When he answered it, he found Alice . . . Lili . . . standing there with a takeaway cup from The Thistle Café. She held it out to him. 'Peace offering. Black Americano. Norina said it was your favourite.'

He accepted it from her without a word, unable to take his eyes off her.

Even though he'd spent a lot of the last couple of days in her company, it was like seeing her for the first time again. It took him right back to that moment when he'd been leaning over his camera in the garden of St Dunstan-in-the-East, how she'd completely taken his breath away, even when she'd been stung by that wasp, and he'd leapt into action, grasping at any excuse to talk to her.

She looked at the floor. 'I shouldn't have shouted at you like that. Not after all you and your family have done for me. All I could think about is finding out who I am. I'm just so desperate to find some answers.'

He nodded. So was he. Even though she was standing in front of him, it made no sense.

He'd been there on the twelfth of July, just as they'd promised they would be. He'd waited the whole stupid day in that garden, right until the church bells had struck midnight, and then he'd sloped off back to his hotel, alone.

But he'd never blamed her for not showing. If there was anyone to point the finger at for messing up what they might have had, it was him. It was all on him. So it made even less sense she was now here in Invergarrig. On some subconscious level, had she come searching for him? And if she had, what did that mean?

'I do understand. A little . . . ' He'd been grumpy and low for ages when he'd come back to Invergarrig. Partly the trauma of losing his sister – although, if he was honest, he'd known how that story was going to end for years; he just hadn't been able to admit it to himself – and partly the sense that his whole life had changed, which meant he'd had to change along with it. For months he'd been unsure of who he was and what his purpose was. How much harder must it be for her, with nothing solid to anchor herself to the life she'd left behind? 'I'm sorry too. I shouldn't have used the word "stupid".'

'Thank you,' she said softly, giving him the merest hint of a smile. 'And you made some really good points. I've spent the last hour or so thinking about it, talking it over with Norina.'

Ben's heart lifted at the thought she might have listened.

'But . . . '

Uh-oh. There was a word he didn't want to hear. 'But . . . ?'

She looked at him bleakly. 'I can't stay here mooching off you and your family. I have to find my way back to my own life.'

He knew she was right. He couldn't keep her here with him indefinitely, even though he now realised that was *exactly* what he'd been hoping for.

'So I'm going to London, and from there on to the wedding venue.' She paused a moment before carrying on. 'Norina and I thought it might be better to aim for the rehearsal on Thursday evening – fewer people and no risk of spoiling the big day. *Someone* there should know who I am. Either the bride or the groom must have added me to the guest list.'

'But what if you're just a plus one? Someone's girlfriend or partner they've never met before?'

She shrugged helplessly. 'You could be right. But then why would I have a note about the wedding rehearsal? I know it's a risk, but I need to do this.'

But I don't want you to go.

He'd only just found her again after more than five years of hoping and searching. Trying to find someone called 'Lili' in a city of nine million people had been impossible, not when all you had to go on was a first name, and even that was possibly a shortening of her name. Hadn't she tried to tell him something along those lines as he'd run away from her at the airport? He'd tried every permutation he could think of: Lillian, Lilias, Emily, even Delilah . . . and nothing. How could he let her leave when even *she* couldn't give him more than he already knew? He couldn't let her disappear a second time.

But he didn't ask her not to go. Partly because of what the doctor had said, but partly because of what had occurred to him earlier: if she *was* a plus one at the wedding, it meant she was probably somebody's girlfriend. Possibly even their wife.

He had no idea where life had taken her in the last five years, did he? He'd travelled all over, and of course he'd met other people after he'd finally given up looking for her. It was logical she might have done the same.

And while she was in a vulnerable state, unable to confirm or deny if there was someone else in her life, it would be totally out of order to make any kind of move on her, to reveal his feelings in any way. He already sensed she felt attached to him. It would be easy to exploit that. But no way was he going to be that guy.

'I'm going to get the bus to Glasgow,' she said, and his stomach hollowed. 'From there, I'll get the train. Norina has given me some wages for the last couple of days, and she bought an advance ticket for me. I'll pay her back when I get back home . . . wherever that is. Please believe that.'

'Of course I believe it.' That was the least of his worries. 'When are you going?'

'The train leaves from Glasgow Central at six-forty.'

'Six-forty *today*?'

She nodded, her eyes large.

'But today is Tuesday. The rehearsal isn't until Thursday. Why the rush?'

Her expression changed, just the way it had done in the garden before she'd stormed off.

Calm down, you idiot, he told himself. *If she leaves now, you might never see her again. Is this how you want to leave things?*

There would be no hope for anything in the future then. And if all her memories did come back in a rush, she'd forget that they'd ever met again. He'd go back to being the guy who'd let her down, and that was the last thing he wanted. 'Sorry,' he said, making himself take a slow breath. 'I don't mean to get so . . . '

'I know you're trying to protect me, Ben, and I really appreciate all you've done for me, but . . . ' She looked away from a second. 'This sounds horrible to say, but I'm not your responsibility.'

Ouch. True, but . . . ouch.

'And I don't need to be told what to do,' she added. 'I can make my own mind up about this.'

She waited, staring intently at him. He nodded just once. Message received and understood. He had to respect that, just as he had to respect her decision not to turn up at St Dunstan's a year after they'd first met.

'Norina has a friend who runs a boutique hotel in Kensington. He's going to put me up for a couple of nights.'

Of course . . . Marco. He and Norina had worked at the same hotel thirty years ago. He'd occasionally taken advantage of Marco's generosity himself when he'd been in London. At least she was going to be somewhere safe.

He had to let her choose for herself and hope that if fate had brought her back to him after all this time, it wasn't for nothing. Not that he actually believed in fate. But he believed in . . . this. Whatever was happening here. What they'd had in those stolen hours in London. Maybe the universe would be kind?

'Will you let us know you get there safely? Whether you find your family or not?'

She pulled a piece of paper from her pocket. 'I wrote the number for the phone Norina gave me down, you know, just in case you . . . ' She trailed off, looking a bit shy.

'Thanks.' He took it from her. 'And let me put mine in yours.' This time he wasn't making that stupid mistake. He quickly tapped it into the handset and gave it back to her. 'Call anytime if you need anything.'

Be patient, he told himself. He'd found her. He had her number. At least this time, they really would be able to keep in touch. And maybe it would be better this way? If she got her memory back, she'd remember him from before, wouldn't she? And then he could explain what had gone wrong five years ago. God, he hoped she'd understand, maybe even forgive him. Maybe they *would* have a second chance; it just wasn't going to be right this very moment.

Besides, there was Willow . . . She needed to be the centre of his love and focus at the moment. The rest could come later.

'Of course I'll call and let you know what happens.' She

stepped towards him, and his heart began to thud like a jack-hammer. 'Ben . . . I'm so grateful. I will never forget what you and your family have done for me.' And then she began to laugh. 'At least, I hope I won't . . . '

His mouth twisted into something approaching a smile. It wasn't lost on him that Lili had promised him that too, to never forget him, and yet, here she was standing right in front of him, having done exactly that.

God, he wished he hadn't let her talk him out of abandoning his year of travel. Yes, it had reaped huge rewards in terms of his career, but it hadn't outweighed what he'd lost.

'Well . . . I suppose this is goodbye.' She smiled, but the light in her eyes dimmed a little. 'Norina's rustled up a little daypack for me for my clothes, so I'm heading over to the B&B in a minute to collect it before I catch the bus at four.'

She made a hesitant move and then raised her arms and gave him a hug. It started out awkwardly, but after a second or so, they clung to each other. Ben felt something inside himself soften and release, something that had been wound tight, yet he hadn't even realised had been there.

'I'll miss you . . . ' she mumbled as they held onto each other. 'For a little while, you were the only person I knew in the whole world.' She squeezed him a little tighter, then pressed a soft kiss to his cheek before pulling away, looking down at the carpet.

'Bye. Have a good journey . . . ' His words sounded hollow to his own ears. So trite and meaningless in comparison to all the big declarations he had locked away inside.

'See you,' she said, holding a hand up to say farewell.

'Wait!' he said as she turned to go. She stopped, looked at him. 'Have you bought your bus ticket yet?'

155

'No.'

'Then at least let me drive you to Glasgow. I won't really be happy until I see you board that train with my own eyes.'

She gave him a huge smile, and he felt his insides light up in response. 'That would be amazing. I was a bit worried about getting the bus on my own and then finding my way to Glasgow Central for the train. Norina gave me a map, but . . .'

'Well, how about you go and get ready, and I'll see you at about four?' That should leave enough time for the ninety-minute journey, and he'd be able to pick Willow up from school before he left.

'See you then. Thanks, Ben.'

CHAPTER TWENTY-FIVE

Eight months before the wedding.

AFTER MY PART in the performance, I hid, tucking myself behind one of the wings, earning myself more than a few puzzled looks from the dancers that flowed past me on and off the stage as the rest of the show continued. I truly didn't know whether I should laugh or cry.

I'd used to think that freezing in front of an audience was the worst possible thing that could happen to me, that I would die of shame and embarrassment if I did it again, yet not only was I still living and breathing, I'd managed to pick myself up and carry on.

But then I'd think about Justin's face as he'd silently pleaded with me to save him from whatever backstage disaster had occurred, how I'd completely failed to do that, and my stomach churned. How was I ever going to face him?

I was supposed to meet him once the programme had ended, but I dithered, waiting until the stage manager shooed me out.

The large foyer in front of the theatre was being used as a bar area, and it was packed. I slithered in, avoiding anyone's gaze, and spotted Justin all the way over on the far side of the room.

I paused behind one of the large pillars, trying to work out the least conspicuous route, and accidentally began eavesdropping on a discussion happening on the other side of it.

'That first piece of the night was . . . ' a deep male voice said, trailing off to find the right word. Unseen, I winced as I waited for him to finish his sentence.

'Oh, I know!' a soft female voice replied. 'It was utter brilliance.'

I blinked. Surely, I couldn't have heard that right?

A third voice joined them. 'The way Justin used the sound – and then the *absence* of it – defying our expectations, was astonishing. It really added intensity to the message of the movement.'

'I thought so too,' the man replied. 'And Haru Morishita's performance was breathtaking. I don't know why Justin didn't finish with that. It was clearly the strongest piece.'

I turned and pressed my back against the cold plaster of the pillar, my mouth hanging open. I must have emerged from backstage into a parallel universe because these people clearly hadn't been watching the same performance I'd been part of.

I brushed my confusion aside and sought Justin out again. Sliding through the gaps in the bodies, I made my way over to where he was standing and ended up hovering behind him, not knowing how to break into the conversation.

After a few moments, Justin turned to replace his empty champagne flute on a waiter's tray, and he caught sight of me. I held my breath. Even if all these people were fooled, thinking the gap in the music had been part of some brilliant creative plan by the choreographer, he and I knew the truth. Felix would probably be upset, and that wouldn't please Justin either.

But his eyes held none of the disappointment I'd sensed when he'd been sitting in the front row. He leaned in, kissed my cheek warmly, slid a hand around my back, and introduced me to the group he'd been talking to.

The rest of the evening went past in a blur. Person after person came up to Justin and wanted to congratulate him on his innovative choreography. His hand was on my waist the entire time, guiding me from one group to the next, introducing me with glowing terms. Every so often, he'd lean in to whisper something in my ear or to kiss me on the cheek. Gradually, my nerves subsided to a manageable level.

I didn't deserve this man. I'd let him down tonight, I knew I had, but he was being nothing but lovely, and I knew, despite the disappointment he must be feeling on his own behalf, that he understood what a breakthrough this was for me. However, it wasn't until we were in the car he'd booked to take us back to his flat that I was able to talk to him properly about what had happened during the performance.

Not long after the driver pulled away, I turned to him. 'I'm so sorry. I tried my best, I really did. Maybe I'd have been okay if the track had played, but—'

'Do you mind if we don't talk about it right now?' His voice was so soft I could barely hear it. I've been putting on a good show, but I have a pounding headache.' Then he turned his face to the window, closed his eyes, and rested his forehead on the glass.

I sat with my hands folded in my lap and stared at the

windscreen between the headrests of the front seats. He was more disappointed than I'd realised. Tears welled behind my lashes. Of course it was okay if he didn't want to talk. After the mess I'd made of things, he didn't owe me anything. But I owed him. Big time. He'd put his trust in me, and I'd let him down. I refused to blink and allow the tears to fall. It would have been selfish to let them.

CHAPTER TWENTY-SIX

Now.

WILLOW CAME RUNNING down the steps of the B&B waving a grey knitted beanie. 'Uncle Ben! Wait! You forgot your favourite hat!'

'Thanks, sweetheart.'

Alice had been about to get into the passenger seat of the car, but she paused to watch as Ben knelt so Willow could put his hat on for him and rose again with it almost covering one eye. He gave Alice a lopsided smile over the roof of the car as he adjusted it.

A thin pair of arms then came around Alice's middle and squeezed her hard. She looked down to find Willow looking up at her. A lump rose in her throat.

'Bye, Alice,' Willow said, holding onto her even more tightly. 'Will you come and visit us again, you know, when you've got your proper name back? And what if it *is* Moana? That would be really funny!'

'It would,' Alice agreed, 'and I'd like to come back to Invergarrig one day.'

Norina peeled Willow from around Alice's waist. 'Come on, wee miss. They've got to get going.' And she leaned in and gave Alice a one-armed hug, then picked Willow up to sit on her hip, giving the little girl a kiss on the head as she did so.

Alice's heart contracted, and her eyes began to sting. 'Thank you so much,' she said. 'I'll miss you both.' It seemed a strange thing to say, seeing as she'd only known them for a few days, but it was true. And then it was time to get in the car, strap herself in, and wave goodbye.

Driving over the humpbacked bridge that led out of Invergarrig opened up a whole new world to Alice, full of new sights and experiences. There were high mountain passes, snow-capped peaks, even a stag watching from an overlooking rock as they drove on the road below, but soon enough, they entered the urban sprawl of outer Glasgow. By the time they reached the station, she was exhausted. Every sound, shape, colour and smell was something new for her freshly scrubbed brain to process.

They stopped a short distance from the wide bank of digital departures boards. She pulled her phone from her bag and snapped a photo of the board that said 'London Euston 18:40' then tucked it into the back pocket of her jeans, noticing that the digital clock said it was five fifty-five. In just over half an hour, she'd have to say goodbye to Ben too, something that made her feel more and more nervous the longer she thought about it. What if he was right after all? What if she should stay in Invergarrig and wait for other people to sort her life out for her, find out who she was?

They wandered around the station for a bit, killing time exploring the shops, but ended up back in front of the departures board. Her attention was snagged by the giant digital display hanging next to it. An ad for Glasgow Botanic Gardens ended, and one for an upmarket hotel began to play. There were shots of a grand facade and luxurious rooms in the slideshow, followed by a shot of a bride and groom embracing each other in the formal gardens. As she watched, it felt like all the blood drained from her body and then – *boom!* – an image appeared in her mind, so clear and fresh it was as if someone had hooked her brain up to an HD video feed.

'Are you okay? You've gone as white as a sheet.' Ben's hands hovered near her, as if he thought he might need to catch her falling body at any second. To be honest, his assessment wasn't far off.

She grabbed onto his arm, shaking her head, and he steered her to one of the solid banks of metal chairs and helped her sit down. 'What's going on?' he asked softly as he crouched down in front of her.

Alice looked back at him. Her mouth moved a couple of times before she managed to form words. 'I think . . . I think I just remembered something.'

'About here? This station?'

'I don't think so . . . I was in a . . . in a . . . ' The image was fluttering around in her head like an elusive butterfly. She screwed up her face in an effort to pin it down and turn it into words. 'I saw a wedding shop . . . a boutique. There were all these dresses hanging up, and there was a mirror . . . I was standing on the sidelines while a bride tried on her dress, but when I tried to focus on her face, it all just kind of . . . ' She wiggled her fingers, mimicking the way the final part of whatever she'd seen had disintegrated and shimmered away. 'Oh, god . . . I think I'm going to be sick.' She leaned forward a little and concentrated on taking in slow, deep breaths, which was no mean feat, given that her heart was racing at three hundred miles an hour.

'I'll see if I can find something to—' Ben frantically looked around. 'Where's a rubbish bin or a plastic bag when you need one?' Failing to spot either, he pulled his grey beanie from his head and held it out, open and upside-down, which made her want to cry, and that wouldn't help at all. She sucked in a little more of the stale station air, then said shakily, 'I think it's passing . . . Thank you.'

'Hold onto this, just in case.' He pressed the hat into her hands.

She nodded reluctantly but clutched onto it, the wool soft against her fingers. 'A bridal shop . . . That *has* to confirm I'm on the right track.' She paused to pat her bag, where the wedding invitation was safely stowed. 'If I was there for a dress fitting, I must know the bride well. I might even be a bridesmaid. This is a good sign, isn't it? It shows my memory might be starting to come back.'

Ben did not look the least bit convinced. 'Yes, it could be a memory. But you can't be sure about that yet. It might be better to wait and see if it happens again, if you get something more concrete before—'

Just at that moment, the Tannoy above their heads sprang into life. Alice didn't really pay attention until the word 'London' drifted past her ears. She quickly glanced at the departures board, willing her eyes to focus properly, and there it was – the 18:40 – now boarding on platform five.

'Time to go,' he said. 'That's your train.'

She pushed herself to stand but reached out for the solid metal arm as she did so, clamping her lips together. For a moment, she really thought she might need to make use of his hat, but then the rolling sensation passed, and she smiled weakly at him. 'It's okay. I'm good . . . '

Ben stared back at her, looking most perturbed. 'No. You are *not* good.' But his tone wasn't hard and frustrated as it had been in Norina's garden; it was warm, concerned.

She reached for her little bee pendant, felt the curve of the wings for comfort, and saw his expression change from worried to . . . she wasn't sure what. It just looked as if he'd made a decision about something.

'I can't let you get on that train on your own,' he said. 'I can't just walk away. Not again . . . '

Not again? But she didn't have time to ask him what he meant. 'Ben, I know you're right, but . . . I *need* to go. I need to find out who I—'

'I know,' he said, glancing around the station, then pulled his wallet from his pocket. 'Which is why I'm coming with you. Stay here . . . ' And then he started jogging in the direction of a bank of self-serve ticket machines.

CHAPTER TWENTY-SEVEN

Seven months before the wedding.

JUSTIN AND I never really did talk about what happened at the preview of his new show. I prepared myself for a big heart-to-heart, tearful apologies, great make-up sex . . . But none of it came about. If I tried to raise the subject, he'd merely kiss me on top of my head and say I should just forget it.

However, my 'mistake' had caused problems that rippled out from that night and affected everything. We'd both agreed I shouldn't try to play live when the programme ran at Sadler's Wells, but if they played the track I'd recorded before the preview, people would hear the difference. If anyone guessed it had all been a giant cock-up, Justin's glowing early reviews about his innovative use of sound would seem hollow. The only solution was to get a new version of the track edited so it mimicked what had happened that night.

Surprisingly, my part in the performance hadn't damaged my career prospects. I was approached by another choreographer who'd been in the audience who wanted me to work on a project with her. It wasn't the path I'd envisioned for myself when I'd begun at the Conservatory, but I was starting to realise there were other ways to play professionally, and I was excited about working on smaller projects with other creative people, rather than feeling lost sitting in the middle of an orchestra.

Justin was thrilled for me, of course, said we should go out to celebrate when we had a night free, but then the shows began at Sadler's Wells in early July, overshadowing everything. I knew this was a big deal for him, so I attended every single night, even though I usually had to sit alone because he was dashing around backstage and would often watch from the wings, only occasionally managing to slide into the auditorium and stand at the back.

When we returned home after the third performance, Justin slammed the front door behind us. He strode into the living room and threw his keys on the coffee table. They skidded across the glass surface and landed on the rug on the other side. 'It was a hot mess! Did you see how the principal dancer messed up her solo on the final piece?'

'I'm sure no one will notice. And the applause afterwards was just as loud as it has been the other nights.'

I hadn't realised that Justin had been careful to invite only friends and supporters, along with a few 'nice' critics, to the preview performance. The reviews that had come out in the last couple of days had not been so complimentary.

'They've got their knives out,' he said darkly, heading for the sideboard that contained the spirits. 'Just like they always have. Because once someone is successful, they have to knock them down again.' He pulled out a bottle of brandy and poured himself a glass, offered one to me.

'I don't like it, remember?'

'Don't start picking at me, Angel, not after the night I've had.'

'I'm not! I . . . Sorry.' I led him to one of the large sofas that stood in the middle of the living room and sat down next to him. He took a large gulp of brandy, placed his glass on the coffee table, then closed his eyes and let his head loll back on the sofa cushions. 'I wouldn't be so frustrated if I hadn't just given the whole company a good talking to. They're just not working hard enough, especially Diya . . . I should never have promoted her to principal. It's as if she deliberately wants to ruin things for me.'

I leaned across and snuggled into him. 'Remember what you say to me . . . ? Don't let what others say upset you. Who cares what the critics say?'

'I do,' he said wearily, not opening his eyes. 'They were vicious about my last show . . . "Justin De la Hay is going stale, churning out the same old dances, rehashed with different lighting and different costumes." Or how about, "De la Hay was the *enfant terrible* of the dancing world when he first arrived on the scene, but now he's settled into conservative hum-drum".' He opened his eyes, sat up and looked at me. 'If the Arts Foundation no longer thinks I'm a trailblazer, they might cut my funding, and I can't afford to float the company on my own – I plough enough money into it as it is. It could be the end of my career!'

'I'm sure it won't. The reviews haven't been *all* bad.'

He humphed, reached for his glass, then stood up and began to pace on the wide stretch of floor between the back of the sofa and the window. 'They like that *first* piece,' he said, staring out into the night beyond the glass.

I turned, bringing my knees underneath me so I could kneel and rest my hands on the back of the sofa and face him. 'There you go!'

'But not because of anything *I* created or decided. Because of your . . . ' He caught himself and looked away. 'And then they consider the rest of the programme and think it doesn't measure up, that it's not a cohesive whole . . . I wish it had never happened.'

I swallowed. So did I. But I hadn't realised until now that Justin felt this way. Did he blame me? 'I'm so sorry,' I said quietly, probably for the thousandth time.

He carried on as if he hadn't heard me. 'It's okay for you.' He took another sip of his drink, his jaw muscles tensing as he swallowed. 'You've got all these exciting opportunities coming your way. Your career is taking off . . , '

That was hardly true. Not yet.

'Whereas I'm just a has-been, a washed-up purveyor of hum-drum. You don't know what it's like to have put years into something and for it to just have it all flushed down the pan.'

I wanted to remind him that if anyone understood what it was like to have your dreams wrenched away from you, it was me, but I didn't want him thinking I wasn't listening, that I was making it 'all about me', as he sometimes said I did – something he and Lo could finally connect about.

His words stung, but I knew he didn't really mean what he was saying. He was just upset, and now he'd explained it to me, I realised he had every right to be. I thought about how I'd felt when I'd just dropped out of the Conservatory, how sometimes I'd lashed out and been grumpy with my parents and my sister. I should try to show him the same patience and sympathy they'd shown me.

With the benefit of hindsight, I realised how horribly

self-absorbed I'd been, how much of a brat. It made me glad we were going round to Sunday lunch the next day because it would give me a chance to apologise.

When I got up the following morning, I found Justin in the living room with his laptop and his phone. He was having a terse conversation with someone, so I snuck past him into the kitchen, where I made us both a coffee from his fancy machine (it had taken me weeks not to be intimidated by it) and then took it back into the living room. While he carried on with whatever he was doing, I made him his favourite omelette for breakfast, then carried it out to him so he could eat it on the sofa.

When he was finished, he handed his plate back to me. 'I've had to call an emergency rehearsal at one o'clock,' he said, adding his coffee cup on top of the plate. 'The whole last piece needs an overhaul.'

'A rehearsal? At one? But we're supposed to be going to Mum and Dad's for lunch.'

'I'm sorry, Angel. It can't be helped.'

I sat down beside him. 'But we put them off last time we were supposed to go.'

He shook his head and gave me an apologetic look. 'I'm sorry . . . '

I made him another coffee and then left him to it while I got ready to go to Mum and Dad's. It was a job to choose something. I didn't want to get all dressed up because it felt as if I was flaunting my new lifestyle in their faces, as if all they'd provided for me hadn't been enough, but I knew Justin wouldn't like it if I dressed too casually. I ended up trying to compromise, which didn't really work. Thankfully, when

I returned to the living room, Justin was too absorbed in his planning to suggest an outfit change.

I went over and kissed him on the top of his head. 'I suppose I'd better be off.'

His arms came around my torso, and he pulled me to him so his head pressed against my stomach. 'Couldn't you stay?'

My hands came to rest on the top of his shoulders. I didn't *have* to go, but I wanted to. Sometimes, with all this luxury around me, all the nice restaurants and fabulous people we socialised with, it felt as if I was living on a different planet from my parents.

'They'll be disappointed enough if you don't show up,' I said, smiling. God, my parents loved Justin. Sometimes, I even felt they were a little bit in awe of him.

'You're the only person who really understands, who gives me any semblance of support,' he said, looking up at me.

I smoothed his floppy fringe away from his forehead. 'You'll be working most of the afternoon.'

He kissed my stomach and pulled me tighter. 'Come with me,' he mumbled into my dress.

I laughed softly at his teasing. 'I won't be of much use! What do I know about contemporary dance?'

'But just having you there will be enough. You're my lucky charm. You know how good you are for me . . . '

He was always saying things like this, making me feel wanted, special. Powerful.

I looked down at his beautiful face. I loved the fact he was a sensitive man, not afraid to show his emotions, to be vulnerable on occasion. And he kept his promises too – not like other men who'd promised the world then disappeared.

If Justin said he'd be my champion, he was my champion. When he told me what we had was special, he stuck around and proved it. This was a man I could trust my heart with one hundred per cent.

'Okay,' I said. 'I'll stay.'

CHAPTER TWENTY-EIGHT

Now.

WHAT ON EARTH was he doing? He should be at home, reading Willow her bedtime story, not sitting here on a high-speed train hurtling through the Scottish countryside. He blamed the adrenaline. He'd looked at Alice sitting on that bench on the station concourse, looking all wobbly but determined to get on the train and travel five hundred miles on her own. Before he'd known it, he'd been running back towards her from the ticket office, and then they'd sprinted for the train together. His heart rate still hadn't returned to normal.

He was travelling again.

Only to London – hardly somewhere new or exotic for him – but the high of heading off to new places, only half a plan in his head, had kicked in hard. God, he'd missed it.

But that was the problem. He wasn't supposed to be enjoying it. He wasn't supposed to be happy to be leaving Willow with Norina while he disappeared into the night. That wasn't the deal he'd made with himself when he'd come back to Invergarrig.

And that wasn't the only hitch in his not-so-brilliantly-thought-out plan.

He wasn't just travelling. He was travelling with Lili. The déjà vu was overpowering, reminding him just how much of an intense experience it had been haring around London together, unable to let go of each other's hands for more than a minute or two.

And now, sitting across a plastic table from her as the train sped through the darkness, it was hard not to remember how soft her skin had felt beneath his fingertips, her lips against his. Not a good idea, Ben. Not a good idea at all. This was going to be a really long five hours.

To distract himself, he pulled his phone out and checked train times for his return journey. He hadn't had time to think about that back at Glasgow Central and had just grabbed a single for the same train as Alice. It turned out there was a sleeper train leaving Euston about forty-five minutes after this train arrived. With any luck, he'd be safely back in Invergarrig just after breakfast.

He felt Alice's eyes on him and looked up just as he was about to press 'Buy Ticket'.

'I was going to ask you something,' she said.

He put his phone down on the table. 'Fire away.'

'About the photos in the cottage, in my— Well, in *your* room.'

'Okay . . . '

'I was wondering where they were taken, particularly the one of the ruined church.'

Ben's stomach immediately fell into his boots.

'I found I couldn't stop looking at it. It just seemed so . . . '

'Magical?' he offered, his insides churning hard.

She looked back at him and smiled. 'Yes! How did you know that was what I was going to say?'

'Lucky guess,' he replied weakly.

Oh, this journey was going to kill him, wasn't it? He was going to silently implode, full of all the things he shouldn't . . . couldn't . . . tell her, and all that would be left afterwards was a puff of smoke and a Ben-shaped hole in the universe.

'It's in London – the garden at St Dunstan-in-the-East. I know that because I took it.'

Alice's mouth dropped open. 'You took it? Ben . . . it's stunning!'

'It's my job. Or it used to be. I was a travel photographer.'

Her eyes widened further. 'I thought you were in the hospitality business, like your aunt.'

'I am now, but I've only been back in Invergarrig for just under a year.'

'You took all those photos in your cottage? Even the ones with the huge icy waterfalls?'

He nodded.

'Ben! You're really, really talented.'

The fact she thought so was bittersweet. Too bad he'd waved that life goodbye.

'You must have been all over the world.'

'A lot of places, yes. I was away more than I was in the country, not even enough to have a flat or house to call my own – although I rented a room at a flat in Glasgow that I used as a base. I suppose not every travel photographer works that way, but I did, doing other jobs like bartending or crop picking between gigs to start with. In recent years, I've made a living solely from photography.'

Alice shook her head, looking incredulous. 'That seems so impossible to me at the moment – to have been to all those places. I mean, I guess I must have travelled too, maybe even as much as you have, but I don't remember any of it. The only place I know is Invergarrig – and I was only there for a few days.' She sighed. 'My world seems so small compared to yours, and that makes me feel even more pathetic than I already do.'

Ben frowned. 'Why should you feel that way?'

'Well, I almost passed out at the station, for a start, and I'm sitting here feeling completely overwhelmed at the idea of making the journey from Glasgow to London, but to you, that's probably like crossing the road!'

'But this *is* a big thing for you. You're not just taking a train to London, like the rest of these people,' he said, glancing around at the quarter-full carriage. 'You're going in search of your whole life. Of course this feels daunting. For all intents and purposes, this is your first time on a train. My first train ride, I cried the whole journey. At least you're coping better than that.'

She stifled a chuckle. 'You cried? How old were you?'

'About three, I think. Norina took me out on a day trip – can't remember where – and I was terrified about sliding down the gap between the carriage and the platform. It was all she could do to get me on the train to come home again.'

'Well, by those standards, I suppose I am doing pretty well . . . Just about.' Her expression grew more serious. 'Thank you, Ben, for getting on the train with me. I'm really, really glad you're here.'

'I am too.' The truth. Even though it shouldn't be.

Alice seemed poised to ask another question when the train juddered. The other passengers in their coach, including a pair of young women across the aisle, frowned and looked around as the train began to slow and then ground to a halt completely.

It could just be a red signal, he reasoned to himself, no reason for the niggle in his gut, even though he'd learned to trust that warning when he'd been on the road. But then the Tannoy system crackled, raising his alert system another notch, and a disembodied voice floated through the carriage. 'We're sorry to inform you that this train has developed an electrical fault. Engineers are on their way, and we will hopefully be moving again as soon as possible.'

CHAPTER TWENTY-NINE

Seven months before the wedding.

I MANAGED TO visit my parents for Sunday lunch the following week. On my own. Justin was too exhausted after the last night of the show to join me. I missed seeing Lo because she was out with a friend, so, the following Saturday, I suggested we go shopping in the West End, like we used to, and then I'd planned lunch at a nice restaurant behind Kensington High Street that Justin sometimes took me to.

'Your hair is so different,' Lo said when we met at the Tube station. 'I can't get over it.'

My hand flew instantly to my head, smoothing the strands down. Even more had come off the length since I'd last seen her. 'Justin knows this excellent stylist in Knightsbridge,' I said. 'He suggested a colour change, and I thought why not?' I'd only had it done the weekend before, and I still did a double-take when I walked past the mirrors in the flat, wondering who this stylish, sophisticated woman with the glossy, honey-blonde bob was.

We started off at Harrods, of course. Lo and I had always loved a Saturday shopping trip up West, and we'd gawp at all the expensive things in the elegant shops before finding a flea market and doing our actual shopping there.

In the middle of the bed linen section, I turned to her and gave her the biggest hug.

Lo chuckled and squeezed me back. 'What's this for?'

'I've just missed you. And it's so good to just be able to let off a little steam, to be silly . . . '

Lo gave me a look I couldn't quite decipher, but then she smiled. 'I've missed you too. We haven't done this in ages.'

We carried on walking, ending up in front of a display of candles in a variety of expensive-looking glass containers. Lo picked up a candle, checked the price on the bottom, then whistled. She showed it to me, her eyes glittering with fun. 'Four hundred quid? For a candle? They're having a laugh!'

'Come on,' I said, chuckling along with her as I took it from her and put it back down on the display. 'I'm starving. Why don't we go and have lunch?'

*

'This is nice,' Lo said, entering the restaurant and looking around at the stripped wooden floors, dove-grey paintwork, and adventurous pieces from local artists. She dumped her handbag on the floor and sat down.

I took the chair opposite her, feeling pleased with myself. 'I just thought it would be good to catch up with each other. Life has been so hectic recently that I haven't seen as much of Mum and Dad – and you – as I've meant to.'

'It hasn't gone unnoticed,' Lo replied, eyeing up the menu. 'Dad keeps joking about only having one daughter – although he has a vague memory there might have been another one, once upon a time.'

I rolled my eyes. 'I was there just last weekend. And I do my best to go round as much as I can. But Justin's been really busy with the show, and it's made him very stressed, so he needs lots of support. It's hardly like I've deserted them!'

'I know that. But you know what Dad's like . . . ' Her expression grew more serious. 'I think he misses you. They both do.'

'I miss them too. But I can't stay at home forever. I've got to start living my life.'

Lo gave me a tentative smile. 'I just hope they're not going to barricade the door when it's my turn.'

I laughed softly. 'They might try!'

We chatted about our lives as we ate. She was getting a promotion. Mum and Dad must be stoked. I told her about my life but skirted around any mention of the unfortunate performance. I'd been too nervous about it to invite my parents, which had definitely turned out to be the right decision. They both preferred *Strictly* to anything too 'arty farty', as Dad called it. I did tell Lo about my upcoming jobs and my hopes for forging a new kind of career in music.

'Justin's changing you,' Lo said, unsmiling.

I felt myself bristle. 'No, he isn't. And if I am changing, it's for the better. I'm becoming who I'm supposed to be. I'm *evolving*.'

Lo snorted softly. She'd always hated anything that reeked of self-help books and psychobabble. 'And it's just a coincidence that you're *evolving* into the sort of woman Justin would like you to be?'

I frowned. 'Well, of course Justin has something to do with it. But only because he's showed me how to like myself again, how to make the best of myself. He challenges me, Lo.

He won't let me be the pathetic creature I was when I left the Conservatory, and I'm grateful for it.'

I saw a shadow pass across my sister's features at that point, and she looked away. I watched her, confused for a moment, and then a thought dropped into my head. 'You don't like him, do you?'

'I'm not the one living with him, so it really doesn't matter what I think about him.'

I felt a flare of familiar irritation. Why did she always have to find fault with whatever I did? Because attacking Justin felt as if she was attacking me – more and more I felt as if he and I were becoming one person. 'Why don't you like him?'

She shook her head, as if she'd rather not have the conversation, which was weird because she was the one who'd brought him up. 'I can't . . . I can't put my finger on it, Lil. He just gives me a weird vibe.' She gave me a rueful smile. 'He doesn't like me much either, that's for sure.'

'Don't be ridiculous,' I said, leaning back and sipping my espresso.

'*Don't be ridiculous* . . . ' she said, mimicking me. 'You're even starting to sound like him.'

'And what's wrong with that?'

'Because he's full of bullshit,' she said, in her usual take-no-prisoners manner. 'And you might think he's the best thing since sliced bread, but I don't think he's good for you.'

I sat there open-mouthed. Lo had had some complete plonkers as boyfriends over the years, and not once had I said anything like that to her about any one of them. 'What is it exactly that you find so distasteful about him?' I asked coolly.

She studied me for a few moments to see if I was serious.

'As much as he charms the pants off Mum and Dad, I see the way he looks at our home when he deigns to come and visit with you. He thinks he's better than us.'

I shook my head impatiently. Lo could be a bit of a reverse snob sometimes. 'He does no such thing. And you don't understand his job – it's not a nine-to-five like yours. Sometimes he's got to work weekends and evenings. Being creative is draining in a way you just wouldn't understand.'

Lo let out a surprised, rather dry laugh. 'Ouch. We're going there, are we?'

I ignored her. She knew I wasn't being funny with her. And I'd rather not get side-tracked off the main subject. 'Give me one example. One time he hasn't been anything but nice.'

She thought for a moment. 'Mum's gravy. I see the way his nose crinkles a little when she offers it to him. Has he never had Bisto before? What's wrong with it, anyway?'

'Nothing!' I said, knowing we all loved Mum's roast dinners more than life itself. 'But you've got to remember Justin grew up very differently from us. He's used to things being a certain way, being . . .'

'*Better*?' Lo suggested, arching an eyebrow.

'No.' I struggled to keep my voice steady. She was starting to irritate me now. 'Just different.'

Lo sat back and folded her arms. 'I knew you'd get like this if I said anything.'

I wanted to stand up for Justin, explain how he'd grown up being used to fine dining and the best ingredients, but I also knew that if I said any of this to Lo, it would just cement how stuck up he was in her eyes.

Unfortunately, my sister took my silence for agreement.

'See? You can't defend him,' she said, then sighed, and her expression softened. 'I'm glad you're happy, Lil, I really am. Please believe that. But that doesn't mean I have to like him. And I don't care if he likes me or not, either.'

I glowered at her, but at the same time, I was thinking back to how Justin had been this morning when I reminded him I was having lunch with Lo. A look of irritation had crossed his face, so fleeting I hadn't really identified it until now.

Okay, so maybe Justin didn't like Lo either. But considering the vibes she was sending out, it was hardly surprising. I watched her sip her coffee. Couldn't she even *try* to meet me halfway? 'You're not really pleased for me, are you? Just because you haven't—'

'Oh, now you're going to tell me I'm jealous – because you've got a man and I haven't?'

'That's not what I was going to say.' But it reminded me of something Justin had said a couple of weeks earlier, and now my mind was running down that track, I couldn't stop thinking about it.

'But . . . ?' Lo prompted, reading me as well as she always did.

'It's nothing.' I played with the teaspoon on my saucer.

'Don't give me that, Lil. I know when you're holding something back. He's said something about me, hasn't he? About me being jealous of you. Because you'd never think that on your own.'

I swallowed. She'd hit the nail right on the head. And my expression said it all.

Lo looked aghast. 'You don't believe him, do you?'

'No,' I mumbled, sounding about only ninety per cent

convincing. 'But I know it's been hard for you over the years, with Mum and Dad giving me loads of attention because of my music—'

'You know that's never bothered me!'

I nodded. I did. At least, maybe not on a conscious level. But maybe Justin was right. Maybe she'd enjoyed being the centre of attention with all her success at work when I'd dropped out of the Conservatory. He said that maybe, on some level, she didn't like seeing me doing better again, and she resented him because he was the catalyst for that. I'd told him he'd got it wrong at the time, even though he'd made a very convincing argument, but now . . . remembering how she talked about him, how she constantly made digs about all the improvements I was making to myself, I was starting to wonder if he was right.

'I can't help that we have different gifts, that I have creative talent and you—'

'Oh, my God! Listen to yourself! You sound just like *him*.'

I'd been going to say she was talented in other ways if she'd let me finish, but all my good intentions about having an adult conversation with my little sister evaporated. 'Well, if you find me – and Justin – that offensive, you don't have to sit here and eat the rather expensive lunch he's actually paying for.'

She threw her napkin down and stood up. 'I'd probably choke on it anyway.'

'Fine,' I said, folding my arms.

Lo practically ripped her cardigan from the back of the chair and turned to go, but after she'd taken a few steps, she turned. 'You know what?' she said, her eyes filling. 'I came here today ready to remind you of something. I know you've been struggling with feeling like you're not good enough since Ben the Bloody Photographer did a number on you and you dropped out of music school, and I was going to tell you that there's nothing wrong with who you are. You don't have to change yourself for him or anyone, but obviously you're too wrapped up in him to see straight.'

'Let me live my life the way I want to, Lo! And if that means putting myself back together with Justin's help and support, I thought you'd be happy for me rather than all . . . judgey. If it offends you so much, you don't have to be part of it.'

Lo no longer looked angry now. She looked hollow, her cheeks drawn. We'd had our squabbles over the years, but we'd never fought like this before.

'If that's what you want,' she said, and her tone was icy, and then she turned and left the restaurant, leaving me staring after her.

*

Justin was in the kitchen when I got home. 'How did lunch go?'

'Not good.' I dropped into the chair opposite him. 'Lo and I had a huge fight.'

'About what?'

I looked away, not wanting to reveal that we'd fought about him. 'It started about something stupid and just . . . escalated. It was horrible, Justin. And before I knew it, I was telling her to stay out of my life, and she . . . Well, she agreed.'

Justin wrapped his arms around me. He was always so wise, so sensitive. He knew how to handle people. Even before he said anything, I could hear the advice in my head . . . *Sleep on it, Angel. Call her in the morning when you've both had some breathing space.*

But when he pulled away and kissed me, he said, 'You can't let her negativity infect you. You're at a turning point, Angel. Maybe it *is* better if you take a break from each other while she adjusts to that.'

I nodded, hearing the logic in his words but also sensing a vague tearing in my heart. Lo and I would patch it up eventually, wouldn't we?

'You don't need her in your life at the moment,' he said, smoothing down my hair, stroking it rhythmically. 'But don't worry . . . I'll look after you. I'll be everything you need.'

CHAPTER THIRTY

Now.

WHILE THE OTHER passengers were discussing the delay amongst themselves, Ben jumped up. 'Keep an eye on our stuff, will you?' he said, then strode off like a man on a mission. Alice turned and craned her neck, watching him until he reached the sliding door at the end of the carriage.

Ben Robertson, she thought as it opened automatically for him then swallowed him up. *You are not who I thought you were.*

She'd thought of him as a static kind of person – solid, dependable – hadn't ever questioned he was anything but a guy who liked checked shirts and soft jeans, who knew how to tile a wall or fix a dripping tap. It was as if she'd been introduced to a whole new person with this information about his former job.

A couple of minutes later, he was back, striding down the carriage towards her, a look of intention about him that drew other people's gaze. Alice ignored the little hiccup in her chest when he sat back down and his knee brushed against hers under the table.

Stop it, she told herself.

Yes, he was very easy on the eyes, with his warm brown eyes and his long legs. Yes, he'd been kind and helpful, her knight in shining armour, but she couldn't let herself develop any sort of feelings because of that.

It was merely her sense of gratefulness because he was the first person she'd met since she'd been this new version of herself, and like a fluffy chick freshly hatched out of an egg, she'd imprinted on him, deciding he was her source of security. It was all completely explainable in terms of biology, this feeling that she knew him, that she belonged with him. She just needed to remind herself of that every time that little hiccup occurred.

'I found the guard,' he said, causing the two young women in the seating bank opposite to prick up their ears. 'He thinks it'll be at least half an hour before we get another update. Possibly more.'

'Great!' the girl with the gentle Irish accent said. 'Stuck in the middle of nowhere for the night.'

Ben looked across at her. 'Hopefully, they'll get us moving, but this is the last train heading this way tonight, so if they don't, the train company is obliged to provide overnight accommodation.'

'What did you do?' the other girl, the one with a Lancashire accent, said. 'Memorise the timetable?'

'Something like that,' he said with a grin, and when the girls returned to their conversation, he turned to Alice. 'Occupational habit, I'm afraid – checking out times, thinking of alternative routes. But it's saved my hide more than a few times when I was away from home.'

She nodded, glad she was with someone who knew what to

do, but she couldn't just keep relying on Ben. Tomorrow he'd be gone. It was time she started doing it for herself.

'I was just thinking I should do a video to add to my diary,' she said to him. 'To explain what's going on. It won't help at all if I just take a picture out the window – you can't see a thing.'

Ben nodded. 'Good idea.'

She lifted her phone up, facing the camera towards him. 'Go on, then, Mr Travel Expert.'

'You want *me* to do it?' He couldn't have looked any more shocked if he'd tried.

'What? Don't like being on the other side of the camera?'

His eyes were warm as he replied, 'Not particularly.'

'It was your clever idea.' The hiccup happened again. Not because he'd accidentally bumped knees with her under the table. Not because she was about to film him, capture a little memory of him, but because she liked what was happening between them – the easy banter, as if they'd known each other for years, not days.

He shot her a look that said *You're really doing this?* then sighed, shook his head gently and launched into a very 'Ben' explanation of the situation – no drama, no frills, just a precise and careful rundown of the facts, finishing off with a smile that turned the hiccup into a stutter.

'It's just gone eight,' he said, checking his own phone. 'Do you mind if I give Willow a call?'

Alice shook her head and waved back at Willow on the video chat when she insisted Ben turn the phone around. But then the begging for a bedtime story came, one of his 'made up' ones, and Ben sighed then launched into a tale about a little girl who had a magic hot air balloon that could visit anywhere in the world and proceeded to tell an adventure involving waterfalls so high that they reached the moon, icebergs that contained vast upside-down underwater cities, and a herd of flying unicorns that got lost when the Northern Lights threw them off course.

'That was so sweet,' one of the girls sitting opposite said when he'd finished and said goodbye to Willow. 'I wish my dad had made up stories for me like that when I was little.'

Ben opened his mouth, and Alice wondered if he was going to correct her about being Willow's dad, but then he just mumbled something and looked out the window.

Alice wasn't sure her heart was in a totally solid state either. This was more than the baby chick theory, she realised. She might not know her name or her address or her date of birth, but she knew – remembered – what it meant when you sat a few feet away from someone and all you could do was *notice* them.

That thought brought her up short.

She'd felt this way before.

That meant she'd felt this way about someone else. No, not someone *else*. Just someone. Because that person had been in her life first. And she possibly did still feel that way about them. Everything she was feeling for Ben right now was only an echo.

The Tannoy system crackled to life again. 'Ladies and gentlemen, we are sorry to inform you that this service is cancelled . . . ' and the guard went on to explain that they would have to be evacuated from the train and buses would be provided to take them to nearby towns.

Alice looked across at Ben, feeling more than a little

anxious at the announcement. The last station they'd stopped at was Carlisle, and that was only just south of the border with Scotland, which meant they were still hundreds of miles away from London. She hadn't doubted she'd make it to the rehearsal on time when she'd left Invergarrig, but now she wasn't so sure.

CHAPTER THIRTY-ONE

Six months before the wedding.

I TOOK THE Tube to Covent Garden and found one of my usual spots to busk. I hadn't been coming out as much since I'd moved in with Justin, and probably not at all in the last few weeks – things had just been so busy – but I was due in the recording studio again in three days, and I wanted to practise a piece I'd been learning so it was perfect.

Agnes, an up-and-coming singer-songwriter, had approached me a couple of days after my horrendous lunch with Lo and asked if I'd record a violin section for her new EP. She'd heard about me from a friend who'd been at Justin's preview.

However, when I'd tried to rehearse, due to the open-plan layout of the flat, it had been hard to find a place where I didn't disturb Justin, who'd pushed back the sofas in the living room and was trying to choreograph a new dance. We'd agreed to work in shifts, and I'd decided to get out of the flat to give him some peace and quiet. I'd just been about to leave when I'd spotted Octavia on the bed, and it had occurred to me that I could kill two birds with one stone.

I changed what I was wearing before I headed out the door.

Justin was so generous. He kept buying me things, especially clothes. I now looked sophisticated, like I belonged with him. That was important to me. I saw women eyeing him up when we went out, the dismissive looks they'd given me when we'd first been together. *Too young, too gauche. Obviously just a fling.* But now, those same women were starting to take me seriously. It was quite a revelation.

Sometimes, I walked into our dressing room in the mornings, and I'd find an outfit hung up in front of my clothing rail, even down to shoes and accessories. He was so thoughtful.

I left my jeans on – no one would be able to tell they were designer – but removed the silk blouse and exchanged it for one of my favourite T-shirts with a band name on the front, a beret and a collection of chains and bangles I hardly wore any more, including the silver bee pendant, which I hadn't thrown away, despite the memories attached to it. It was beautiful, really me, and it made me angry to think of getting rid of something I loved because of *him*. So I'd decided to reclaim it, wore it every day for months, deliberately creating new memories with it, diluting the impact of the ones I didn't want to think about. *I don't need those memories of you any more,* I whispered in my head as I raised my hands behind my neck and did the clasp up. *I have a new man now.* One who wasn't afraid to stay.

I played to my heart's content when I arrived in Covent Garden, doing loads of the old favourites and popular classics, and I returned to the flat two hours later brimming with joy and optimism.

The first thing I did when I got inside was to head straight to the dressing room. I'd only just peeled my beret off when

I sensed someone standing behind me. Justin choreographed in his bare feet or socks, so he often managed to creep up behind me without me knowing. Well, not *creep*, exactly. Just appear, as if out of nowhere.

Even though I'd had a feeling he was there, I still jumped when I turned around and saw him. I laughed, pressing my palm to my chest. 'You've got to stop doing that!'

Justin didn't laugh with me. 'What are you wearing? And why are you so late? You've been out all afternoon. I was starting to get concerned.'

'Oh, sorry! I didn't mean to worry you.' I gestured to my T-shirt. 'Thought this was more in keeping with a busking vibe.'

'You went busking? Without telling me?'

I nodded. 'I did say I was going out . . . '

'But not busking.'

'No. That was a spur of the moment thing.' I frowned. 'Is something wrong?'

His cheeks pulled into a tight smile. 'No. Of course not.'

We stood there, looking at each other awkward. 'Well, I'll just go and hop in the shower, wash the city grime off and get ready to go to Penge.' It was Dad's birthday, and the family tradition was to go out for a Chinese to celebrate. 'You don't have to come tonight if you don't want.' I had a feeling Justin's palate was a little too sophisticated for The Peking Duck.

'No, I'll come.' He sounded oddly resigned. 'Where you go, I go . . . That's what supportive couples do for each other, isn't it? They stand by each other, back each other up.'

I frowned as I got undressed and headed for the en suite. Justin's words had been just what anyone would want to hear from a partner, but I'd sensed something else, something I couldn't quite pin down.

When I was finished, I got dressed in a soft, chiffon sleeveless blouse and wide-leg trousers that Justin had picked out on a recent shopping trip. Instead of putting the bangles back on, I opted for a fine gold chain and left the rest of myself accessory free. Justin liked uncluttered.

I wandered through the flat looking for him and eventually found him nursing a glass of red wine in the kitchen. I went to sit beside him on one of the stools that flanked the breakfast bar. 'What's up?'

'Nothing,' he said, staring into his wine.

'Talk to me . . . You know you can tell me anything.'

He shook his head in short, staccato movements. 'I can't. You're going to think I'm pathetic.'

I reached over and kissed his temple. 'Never. You're sensitive and emotionally open. That's what I love about you.'

He turned to face me. 'You really don't need to go busking any more. I have enough money for both of us.'

'I know. But you also said you thought it would be good if I contributed, and until more session work comes in . . . '

'It's hardly worth it. I mean, it's just pin money.'

I thought about the notes and coins in my violin case, and I knew he was right, but it still felt as if he was squashing my accomplishment. And it wasn't just about money; it was about healing, moving forwards, getting stronger.

I decided to try and jolly him out of his dark mood. 'I made enough for a decent bottle of wine. I'll treat you.'

He sighed and turned to face me. 'You only get that kind of cash because the men in the audience think you're stunning.

Remember that I've been there . . . I've seen them watching you.'

I blinked, taken aback. First, I wasn't stunning – I'd have placed myself at 'distinctly average' on the beauty scale – and second, I hoped there was a more important reason people threw money into my violin case. However, I knew Justin could get a little insecure because of his ex-wife's infidelity, so I ignored the edge in his voice and looped my arms around his neck.

'You used to be one of those men, remember?' I smiled up at him, willing him to laugh along with me. 'You didn't seem to mind it much then.' I kissed him on his lips softly, and he closed his eyes, so I kissed each of his eyelids too, and his arms came around me, pulling me even closer.

'That's kind of my point,' he said wearily into my ear. 'I just can't . . . '

'Shh . . . It's okay. I understand. But it's you I love. I promise you I'm not going anywhere.'

'Can I ask you something? A favour?'

I rested my head against his shoulder. 'Anything. You know that?'

'Will you stop?'

I raised my head to look at him. 'Stop what? Stop *this* . . . ' and I began to move my hand up his thigh. However, the look he gave me was so heartbreakingly forlorn, I paused.

'Will you stop busking? I know I'm an idiot . . . And I know I'm not being reasonable, but I just can't stand the thought of other men looking at you that way, *wanting* you the way I want you . . . wanting all of you.' And he pulled me into his arms and crushed me against his chest, his breathing ragged.

'I . . . Justin . . . ' I understood what he was saying, but even though I'd just said I'd do anything for him, I felt a kernel of resistance inside. 'It's really not fair of you to ask that. I've never even *looked* at another man since we've been together. And you know how much busking means to me . . . It's the only way I can properly let off steam.'

He moved me away from him, and suddenly there was cool air between our bodies. 'I thought you said you loved me.'

'I do!'

'Then can't you do this for me? I do so much for you.'

I looked down at my feet. He was right. He did do so much for me. Wasn't I always thanking my lucky stars how supportive and encouraging he was? He'd made it possible for me to follow my dreams.

Was I being selfish?

He slid off the stool, took his wine glass and walked across the room to stand in front of the vast fireplace. 'I didn't want to say this, but all the time you're putting your creative energy into busking, it's diverting it from other things you could be doing – *should* be doing. It's a safety net, and you need to get rid of it. You need to be brave, not weak, Angel. You've got to push yourself to do more than the things you find easy, palatable. That's not what a true artist does.'

'You think I'm weak?'

He gave me a pleading look as I walked towards him. 'Not weak, but . . . I just think you're very afraid sometimes. You're not going to get anywhere unless you push yourself. Look at the preview . . . You did more than you ever thought you could do, even if it was a shaky start. I *knew* it was a better decision for you to play live instead of using the track.'

Did he have a point? I thought I'd been doing so well, but was I still a scared little girl, hiding from what life wanted to give me? But then something he'd said snagged my attention. 'What do you mean, "instead of using the track"? I was supposed to play along with the track and something went wrong. There was no "decision" to do that . . . Was there?'

Justin shrugged noncommittally.

'Justin . . .'

He took a sip of his wine, breaking eye contact as he did so. I could read him well enough by now to sense there was something he wasn't telling me. But what could . . . ?

Oh.

An icy feeling began to bleed through me, my instincts catching onto something a couple of seconds before my conscious brain registered it. 'Did you . . . ? Did you *tell* them not to play the track? On purpose?'

He wouldn't meet my eye.

'Oh, God . . . I can't . . .' I walked away, back to the windows and placed my palm on my abdomen to quash the vaguely breathless feeling creeping over me. I felt like I was a snow globe, like someone had just picked me up and shaken me violently, and now everything inside me was flurrying in different directions. 'You did, didn't you?'

For a long moment, Justin said nothing, and then he blinked slowly and turned to look at me. His face was unmoving, his eyes expressionless. 'Yes, okay. I did it. I told them not to play the track.'

'Why? Why would you do that?' The tears were thick in my voice. 'You knew how terrified I was, and you didn't even warn me! You left me standing there like a lemon, and then

I . . . ' I trailed off as my brain started working overtime, thinking back to that night and the conversations we'd had since, trying to piece it all together like a rather complicated puzzle. 'You blamed *me* for messing up!' I let out a hollow laugh. 'And look where it got you! If you'd played the track as planned, it wouldn't have mattered that I'd made a mistake! It would never have been a problem.'

'Angel, you're becoming hysterical.'

I stared back at him, hardly knowing what to think or say. I did have a tendency to go off at the deep end when I got wound up and, yes, I was getting emotional, but I had good reason: the man I thought was my rock, my foundation, had just admitted to sabotaging me. He'd known how terrified I was about even being on stage that night, and he'd done it anyway.

I didn't understand how he could be so calm, so *un*emotional. This was our first fight, and I was hating every second of it.

He put his wine glass down and came closer, laid a hand on my shoulder. 'I did what we agreed. You said you were feeling confident, that you wanted to do it for me . . . '

I shook his arm off. 'I didn't say that.'

'You didn't?'

I thought back to that night, to the few words exchanged between us as we arrived at The Fire Station. 'Okay, I may have said *something* like that, but that wasn't what I'd meant. You knew that.'

He looked wounded. 'Those were your exact words. When I asked you if you'd do it, you said, "I want to – for you. I really do . . . " Don't you remember?'

I stared back at him, unable to either nod or shake my head. 'No . . . ' I murmured, even though I couldn't quite get the whole thing straight in my head.

He stepped towards me. 'And I think it's unfair to blame me if you were overoptimistic. If you'd have said no, I'd have gone with it. But you didn't.'

I shook my head. 'I'm sure I did!'

'You really didn't.'

It was true, I realised. I hadn't actually said the words, but thinking back, I could see the expression on his face, the nod that signalled his tacit acceptance of my refusal before we'd walked into the foyer. I knew I was right about that, no matter what he said.

'I'm finding these accusations of yours really quite hurtful, Angel. Like I said earlier, I did it for you, not me. Haven't I been your biggest supporter? I mean, I gave you the job in the first place. And now you're doubting me?'

He was turning this back on me so that I was in the wrong?

I stared at him. Who was this man? Where was the Justin I knew and loved?

He turned and headed for the bedroom at that point, effectively ending the discussion. 'If we don't start getting ready now, we're going to be late to meet your parents.'

And just like that, it was over. For him, at least. Dumbfounded, I followed him, then watched him peel off his practice clothes and pull a suit from the dressing room rail.

I stood there, aware of nothing but my own heartbeat for a few moments, and then I said, 'Actually, I think it's better if I go on my own.'

Justin stopped, one foot in a trouser leg. 'What do you

mean?' For the first time since we'd started arguing – well, not exactly arguing; he'd been too calm for that – since we'd been *disagreeing* about this whole situation, he looked worried.

I took a breath, tried to calm myself down. 'I mean it's probably a good idea to give ourselves a bit of breathing space, and I don't want to spoil Dad's night with an atmosphere.' Before he could argue with me, I picked up my bag and walked out the door.

CHAPTER THIRTY-TWO

Now.

ALICE READ THE hotel sign overhead – Travel Inn, Penrith. Tiny, pale flakes spiralled in the air above her head. 'It's snowing.'

Ben looked up. 'The forecast said it wasn't going to be heavy. It probably won't even settle.'

They made their way into the lobby along with almost two coachloads of other stranded passengers.

'Right,' the receptionist said when they got to the front of the queue. 'Room one-o-three.' And he handed over a key card, then looked expectantly at the family standing behind them.

'What about the other key?' Ben asked. 'For the other room?'

The receptionist frowned and checked some papers on the desk in front of him. 'Ben and Alice Robertson?'

'Yes,' Alice said.

'No,' Ben said simultaneously.

When the railway staff had been taking names and details for overnight accommodation, it had become apparent that she was missing a surname. Ben had suggested she just use his to save long explanations.

'We're not . . . together,' she said to the receptionist and felt her cheeks heat as she kept her eyes away from Ben's.

'You're not married?

They both shook their heads.

'Brother and sister?' the guy asked hopefully.

A blush crept up past Alice's chin to warm her ears.

'It's complicated,' Ben said.

The receptionist merely blinked, then said, 'Of course, West Coast Rail may well be happy to sort out another room for one of you, but it won't be at this hotel. We're fully booked now, and they're sending everyone else to Carlisle. If you'd like to stand to one side, I can get them on the phone for you.'

There was shuffling in the queue behind them. People were getting restless. 'Carlisle is north of here,' Ben said to her. 'We'd be heading in completely the wrong direction.'

Alice nodded. It made no sense to go back there. It also made no sense for her and Ben to split up. 'I don't suppose you have any twin rooms left?'

The receptionist shook his head. 'But some of our rooms have a sofa bed. I can put you in one of those?'

She shot a look at Ben. He met her gaze and nodded. 'I'd have slept on the floor if need be,' he told the receptionist, 'but that would be great. Thank you.'

*

While Alice was in the bathroom, Ben slipped out of his jeans and slid between the sheets of the sofa bed situated next to the window. One of the hotel staff had come and removed the back cushions and made it up not long after they'd got to the room. It was turning out to be surprisingly comfortable.

The bathroom door opened. Alice emerged looking a little awkward in a pair of too-large pyjamas. He opened one of the reading apps on his phone to both distract himself and give her a little privacy.

The sheets on the bed rustled. 'Are you okay if I turn out the light?'

'Of course.' She flipped the switch, and then the only source of light in the room was the dull glow of his phone screen. 'Will this disturb you?' he asked.

'No, it's okay. I think I'll be out for the count once my head hits the pillow.'

Alice predicted well. Her breathing slowed not long after he heard her plumping up the pillow, but while she was right about the speed with which she fell asleep, she was wrong about the quality. He read on his phone for the next hour or two, during which she had patches of tossing and turning. He'd just about nodded off, his phone lying on his chest, when she suddenly gasped and sat up.

Ben also lurched to a sitting position. 'Are you okay?'

She breathed heavily for a moment, then said, 'Yes . . . Just a bad dream.'

He knew all about bad dreams, had been plagued by them for a good while after Cat had died. They hadn't been identical, but they'd all run along the same theme: she was in danger – locked in a house, being sucked under swampy mud, flailing far out at sea – and he could never get to her in time to save her. 'What was it about?'

He heard her inhale and then exhale, and then she began

talking. 'I can't remember. It was a feeling more than any-thing . . . of being breathless. And being trapped. I was trying to get away from something when I woke up. But it's like the atmosphere of the dream is still with me now I'm awake.'

He hated it when that happened. 'This is a stressful time for you. It's not surprising it's leaking into your dreams.'

She was quiet for a moment. 'It's not just the dream that's making me feel this way,' she replied quietly. 'It's real life.'

He propped himself up on his pillows and turned towards her. 'In what way?'

'All I've wanted since that day I met you outside the café was to find out who I am, to slot back into the life I left behind. After talking to the doctor, I have to acknowledge that I might not like what I find. Things might not be perfect. I thought I was ready for that, but now we're on the way, now we're getting closer, it's all becoming very real. And I'm scared. Does that make sense?'

'Yes,' he said softly.

'It does?'

'It was hard to come back to Invergarrig when my sister died. I thought I knew what my future looked like, and then one day – *poof!* – it was gone, and I had no idea what would replace it. I still don't, really . . . That was daunting enough, even when I knew who I was and where home was supposed to be. I can't even imagine what it must be like to not know those things either.'

She nodded, and he thought he could see a rather wobbly, grateful smile curve her lips. 'It just feels very . . . '

He waited for her to finish her sentence, but the room was completely silent for almost a minute, and then he realised why. In the dim light, he could see she'd covered her face with her hands.

'Alice?'

She tried to answer, but all that came out at first was a gurgling sniff, and then she managed, 'I just f-feel so *lonely*. All the time. It's like I'm in this world with everybody else, but I'm from a separate planet, a place no one else understands because they've never been there. I just . . . I just want it all to *end*!'

It was all Ben could do to stay anchored to his stupid sofa bed and not leap over to where she was and gather her up in his arms. But he kept his backside glued to the mattress.

When she'd composed herself, she said, 'I keep thinking about that image I saw so clearly in my mind back at the station. It could be a memory, but you're right – it could just be my addled brain playing yet another horrible trick on me. But then I think, "What if it isn't? What if it's real?" and I go round and round in circles trying to work the answer out. It's exhausting. And I keep thinking: all I want is one thing, just one fact to know about myself to anchor me in place, to make me actually feel like a real person . . . not a figment of someone's imagination that might disappear at any second.' She buried her face in her hands again, and her shoulders began to shake. Ben's eggshell-thin resolve cracked.

Don't do it, don't do it, a voice warned inside his head as he threw his duvet back and stood up. *She needs a friend, not . . .*

Shut up, he argued back. *I know that. Don't you think I know that?* And to prove his point, he didn't get into bed beside her but stayed on top of the duvet, putting an arm around her from the side so she could lean into him. She let out a strange little sob, and then the floodgates opened.

He'd never been that good with other people's emotions. Not really, even though he was definitely a people person. There was getting deeper, connecting, and then there was . . . this. It reminded him of his sister, how she'd worn all her feelings on her sleeve for the world to see, how he'd tried to tell her over and over to buckle them up inside when she got upset because you never knew when the door would slam open and an angry voice would tell you to shut up or they'd give you something real to cry about.

But, somehow, he didn't want to crawl away, find an excuse to do something else, *go* somewhere else, while Alice turned the front of his T-shirt into a lake. He didn't know what to do or what to say to solve her problem, although he desperately wished he could, but he could do this. He could hold her. He could try and absorb some of her pain.

She eventually ran out of steam, becoming heavy against him. 'Why don't you try and get some sleep,' he whispered, but when he tried to pull away, she grabbed his arm, kept it pinned against her.

'Please . . . Don't go. Not just yet.'

He remained still for a couple of heartbeats, then said, 'Give me a second . . . ' before putting one foot on the floor and reaching over for the single duvet on his bed. When he returned, pulling the duvet with him, Alice had sunk onto the mattress, facing away from him. He scooted in close, staying on top of her duvet but pulling his over him until he was spooning behind her. Close but not too close.

There. All very platonic. No skin was touching skin, except if you counted where his forearm lay across hers.

He lay in the darkness, feeling her heat seep through the duvet, hearing the soft rasp of her breathing. 'Sorry . . . ' she finally whispered, and it was that one tiny, scratchy word that broke him.

She didn't need to be sorry about anything. If there was anyone who was sorry, it was him. Because he had the power to solve her problem. He could give her that one thing she'd asked for, no, practically *prayed* for. He could give her one fact. At the very least, he could give her a name. One that actually belonged to her.

The doctor had said it might upset her, make her emotional state worse, but what was this if it wasn't 'upset'? More than that, if this wasn't 'downright heartbroken'? As far as he could tell, *not* knowing was causing way more damage.

Now the idea to say what he'd been holding back ever since he'd seen her bee necklace in the garden had planted itself in his brain, his heart began to hammer. There was no going back if he did this.

She let out a long, slow breath, but he could tell she was still aching inside, felt the quiver of her ribcage at the point between breath leaving her lungs and new air being sucked in again.

That was all it took.

'When I first met you outside the café, I thought you were someone I'd met before.'

Alice went very still. 'You did? I don't . . . I don't remember much about that. Pieces of that morning are all a bit blurry.

The first thing I remember really clearly after leaving the café is sitting in an armchair by the fire at the B&B.'

He heaved in a breath and carried on. There was no point going only halfway. 'But then I thought I must be wrong because you didn't recognise me, and other things didn't add up either. Your face was similar, but your hair is very different. Even your voice isn't the same as the woman I remembered.'

'This was someone you knew? A friend?'

He shook his head and smelled the lemon of her shampoo as his jaw rubbed against her hair. 'Not quite.'

'If it *was* me, would I have known you too? Would I have remembered you?'

He let out a heavy sigh. 'I think so.' He hoped so, even if it would have meant she'd taken one look at him, walked away and never given him the time of day.

She was quiet for a few moments, and then she said, 'Why are you telling me this?'

'Because . . .' *Oh, Lord. Here goes.* 'Because I'm starting to think I was right. I'm starting to think we met before.'

Up until that moment, it was as if they'd been curled up in a little cocoon of darkness and warmth, but Alice shattered it completely by sitting bolt upright, tearing herself out of his arms and turning the light on. He blinked in pain as an imprint from the harsh little reading light above the bed seared itself into his retina.

'What? How . . . ?' She looked as if she was about to cry again. This was *not* the way he'd thought this would go. 'Why didn't you tell me this before?!'

CHAPTER THIRTY-THREE

Six months before the wedding.

I ARRIVED FAR too early at my parents' house and fudged an excuse about Justin not feeling well to explain his absence. Mum and Dad bought it, I think. The only person who might have looked a little deeper was Lo, but when she got home from work, she barely glanced at me, let alone spoke to me. It cut like a knife, but at least she wouldn't notice something was off.

I should have been enjoying one of our favourite family nights of the year, but I couldn't wait for the evening to be over so I could hide in my bedroom and have a chance to process what had happened. Had Justin really admitted to not using the recorded track for his performance on purpose? I played our conversation back in my head in crystal-clear detail.

He had. He'd definitely said it.

The knowledge cut me to the core, but I found it hard to verbalise exactly why that was. It was . . . It was as if I'd had a picture of Justin in my head, one that I had believed was a faithful and true representation of who he was, the man I loved, and somehow that picture didn't fit the person I'd had that conversation with. That scared me.

While we were at the Chinese restaurant, I could feel my phone vibrating every couple of minutes. Eventually, I couldn't stand it any longer. I excused myself and went to the ladies', where I fished my phone out of my bag. There were six missed calls from Justin and fourteen unread messages. The latest read: *Angel, please come back home. We need to talk about this.*

I agreed with him. We did need to talk. But not yet. Justin was much better at coming up with logical reasons why he was right than I was. I needed more time. Not only to work out how I felt, but how to express it clearly. There was also a second reason that was fairly obvious. *It's Dad's birthday dinner,* I messaged back. *I can't talk right now.*

A voicemail arrived as I was washing my hands. He wanted me to come home. He loved me. He wanted to talk about this and work it out. It went on and on and on.

I've asked Mum if I can stay over tonight, I replied. *We could both do with cooling off a little.*

He texted back instantly, saying that he understood completely but also asking if he could come round the following morning.

I don't know. I will talk to you soon, I promise, but could you stop messaging and calling for now? As I read the words back, I realised it might sound a bit sharp, so I added, *Sorry. Not trying to be funny. I just need time to get things straight in my own head.*

Okay, the reply came, and then my phone was blissfully silent. I closed my eyes, let out a breath, and went to re-join my family.

By the time we got home just after ten, I was ready for bed.

I changed into a nightshirt I found in my chest of drawers. It had been one of my favourites, old and soft, with a stupid slogan on the front. It had hardly screamed 'sophisticated new life', so I'd left it behind when I'd moved to Justin's. It was just what I needed at that moment, a bit of comfort in the form of a misshapen bit of cotton jersey.

I was just about to shuffle down in my single bed and tuck the duvet under my chin when I heard a soft knock at the door. 'Lil?'

'Yeah?' I whispered back.

Lo's head appeared around the door. 'Want to talk?' Her manner was still frosty, but there was genuine concern in her eyes.

I so wanted to say yes, to pat the bed so she'd come and sit at the end, as she always used to do when we'd had a good gossiping session. We'd both been too stubborn to pick up the phone to make the first move since our falling-out almost four weeks ago, but it was time to make amends. 'I'd like to put that stupid fight behind us,' I said.

'Me too.' She slid inside and perched on the end of my bed. 'So, what's up? You weren't yourself tonight.'

Unsure of what to say, I made a face, rehearsed and then discarded a few opening phrases in my head.

She looked me in the eye. 'Is it Justin?'

I swallowed. 'I . . . I overreacted to something he did. We had a fight.'

'You overreacted?' Lo gave me a suspicious look. 'Are you sure that's what happened? You can tell me, Lil. I—'

'Yes, I'm sure that's what happened,' I snapped back. Even though she'd hit the nail on the head, I didn't like the fact she'd been so quick to think badly of Justin. She hadn't even heard the whole story.

Lo stared at me for a couple of seconds, her expression pinched. 'You're lying.'

'I'm not!'

'Yes. You are.' She pushed herself up from the end of the bed. 'If you're not going to have an honest conversation with me, there's no point.'

'Lo!' I called out in a hoarse whisper as she headed for the door, but she didn't stop, didn't turn round. She just closed the door firmly behind her. Seconds later, I heard her bedroom door shut. I sank back onto my pillows and stopped trying to hold back the tears.

I couldn't deal with both her *and* Justin tonight. My sister would just have to wait until I'd untangled the mess I'd made of the other important relationship in my life.

*

I crept past my parents' bedroom, avoiding the creaky floorboard at the top of the stairs, then tiptoed down them and made my way into the kitchen. The overhead light would have been too jarring, so I turned on the strip light under the top cabinets and pressed the button on the kettle. I'd slept for about two hours before waking up, and the events of the previous day played in my head on a loop as I sat there, blearily sipping herbal tea.

About five minutes later, the kitchen door opened, and Mum peered round it. 'Oh, it's you! Can't sleep?'

I shook my head.

She pulled a mug from the cupboard and set about making herself a hot drink, then sat down opposite me, cupping it in her hands. 'Justin's not really ill, is he?'

'How did you . . . ?'

She gave me a knowing smile. 'I could tell you were stressed all evening, and your phone was going off almost constantly, and you normally jump to attention every time Justin texts or calls, yet you didn't once pick it up and look at it.'

Busted.

'We had a fight . . . ' I frowned. 'Do you think Dad noticed? I didn't want to ruin his night.'

Mum laughed softly. 'You could have worn a flashing neon sign broadcasting the news, and your dad still might only have a vague inkling something was up.'

I laughed too, just a little bit. It felt good.

'You had a fight?'

I sighed. 'Well, not even really a fight.' I'd been the one doing all the shouting, after all. 'More of a difference of opinion over how something happened.'

'Relationships aren't easy,' Mum said, looking back at me with a mixture of love and concern clouding her eyes. 'But I can tell he adores you.'

I nodded. I knew he did.

'No person is perfect. I know it can all seem like a fairy tale in the beginning, but that's not how real life – real love – works. Me and your dad have had our share of ups and downs over the years, but you work on stuff. You pull through together.'

This was exactly how I felt, that some of the glitter had been rubbed off my fairy tale. Was I being unfair to Justin, expecting him to be perfect when I so clearly wasn't? 'What do you do when someone does something that really hurts you, something unexpected?'

Mum thought for a moment. 'Did he intend to hurt you?'

'No . . . He said he was trying to help me. I just . . . I suppose I didn't appreciate the way he went about it.' Hearing those words coming out of my mouth made me question my dramatic exit from the flat. Was I overreacting? Should I accept what Justin said and forgive him? Part of me wanted that more than anything but another part was stubbornly clinging to the idea that this was something important, that I shouldn't ignore it, even though I couldn't really put it into words.

'I suppose what you have to ask yourself is this . . . ' Mum reached for the biscuit tin, took the lid off and offered me a Hobnob. 'Is the rough so bad that you can't put up with the smooth?'

No, I answered silently. As much as I hated this fight I'd had with Justin, I still loved him. I still wanted to be with him. And that's what Mum was saying, wasn't it? That sometimes, you have to compromise, you have to tuck away what you want, and think about the other person. So far, all I'd done since storming out of the flat was think about myself.

CHAPTER THIRTY-FOUR

Now.

THEY'D MET BEFORE?

Alice studied Ben's expression for a hint that she'd misheard him or that he was telling a horrendously inappropriate joke, but she saw the truth in his eyes. 'No,' she said, although she had no idea what question she was answering. Keeping her gaze locked on him, she scrabbled out from under the covers and away from the bed. She didn't want this. She wanted him to take it back.

Because for the first time since she'd found herself at that bus stop in Invergarrig, she'd felt safe. All the whirling thoughts and questions inside her head had come to rest. And now it felt as if her whole world had been upended again. That Ben was the one who'd done it ripped her heart in two.

'Who are you?' she practically shouted at him. For the first time in his presence, she felt scared. She was in a hotel room with a stranger, a stranger who'd been lying to her.

'If you just let me—' He pushed himself up onto all fours, made a move to come closer. Alice backed away, clutching her arms around herself until she was prevented from going any further by the wall.

He held up his hands, as if to say, *Whoa. It's okay*, looking so conflicted and confused that she wavered. On one hand, her heart told her that this was still the same man who had held her gently while she'd sobbed, but on the other, alarms were going off inside her head like World War III was about to start.

'You've been lying to me.'

'I—I haven't been lying.' Ben's eyes were pleading. 'I just didn't tell you the whole truth. I didn't even realise it myself at first. I thought my brain was playing tricks on me.'

Alice hugged herself harder. If there was one person who knew how unreliable a person's mind could be, it was her. Memories weren't concrete things. They were insubstantial, malleable. Prone to error or even complete erasure.

'I mentioned it to the doctor at the hospital and he said I should wait for the specialists at the memory unit to decide what to tell you. He wasn't sure if it might upset you further.'

'Then why . . . Why are you telling me now?'

He sat back down on the mattress heavily, ran his hands over his face and through his hair before looking back at her. 'Because I thought *not* knowing was making it worse. Because . . . Because I couldn't stand to see you tearing your heart out when I could do something to stop it.' His arms fell by his side helplessly. 'Maybe it was a mistake . . . Maybe I shouldn't have said anything. But I did. I can't take it back now.'

He was right about that. While it felt as if her whole life had been razed to the ground yet again, whatever happened next would be built on the foundation of this knowledge.

'While the doc said not to say anything to you, I told PC

Wilson everything I know. I hoped it might speed up her enquiries, point her in the right direction.'

Alice's brain began to tick away. 'Is that why you . . . why you were so insistent about me staying in Invergarrig and waiting for her to finish her investigation?'

He nodded.

And the doctors in Glasgow. He'd tried to convince her not to leave before seeing them. It all made sense. She didn't like it, but it all made sense. Her heart rate began to slow.

He shuffled off the bed, taking his duvet with him back to his sofa. With one arm, he gestured towards the empty king-size. Alice looked longingly at it. The air in the room was a couple of degrees lower than comfortable, standing-there-in-your-pyjamas temperature. She inched forward a little, keeping her eyes on Ben. 'Tell me,' she said. 'Tell me how we met. Did we know each other? Were we friends?'

He shook his head. 'We met in London five and half years ago. In July. I was only supposed to be there for a day, doing a bit of work before I headed off elsewhere. I . . . I bumped into you while I was sightseeing.'

'Sightseeing? Was I a tourist? Do you know where I came from?'

'All I know is that you lived somewhere in Greater London – south of the river, I think – and your first name.'

That information washed over her like a shower made of ice cubes. 'You . . . ' Her throat was so tight she could hardly get the words out. 'You know my *name*?'

He nodded, and she swore she got a glimpse of what he must have been like as a boy, in the midst of being told off, but desperate to smooth it all over, make everyone happy again.

'Kind of . . . You said something about it not being your full name, or your proper name, as we said goodbye, so if there was more, I never knew it. Do you want me to tell you what it is?'

She opened her mouth and then did nothing for a few seconds. 'I . . . I don't know.' And she really didn't. It felt like too much. Yet another piece of knowledge to send her brain spinning out of control, even though this was exactly what she'd wished for not ten minutes ago.

She reached behind her and placed the flat of her palm against the wall, something solid to steady herself against. 'Yes,' she whispered. 'I want to know.'

Ben nodded. 'You told me your name was Lili.'

Lili.

Such a short word. So simple. Yet it felt like a discovery on the same scale as the law of gravity or that the earth revolved around the sun. It was world-changing.

'It's been killing me not being able to tell you, it really has. You don't know how many times I almost cracked. And the longer it went on, the worse I felt about it, you've got to believe me.'

'I don't *have* to believe you.' But she did. Even though the echoes of air raid sirens were still ringing in her ears, deep down in her gut, she did. She knew this man. Even without the memory of ever having seen his face before Saturday morning, she knew him.

And Ben hadn't planned to come on the train with her, had he? He hadn't known she was going to have a meltdown on the station concourse. He couldn't have anticipated that. There was no reason to suspect he had any ulterior motive. 'Is there anything else you know about me? Anything at all?'

'Not much,' he said wearily. 'You said music was your passion, that you played the violin.'

'The violin?'

He nodded. 'You were studying it somewhere in London, but I'm not sure you ever mentioned the name of the music school, or if you did, I forgot.'

Well, she could hardly blame him for that, could she?

Despite the fact she still felt a little shaky, she peeled herself from the wall and went around the other side of the bed, sat on the edge and faced him so they were only a few feet apart. 'You said you weren't sure at first . . . '

'No,' he said, dark eyes fixed on hers, unblinking. Honest.

'What made you sure?'

Ben swallowed, and then his gaze drifted lower. Was he . . . ? Was he looking at her *boobs*? She was about the jump up, run and lock herself in the bathroom when he reached out and pinched the thin silver chain where it sat on her clavicle and pulled it so he was holding the little bee pendant away from her chest. 'Because I gave this to you.'

Oh. Her mouth made the shape, but her vocal cords declined to provide the sound. Their faces were almost touching as he held the tiny silver charm so gently between his fingers and her whole body felt as if it were humming with electric current.

'I thought you said we met sightseeing. Do you usually buy presents – jewellery – for women you meet sightseeing?' And since he'd told her that very day that he'd travelled all over the world, that would be an awful lot of bee pendants.

'No,' he said quietly. 'I only did it once.'

Even though it was past two in the morning and the hotel was utterly quiet, the silence around them thickened. Ben seemed to notice it too because he dropped the silver charm as if it had grown lava-hot, then scooted away, pressing himself against the back of the sofa bed, putting as much distance between them as possible.

Oh.

'Were we . . . ? Did we . . . ?'

The discomfort on Ben's face almost told her the answer to her question. She could have left it there, but she knew she needed to hear him say it out loud. 'Were we in a relationship?'

For a second, he looked concerned, as if he was thinking hard about what to say next, and then his features relaxed, and he breathed out. 'No. We never dated. And we never . . . ' He paused, shook his head. 'We only spent a day or so together, and then I carried on with my life, and you carried on with yours.'

'Ships in the night,' she whispered.

He gave her a lopsided smile that looked slightly pained. 'It was a very hot and sticky July, so mostly in the sunshine but, yes, something like that.'

Alice closed her eyes and yawned. Her head was starting to ache. After feeling as if there had been nothing inside her skull for so long, it now felt rammed full of information, and she wasn't sure she had any energy to process a single bit of it. 'I need some time. I don't even know where to start unravelling all this at the moment. Do you think . . . do you think we can just . . . shelve this for now, talk some more in the morning?'

'I think it might be best,' he answered, hiding a yawn with his hand. 'We've to be up in a few hours. Do you think you'll be able to sleep?'

I will if you climb into bed beside me, if you hold me the way you did before.

Where had *that* thought popped up from? 'Um . . . no . . . I mean, yes,' she stammered. She shook herself and started again. 'I hope so.'

He nodded, lay down on the sofa bed and pulled the duvet up over himself and looked at her expectantly. What? Was he waiting for her to join him?

She stalled for a moment, and then she followed his gaze. Oh, the light! Feeling her cheeks heat, she clambered back into her bed, reached over, and turned out the light.

'Night,' he said softly.

'Night,' she whispered back.

When she finally fell asleep again, her hand was closed around the tiny silver bee on the end of the chain around her neck.

CHAPTER THIRTY-FIVE

Six months before the wedding.

THE TEXTS FROM Justin didn't stop completely, but they did slow to a trickle. I only replied to one, standing my ground about needing space, telling him I was going to stay at my parents' another night. The following morning, a bouquet of red roses arrived. It was so huge I could hardly see the delivery guy struggling to hold them. I thanked him and took them through to the kitchen so I could read the card.

To my darling Angel – I love you more than I can express. Justin x.

I read it three times and then carefully tucked it into my jeans pocket, and later, when a text arrived asking if I'd received them, I almost called him back. But when I pictured myself standing on that stage, the silence cloying around me as I waited for the backing track to play, Justin silently begging me to help him from the front row, I put my phone down again.

Just as I'd been struggling to reconcile the two versions of Justin in my head, I now felt as if there were two versions of myself. One was Justin's 'Angel', and the other was a suspicious, paranoid little devil. They were waging war against one another.

Lo disappeared off to Bluewater shopping centre and didn't invite me to go with her, so while I tried to work it all out, I mooched around the house in joggers and an oversized T-shirt that Justin would have described as 'hideous'.

Mum got fed up with me getting under her feet while she was trying to do her Saturday clean and suggested I go and have a bath to help me chill out.

I'd only been in the tub for about five minutes when the doorbell rang, followed by persistent knocking.

'Hold your horses!' I heard Dad yell, followed by Mum telling him to calm down and that she'd get it. I was just about to settle back down into the suds with my book when I heard a different voice in the mix. Justin's.

What was he doing here?

I stayed there, frozen for a few seconds, and then I put my hands on the edge of the tub and pushed myself out of the water. Once I'd wrapped a towel around myself, I tiptoed along the landing and peered around the wall to look down the stairs. I was hidden from Justin's view but Mum spotted me and shot me an enquiring look.

I shook my head. I didn't know if I was ready to see him yet, especially not when he'd turned up out of the blue and I'd had no chance to prepare myself.

But instead of asking Justin to leave, Mum ushered him into the living room, where they started talking with Dad. The door was closed, so I couldn't hear the exact words spoken, but it was clear Justin was talking passionately and emphatically. When the door finally opened again, I flattened myself against the wall so I couldn't be seen from the bottom of the stairs and held my breath.

'She's her own worst enemy,' I heard Justin say as he exited the living room and walked towards the front door. 'I want so much for her to believe in herself the way I do, and I know that causes friction. She's wasting her time with all this busking, but I can't get her to see that.'

Mum's tone was puzzled. 'You don't think it's helping, even though she's finally managing to play in front of an audience?'

'No. I think it's another version of what she did last night. She's running away when things get too difficult, choosing what's safe and familiar instead of challenging herself. I know she's capable of more.'

Dad made what might sound like a non-committal noise to the untrained ear, but I could tell it was a huff of agreement.

'Will you let her know I'm ready when she is?'

'Of course,' Mum said. 'Bye, love . . . '

His words touched me. Hearing him say it to my parents somehow made it seem more reasonable, more logical. After all, he wouldn't be here if he didn't care, would he? And he always had been so supportive of my music. Why was I doubting his motives now?

'Wait!' I said, jumping from my hiding place.

Justin was standing at the bottom of the stairs, and my eyes met his. 'I'm ready. If you can wait a moment while I get dressed, we can talk now.'

He nodded, and I turned and ran back to my bedroom. A quick check of my wardrobe revealed there were plenty of my clothes there, but none of them seemed right. They were things the 'old' me would have chosen – bohemian and individual, yes, but also cheap and poorly made. Anything Justin would have liked was hanging in the dressing room in

Kensington. I ended up following his rules for effortless style as much as possible, sticking to jeans and a white T-shirt and leaving the accessories alone.

When I came back down, he was standing where I'd left him at the bottom of the stairs. Mum and Dad had made themselves scarce, so he cut a lonely figure. I felt a pang of sadness. I'd been selfish again, hadn't I? Thinking about myself and my feelings and hardly giving any thought to his.

'Would you like to go for a walk?' I said. The weather wasn't wonderful for August. The air was warm but slightly sticky, the overcast sky keeping the humidity high. Rain would be more welcome than not, but there wasn't really anywhere to go away from listening ears inside our house.

I led the way to nearby Crystal Palace Park. The wide avenue at the entrance was teeming with people and we waited until we'd passed the playground and the overflowing café before we began to talk.

'I know I upset you,' Justin began, 'but I really hope that you'll see that this is all a storm in a teacup, really it is.'

I bristled, but I'd told myself I'd stay calm, that I would hear him out. Mum's question about whether he'd intended to hurt me or not echoed in my head. I didn't think he'd meant to, and I wasn't ready to throw what we had away just yet. 'You should have told me what you were planning.'

'There's no point us going round and round on this point again,' he replied, very gently, very reasonably. 'We both have different memories of the situation, and we're probably never going to agree exactly on what went on.'

I'd been so sure that the conversation we'd had when we'd arrived at the theatre had gone the way I'd remembered it, but

Justin seemed to be so confident in his version of events that I started to wonder if he was right after all.

The main path was busy with meandering families, so Justin grabbed my hand and led me down one that took us to one of my favourite parts of the park. 'What's really important is *why* it happened,' he said. 'Whatever muddle got us in that situation, you need to accept that my motive was to do something good for you.'

'Good for me?' I turned my head to look at him, confused and incredulous. On what planet had leaving me centre-stage, alone, poised to fail . . . been a good thing for me?

'You're so talented, but you've got into such a negative headspace about playing. I just wanted to prove to you that you could do it.'

'But I didn't, did I? I ruined the piece!'

'This is getting us nowhere,' he muttered, and we walked in silence for a couple of minutes. I could tell he was thinking hard. Eventually, he stopped and turned to face me, grasping both of my hands and holding them in his. 'What it boils down to is this . . . I love you, Angel. Do you believe that?'

I nodded. Even if I was very confused about what happened at the theatre, I didn't doubt that.

'Then why would I deliberately put you in a situation that would do you harm? Do you really think I'd do that to you?'

I looked back at him, all sorts of feelings swirling around inside me. 'No, but . . . '

'I want you to succeed, don't you believe that? I've made that clear right from the very start.'

Had I let my insecurities colour everything, even what I believed he felt for me? Fear had stolen too much from me already. I didn't want it to take Justin from me too. He was the only thing that had made my life bearable in the last six months. 'I know you've been there for me,' I said softly, 'and I really appreciate that, but you have to realise that what you did wasn't fair to me, no matter how well-intentioned.'

He moved his hands up to either side of my face and leaned in to kiss me softly, slowly. I melted. It was as if he could cast a spell over me, and when he pulled back and smiled at me, I knew he knew it too. 'What I'm trying to say, my angel, is that I want to— Holy crap! What *is* that?'

I glanced over my shoulder, saw what had startled him and laughed. A fifteen-foot metal sculpture stood on an island in the middle of a small lake. 'It's a dinosaur – an Iguanodon if I remember rightly.'

He was still staring, open-mouthed. 'It's the weirdest-looking dinosaur I've ever seen!' he said, scanning the length of the muddy shore and realising there were more.

'The Victorians put them there,' I said with a shrug. 'Let's just say modern science is a little more accurate regarding giant extinct reptiles. Lo and I used to beg Mum and Dad to bring us to see them almost every weekend.'

The fact Justin had been shocked out of his big speech, that we'd started talking about something else calmly and naturally, had caused the atmosphere between us to shift. All of my anger faded away, and I focused on the one thing I really did know for sure – Justin loved me. And what couple didn't have their share of fallings-out?

I followed him as he walked along the path, reading the signs of the various cast-iron sculptures with wonder. There were ones that looked like crocodiles, another winged one perched on a rock with a long beak-like snout. They must have seemed like monsters to the people who'd come to see them in the mid-1800s, but really they were just animals, larger and different to what we were used to, but animals all the same.

I turned to look at Justin. And this, too, was just a man. Not a monster with a nefarious plan. I could see that now. A man who'd let his passion run away with him and cloud his judgement. But wasn't that passion one of the things I loved most about him?

'What were you going to say?' I asked gently. 'Before you spotted the dinosaurs?'

Justin regarded the motley collection of half-scientific, half-fantastical creatures for a few seconds more, and then he turned back to me. 'I've been doing a lot of thinking since you left the other day. About us, about how much you mean to me . . . I love you so much, and if this stupid fight has taught me anything, it's that I know I don't want to be apart from you ever again.'

He kissed me again, more passionately this time, and I leant against him, savouring him, feeling as if I'd finally come home. He looked into my eyes, the way he always did when he was about to say something heartfelt. 'Angel, will you—'

I planted a huge kiss on his lips, cutting him off. 'Of course I'll come back home. I just needed some time to—'

'No,' he whispered against my lips as he kissed me again. No? He didn't want me to come back? I must have looked distraught because he added, 'Well, yes, of course I want you to come back, but that wasn't what I was about to say . . .'

And, suddenly, he was kneeling on the tarmac in front of

me, pulling a box from his pocket. 'I want you to be my wife. Will you marry me?'

Time stopped at that point, at the moment right between heartbeats. I stared back at him, trying to make sense of the words he'd just said, and then he picked me up and spun me around. I don't even remember exactly how I phrased my answer, but I must have agreed because seconds later, I was wearing a massive diamond ring on my left hand.

'Really?' I said, stretching my left arm out so I could look at it properly. 'You really just asked me to marry you? I'm not dreaming it?'

'No.' He hugged me tighter. 'You're not dreaming. Or if you are, I am too.'

Beyond his shoulder, across the lake, the iron monsters cast their eyes on me, seemingly unmoved by the romantic scene before them.

CHAPTER THIRTY-SIX

Now.

A THIN STRIP of cold, silvery light carved its way through a gap in the blackout curtains. Alice's eyelids fluttered, and the conversation from the night before came back to her in snatches as she swam up through the layers of consciousness. She rolled over to look at the sofa bed. There was a lump under the white duvet, a dark head on the pillow.

Had that really all happened? It hardly felt real.

Her fingers instinctively sought the bee pendant around her neck. If they'd only met for a short time, why had he bought it for her? And why was she still wearing it five years later? She believed his reasons for not telling her what he knew sooner, but she still had a niggling feeling that something wasn't adding up, that there was more to the story.

The sleeping lump began to stir. Her stomach quivered. 'Morning,' she said softly enough not to startle him awake.

'Morning,' he replied, his voice rough with sleep, then he frowned and looked at the window.

Alice followed his gaze. It was almost seven, but it seemed awfully bright outside for February. Was the digital clock on the bedside wrong? Had they overslept?

Ben suddenly swore, then jumped up to kneel on his sofa bed and looked out of the window. He pulled the curtain back, then shuffled out of the way. Her eyes widened when she saw what was waiting outside.

Snow. And lots of it.

She turned and looked at Ben. 'I thought you said it wasn't going to settle.'

'I did,' he said grumpily, picking up his phone, as if checking the forecast again might change what was outside the window. 'But when these apps get it wrong, they really get it wrong.'

'Do you think it's going to affect the journey?'

He sat back down on the bed, exposing quite a lot of his long, rather nicely toned thighs. 'If we were in Alaska or Calgary, I'd say not, but we're in England.'

Even though she'd lost all knowledge about her life up until that point, she still remembered that three flakes of snow were enough to bring the entire British rail network to a halt. 'Crap,' she said.

'Exactly,' he replied. 'We'd better get going, see if the train company has anything to say about it.' He began to rummage for his jeans, but then he paused. 'But before we go any further, I just want to apologise.'

'What for?'

'For last night. I thought I was doing the right thing telling you what I knew, but . . . now I'm not so sure. It didn't seem to help much in the "not upsetting" you stakes. I should have listened to Dr Manzar.'

'It's okay,' she said, realising she wasn't just smoothing his ruffled feathers. She really meant it. 'It was just a shock.

I'm starting to get my head around it now. And I suppose what you told me does help . . . If I come from the London area, then it would make sense I might know people having a wedding just outside it.'

'I suppose so.' He pulled his jeans on, and she eased herself off the sofa bed and headed for the chair where she'd left her daypack.

'There's another thing . . . ' he added.

'Yes?' She pulled some fresh clothes from the bag and headed for the bathroom.

'I don't know what to call you any more. Do you want me to use Lili? Or should I still call you Alice?'

She stopped, jeans and chunky-knit jumper clutched to her chest. She definitely was Lili, wasn't she? Unless there was another woman who looked just like her and who also owned an identical bee necklace, which seemed too much of a coincidence. It would make sense to use her proper name.

But when she opened her mouth to tell Ben that, she found herself saying, 'Let's stick with Alice.' At least she was *beginning* to know who that person was. Lili still felt like a stranger.

*

The uniformed man standing by the ticket office cleared his throat. 'I'm afraid the first few trains this morning have been cancelled, and those running later will be subject to delays.' A collective groan rippled through the crowd of stranded passengers. 'However, we will endeavour to get all of you to your destinations later today, but please bear in mind that the first trains that run this morning may be quite crowded.'

Ben closed his eyes and gave himself a mental slap. They should have asked to stay overnight in Carlisle, after all. Any trains travelling from Glasgow to London would stop there first, meaning there'd be a lot fewer seats by the time they got to Penrith.

'We'll have another update for you in about an hour,' the railway company employee said, then scurried away behind a door marked 'Staff Only' before anyone could moan at him further.

'Great,' Alice muttered. She waved her phone listlessly at him. 'I suppose I'd better update my travel journal – although it's turning more into an epic saga. Do you think there'll be dragons or a giant squid later on? Because I feel it's becoming that kind of trip.'

Ben hid a smile. Despite the difficult conversation they'd had last night, it seemed as if things were edging back towards normal between them, although, whether that was 'normal for him and Lili' or 'normal for him and Alice', he wasn't sure.

They eased their way through the collected bodies and out of the ticket office. 'Video, I think,' Alice said. 'This one's a bit too complicated for a string of pictures.' She was about to hand her phone over to him but then glanced at the huddles of muttering people near the station entrance. 'Do you think we could go somewhere a little more private?'

'Sure. What about over there?'

Alice turned and looked to where he was pointing. Beyond the small car park, partly obscured by trees, a ruined building sat in what would have been a spacious lawn if it hadn't been covered in ten centimetres of snow.

They trudged their way across the forecourt, onto the newly

gritted road, then walked a short distance into the parkland. Once they were far enough away from nosey onlookers but close enough to keep the station building in shot, Alice blew out a breath and handed her phone to Ben. He framed the shot, then gave her a nod.

'I'm . . . um . . . here in Penrith,' Alice began, doing anything but making eye contact with the lens. 'It started to snow and— Oh, maybe I ought to mention . . . ' She turned away from the camera, screwed her face up, then tried again. 'Well, before the snow, there was the train and the . . . ' She mimed 'cut it' by pulling a finger across her throat, and then her shoulders sagged. 'Clearly, my career is *not* in television. Okay . . . give me a moment while I get it straight in my head.'

The second attempt wasn't much better than the first. She got the events in the right order, but it was all a bit jumbled.

'Just be yourself,' Ben said.

'Easy for you to say. I have no idea who that person is.'

'You do,' he replied softly. 'Deep down inside.'

She sighed and reached to take the phone from him. 'We haven't got time for that amount of soul searching – even if I did think it was possible.'

He batted her hand away. 'Don't think about talking to a lens or a camera, some faceless person who might see this video one day. Talk to *me*. That should be easy enough – you and I have discussed nothing else all morning.'

'All right then . . . Just hold the phone down a little bit so I can see your face. That'll help if I'm supposed to be talking to you.'

Attempt number three still wasn't professional broadcaster

quality, but Alice got through it. 'Right,' she said when she finished, turning in the direction of the park exit.

Ben glanced around at the remains of walls and tall chimneys poking up from the crumbling brickwork, all capped with a thick layer of fresh snow. 'Don't you want to take a moment to look around?'

'What about the update from the train company?'

'We've still got another fifty minutes before we learn anything new.'

She took a moment to look around. 'It *is* really pretty here . . . '

Ben handed her phone back to her and set an alarm for nine fifty-five on his own. They walked closer to the ruined building and found a sign that informed them this was what was left of Penrith Castle.

'Don't put it away just yet,' he said as she went to tuck her phone back into her jeans pocket.

'Why not?'

'A journey is more than merely getting from A to B. It's more than trains and buses, boats, and aeroplanes. Each journey, even on the same route but on a different day or in a different season, has its own unique flavour. You'll never have a moment exactly like this again. Why not capture some of this for your travel journal too?'

She blinked. 'You're right. I suppose I've just been focusing so hard on the mechanics of the journey that I didn't even think about that. And the castle does look stupendous in the snow.'

She was right about that. The sky was a clear, shocking blue against the icy whiteness, setting off the warm tones of the bricks and fallen stones. Alice walked a short distance away, held her phone up, and pressed the screen to take a photo.

As Ben watched her, he realised she was instinctively finding the right direction for the light, using things like drooping tree branches to frame her subject, getting down low or climbing up on something to give her a different perspective. All things he'd shown her the first day they'd met. Could it be that there was some small part of her that remembered *something* from their time together? The idea settled like a bright glowing seed inside him.

Ten minutes later, they compared their results. 'Not bad,' he said, swiping through her phone. 'I'd better watch out.'

She gave him a cheeky look, took the phone from his hands, backed away and held it up in his direction. 'Say cheese!'

'Really?' he said, realising even though it was her, he still didn't like being this side of the lens. The camera saw everything, and he preferred to be tucked away out its eye-line if possible.

'Really. Someone once told me that a journey is more than just getting from A to B.' She glanced up, her expression playful.

'Okay,' he said, laughing. 'You got me there.'

'But it's more than other places too, isn't it? It's the people you meet. That means you're part of my journey, Ben. A big part of it.'

It wasn't lost on him that he'd said something very similar to her in that hidden garden back in London all those years ago. It made him feel that if he could reach out and scratch just a few thin layers away, her memories of him might be hiding there, just under the surface. What if they did all come back in a rush, wiping the current ones away? Part of him wished for that, so she could remember how it was before, so he could explain and seek forgiveness, but another part of him didn't. He didn't want to lose the time they'd had together over the last few days, either.

Out of the corner of his eye, he was aware of Alice moving away, balancing her phone on one of the tumbledown walls.

He was about to ask her what she was doing when, in one smooth motion, she scooped a handful of snow off the corner of the wall and pressed it between her hands. A second later, his face was full of ice, and he was spluttering for breath.

Alice laughed. And it wasn't the soft chuckle he'd heard her do before. This time it came right up from inside her, rough and dirty and unstoppable. He couldn't help joining in. He also couldn't help reaching down, finding his own handful of snow, and flinging it back at her.

She was too quick for him, darting to the side before it made impact. But he was pretty sure he had a better throwing arm and longer legs. It took three attempts, but he finally got her, and then all-out war ensued. After ten minutes, they were both breathless and feeling the chill of melted ice down the backs of their necks.

While he brushed himself down, Alice looked up. Clouds had drifted in since they'd arrived at the ruined castle, and now both land and sky were painted with the same soft white palette. 'Do you think it's going to snow again?'

He came to stand beside her. 'Probably.'

'My ears are freezing.'

He thought for a moment, then reached inside his coat pocket, pulled out his grey beanie and pulled it down over her snowball-tousled hair. Her eyes widened, and she moved to take it off again, but he shook his head. 'Keep it. For now.'

They walked around, looking at what must have been the remains of the different rooms inside the castle, most only low walls unless they were part of the exterior of the structure. Alice took a few more shots of different things but frowned when she looked at the results. 'Some of my shots look washed out. What am I doing wrong?'

'It's all about lighting, mainly,' he said. 'And contrast – finding an area of dark and shadow to feature, so it's not just different shades of white in the shot.' He took a couple of shots of a snow-covered bush from different angles and showed her the difference.

'Oh, yes. I see what you mean now!' She handed his phone back to him, and her expression grew serious. 'This is your passion, isn't it? Taking photographs?'

'Um . . . Well, yes.' There wasn't much he could do to deny it now.

She was looking at him the same way she had done countless times when they'd hopped around London together – like she wanted to get a screwdriver, unlatch his skull and peer inside at his brain to find out what made him tick. Ben steeled himself for the next soft probe.

'When we were on the train, you said you used to be a travel photographer. *Used* to be. If you love it so much, why did you give it up?'

CHAPTER THIRTY-SEVEN

Five months before the wedding.

'JUSTIN . . . ' I SAID laughing, 'do I really have to wear this thing?' I reached up to touch the silk covering my eyes. I was sitting in the passenger seat of his Range Rover, and he'd been driving for about forty minutes. Five minutes ago, he'd pulled over and insisted he knot one of his ties firmly around my head.

'It won't be long now,' he said, and I could hear the smile in his voice. 'I don't want to spoil the surprise.'

I relaxed back into the comfortable leather seat and smiled to myself. However high maintenance Justin could be sometimes, he was also loving and romantic, and when he pulled out all the stops, he made me feel like a princess.

A short while later, he came off the motorway – I felt the car slow, and then we took much more winding roads for a few minutes, before turning into what I guessed was a drive of some kind, because he kept his speed low and now and again we had to bunny hop our way over little speed bumps. Finally, he parked. I went to push the tie up onto my forehead, but his hand shot out and stopped me. 'Not yet, Miss Impatient.'

I laughed, but I did as I was told. He came round to my

side of the car, opened the door, and helped me down. I could feel rough, slightly stony ground under my feet. The summer was heaving its last dying breaths, evidenced by the cool breeze that rippled around me. I could hear voices, birds, trees rustling, but none of them gave me any clue to where we were. I gripped onto his arm tightly when he offered it to me.

Justin put his arm around me and led me along a firm, tarmacked path. It was just as well because, since I hadn't known where we were going today, Justin had picked my outfit, and I was wearing nude pumps with four-inch heels. They were beautiful but not very practical for being out in the countryside.

'I thought you said you were going to trust me when I put the blindfold on you,' Justin said softly, but there was no irritation in his voice, only humour.

'Sorry.' I did my best to let him lead me, discovering it was easier if I stopped thinking for myself, trying to work out where we were and how I should put my feet, and let Justin think for me. After a while, I kind of checked out, and it was like waking from a daze when he finally brought me to a halt and lifted the blindfold from my eyes.

'What do you think?'

I blinked, trying to get my blurry eyes to adjust to the light of the bright September morning. The first thing I saw was water – so flat and calm it had become a mirror for the cloudless blue sky above. The only hint that it was a lake were the tiny ripples fluttering across the surface in the wake of a pair of swans.

My gaze travelled upwards and I saw . . . I inhaled sharply. A castle. With turrets and windows and crenelated walls, all shaped in soft yellow sandstone. What I'd thought was a lake was actually a moat, and the main part of the castle was joined to the shore by a small, arched bridge.

'Do you like it?' Justin said in my ear.

'I love it!' I turned and gave him a quick but heartfelt kiss. When he'd said he was taking me for a day out, I hadn't expected this. I thought it would be a fancy lunch at one of his favourite haunts or an art gallery. While I didn't mind those things, this was much more up my street. How wonderful that he'd realised without me even telling him.

'Come on,' he said, grabbing my hand and leading me towards the castle. 'There's someone I want you to meet.'

I didn't have time to raise my eyebrows in surprise because we were instantly hurrying along the path, over the bridge, and onto the island. The castle itself sat just beyond a large, clipped lawn surrounded by a path. Justin tugged my hand and pulled me into one of the large gatehouses that sat just beyond the bridge.

A woman in a gorgeous cream suit greeted us as we reached the nail-studded wooden door and led us into a spacious room with a large brick fireplace at one end, tapestries on the walls, and wrought-iron chandeliers hanging from the ceiling. A waiter appeared from nowhere and offered each of us a glass of champagne.

'Mr De la Hay,' she said warmly, and I detected a hint of an American accent. 'Welcome to Hadsborough Castle. Why don't I give you a tour first, and then we can talk in more detail about our wedding packages?'

'Perfect,' Justin said and squeezed my hand.

I just smiled back. Had she just said 'wedding'? The concept of this even being a *possible* venue blew my mind.

The next twenty minutes were a blur. We inspected a spacious barn situated a short distance from the castle, the more affordable of the castle's two wedding venues, and then Faith, our guide, brought us back into the castle itself, where she showed us a large panelled banqueting hall with mullioned windows overlooking the moat, a dressing room for the bride with a proper four-poster bed, and promises of a drinks reception and photos on the lawn outside if the weather was fine. Once all the talk was over, she withdrew to a discreet distance.

Justin led me to the long windows overlooking the moat and took my hands in his. 'So . . . what do you think? Don't you think this is the perfect place to get married?'

I nodded, swallowing at the same time. It *was* gorgeous, a dream come true. But that was half the problem. 'I . . . I don't think my mum and dad would be able to stretch to something like this,' I said quietly, not wanting Faith to overhear. 'Not even the barn.' And I looked back at him, willing him to understand, so I didn't have to spell it out in front of a stranger. To be honest, I'd hoped he might have worked this out for himself.

Justin reached up and touched my face with his hand. 'Darling, of course I'm going to chip in! I wouldn't expect your parents to bear the cost of this alone.' He smiled back at me, as if that solved everything.

My throat tightened further. Only the other week, Mum had told me how hard she and Dad had saved for my and Lo's weddings. Our family wasn't going to let the side down. They were going to put on a good 'do'.

'I think I need to talk it over with Mum and Dad,' I said quietly.

Irritation pinched Justin's features. Even though he was an incredibly structured kind of person, sometimes, he also had these . . . what did I call them? 'Whims' didn't fit. The word made it sound as if his ideas were flighty or airy when, in fact, they were often solid and intractable, projections of his steely will. I could tell he'd come here expecting to book this place today, and he'd be upset if we didn't.

'My dad grew up with nothing,' I explained. 'He's worked all hours to build up his plumbing business, and he's proud of what he's achieved, and he might be a bit . . . *sensitive* . . . if we rock up and say what he'd been planning isn't good enough. I think he and Mum had been thinking of The Maple Court Hotel.'

'What? That place where your cousin had her engagement party? Don't you think it was a little tired?'

I bit my lip. At the time, I hadn't thought anything of it. The Maple was the poshest hotel in the area, which wasn't saying much, I suppose, since our bit of south London wasn't exactly a thriving tourist hotspot. However, when I looked around at where we were – an actual *castle* – and thought about the kind of places Justin frequented, I could see his point.

'You're right. Of course you are.' Justin always was when it came to matters of taste. 'But I don't want to offend my parents . . . They've done so much for me over the years.'

His face fell. He shoved his hands in his pockets and walked off to stare into the vast, empty fireplace. I waited for a minute or two, unsure what to say or do, and then I followed him.

'Justin?' I said, rubbing his arm gently.

'I know I've got ahead of myself,' he said, gazing in the direction of the grate, 'but I wanted to give you this. I want you to have the fairy tale, Angel, because you deserve it. It doesn't matter what it costs, not to me.'

He looked so dejected that I walked round to stand in front of him and drew him into a hug. 'You're right,' I said quietly. 'I do love it. It's everything I've ever dreamed of, but . . . '

'But?'

He looked at me with those big blue puppy dog eyes of his, and I felt myself begin to crumble. 'Maybe we could take Mum and Dad out to lunch at the weekend, talk it over and get their blessing, rather than just presenting it to them as a done deal? If we make them part of the decision, maybe ask them to chip in for something they could afford . . . '

I wasn't convincing myself they wouldn't be hurt, but what could I do? I had to find some compromise. I was stuck between two sets of people I loved to distraction.

Justin looked sheepish. 'The thing is . . . I might have already booked the castle. There was a cancellation at the end of February. Other than that, it was a two-year wait, so I just . . . did it. I thought you'd be pleased.'

'February? That's only five months away!'

'I know it'll be a rush to get things done, but if you scale back on work and concentrate on planning, I'm sure we can get it all done. You can build things up career-wise again after we're married. While I appreciate you contributing to the household, it's not as if we need to rely on your income.'

'I . . . '

I didn't know what to say. I'd been getting more and more interest in session work in recent weeks. It had made me feel like someone again, someone useful and productive. I didn't want to let go of that unless I absolutely had to. I was also juggling thoughts of Mum and Dad, the fact I'd always wanted a summer wedding, not a February one, and that Justin had, with all the best intentions, done all this without consulting me.

'Yes?' He looked at me with such boyish adoration in his eyes, it reminded me of how it had been when we were first together, and I was struck by how much he loved me, how much he saw the real me. It wasn't that he'd planned to upset me, was it? He'd tried to do something wonderful, and I was making it seem as if I didn't appreciate his thoughtfulness.

'Okay, yes. Let's get married here.'

Justin kissed me properly, showing me just how grateful he was, how much he loved me. 'You wait, Angel . . . This wedding will be just as perfect as our happy, wonderful lives together.'

CHAPTER THIRTY-EIGHT

Now.

'I THOUGHT I'D already explained why I gave up photography,' Ben said as the snowy breeze whipped around them. 'I had to come home for Willow.'

Alice frowned. 'But aren't there photography jobs you could do based in Invergarrig, even part-time?'

'It wouldn't work. I'd be . . . distracted. She needs me to be one hundred per cent present. I failed her mother. I won't fail her.' He stuffed his hands in his pockets. 'Come on . . . If we go back to the main road, we can find the standing stone that's supposed to be around here somewhere. I saw a sign.' And he began trudging back towards the entrance.

Alice jogged after him. She wasn't letting him run away from the conversation that easily. Not just because she was feeling nosey, which she was. Hugely. But because he was doing just that – running away. If anyone understood just how much trouble fleeing from your problems could cause, it was her.

She caught up to him and did her best to match his stride. 'Ben . . . We haven't got time to hike to a standing stone, and what do you mean you failed your sister?'

'Oh, it's true,' he said, a biting edge to his words.

'But you're looking after her child!'

He stopped walking. 'Yeah, well, she should have named Norina as Willow's guardian, not me. It was a mistake.'

'But you're devoted to Willow, anyone can see that – and she adores you. And surely your sister wouldn't jeopardise her daughter's future by asking someone who wasn't up to it to do the job.'

He let out a short, hard laugh. 'You think? I wouldn't be surprised if it was Cat's way of getting revenge from beyond the grave, for all the times she moaned that I wasn't around enough, that I didn't care.'

'You can't honestly believe that,' she said, trying to interject a bit of sanity into the conversation. 'Anyone can see why your sister chose you to be Willow's guardian.'

'You don't know me,' he said in a low voice. 'Not really.' And then he began striding again.

Alice let out a growl of frustration and jogged to catch up. 'It's true that we only met four days ago, but I *do* know what kind of person you are – by your actions, not by who you say you are. Look what you've done for me in that short time: taking me to the hospital, giving me a place to stay, even coming to London with me when you knew I was feeling shaky – and I'm a stranger . . . well, *almost a* stranger. So, don't tell me you wouldn't go to the ends of the earth for someone you loved.'

That got his attention. He stopped again and turned to face her, his gaze searing. 'Yes, I went to the ends of the earth, but not to save my sister – I went to get *away* from her, from everyone back home. I did it because I was selfish. Deep down, I knew I should have done more for Cat, and I didn't. But admitting that to myself would have meant admitting she needed me close by, not always on another continent when a crisis occurred.'

He was acting as if this was all on him, that he was the only one who had any responsibility in the matter. 'What about your dad? Couldn't he have stepped in?'

He let out a short, hollow laugh. 'My mum died when Cat was seventeen. Losing her was what really started that downward spiral, and my father moved away when he remarried. Last I heard, he was in Edinburgh. But even if he weren't, it wouldn't have mattered. My father—' his features twisted his face into something resembling a snarl '—was a big part of the problem.'

'I'm so sorry about your mum,' she said. 'I didn't know.'

He gave her a lopsided shrug. 'How could you have done, but . . . thank you.'

People were walking along the pavement near the entrance. Not many, but Alice felt they needed a little more privacy for this conversation. She led Ben back towards the ruin. Soft flakes of snow had begun to fall from the sky, just here and there, and they sheltered under a wide, low arch built up against a wall. She guessed it might once have been part of a cellar or a vaulted kitchen. 'Tell me,' she said.

'Can't we talk about you instead?' he said wearily. 'I'd much prefer that.'

'What's left to say, Ben? I'm an open book to you. You know everything I know about myself, which isn't much. You've seen me at my worst and my most vulnerable. You know it all. I have nothing else left to share.' Except maybe that she was developing a crush on him the size of Ben Nevis, but that was hardly relevant to the current conversation.

She trusted him so much, which probably would sound stupid to someone else, but what she'd said to him was true. She knew him. Now she wished he'd trust her with something too, let her help him just a little bit.

'Please?'

Ben let out a ragged sigh. 'I don't talk about this much. I don't talk about it, well . . . ever. I'm not even sure I know how to.' And then, in fits and starts, he began to tell her a story about an autocratic father who ruled with a rod of iron, two children who desperately wanted to please him but could never match up. He wiped a hand over his face then rested his long frame against a ledge in the curving wall. 'Mum was amazing, filling in all the gaps he left with love and acceptance. While she was still around, things were okay, but later I always wondered why she stayed. He wasn't always nice to her, either. She did it for us, maybe.'

Alice nodded, not wanting to interrupt him, but her heart was speared by an image of a young, lanky boy, full of creativity and passion but paralysed by fear and judgement.

'He told me that if I wanted to waste my life taking "snaps" instead of joining him in his insurance company, then I could get out the day I turned eighteen. For once in my life, I was pleased to do as I was told. I packed my bag and left. Got the first bus out of Invergarrig, not caring which way it was going. And I never went back. Not to his house anyway . . . Norina had always doted on us, and she didn't have any children of her own, so when her sister died, she said her door would always be open to me and Cat. She became something of a stand-in mum for me, but Cat . . . She loved Norina, but by that point, she'd lash out at anyone she perceived as an authority figure.'

She reached out, gently laid her hand on his arm. 'No one would blame you for not doing what your dad wanted as a career. It would have been such a waste if you had.'

Ben looked away. 'But it wasn't just me, was it? While I was off having fun, travelling the world, building a career . . . I'd left Cat there on her own. She started letting off steam the only way she knew how – at first it was drink, but later she got on to harder stuff.'

'Ben?' She waited until he met her gaze. 'You are not responsible for your sister's addiction.'

He stared at her bleakly. 'If I hadn't left, things would have been different . . . '

'Yes, and if your father had been a different man, things would have turned out differently, or if your mother hadn't died, maybe Cat wouldn't have rebelled, or if she'd had different friends . . . There are so many variables. You can't lay it all at your own door.'

He gave her a look that said, *Can't I?*

'The last time Cat went into rehab, about a year before she died, Norina and I did a programme too. Cat had been turning up at Norina's, talking about taking Willow, and the staff helped us work through setting boundaries, outlining dealbreaker behaviour with her. I'd always felt so guilty where Cat was concerned that she sometimes could talk me into giving her money. I knew deep down it wasn't helping her, that I was just enabling her, but it was so hard to say no.'

'I can't even imagine . . . '

'So I set boundaries and I stuck to them. No more money. No more bailing her out of her own mess.'

'That sounds healthy. Especially if that's what the experts told you to do.'

Ben looked away. 'A month before she died, I was back in Glasgow, staying at my friend's flat, and she found me. She was clearly off her face, and she begged me for more money. I said no.' He shook his head. 'I turned her away . . . '

Alice's heart lodged in her mouth. She so badly wanted to reach out and touch him, to smooth that torment from his brow with her fingertips.

'I wasn't there for her when she needed me. And not for the first time. It had always been a disaster waiting to happen, and I could have stopped it, but I didn't. I chose not to.'

Alice stepped closer, almost between the long legs anchored against the floor to keep his backside resting on the ledge.

When he met her gaze, the rawness in his eyes tore at her soul. 'What if I do it all over again? What if I let Willow down too? I couldn't bear it.'

Even though it was gloomy in their little shelter, she saw his eyes become shiny, heard the catch in his voice. A single tear leaked from the corner of his eye, and she reached up and brushed it away with the pad of her index finger.

He grabbed her hand and held it between both palms, pressed it to his cheek. Alice's heart began to pound. 'Don't,' she whispered, and tears welled in her own eyes at the thought of how this wonderful man's heart was ripping in two. 'Don't do this to yourself.'

Their faces were close now. She could feel his warmth, the

juddering of his ribcage as he drew in a breath. His pupils were large and black, only a thin sliver of brown remaining.

Alice didn't know how many kisses she'd had in her life, but she knew she was on the verge of one at that moment. For her, it would be like a *first* kiss, the kind that marks you forever purely because it's just that. Her eyelids drifted closed, and she held her breath.

'This is a bad idea,' Ben murmured, his voice low and rumbly in the confined space.

'I know . . .' For all the reasons she'd already told herself. But that had been when she'd thought this was a one-sided thing, when she was just crushing on someone who'd been kind to her.

There was a moment when everything felt suspended, as if they were at the top of a giant roller coaster ride, about to plunge into something deep and scary and thrilling, and then Ben shifted, and she knew he was about to move away.

'Can we just . . . you know, stay like this for a moment?' she whispered.

Ben's breath came out shakily as he nodded, and he rested his forehead against hers. They stayed there in silence, sensing the rise and fall of each other's chests, only the tiniest patch of skin touching, but it felt . . . like an admission. Like the start of something.

Alice was just wondering if they could climb back to the top of that roller coaster, ready to start the wild and heady ride, when Ben jolted and pulled away from her and reached for his phone. Now she thought about it, her brain had registered a soft electronic pinging a few seconds earlier, but she'd been so absorbed in being close to him that she hadn't paid any attention to it.

It was the alarm he'd set to go back to Penrith station. He tapped his phone to silence it. 'Time to go and find out what our immediate future holds.'

CHAPTER THIRTY-NINE

Three months before the wedding.

I KNEW I'D promised Justin I wouldn't busk any more, but I had to. Not for the money, but because playing the violin was the only time when I really felt like me nowadays.

Planning the wedding was filling all of my time, so I'd had to turn down quite a few offers of session work, some of them jobs I would have killed to do. The awful thing was that even with all the extra time on my hands, I wasn't doing a very good job of getting the wedding sorted. Everything I picked or booked often needed to be tweaked or changed completely, and I'd begun to second-guess every decision I made.

Last night Justin had sat me down and had a talk to me about my attitude. He knew I was finding it stressful, but it wasn't fair if I was moody and tense with him if he tried to make suggestions on how I could do things better.

I couldn't deny it. I *was* stressed. Which is why I needed to play, why I *needed* to busk. We were only a couple of months away from getting married, so I was proving my commitment to him. Surely he'd be more secure about the whole thing now? Besides, if I slipped away quickly and was only out for an hour or two, he'd never know.

It was a bright, chilly November day, so I dressed up warmly, adding a crocheted scarf my nan had made me. I'd hidden it underneath some other things in the dressing room, so Justin didn't find it and chuck it away. As I left the flat, I felt buoyant but also jittery, as if I was doing something vaguely illegal.

Initially, I headed west towards High St Ken Tube station, but when I was standing in front of it, looking at the large blue-and-white sign, I reconsidered. I'd told Justin I wouldn't busk, so maybe I shouldn't. But he'd never said anything about playing outside, not for money or practice, but just for fun. It was a technicality, I knew, but I was prepared to run with it.

Instead of descending into the dusty depths of London's Underground, I turned and headed back the way I'd come, towards Kensington Gardens.

Once inside the park gates, I headed away from the palace and formal gardens, choosing one of the broad wide paths. On a hot summer's day, the park would be packed, but at this time of year, there were only a few lone souls strolling along, eclipsed every now and then by the occasional runner, puffing small, hot clouds as they passed.

I ended up on a broad expanse of lawn not far from one of the park's lakes. Right there, I saw the perfect spot to play. An old-fashioned bandstand with delicate iron struts holding up the onion-shaped roof. Nobody was about, so I ran up the steps to the small raised platform, pulled Octavia out of her case and began to play.

At first, I gravitated towards the old favourites from my busking days, familiarising myself with the feeling of the instrument in my hands, but, eventually, I moved onto pieces that spoke to me, that required me to reach into my soul and pull something out of it to make the music come alive. I closed my eyes and totally lost myself.

I had no idea how long I'd been playing when I came to the end of a piece and heard a smattering of applause. I opened my eyes to see a mum with two designer-clad children, an elderly gentleman and a female runner standing there. I coloured, taken aback by their presence, but managed to smile and give a small bow.

'Play something else,' the little boy said. 'It makes me feel tingly inside.'

How could you resist a request like that, even if it did mean I was performing to a very small audience? But there wasn't a man of datable age in the vicinity, so no one to gawp or ogle. 'Okay,' I said, and I began a couple of pieces from *Peter and the Wolf*, ending with the swan's melody. I kept my eyes open as I played this time, enjoying their smiles. I didn't feel like my audience had teeth and fangs, that they were an enemy to be faced.

It made me realise that not much in my life felt simple any more, and I wasn't sure why. When had things got so complicated? At the Conservatory? Afterwards? I thought things had become more straightforward for a while when I'd first got together with Justin, but now everything felt . . . tangled.

And I supposed I might have to get used to the fact that, as much as I loved him, Justin was not a simple man. Maybe that's *why* I loved him. But his darker moods were becoming more and more frequent, and sometimes I felt exhausted from constantly walking on eggshells around him.

He said the same of me, of course – that I was oversensitive, that I took the littlest thing he said or did out of context or made a big deal about it. I suppose I did. Sometimes.

It was the stupid wedding that was making us both tense. My parents had been wonderful about the venue, but I could tell it had hurt their feelings, which had taken some of the excitement about getting married at the castle away from me. I was tempted to suggest jetting off somewhere warm and getting married on a beach, just the two of us, but Justin was far too invested in the wedding we'd already planned for that. Besides, he'd lose loads of money if we backed out now.

My audience soon drifted away, off to resume their busy lives, and I played for a while more, standing in the middle of the bandstand, enjoying hearing the notes soar out and across the lake and into the frosty autumn air. It was like I drifted into a different zone where it was just me and the music. Time stopped. And when I checked the time on my phone, I realised more than a couple of hours had slipped by. I quickly packed up my violin and headed back to the flat.

*

When I went to hang my coat up and saw Justin's back in the hall cupboard, I grimaced to myself. This was going to be awkward.

'Where have you been?' he said when I found him searching for something in one of the kitchen drawers, his brows drawn, mouth a thin line. I tried to come up with an answer, but there were literally no words inside my head. He stopped what he was doing and came to stand right in front of me. He didn't shout. Instead, his voice got smooth and low, a tone I'd come to recognise as my least favourite of his. 'Sorry for surprising you, Angel. It's clear you weren't expecting to see me here.'

I stared back at him, unable to disagree.

He looked down at the violin case in my hand. 'You've been busking, haven't you?'

I swallowed. 'No. Not exactly.'

'Did you take your violin outside and play it? Did people watch?'

'I didn't do it to get any money! I just wanted to play, so I went to the park.'

'What's wrong with playing in the flat? There was no need to go out. You know I'd rather you didn't. And you agreed not to, Angel.'

'I know . . . I just . . . ' How could I tell him that the reason I couldn't play here was that I'd needed to go somewhere I could be myself, and it was becoming harder and harder to feel that way inside this flat. He would only think I was blaming him.

'I'm really disappointed with you, my darling. I thought we loved each other. I thought we *trusted* each other. And yet here you are, disrespecting me, sneaking around behind my back.'

'It wasn't like that,' I mumbled.

'Oh, no?' he said, his tone still smooth, but there was something underneath, an emotion I couldn't name. 'You didn't wait until I'd left so you could go out without me knowing?'

I swallowed the huge lump in my throat. While I hadn't *exactly* been as calculating as Justin made it seem, that pretty much had been the result. 'I . . . What are you doing back here this early, anyway?'

'Class got cancelled – broken water pipe upstairs dripping into the studio – but that's hardly the point. I'm not going to allow you to deflect, to wriggle out of giving me a straight answer . . . And if you're going to try to run rings around me rather than tell the truth, then maybe I need to do something concrete to stop it happening again.' And before I could even twitch in reaction, he pulled the violin case out of my hand and backed away. 'From now on, you will have to ask for your violin if you want to play it, and I will decide if it is appropriate for you to have it or not.'

'Justin!' I said, half laughing at the ridiculousness of what he was saying but feeling panicky at the same time. 'This is stupid! Just let me explain—'

'Don't turn this on me,' he said softly, and I could see the hurt in his eyes. 'You're the one who's been dishonest. Do you deny it?'

'Well, no . . . ' When he put it like that, it didn't really sound that good, and while I'd convinced myself at the time I wasn't exactly breaking our agreement, I knew I'd been breaking the spirit of it. I didn't have a leg to stand on.

'I trusted you, Angel. And you know how important trust is to me, especially after the way my vicious, cheating ex betrayed me.'

He looked as if he was about to cry, and I stepped towards him, lifting a hand to reach for him. 'Justin, I'm so . . . '

He backed away, clutching the violin case to his chest. 'Is this what our marriage is going to be like? Full of lies and deceit?'

'No! Of course not! I wasn't thinking . . . I wasn't . . . ' I stared at the violin. Playing in the park that day had been the only time I'd felt truly carefree in weeks. 'Please, Justin – I know I was in the wrong, but you don't need to take Octavia away from me, you really don't!'

'This is what makes me the saddest. If I didn't know better, I'd say you love that violin more than you do me. And call it what it is, will you? Giving an instrument a name is something a child does. But maybe that's indicative of what's going on with us right now – you're just too immature to be in an adult relationship.'

Was this it? Was he going to say it was over? That he didn't want to marry me after all? My stomach plummeted.

'And until you can grow up a little, I will take custody of *Octavia*.' He turned and, with great control, walked out of the kitchen, across the living room, towards his study. I jogged after him, trying to work out what I could say to put things right.

I watched helplessly as he pulled papers out of the bottom drawer of the filing cabinet. When it was empty, he placed the violin case inside and locked it closed.

CHAPTER FORTY

Now.

ALICE WALKED IN silence beside Ben as they crossed the forecourt of Penrith station. She was trying very hard not to think about what had almost just happened between them. *I know it feels like Ben is the missing piece of the puzzle you've always been looking for,* she told herself, *but you can't trust your instincts at the moment, remember?* Without any knowledge of her personal history, she had no context for these feelings.

What if she got home and found out she was in a long-term relationship of some kind? What was she going to say then? *Hi honey . . . Yes, my memory's back now, but while it was missing, I accidentally fell for someone else. Sorry 'bout that.*

As they neared the station entrance, the two girls who'd been sitting opposite them on the train appeared, deep in conversation. 'I told you calling my brother to come and get us was going to be a good idea,' one said.

'Did we miss the update?' Ben asked them.

The other girl nodded. 'What there was of it. First train through isn't going to be for almost another hour, and then after that, it's delays and cancellations all day.'

He nodded thoughtfully. 'Where're you heading?'

'Blackpool.'

Ben tapped away on his phone for a few seconds. 'And your brother's going to be here in a wee bit?'

The girl looked puzzled but nodded. 'In about forty-five minutes.'

'Do you think he has room in his car for another two bodies?'

The girl shot a look at her partner, who just shrugged. 'Yeah, why not.'

'If we can get to Blackpool,' Ben said to Alice, 'we'll have other travel options, including coaches. What do you think?'

Both the girls and Ben looked at her. Alice felt herself shrink a little. 'I don't know . . . '

She preferred the idea of something known in favour of a nebulous plan. The trains couldn't be delayed forever, could they? Having no memory meant that she had to take every bit of information that came her way on faith, so she found herself reluctant to release this one concrete detail she'd been hanging on to.

Looking at Ben's face, she could tell he was full of good reasons why they should adopt this plan. It would only be moments before he started laying out his argument, explaining why she was wrong, and he was right, chipping away at what she thought was real until she didn't know what to think any more . . .

She steeled herself, a familiar and inbuilt instinct telling her to dig deep and find a good reason, something he couldn't swat away with a clever twist of words.

'Alice . . . ?' Ben said.

She looked up.

'I'll be by your side no matter what. But it's your journey. It's your choice.'

He was just letting her decide? Just like that?

But why had she doubted he would? This was Ben, after all. Whatever certainty she'd been clinging to about the train crumbled like the dusty snow they'd been flinging around not half an hour earlier. It wasn't the train she believed in, she realised. It was him. And, even more astonishingly, he trusted her to make the right decision – or maybe even a wrong decision – about what they should do next. The thought was terrifying and exhilarating at the same time.

Heart thudding, she turned to the girl and said, 'If there's room in your brother's car, that would be amazing.'

*

Alice's fingers kept wandering to the bee pendant hanging just below the neckline of her jumper, but every time she discovered herself stroking it, she made herself release it. She was in the back of Aoife's brother's car, sandwiched between Ben and Rashida as they left the Lake District behind.

Ben's thigh was pressed against the length of hers. It was making it very difficult to think properly, which was unfortunate because the monotony of the motorway offered a chance to process things she'd either been too busy or too blindsided to dissect up until that point.

Why had Ben given her the necklace? She must have been more than an acquaintance for him to have done that. It had to have been more than bumping into each other, maybe sharing a coffee or a quick bite before they went their separate ways.

And then there was this bizarre chemistry between them.

Had they felt it when they'd met before? And if they had, why had nothing happened between them? She hadn't questioned it earlier because she'd just thought it was just her who felt the air shimmer every time they got close to each other, but that *almost* kiss in the castle ruins had changed everything.

Patrick dropped them at the bus station in Blackpool. They thanked him and the girls and said their goodbyes. The next bus to London – with a change at Manchester – wasn't until two-fifteen. There was a fish and chip shop across the road from the bus station, so they grabbed some lunch but opted to take their food away, making the short walk to the nearby seafront, past brightly painted frontages of penny arcades and amusements, all shuttered up for the winter.

There was a thin dusting of snow on the deserted promenade, criss-crossed with footprints of different sizes and tracks from bikes and pushchairs. Ben and Alice walked to the railings overlooking the pale sand and stared out across the Irish Sea as they opened the paper parcels containing their lunches. The waves were the colour of steel, frothing gently at the edges, the sky so white it was almost painful to look at.

Alice picked a hot chip soaked in sharp malt vinegar and dusted with salt from her paper parcel but held off putting it in her mouth. 'Ben?'

He turned his head to look at her. 'Yeah?'

Alice bit the chip and swallowed. If she wanted answers to her questions, it was now or never. In a few hours, she'd be in London, and he'd be on his way back to Scotland. 'When you said there was nothing between us . . . ' She paused, unsure how to phrase the next bit.

He looked at her carefully. It seemed he was weighing up whether to say something or not, but he eventually replied, 'I said we weren't in a relationship.'

She stopped leaning on the railing and faced him fully. She discovered she didn't need to find the right words because she had her answer. It was there, written all over his face. 'Oh! Then that's why I . . . How you always . . . ' She looked at him, eyes pleading. 'You know what I'm talking about, don't you? You feel it too.'

He held her gaze for a few intense seconds. 'Yes. I feel it too.'

She nodded. For some reason, it felt as if a weight had been lifted from her with his admission, even though it didn't make anything less complicated, probably the reverse. 'It all makes sense now,' she said quietly. 'Why you have *never* felt like a stranger to me, not even from the first moment I met you, why there's this pull inside . . . Why, maybe, I came to Invergarrig in the first place.'

'Yes,' he said again.

She sighed and wrapped up her remaining scampi and chips. She'd been ravenous twenty minutes ago, but now she couldn't eat another bite. 'Then why didn't you tell me that?'

'Because it's five years later, and neither of us knows if you're single any more. Because you were upset last night, and you said you needed a break before we carried on talking and I was waiting until you told me you were ready for more. But I want you to know that I told you the truth, Lil— Alice. We were never boyfriend and girlfriend. I didn't lie to you about that, about anything . . . '

'But it was *something*,' she said as they began to walk towards the pier, the blustery wind from the sea blowing her hair over her forehead. 'Something unusual. Something special.'

'It was,' he said, and his eyes held no more secrets. 'For two days and one night, it was.'

She nodded. They walked in silence for a couple of minutes and when they passed a bin, Ben dumped both their rapidly cooling fish suppers inside.

'Why such a short time?' she asked. 'Why never anything more? Was I having an affair? Were you?'

He looked so affronted she almost laughed. 'No, it was nothing like that. It was . . . ' He turned and stopped in front of her. 'I've been waiting more than five years to say this to you, rehearsed it a million times inside my head. If I'm going to do it, I may as well do it properly. Do you want to know everything, absolutely everything?'

She swallowed the lump that had lodged itself in her throat. 'Yes, I really do.'

CHAPTER FORTY-ONE

Six weeks before the wedding.

THE MOTION OF the train lulled me, and my mind drifted. When the sliding doors whooshed open, and I realised it was my stop, I hopped off quickly and headed for the exit. It was only when I emerged from the ticket hall onto the road outside that I realised something was off.

I recognised the place instantly – Penge East station – but that hadn't been my intended destination when I'd left Kensington. I'd planned on heading up to Oxford Street to find some bikinis and flip-flops for my upcoming honeymoon in St Lucia, and then I was due to have a fitting for my wedding dress near Bond Street.

How odd. I must have just been on automatic, so lost in thought that I'd headed home, a route I'd taken hundreds of times before.

I checked the time on my phone and then, instead of crossing the footbridge to get the train back into central London, I set off for my parents' house. If I ditched the bikini shopping, I could still make the dress fitting. It seemed stupid to turn around without paying them a visit now I was here.

'Oh!' my mum said when she saw me standing on the

doorstep. 'I thought it was the postman.' But then she gathered me into her arms. 'I've missed you.'

I held on tight. 'Me too,' I said. 'I was thinking about you this morning.'

Maybe that's why I'd ended up there? The idea must have got stuck in my subconscious. Justin's Christmas present to me had been a week in a gorgeous old cottage in the Cotswolds, just the two of us, so I hadn't seen my parents over the festive period. And by the time he and I had got back, they'd been in Margate seeing in the New Year with Auntie Lisa.

Mum bustled me in out of the cold and put the kettle on. 'Are you okay, love? You're looking a bit peaky . . . and you've got bags under your eyes. Haven't you been sleeping well?'

'Not great.'

'What's got you stressed?'

I hesitated. I knew she would worry and fuss if I told her Justin and I had been arguing a lot recently. I was still upset with him for locking Octavia in his filing cabinet. Justin was all drama, highs and lows . . . *I'd crushed him unbelievably . . . I was the love of his life* . . . I could hear both those things in the space of an afternoon. Anyway, I'd assumed that once he'd calmed down, he'd see sense and give the violin back to me.

I'd been wrong.

Asking about it had prompted most of the arguments in question, so eventually, I'd just stopped. But I didn't want to tell Mum any of this, so I just made up an excuse about it being wedding nerves. I *think* she bought it.

'Why don't you take your cuppa into the living room and keep your dad company for a bit? I'll be with you in just

269

a sec . . . Ooh, and I'll show you the outfit I've bought for the wedding! I found something last week.'

When I arrived in the living room, Dad gave me a swift hug but quickly turned his attention back to a gardening programme on the telly. Lo was in there, engrossed in her phone. 'Aren't we supposed to meet in town in an hour and a half for your dress fitting?' she said. 'Did you decide to escort me there in case I forgot to go?'

Not the usual hug-filled greeting we would have had before our fight, but things were thawing slowly since I'd waved a long-overdue olive branch and asked her to be my maid of honour. 'I just . . . wanted to visit.'

While it hadn't been my plan when I'd left Justin's flat that morning, it was the truth. I sat with Dad and Lo and watched someone talk about lining ponds properly on the TV for a while, but then my stomach growled, so I decided to go and get a biscuit to go along with my tea.

I'd just headed out the living room door when I heard Mum talking in low tones at the top of the stairs. 'Yes, it's okay. She's here. She's safe . . . Are you going to come here?' It sounded like she was on the phone. There was a moment of silence while she listened to the person on the other end of the phone, and then she added, 'Yes. Yes . . . I think that's a good idea.'

I knew I should have kept walking to the kitchen, but now I was intrigued.

'Okay. Well, I'll see you when you get here, love. Bye, Justin . . . '

My eyes widened. Since when had my mum and Justin had each other's phone numbers?

I heard the creaky floorboard on the top of the staircase go, so I quickly slid back inside the living room. When Mum came downstairs, I followed her into the kitchen. 'Did I just hear you talking to Justin?'

She'd been stirring the sugar into her own mug of tea, and the spoon stopped moving, then started again. She turned, looking a little sheepish. 'He said you hadn't been answering your phone, so he'd checked that app thingie that lets you know where people are, and it said you were here instead of up in London somewhere. He sounded a bit worried.'

Oh, crap. Justin hated it when he couldn't get hold of me. I was surprised I hadn't noticed my phone vibrating in my bag. 'How did he get your number?'

She frowned. 'I presumed you must have given it to him. Didn't you?'

'I don't . . . ' I began, but then I trailed off. With all the turmoil with Justin recently, everything was getting a little bit hazy. I couldn't remember giving Justin Mum's number, but I also didn't remember *not* giving it to him. 'I must have,' I said. It was the only explanation.

'Anyway, he says don't worry . . . he'll come and collect you then take you to your fitting.'

I'd got a lovely cosy feeling when Mum had hugged me at the front door, but I realised it had been leaking out of me like a slow puncture since I'd heard her talking to Justin on the landing. The last of it drained away, leaving me unsure what I was doing there.

I went back into the living room and broke the good news to Lo. 'Justin's going to give us a lift to the dress fitting.'

To my sister's credit, she managed not to roll her eyes. 'How nice of him. I suppose I'd better get ready.' She disappeared up to her room.

When I heard Justin's knock at the door, I instantly tensed up, knowing he wouldn't be pleased I'd gone AWOL or that I hadn't answered my phone. It had always been natural for me to let my feelings spill out, but Justin was different. Everything simmered inside. Sometimes, I thought things were perfectly fine, and then he'd get upset with me about something that happened days, sometimes weeks, earlier. I'd underestimated his ability to *stew*.

I stood up as I heard him enter the front door, ready to appease . . . but when he came into the living room he smiled, holding his arms out for me to walk into them and kissed me fondly before releasing me and greeting my parents. He refused a cup of tea, saying we needed to be on our way to the fitting, but added he had something he needed a quick word about first.

'I've been concerned about your daughter recently,' he said, eyes full of sincerity as he looked from Mum to Dad. As we all took a seat in the living room, I was glad Lo wasn't here to witness this. It would have only made the car journey to the dress fitting more uncomfortable.

Mum nodded. 'She was always sensitive that way, ever since she was little. Never found it easy to get over things. I used to try to talk to her—' she glanced over at me sadly '—but sometimes nothing I said or did helped. I didn't know how to get through.'

'Oh, Mum . . . ' I said, wishing I was sitting nearer her so I could reach out and touch her.

'I just wanted to help you,' she continued, her voice getting thick. 'Especially after you left music school. I could see you were struggling, and I didn't know what to do, and if I tried to say anything, you'd just get angry and push me away.'

'I'm so sorry. I didn't realise.'

Justin was sitting next to me on the sofa, and he reached for my hand and gave it a squeeze. 'I think we've been experiencing some of the same issues. I've been able to see that she's not herself at the moment, but if I try to help, point it out, she just flies off the handle.'

I avoided eye contact with anyone. It was true. I had been more snappy with him recently. But it wasn't me on my own causing the problems. It was just . . . everything I did seemed to be wrong. From the clothes I wore to the way I kept pushing my sleek bob back behind my ears (they were too big to be elegant, apparently). What time I got up in the morning (later than him), to how I wiped the sides down in the kitchen. I suppose it was the way Justin showed his stress, but, eventually, he'd pick and pick and pick, and then I'd show *my* stress by snapping back at him.

It would be better after the wedding, he'd said. When it was all over, we could just go on honeymoon – no more organising, no more running around – and enjoy each other. That was the thought that kept me going.

'You're very lucky to have such a great guy looking after you,' Mum said.

'I know.'

His eyes were fixed on me with such adoration that a warm glow settled inside me. When he looked at me like he was doing at that moment, I felt like the most treasured and beautiful woman in the world.

Lo appeared at the doorway, dress and make-up immaculate. 'Hey, there,' she said, nodding at Justin, and I was grateful for the effort she was making. 'Shall we get this show on the road?'

CHAPTER FORTY-TWO

Now.

BEN AND ALICE walked along the seafront as he told his story. When they reached Central Pier, he gestured towards it. Alice nodded, so they crossed the threshold into a large space full of dinging slot machines but empty of all but a handful of customers. They weaved through the lights and noise and emerged onto the weather-roughened boards of the pier, where they strolled past row upon row of sideshows and fast-food kiosks, all with their shutters firmly bolted down.

Alice listened without interrupting, which Ben found slightly unnerving. By the time he'd covered everything, starting with a wasp sting in a secret garden and finishing with a heartfelt goodbye in Heathrow's departures hall, they were passing the Ferris wheel at the centre of the pier. The entrance was boarded up, and it sat completely still, its white struts skeletal against the sky.

Alice merely nodded, her pace steady and even, and when they finally reached the end of the pier, they circuited a pirate-themed bar, found a piece of railing they could lean on and looked out across the sea.

'That was the last time we saw each other?'

He nodded. 'Yes. Until four days ago.'

'What happened? Why did we never meet up again a year later?'

He sighed and turned away from the waves to look at the weather-beaten building behind them, leaning his backside against the railing. 'I'd like to be able to tell you that fate swooped in and did something grand to keep us apart because then I wouldn't have to admit it was down to sheer stupidity – *my* stupidity.'

She raised her eyebrows, and he carried on.

'I lost my phone.' He still smarted with frustration about that day. 'Running through the airport at the speed of light, reaching the gate with nanoseconds to spare, I must have dropped it somewhere, or left it in a plastic bin at the X-ray machines . . . I don't really know. I contacted Heathrow multiple times, but it never showed up, and without it I had no way to contact you, and you had no way of contacting me – your phone had died before we'd even got to the airport, so you hadn't put my number in it. So that was it. My own stupid fault.'

Alice frowned, looked at the glassy slate sea for a moment. 'But we arranged to meet a year later – did you turn up?'

He nodded. 'I did. I waited all day, but you never showed. And I couldn't blame you for that. I mean, I left promising the world and then . . . nothing. It must have looked like I'd ghosted you. You probably wrote me off as a complete loser and moved on with your life.'

She sighed heavily. 'That would be a reasonable assumption. But you know what?'

'What?'

'I'd like to go back and give Past Lili a slap, tell her to get over her hurt feelings and just have a little faith that things would turn out, that life didn't always have to be the worst-case scenario, and then we'd have met up, and we'd have known whether it was meant to be or not. I might not have ended up in the mess I'm in now if we had.'

'What mess would that be? Standing on the end of the pier with a complete and utter numpty?'

She laughed at that.

'No. You know what I mean . . . ' She turned to look towards the town and vast cast-iron tower that dominated the Blackpool skyline. 'But I obviously never forgot you.'

His chest squeezed at her words. He'd never forgotten her either, no matter how hard he'd tried.

'I'm still wearing this . . . ' she said, looking down to pick up the little silver bee between thumb and forefinger, feeling its wings and body with her fingertips. 'And when I was lost and alone, when I was most vulnerable . . . ' She looked up and met his eyes. 'I came and found you.'

Even with the brisk sea breeze, there was a stillness to the air around them. He looked into Alice's eyes and found everything he'd ever hoped to see there. Forgiveness. Understanding. Not just for that one stupid mistake but for everything, even who he was. It felt like slipping under, and it would be so easy to get caught in that riptide and be swept away.

'I apologise for being such an idiot. If I hurt you in any way, even though it was never my intent, even though you don't remember any of it, I'm so terribly sorry.'

'It's okay.' The smile she gave him was so sweet, so soft, that he knew it really was. But then her eyes took on a cheeky glint. 'Now . . . did you mention that I could whoop your ass at pinball? Because I saw a couple of tables when we walked through the amusements . . . '

*

Alice and Ben collapsed, laughing, into a pair of seats onboard the London-bound bus as the doors hissed closed. The service from Blackpool had got in almost an hour late, and they'd had to sprint through Manchester bus station, Ben dragging her along behind him. They'd made it with thirty seconds to spare.

Alice's heart was hammering. She looked across at Ben, also breathing heavily, and they smiled at each other. It was only then that she realised they hadn't let go of each other's hands.

He looked down to where their fingers were joined, his much larger hand entwined with hers, and his expression grew serious. *This is stupid,* they both seemed to say to each other without words, without even breathing. *We should probably let go.*

Ben dragged his eyes from hers, turned to look out the window, and she felt the wrench of it. But his hand remained wrapped around hers. Warm. Solid. Comforting. Like it belonged there. Like it had always belonged there.

We're going to ignore it, then. We're going to pretend we're not doing this.

All she could think of, as the bus pulled away and edged its way out of the city, was how terrified she'd been when she'd set out on this journey, so much so that she'd practically fainted in the middle of Glasgow Central. It felt like she'd lived a year since then.

What a difference to the woman who had just run through Manchester bus station, adrenaline pumping, eyes sparkling. She didn't know how, and she didn't know why, but she was changing. And she had a sneaking suspicion it had something to do with the man sitting beside her.

And it wasn't because he'd done anything or said anything to make her change. She didn't feel as if she'd become someone else. How could she, when she didn't even know who she was in the first place? Ben hadn't defined her. He hadn't presented her with a version of herself to be swallowed whole and accepted. He'd merely given her room to find out, had been by her side for the journey.

She moved her thumb, running it over the skin at the base of his knuckle, and felt him shiver in response. His fingers hugged hers more firmly. She glanced up at him. He was still staring out of the window, but his expression had taken on a fierceness that made her heart ache.

When they got to London this evening, it couldn't be goodbye. It just couldn't.

And she couldn't let herself forget him again, either. She had to hold on to the memories of what had happened over the last few days and learn to mesh them with the memories of her old life, like the doctor had said. Otherwise, all these wonderful moments, snowballs and frosty piers, would be swept away, and he'd go back to being the jerk who'd never called her. It made what she was doing with her travel diary even more important.

But you don't know if you're free . . . Maybe it would be better to forget? Why torture yourself yearning after something you can never have?

Slowly, she eased her fingers from Ben's, pretending she needed to reach inside her handbag for a tissue and blew her nose, even though there was no desperate need. He moved his hand back into his lap. She could tell he understood.

Oh, this *not knowing* was really starting to get to her. How could she make any choices, take charge of her life in any real sense, if everything in it remained a total mystery?

But at least she was learning to trust herself. And her gut said this thing between her and Ben was good. It was right. Surely she wouldn't be feeling like this – wonky memory or no wonky memory – if she truly loved someone else? There were some things a heart didn't forget.

CHAPTER FORTY-THREE

Six weeks before the wedding.

JUSTIN WANTED TO come into the bridal boutique with Lo and me, but I put my foot down. If I hadn't wandered off and ended up at Mum and Dad's, he wouldn't even have been here with us. It was bad luck for him to see the dress, I reminded him. He'd just have to trust that I would pick well. And by that, I meant nothing strapless or backless, or with a short skirt. Something classy and traditional. Those had been his preferences. In the end, I opted for something that looked a bit like Grace Kelly's wedding gown. You couldn't get much more classy and elegant than that, could you?

However, as I stood in front of the long mirrors, the dressmaker checking and adjusting the fit, I began to doubt my choice. The lace at the top of the bodice rose into a high collar, and while it wasn't cheap, scratchy stuff, I kept wanting to undo the button to allow myself to breathe.

'You look beautiful,' Lo said behind me.

I looked at our reflections in the mirror and smiled at her. Maybe I was making a fuss over nothing. I'd blown most of Mum and Dad's wedding budget on this dress, seeing as

Justin had insisted on covering almost everything else, and I had a feeling it would be a double blow to their pride if I said I wanted something different. Even if I did, there was no money or time to go back to the drawing board now.

Besides, I wasn't sure it was the dress that was the problem. Lo was right. It looked amazing. So what if it chafed a little, if it didn't *feel* right. No pain, no gain, right?

When I caught Lo's gaze again, she was looking thoughtful. 'You okay?'

I nodded. 'The dress is perfect.'

'I wasn't asking about the dress. I was asking about you.'

That was the problem. I didn't know how I was. If I was honest, the fact I'd wandered off, found myself somewhere else over an hour later scared me. Even if I tried, I couldn't remember anything that had happened between Kensington and Penge East. It was as if I'd completely zoned out and done everything on automatic.

'I'm fine,' I said and went back to studying myself in the mirror, wishing I could airbrush away the dark circles under my eyes. I didn't look much like a glowing bride today.

Then I had the strangest sensation . . . I felt as if I was standing outside myself, looking on, and someone else was standing in a wedding dress in front of the mirror. Even when I snapped back into myself, looked myself in the eye, there was still a lingering feeling that it was a different person staring back at me. Someone I didn't know.

I reached for the buttons on the collar and asked Lo to undo the back of the dress. I needed to get out of it. Now.

'Justin's probably getting bored in that café across the road,' I said, as we peeled it off me and I handed it back to the designer. I got back into my normal clothes, said goodbye to my sister and went to find my fiancé.

When we got back into the privacy of his car, he reached across and laid his warm palm on my thigh. I looked across at him.

'Now we're alone, there's something I need to talk to you about . . . '

'I'm not showing you a picture of the dress, no matter how hard you beg me.'

Justin didn't smile at my feeble attempt at a joke. 'You really gave me a scare earlier on, Angel. I had no idea where you were.'

'I'm sorry. I don't really know how to explain what happened. I just kind of . . . drifted off . . . and the next thing I knew I was getting off the train at Penge.'

'You know that's not normal, right?'

I did, but I stayed very still, my gaze focused on my hands sitting in my lap.

'Don't take this the wrong way, Angel, but I think that maybe when we get back from St Lucia, you ought to see someone.'

I looked up. 'See someone?'

'A professional. Someone who can understand what's going on inside your head and with your emotions. Someone who can help untangle it all for you.'

'You think . . . You think I need psychiatric help?'

'Possibly.'

'Oh.' I looked down to where his hand was rhythmically stroking my thigh. 'I thought it was just wedding stress,' I mumbled. 'I thought I'd be okay once the wedding was over.'

'Maybe it is,' he said, but his eyes told me he wasn't sure he believed that. 'But we need to make sure, okay?'

I fought back the urge to cry because that would only cement his opinion that I was horribly broken, wouldn't it? If I got all emotional and upset about him suggesting something so caring? And aside from today, I had been feeling a bit . . . well, low, recently. I should welcome this chance, shouldn't I? See it as a positive.

'Don't be sad, Angel,' he said, hooking a finger under my chin and gently lifting it so I could meet his eyes. 'I'll be right beside you. I'm here for you . . . No matter what.'

CHAPTER FORTY-FOUR

Now.

SOMEWHERE BETWEEN MANCHESTER and a service station on the M40, where the coach stopped to change drivers, Ben came to a decision. When Alice took advantage of the rest break to visit the ladies', he pulled his phone out of his pocket and called Norina's friend with the hotel, and asked him if he had another room.

He was in this now, whatever 'this' was.

He felt guilty about not being back in Invergarrig when he said he would, but he was already going to be a day late, thanks to the snow, and when he'd called Norina, she'd said Willow had hardly batted an eyelid. Of course she'd be fine if he stayed a bit longer. Which was just as well because, until he was absolutely sure there was no hope, he wasn't letting Alice out of his sight.

Inside the service station, he and Alice opted for the coffee shop, grabbing a couple of sandwiches and hot drinks, then sat down to eat them while listening to the music being piped from speakers hidden amongst the exposed heating vents in the ceiling. An eighties mix, he guessed, as he made short work of his ham and cheese toastie.

When he finished it, he leant back in his chair, stretching his legs out and crossing one foot over the other, and his eyelids drifted closed. It was tempting to let himself nod, seeing as he'd only snatched a few hours' sleep the night before. 'Every Breath You Take' by The Police was playing, and he was mulling over the haunting, slightly claustrophobic mood of the song when a chair leg scraped against the floor. He opened his eyes, but it took him a second or two to realise that while Alice's coat was hung over the back of her chair, Alice herself was nowhere to be seen.

A cold spike of fear shot through him. So much for not taking his eyes off her! Where was she? He stood up to see above the heads of the other diners and spotted her jogging towards the entrance. When the automatic doors slid open, she kept running out into the night. Ben didn't stop to think. He took off after her.

'Alice?' he called out as he neared the exit, and spotted her standing on the kerb overlooking the car park, arms wrapped around herself. She didn't turn, didn't answer. He picked up speed.

When he reached her and touched her arm lightly, she jumped as if she was surprised he was there, maybe even as if she was surprised that *she* was there, instead of listening to the music in the warm café. While it wasn't snowing this far south, the temperature was still icy.

'Are you okay? What's going on?'

Alice inhaled a jagged breath. 'I don't know. I think I need to . . . to . . . ' She looked up at him helplessly. 'I don't know. I just . . . It was that song . . . ' Her eyes widened, as if the words she'd just said were a revelation to her just as much as they were to him. 'I really hate that song!'

'You hate The Police?'

Alice pressed her lips together and shook her head. 'No. I don't . . . I don't hate the band, not at all. It's the song. That particular one. And now I feel a bit . . . strange. Like my head is buzzing. Racing. I think I might— Oh!'

Ben stepped closer.

'I just saw . . . ' She looked at him with terror in her eyes. 'I just had another one of those flashes . . . an image of something. But this time it was longer. Clearer. And I could hear that song playing in the background. *Every move you . . .* ' She trailed off and hugged herself tighter.

'What did you see?' Ben asked quietly.

She swallowed. 'It was the same thing, almost, as the last time . . . the bridal shop, the mirror. I was wearing a . . . Oh, God! I was wearing the wedding dress. It was me!' Her fingers moved to her neck, touched the skin there. 'The collar was scratchy and tight . . . But I wasn't really looking at the dress. I was looking at my reflection. It was as if I was looking at another person . . . ' She swallowed. 'I think she was trying to send me a message.' Her lips trembled. 'I think she was telling me to get out of there. To run.'

Ben reached out and pulled Alice into his arms, where she stood, shivering. It wasn't like earlier, he reasoned. This was about safety, about making a friend feel better when they were having a wobble. 'It's freezing out here,' he said. 'And the coach is going to leave shortly. Let's just grab our coffees and get back on board.' He was much less likely to lose her again there, especially as she preferred sitting next to the window.

When they got on board, Alice slid into her seat. He sat beside her in silence, knowing that she needed time to process what she'd remembered, giving her space, even though he was desperate to ask questions.

After about ten minutes, she picked her handbag up from beside her feet, unzipped the side pocket and carefully pulled out the crumpled invitation. 'The wedding . . . ' she said, her voice trembling. 'The one I'm trying to get to . . . I have a horrible feeling it might be mine.'

CHAPTER FORTY-FIVE

Now.

ALICE STARED AT the invitation in her hands. She studied every word, taking in the play of light on the gold foil on the bride and groom's names, following each scrolling letter with her eyes until the words became nothing but shapes and lines without meaning.

Was that her name? Her full name?

She felt no connection to it at all.

No. It couldn't be true.

The coach rumbled on towards London, joining the M25 near Heathrow Airport, then coming off again to head into the urban sprawl, through the city towards Victoria Coach Station, just a stone's throw from Buckingham Palace.

It had to be a memory that she'd experienced standing outside the service station. Something real. Otherwise, why would the same image keep slapping her around the head, getting stronger each time, getting clearer? It was as if her brain was trying to say, *Wake up! Listen!*

She ran her fingertips across the embossed lettering of the invitation, then slid it carefully into the side pocket of her handbag before staring at the back of the seat in front of her.

She wanted to put her hands over her ears and go 'la, la, la'. She wanted to take Ben by the hand when the coach stopped and just get the first one back to Scotland.

Was she right? Was she really about to get married?

A wedding should be the happiest day of someone's life, full of joy and excitement, so why did the images in her head trouble her so much? Of course, this uneasy feeling could just be a hallucination, her brain misfiring. There might be a groom, searching frantically for her, worried sick. If there were, she'd probably put him through the worst week of his life. But, somehow, even if she managed to squash this sense of foreboding, she couldn't bring herself to care about him. He was a stranger.

She sure as hell didn't want to marry him.

A tear leaked from the corner of her eye, and she bowed her head. Ben pulled a small packet of tissues from his pocket and handed them to her. Warmth flared inside her chest. She looked at him gratefully, then she wiped her eyes and blew her nose.

'Are you okay?'

He asked her that a lot, didn't he? Which hinted she was becoming a responsibility to him, one he shouldn't have. Other things should be his priority right now, like an adorable little girl who desperately needed a father figure. And helping her get to the wedding rehearsal was taking him away from that.

'I'm okay. Just feeling a bit weird. As if none of this can be real.'

Ben nodded sympathetically. 'I wasn't sure if I should say anything, but I had an idea of a way – possibly – to get more information.'

'You do?' Her heart did a little leap. Maybe they could find something that would prove she was wrong?

'If we assume these "flashes" can be trusted, that they're real memories, it tells us a few things. Leaving aside whether you're the bride or not, if you were at a dress fitting, you're not just a plus-one that somebody's cousin is bringing along. What if we phoned the venue again? Not to ask for information about the wedding itself, but about the rehearsal. We know things that only someone with an invite would know. We might be about to find out something useful. What do you think?'

'I'm willing to give it a shot.' Anything to disprove her theory and make it all nonsense.

'It's probably after hours, but if they do evening events, we might get hold of someone. If not, we'll just try again in the morning.' He pulled his phone from his jacket pocket, found the number on his list of recent calls, then put the phone on speaker, the volume on low.

The receptionist who picked up didn't sound as chirpy and well-scripted as Alice expected her to. She sounded like somebody's grandma – someone's *Scottish* grandma.

Ben introduced himself and said he was checking on the exact location of the rehearsal tomorrow night. The invite had been lost, and he wanted to make sure he was going to the right place.

The woman's tone brightened considerably when she heard him. 'Och, don't worry about that,' she said, and Alice could hear the clacking of fingernails on a keyboard. 'I'll soon find that out . . . Yup, it's six-thirty p.m. at the Tithe Barn. Use Car Park C because that's the closest, and just follow the signs. Turn left after the maze. And don't forget to bring the confirmation email because you won't get in without it – the castle grounds close to the public at six.'

'That's great. Thank you so much.'

The woman sighed. 'But keep an eye on your inbox . . . You know, in case they actually *do* cancel.'

Alice looked at Ben, eyes wide. He didn't break eye contact as he replied to the woman on the phone. 'Of course. It's . . . It's definitely keeping us all guessing.'

The woman laughed. 'So it would. The phones have been ringing off the hook about it all week. It's not every day someone from the bridal party goes AWOL.'

Alice's stomach dropped. She felt as if a trap door had opened up underneath her, that she'd fallen through the belly of the bus and hit the motorway tarmac with a splat. Oh, God . . . Where was fresh air when you needed it? She reached up and fiddled with the array of knobs and buttons above her head, trying to find a blast of cold air, but only succeeded in turning on the reading light.

Ben frowned but carried on. 'I know . . . It's all been very shocking. Can you tell me how likely it is the wedding's going ahead?'

'Hm, I shouldn't, really. It would only be speculation . . . '

Ben's accent thickened a little. 'I know,' he said smoothly, 'but I'm just trying to work out if I should return my gift or no.' With all those rolling 'r's and lilting words, he might as well have been purring into the phone.

'Well now . . . ' Her voice lowered in the same way it might have done if she'd been having a good old gossip with a friend. 'I don't think it's likely. Management have been pretty hush-hush about it, but I did overhear someone saying they're not holding their breath that the missing woman will turn up. We're all pretty sure it's the bride.'

Alice's lungs stopped working. She couldn't take any more . . . She pulled the phone out of Ben's hand and jabbed her finger on the screen to end the call and then shoved it back at him and stared at the seatback in front of her, heart hammering.

Since the train had broken down the night before, she'd been scared she wouldn't get to the wedding rehearsal on time. But, at that present moment, she was terrified she would.

CHAPTER FORTY-SIX

Two weeks before the wedding.

'MORE COCKTAILS!' LO yelled at a passing waiter. No one defied my sister when she was in one of her strident moods, so he obediently arrived with another round of mojitos a few minutes later. She handed me one. 'Bottoms up!' she said, grinning, before taking a large slurp. If there was one thing to say about my sister, it was that she knew how to throw a party.

And this party was for me, my hen night. Lo had originally wanted to do a weekend in Dublin, as my cousin had done, but Justin hadn't liked the idea of multiple nights away, lots of girls behaving badly and getting drunk. It wasn't classy, he said. Why not do something more low-key?

However, I'm not sure my maid of honour had understood the assignment. Or maybe she had, and just decided to book a noisy, colourful South American restaurant in Soho, full of partying groups, because she knew it was *exactly* what my fiancé would object to.

Whatever the reason, she was doing her best to work her way through the cocktail menu. Maybe she was a bit nervous? I certainly was. Although things had been better between us recently, they still weren't back to normal.

We were a small party, only seven of us. Lo, plus her best friend Maddy, and then four of my old school friends, whom I hadn't seen in a couple of years. It wasn't until I'd had to put a guest list together that I realised how few friends I had, especially female ones. I hadn't really made any at the Conservatory, and after that, I'd been pretty much a hermit. Nowadays, nearly all my time was spent with Justin, and I lived in a different part of London, so I supposed it was hardly surprising.

However, I was enjoying celebrating with people my age, being silly and not thinking about what the most elegant or well-mannered thing to do was. After all the stress of preparing for the wedding, it was a wonderful way to let off steam.

'I know!' Lo yelled, even though we were sitting very close together at our table. 'Let's go to a club!'

The rest of the girls began throwing out possible names, but I leaned closer to Lo and said, 'I told Justin I'd be home by eleven.'

'Oh, come on . . . You love dancing. And it's your hen night. Besides,' Lo added, waggling her eyebrows, 'I've got a surprise lined up.'

When I saw the naughty smirk she was wearing, my stomach dropped. 'Lo . . . No strippers! We agreed that, remember?' Justin had been very clear about that.

My sister mimed crossing her heart with her finger. 'Wouldn't dream of it,' she said, her eyes wide and innocent. 'Come on . . . We're having such fun!' She leaned in, put her arm around me, and gave me a sloppy wet kiss on the cheek. Yep. Lo had definitely had quite a few cocktails. However, the alcohol had loosened us both up a little bit, and I was enjoying laughing with my sister after the months of frostiness.

'Let me go and call Justin.' I stood up so I could go and find a quieter spot.

'Just send a text!' Lo said, grabbing my arm and pulling me back down again.

'No, it would be better if I call. Justin's just a bit sensitive after all the things his ex put him through.' Also, I knew I needed to lay the groundwork, break it to him the right way so he wouldn't get upset later on. It was much better to head things off at the pass than have to deal with one of his moods.

It took me about twenty minutes to convince Justin I'd be all right staying out longer. I could tell he really didn't want me to, but Lo was right. It was my hen night. When was I ever going to get to do this again?

*

Lo lied. We did indeed go to a club, and there were indeed strippers. She had a whale of a time egging them on. I vacillated between cringing and laughing and was glad when the whole thing was over so we could get back to dancing. Lo had been right about that too – I really did love to dance.

More cocktails were consumed, and when we spilled out onto the chilly street outside the club, to join the queue for taxis, I looked at my phone and gasped. 'It's two-thirty! Justin is going to be frantic!'

Lo swayed on her stilettos and placed a palm on a nearby lamppost to steady herself. The other girls were deep in some gossip about someone they all knew back in Penge. 'Sensitive, my arse,' she said, blinking slowly and trying to focus on my face. 'That man is controlling.'

Really? This again? 'Don't start, Lo. *Please*. We've had such a nice night . . . '

Lo held her hands up in surrender. 'Okay, okay. I didn't mean to . . . you know.'

I sighed. I did know. My little sister was a straight shooter, and nothing was going to change that. And while it irritated me no end, I knew she wasn't coming from a bad place.

'But don't you think he's just a little . . . ?'

Unfortunately, drunk Lo was even more reluctant to let things lie than Sober Lo. The only way I could think of to shut this conversation down once and for all was to face the matter head on, just this once. 'Okay,' I said firmly, so she knew I was making an important point. 'Maybe he is a *little* controlling. But it comes from his past. He's still healing. And I love him, Lo. Mum said I needed to learn to take the rough with the smooth, so that's what I'm trying to do. In time, I'll prove to him how much I love him, and things will change. He'll feel more secure.'

Lo looked away, weighing up her next words, I guessed, then looked back at me. 'You don't think how he acts some-times – and I'm sure I only see the tip of the iceberg – is a little worrying?'

'I know he's high-maintenance, but so am I – you've always said so.'

Lo rolled her eyes, and then one side of her mouth hitched up in a smile. 'Well . . . you are.'

'You don't see the side of him that I see.'

Although Justin had been super picky about anything to do with the wedding recently, everything else had been fine since the day of my dress fitting. It was just like when we'd first been together, and finally, I'd thought, *This is what it's supposed to feel like just before your wedding.* We were in a really good place, ready to put the wrinkles of the past behind us.

'He's being so sweet and caring at the moment. I've lost count of the number of flowers he's bought me, and he's always taking me out, buying me nice things . . . ' I saw Lo's face and knew instantly where her mind had gone, so I quickly added, 'and it's not about the money. That's just an outward show of how he feels about me. He's so supportive: he listens to me when I need him to, tells me I need to believe in myself more . . . ' I trailed off, unsure of what more I could say to convince her.

Lo swayed again as she tried to reach out and touch me. She missed the first time but then grabbed onto my coat sleeve. 'I'm only saying this because I love you, because I'm looking out for you . . . Sometimes I wonder if his behaviour isn't a little abusive.'

I was so shocked by what my sister said that I laughed really loudly, causing a couple of other people in the queue to turn round to see what was going on. 'What? No! What are you talking about? Justin has never hit me. Don't be daft.'

Lo took her hand off me and concentrated on balancing as the queue moved forwards. 'Abuse can be more than just hitting, Lil. It's about patterns of behaviour, about control, about erasing someone's sense of self so completely that they are totally under your spell.'

'No. You're wrong. It's not like that between him and me. What makes you such an expert, anyway?'

'Remember that girl I worked with a few years ago – Priya? Well, she had a girlfriend who was like that with her. I dunno . . . ' She shrugged and raised her hands, which was a bit more than her impaired balance centre could handle, and she had to step back to stop herself from falling over. 'Sometimes, Justin gives me the same vibe.'

I shook my head and smiled, knowing she was going to be horrified with saying all of this in the morning. It was so utterly ridiculous I found I couldn't even be angry about it. Yes, I knew Justin wasn't perfect, that there were moments when he really upset me, but it wasn't as bad as all that.

'I mean, does he ever sulk or give you the silent treatment when he doesn't get what he wants, keeps it up until you give in?'

I stopped smiling. 'Well . . . Sometimes. But so did you, Lo, when we were growing up!'

Lo narrowed her eyes and looked at me. 'I was a temperamental teenager, not a grown man in his thirties.' She stayed silent for a moment, and I'd hoped she'd drop the subject, but then she said, 'Okay, well, you've got to admit that he's changed you since you started seeing him. The latest thing is the voice – what's up with that, going all posh on me?'

My cheeks heated, and I looked away. 'I've been having lessons from an actor friend of Justin's, and he's not *forcing* me to do it. I want to do it.' I looked back at her, begging her to understand. 'You don't see the way some of the people he mixes with look at me when I open my mouth.'

'But I bet it was his idea, right?'

I sighed heavily. Yes, Justin had suggested it, and I suppose I'd been a little bit offended at first, but when he'd explained it to me, I'd agreed to go along with it. In the end, I'd been grateful for it. People were taking me more seriously. 'That doesn't prove anything.'

Lo leaned in and said, 'Are you sure you want this?'

'Want what?'

'To marry him! It's not too late to back out, you know.'

'Lo . . . ' I was getting irritated now. She was taking this too far. 'Drop it, okay?'

We reached the head of the queue, and the next taxi in the rank pulled forward. 'You have this one since you're going a different way,' she said. 'The girls and I will get the next.'

'Thanks,' I said, giving her a brisk hug, glad I was about to be whisked back to Kensington, and the conversation would be over.

She tugged my coat sleeve as I opened the door and leaned into the cab to tell the driver the address. 'Okay, one last thing and I promise I'll drop it . . . I know you say he's not physical with you, but does he ever make you feel like you're losing your mind, that you're doubting yourself about everything. Does he ever *scare* you?'

I kissed her on the cheek, and as I clambered into the back of the taxi, I thought about what she said. Justin made me feel many things. Yes, sometimes I felt frustrated, confused, upset. But show me anyone in a long-term relationship who *didn't* feel that way on occasion. And, yes, sometimes, in his more intense moments, I found myself wanting to back away, but that was just his passionate nature. The flip side of that very same passion was what made me feel cherished, loved, worshipped.

'No,' I said as I sat down and reached to pull the door closed. 'Justin has never scared me. Now go home, take two paracetamol and put a pint glass of water next to your bed.'

CHAPTER FORTY-SEVEN

Now.

THEY SAT IN silence for the rest of the journey to London, both too shell-shocked to utter a word. What could he say anyway? 'Congratulations?' He wasn't feeling particularly overjoyed about the idea of Alice getting married, but she looked . . . Well, she looked devastated.

'I can't get my head round it,' she kept saying, staring blindly out of the window.

Neither could he. Why hadn't he found her a year ago, or two years ago? It was crappy, crappy timing. He'd thought the universe had been smiling on him. Hah! This wasn't a second chance. This was fate rubbing his nose in it.

Despite Alice's flashes of memory, he hadn't even considered the wedding she was trying to get to was her own. However, now he thought about it, he realised that the times she'd been most wobbly were when she'd come across something connected with a wedding. All the clues had been there. He'd just ignored them.

Like he had done with Cat. He had a talent for deluding himself, for refusing to see the disaster that was upon him until it hit. Despite all his efforts to change, to be more present for the people he cared about, he hadn't made any progress at all.

Alice's hand rested on her thigh, so close to his that he could stretch out his little finger and touch her if he'd wanted to. He picked up his phone to keep his hands busy. No more touching. No more believing this could go anywhere. But he still wasn't leaving her side. Not yet.

And not for his own selfish need to be with her as much as possible. Because, even though she might only be days away from getting married, something clearly was wrong for her to have ended up in this state. Until he knew she was safe with people who loved her and would take care of her, he wasn't walking away. He was going to stay, no matter how gut-wrenching it got, and he had no illusions about how hard it was going to be to see her walk away into the arms of another man.

'Ben?'

'Uh-huh.'

'Do you think . . . ? Do you think the wedding will go ahead with me like this? It can't, can it? Not if I don't remember who I'm supposed to be marrying?'

Hope flared in his chest, but he squashed it down again quickly. It didn't change anything, not really. When her memories came back, she'd be ready to pick up the reins of her old life. He wouldn't be needed. 'I don't know,' he said truthfully. 'All we can do is turn up at the rehearsal and find out.'

'We?' she almost whispered.

He nodded. 'I've already spoken to Marco about staying tonight, but I'd like to come with you, make sure you get to Hadsborough Castle, okay . . . If that's all right by you?'

She smiled, her eyes full of warmth and sadness. 'Yes, that's all right by me. Thank you.'

'It's settled, then.'

She bobbed her head gently. 'You were there at the start of my journey. It only seems fitting for you to see it through to the end.'

*

The Sonata Hotel had had a revamp since Ben had last visited. It had always been a quirky little boutique hotel, but the owners had obviously decided to renovate and go all-out on a musical theme, possibly due to its proximity to the Royal Albert Hall. The lobby was full of busts of famous composers, sheet music and draping red velvet.

Marco was at the reception desk when they arrived, and Ben could have kissed him when he told them he had two rooms ready for them with comfy beds and hot showers. He'd been wearing the same clothes for a day and a half now, and he couldn't wait to get under the hot spray. Thankfully, Kensington High Street was within fifteen minutes' walk, and he should at least be able to grab underwear, socks and a fresh T-shirt in the morning. Maybe even a backpack to put his gear in. He always felt a bit naked when he travelled without a backpack.

'So,' Alice said, clutching her key card and forcing a bright smile onto her lips, 'this is it. Hopefully, it'll be a less eventful night than last night, and you'll actually be able to get a bit of sleep.'

'Hopefully,' he said, playing along, although he doubted

sleep would bless him much that night. 'I'll see you in the morning.'

She nodded and walked across the lobby, heading for the compact elevator. Ben thought about the amount of space inside, how close they'd have to stand, and took the stairs.

The first thing he did when he got into his room was hang his coat on the back of the door, strip off his clothes, and head for the shower. When he returned, he folded his T-shirt and jeans, then went to retrieve his wallet from his coat pocket. He always liked to keep it on the bedside table when he was travelling, but when he rummaged in his pockets, he came up empty.

What?

He went back to his jeans, patted down his pockets.

Oh, God. Where had he been the last time he saw it? He mentally rewound through the day. He'd last see his wallet when . . . When he'd run out of the service station café after Alice. He'd popped it down on the table after paying for their drinks and toasties. Flicking through his memories of that time, he had a vague image of the table being empty when they'd dashed back to grab their coats before getting back on the coach. Someone had obviously lifted his wallet whilst he'd been outside, and he hadn't even noticed.

He didn't know who he was angrier with: the bastard who'd taken it, or himself, for making such a rookie mistake. Again.

CHAPTER FORTY-EIGHT

Two weeks before the wedding.

I HAD A little trouble lining my door key up with the lock when I got back to the flat after my hen night, which I seemed to find funny rather than annoying, but I eventually got inside and instantly kicked off my stilettos. The smooth marble tile of the hallway was blissfully cool against my aching feet. I dropped my handbag and jacket on the floor, dimly aware that I might get an earful for doing so the next morning, and tried to creep as quietly as I could down the hallway.

My eyes were beginning to adjust to the darkened flat when I nudged the bedroom door open. The lights were off in there too, Justin a shadowy lump on his side of the bed. *Shhh . . ..* I told myself and squashed the urge to giggle, but when I'd brushed the hilarity away, I realised there was an uncomfortable knot in my stomach that had nothing to do with the number of cocktails I'd drunk.

It would be better if I didn't wake him.

I sat down on the edge of the mattress and shimmied out of the sequinned dress I was wearing. Too tired to peel my underwear off, I slid underneath the covers with it on.

'You bothered to come back, then?'

The low voice surprised me so much, I squealed and almost jumped out of bed again, pressing my palm to my pounding chest. 'Justin! You almost gave me a heart attack! I thought you were asleep.'

'No such luck, Angel.'

Oh, dear. I knew that tone. I began to sober up pretty quickly.

'Sorry,' I said, although I wasn't exactly sure what I was apologising for. Although I'd been worried about how late it was, we'd agreed I could stay out later, and he hadn't specified an exact time to be back. Sometimes, he just expected me to *know*, but I often guessed things wrong, which only led to an argument.

'It's a bit late for apologies.'

I pulled the duvet up under my chin for protection. 'Had a few cocktails,' I mumbled. 'Lost track of time.'

'Too busy having *fun*?' His words were dripping with disgust.

I went still. I knew I had to be very careful about what I said next. When Justin got sensitive like this, any little slip could set him off. 'I was *supposed* to be having fun with my girlfriends. It was my hen night. But I behaved myself. You don't have to worry.'

'Were there men there?'

'I just told you. It was just me and the girls.'

'What about strippers?'

A cold sensation washed through me.

'Angel?'

There was no point in lying. He'd just keep needling me, finding inconsistencies in my story until I had to come clean

306

anyway. 'Lo hired a couple. She did it because she thought it would be funny . . . ' or possibly because it would piss Justin off, but I wasn't going to tell him that, not when they had to play nice together on the top table at our wedding reception in fourteen days. 'But I didn't have anything to do with it – and I told her she shouldn't have.'

He was quiet for what seemed like ages. I knew he was picturing the scene in his head, and anything he was thinking of probably wasn't that far off base. Yes, I had blushed and felt awkward – it really wasn't my kind of thing – but I would have come off as a spoilsport if I'd shut it all down. And it had been harmless fun. I hadn't been even vaguely attracted to either of the two dancers.

'Why would you do that to me? When that was my one stipulation about letting you have a hen night.' All trace of anger gone in his tone. He just sounded incredibly wounded. 'I give you everything I have, Angel, everything I am . . . Why do you deliberately try to upset me?'

'I explained . . . It had nothing to do with me.'

'You didn't watch them? You didn't let them come up close to you and wave their arses in your face? And more!'

I swallowed, and then I turned to him and slid my palm across his bare chest. 'Justin . . . It's you I love, don't you know that? I'd do anything for you. I'm marrying you in a fortnight.'

'But even that's spoiled now because you've invited *him* to the wedding.'

Oh, god. Here we went again, I thought. Ever since Justin had discovered my old next-door neighbour Sam was on the guest list, he'd been going on about it. 'I've explained about that too – the Baxters are my mum and dad's oldest friends.

They're like family – closer than most of my actual aunts and uncles. I couldn't leave them off the guest list. And I told you . . . It was just a silly teenage thing between Sam and I that neither of us barely remembers. We see each other when our families get together, but we don't have a friendship outside of that.'

'So you say . . . ' Justin huffed, and then he threw the duvet back and got out of bed.

'What are you doing?'

'I'm getting up. I can't sleep next to you feeling the way I do at the moment.' And he grabbed his robe and strode from the room. I lay there for a few moments, and then I sighed. I was tired and headachy and, unfortunately, feeling a lot more sober than I had been when I'd slid my key into the door.

No way was I going to get to sleep knowing Justin was in another part of the flat, *stewing*. There was no telling what kind of state he'd have worked himself up into come morning. I was going to have to go and find him. However, having this conversation in just my underwear seemed to hit the wrong note, so I quickly pulled my pyjamas on before heading out of the bedroom.

I didn't bother turning on any lights but walked around the flat in my bare feet. I found him sitting on one of the sofas in the living room, the glow from the city outside picking him out in the dark. I went and sat down, close but not right next to him, sensing he might need a little space.

His voice was hollow when he spoke. 'I put you above everything . . . Have I invited any of my exes to the wedding? No. I wouldn't do that to you. But I always feel I'm last on your list, that there are so many other things you put above me.'

It broke my heart to hear him talk like this. Didn't he understand how much I'd twisted myself like a pretzel trying to be the kind of woman he deserved? I was *always* thinking about what he wanted, what would please or displease him. My whole life revolved around him. 'Justin,' I said, and my voice caught. 'You are my world! Please believe me!'

He turned his head sharply to look at me, and I wondered how someone so perfect, so handsome and talented and sensitive, could believe in himself so little. 'Prove it, then.'

I shook my head gently in bemusement. 'How?'

'Prove that you love me above absolutely everything . . .' He got up and headed for the study, and I followed him. I had a bad feeling about this.

He walked over to his desk, unlocked the bottom filing cabinet drawer, and pulled my violin case out. I instinctively reached for it. What had Octavia got to do with this?

'This,' he said, pulling the violin from its case. 'This is what you love more than me.'

I gave a little half-laugh, more out of nerves than out of humour. How on earth could he be jealous of a violin? 'Don't be silly, Justin.'

His expression grew even more furious then, and I knew instantly that I'd said the wrong thing. My stomach chilled to ice as he glared at me, strode into the living room, and unlocked the sliding doors that led onto the balcony. It was early February and the coldest part of the night. My skin instantly puckered into goosebumps.

He shot me a scathing look, then walked outside and stood at the railing. When I joined him, he shoved the violin at me, bumping it painfully into my chest. 'Hold it out,' he ordered.

'What?' He couldn't be saying what I thought he meant. It was ridiculous.

'Hold the violin out, over the edge. Or the wedding's off.'

I was tempted to laugh, to think I was still tipsy, but standing there in the icy night air, I knew I was stone-cold sober. This was all just so surreal. I took a few moments to consider my choices. This was a test. Justin was big on tests, another hangover from his failed marriage, I supposed. It might be better to play along. He wasn't *really* going to make me do anything to Octavia.

Keeping my eyes on him, I let out a steadying breath, and then I gripped the neck of the violin with my left hand and extended my arm, so it dangled over the railing.

'Let go,' he said. There was no hint of rage or despair or any emotion at all in his tone now. It was as cold as the air wrapping itself around us.

I did laugh then, a tiny nervous bubble of sound. 'Justin . . . You don't seriously expect me to—'

'It's your choice, Angel. Do you want me, or do you want the violin?'

Why was he being so nonsensical? I pulled my arm back and hugged the violin to my chest.

He blinked and then said, so, so smoothly, 'Or do I have to do it for you?'

Before I could answer, he reached across, wrenched Octavia out of my hands and held her over the railing.

'No! Please don't! Justin, you don't need to do this!' I looked at his face, a face I thought I knew so well. A face I loved so much. But I was staring into the face of a stranger.

'Any last thing you want to say?' he asked, keeping his eyes on me.

I was frozen, unable to do anything but tear my eyes from his and look longingly at the instrument dangling over the railing.

One by one, he released his fingers. When thumb and forefinger were all that was left, I couldn't take it any more. I lunged for Octavia just as he let go, letting out a scream of pure despair as she disappeared out of sight. A second later, I heard the sound of splintering wood on the paving stones below.

CHAPTER FORTY-NINE

Now.

ALICE WOKE WITH a sick feeling in the pit of her stomach. Today was the day of the wedding rehearsal, the day she'd been waiting for, but now it was here, all she wanted to do was climb back under the lovely soft duvet and hide. This life – the only one she knew and remembered – was about to collide with her real one, and she couldn't help but fear that she'd be crushed between the two when the moment of impact arrived.

Ben was already in the hotel breakfast room when she went downstairs. She slid into the seat opposite him. From the looks of the circles under his eyes, he hadn't slept any better than she had.

They ate breakfast in silence, punctuated by requests to pass the milk or the teapot, neither of them wanting to raise the subject of her impending nuptials. The easy conversation was gone, and Alice mourned it. Even though he was only a couple of feet away across the breakfast table, she missed him.

But when she caught his eye when they both reached for the toast rack at the same time, she saw everything she was feeling – the sense of loss, of the unfairness of it all – mirrored back to her. She pressed her lips together in a wonky sort of smile, and he dipped his chin almost imperceptibly in rely.

The only thing they could do was focus on the day's journey and all the practicalities that came along with it. Those, at least, were safe topics.

'I think we may have a problem,' she told him, pulling her phone out of her bag. 'That receptionist yesterday evening said we need a confirmation email to get into the castle grounds.'

Ben put his toast down and looked thoughtful. 'There must be a way around it . . .'

Alice nodded. She'd been thinking about that last night while sleep had evaded her. 'The only other option is to buy tickets, just like regular visitors, but even that has a snag because she also said the castle closes to the public at six, which is half an hour before the rehearsal starts. I suppose we could just get there before closing time and hang around. If we position ourselves near the barn, we're bound to see people arriving.'

One side of Ben's mouth hitched up. 'Look at you, doing my job for me and ironing out all the travel kinks. Seems like you've thought of everything.'

'The only other problem is the tickets are quite expensive – almost thirty quid per person. I've got enough to pay for mine, but I don't think I can stretch to yours.'

'You're right about it being a problem,' Ben said, grimacing slightly. 'When I got to my room last night, I realised someone had stolen my wallet – or I lost it – at the service station on the M40.'

Alice's hand flew to her mouth. 'Oh, no! Can we go back there to look for it? Have we got time?'

Ben shook his head. 'No point. I phoned my bank and cancelled all my cards, but it means I'm limited to the contactless payments I can make with my phone. When I moved back to Invergarrig, I switched to the tiny Scottish bank that has a branch opposite the church, and I don't think they partner with any banks in England so I could draw cash out of an ATM, but I can double-check that.'

'That's the only bank card you have?'

He shrugged. 'I have a couple of credit cards I use when I'm travelling, but I wasn't expecting to be making last-minute five-hundred-mile trips, so they're in a drawer back at the B&B.'

'Well, you can probably manage a ticket to the castle, but what about the train fare back to Glasgow?'

'I guess I'm just going to have to come up with something clever. In the meantime, I could do with some fresh clothes, so I'm going to see if I can find a cheap store where I can get a few basics without exceeding my contactless limit.'

She nodded. 'There's no rush. We don't have to be there until late afternoon. I'll wait for you here.'

They finished their breakfast, and when Ben left in search of clothing, she Googled travel info for the castle – with a backup route, just in case of delays, even though there wasn't a speck of snow on the ground in London.

On the way back to her room, she passed the small lounge opposite the reception desk and decided to go in to see if there was a bookshelf. Reading would help kill some time until Ben returned. The walls were papered with sheet music, and it had rows of dark mahogany bookshelves. However, when she tried to pick up a dusty looking hardback, she discovered they were all fake. Just the spines of old books glued onto a board and shoved into the recess to make it look like an old-fashioned library.

However, there were also other shelves filled with ornaments and music-related objects. An instrument case lay on the shelf below. Was that fake too? She pulled it towards her and unclipped the catches. Much to her surprise, she found a real violin inside.

What had Ben said in the early hours of yesterday morning? That she'd been at a music school somewhere in this city?

Holding her breath, she ran her fingers over the strings, over the scrolling woodwork at the neck. It was just so beautiful. And there was something about it that called to her. A thought came to her, one that might solve all their problems at once.

*

Ben strolled back to the hotel with some fresh clothes and a cheap rucksack that would probably fall apart before he reached Glasgow. He still wasn't quite sure how he was going to get back to Invergarrig, but he might be able to get a coach ticket. Twice the journey time of the train, but at a fraction of the price.

The weather was cold but clear, so instead of drenching himself in exhaust fumes walking along the busy main road, he cut through Kensington Gardens, planning to exit back onto the street opposite the Albert Memorial, only a short walk to the hotel.

He'd only just entered the park when he heard music, the sweet, soulful strains of a violin drifting through the trees towards him. Curious, he veered from the path and crossed the grass towards the sound, emerging from a more densely planted area onto a wide lawn. A small, ornate bandstand stood a short distance away, a handful of people gathered around it. Ben walked round to join the back of the crowd, but when he saw who was standing on the raised platform, he almost fell over with surprise.

It was *Alice* standing up there, playing the violin.

Her eyes were closed, and she held the instrument as if she was born to do it, her body swaying and dipping with the sound. It was electrifying. He couldn't have stopped watching even if he'd wanted to.

When she finished the piece, the audience applauded. She beamed at them and bowed, as if it was completely natural for her to be standing in front of people, sharing her gift with them. He didn't know how to describe it. The best he could come up with was that, while he'd thought she was pretty wonderful, it was as if the Alice he'd known up until now had only been in black-and-white but now . . . now she was a Picasso or a Kandinsky, full of bold and bright colours. Astounding. Glorious.

And today was the last day he'd ever see her.

She spotted him and ran towards him, her face lit up. 'I had an idea to drum up some extra cash. Look . . . ' She pointed to his grey beanie hat, upside down on the floor of the bandstand, dotted with lots of coins and a few notes. 'We've definitely got enough for another ticket to Hadsborough Castle now, and I reckon if I move along to outside the Albert Hall, I could probably get even more, probably enough for your train ticket home.'

Ben stared at the hat and then the violin and then back into her bright, shining eyes. 'How did you . . . ? Where did you . . . ?'

'The violin?' She laughed. 'I found it in the hotel lounge. I asked Marco if I could borrow it.'

'You're *really* good,' he said, aware how much of an understatement that was. 'I mean, I don't know much about music, but . . . '

'I am, aren't I?' she said, glowing again. There was no hint of shyness or embarrassment about her answer, but also no arrogance. She was simply stating a fact.

'Oh, Ben,' she said, jumping back up onto the bandstand to collect the hat full of cash. 'It was wonderful! When I was playing, it was like I was flying. It was like nothing else mattered. I might not know much, but I know that *this* is who I am. This is what I love to do.' Her voice grew hoarse at the end of her sentence, and her eyes glittered with a jubilant ferocity.

Ben could hardly resist her. He wanted to kiss her so badly it hurt.

'Play something else,' he said. 'But before you do it, give me your phone.'

She shot him a puzzled look but did as he asked, and when she raised the violin and bow, he held up the phone and started to film.

'If you want memories of your trip. You're not going to want to miss this one.'

CHAPTER FIFTY

Now.

THE SUN WAS hovering low in the sky when Ben and Alice arrived, casting a golden glow over the warm sandstone bricks of what was possibly the prettiest castle Alice had ever seen. It sat on an island in the middle of the moat, reached by an arching bridge, and the vast array of tall leaded windows reflected the golds and pinks of the gathering sunset.

'It's the perfect place for a wedding,' she said, swallowing down the knot in her throat. Ben's only reply was a soft grunt.

Nothing felt real any more. She'd been on such a high after busking in Kensington Gardens earlier that day. How had her fingers known how to hold the bow and cause it to fly over the strings? But know they had, and she'd played tune after tune after tune with hardly a wrong note, her muscles remembering something her conscious brain could not. The endorphins stampeding around her system had made her feel as if she was about to explode with joy, but now, in the aftermath of all those rushing emotions, she just felt weird. As if she was watching the world go by from inside a goldfish bowl.

Hadsborough Castle . . . Getting here had been the focal point of her whole existence, it seemed, but now the moment had come, she'd rather be anywhere else on the planet. *Run*, a little voice inside her head whispered. *Just go . . .*

But she couldn't. What was she going to do? Run forever?

No. Despite the feeling that another panic attack might swallow her up at any second, she wasn't going anywhere. She was going to see this through. It was time to get the answers she could no longer avoid.

'What's the time?' she asked Ben.

'Coming up for half five.'

She nodded. Only an hour now. She could hear the seconds counting down, ticking loudly inside her head. They walked up the gatehouse that led onto the island and, with the absence of anything else to do, decided to go and look around the castle to kill some time. Anything was better than standing around just waiting.

The inside of the building was just what you'd expect – suits of armour by the dozen, spears on the wall, tapestries, and hefty oak four-poster beds, one of which Henry VIII was supposed to have slept in. Alice was happy to allow herself to be distracted by it all, but then they entered a long, panelled gallery at the far side of the castle. It had a vast stone fireplace and tall windows that looked out over the moat, which was as still as a sheet of glass, the only imperfection the V-shaped ripples trailing out from behind a pair of black swans.

It was easily one of the most picturesque rooms in the castle, but Alice went cold all over. 'Now, this is one of the locations in the castle where we hold weddings,' a guide directing a tour began to say. 'It can seat up to—'

And, just like that, Alice was striding away. She walked out of the banqueting hall, down the corridor and out onto the neat lawn catching the last glowing rays of the setting sun. A few moments later, Ben appeared beside her.

'Just . . . needed some fresh air,' she said, still not sure if that had been the reason for her swift exit, but she was awfully glad to feel the chill of the February breeze.

He nodded, and she knew he understood why she had the jitters. 'It's almost six. Do you want to cut the hanging around and go and stake out the barn?'

'That's a good plan,' she replied. 'People might arrive early, and the sooner we find someone, the better.'

They made their way off the castle island and, following the guidance of a signpost, took a path up the hill behind the castle. 'There it is,' Alice said when they'd rounded a wooded area. She could see the rough, dark-stained wood of the Tithe Barn just opposite a cluster of stone buildings. While it looked pretty ancient at first glance, when they got closer, it became clear this was a modern structure built with traditional techniques. It had a high, vaulted roof, and a whole side of the building was constructed of timber and glass instead of overlapping wooden planks.

'There's someone inside,' Alice said, as they reached the large glazed doors. 'Looks like a member of staff.' The woman wore a skirt and waistcoat the same shade of burgundy as the banner on the castle brochure, and she seemed to be inspecting the layout of tables and chairs.

Alice pulled her coat tighter around her neck. 'Shall we ask if we can wait inside?' Now the sun had set, the temperature had dropped considerably. 'I have the invitation with me – I can show them the note about the rehearsal. I wouldn't have that if I wasn't supposed to be here, would I? And, look . . .'

she pulled the brochure out of her bag. '*Hadsborough Castle – the home of chivalry and beauty*. That's got to count for something, hasn't it?'

Sadly, it turned out to mean nothing.

'Nope,' the woman inside said when Alice began her story and waved the crumpled wedding invitation at her. 'No one attends out-of-hours events except with the proper email confirmation. We can't have Tom, Dick and Harry running around the castle grounds of an evening, doing what they like.'

'But . . . You don't understand! I know the bride and groom. I might even *be* the bride. We phoned up yesterday, and the woman on the phone told us the bride had gone missing – that's me!'

The starchy looking middle-aged woman, her hair still stuck in the nineties, by the looks of the amount of hairspray on it, gave Alice a disbelieving look. 'Well, if you were the bride, madam, you'd have one of them emails, wouldn't you?'

Alice shot a look at Ben then launched into the entire story of the last week, starting with the bus stop in Invergarrig and ending up with arriving at the castle, and the longer she talked, the more sceptical the woman's expression became. 'Nice try,' she said when Alice finally ground to a halt, then she unhooked a walkie-talkie from her waist. 'Security?' she said, 'Is that Mason . . . ? Can you come to the Tithe Barn? I've got a situation . . . '

*

Ben looked across at Alice. He could just about make out her face in the moonlight. She pressed a finger to her lips. 'Shh . . . '

They both went still. Yew twigs dug into his face as he hunkered down in a corner of the castle's maze. Alice had been distraught when a bald-headed pit bull of a security guard had escorted them away from the Tithe Barn. What was she going to do if she couldn't get answers tonight? she'd said. She had no home, no family . . . Not even a full name of her own. It had to be now.

After looking at the map of the castle grounds, Ben had a pretty good idea of the layout in his head, so he'd managed to convince 'officer' Mason they wouldn't need an escort all the way to Car Park C. Once they were right on top of it, the security guard had glowered at them and had turned back, at which point, instead of making their way to their fake car and fake driving off, they'd ducked into the maze next door.

Had they come far enough inside not to be discovered? He hoped so. The plan was to wait here until just before six-thirty, then they'd make their way back to the barn. Hopefully, they'd spot someone who could vouch for Alice before they ran into another security guard.

Just as he was starting to relax, there was the sound of boots on gravel, and they heard low, gruff voices getting closer. A torch beam swung through the air somewhere near the entrance to the maze. Alice looked at him with wide eyes and pressed herself further into the corner of the hedge. There was a clank of metal, and then the footsteps retreated, and it was quiet again.

'That was close,' Alice whispered when enough time had passed. 'I thought they were going to come inside.'

Ben breathed out. 'Me too.'

Once they were sure the security patrol had gone, they

stood up. 'We could probably find our way all the way to the centre if we wanted to, even in the dark,' Alice said, glancing in the direction of a high mound with a view over the maze – the reward for anyone that reached the middle. 'Did you know that you can solve a maze by keeping one hand on the hedge at all times, either left or right, it doesn't matter which, and then you just follow it around until you find the centre?'

Ben's chest tightened. 'Yes,' he said, his words sounding a little strained, 'I did hear that somewhere.'

'Strange the things you remember, isn't it?' Alice said with a gentle chuckle. 'I can't remember where I live or if have any brothers and sisters, but I know that. I wonder where I learned it?'

All Ben could manage in return was a tight smile. While it warmed him to know that she'd remembered what he'd told her – more evidence that their time together hadn't been completely erased from her mind – there wasn't any point in mentioning it now.

But he couldn't help thinking about the last time they'd been in a maze, how she'd walked up to him and kissed him. No fear in her eyes, no doubt in her heart. It was at that exact moment that he'd known he wasn't going to fly off, never to see her again, that he'd find a way back to her. He sighed. If only history could repeat itself.

Just one kiss . . . a little voice in his head whispered. *Surely you deserve that? And she'd kiss you back. Willingly. You know that.*

Yes. But the other thing he couldn't stop thinking about was the man who'd be waiting for her at the altar in just two days' time. While he didn't know that guy, didn't owe him anything, he kept imagining it was him in that suit turning to the back of the church when the organ struck up, strangely breathless as she walked towards him . . .

How would he feel if she was his bride and she'd lost her memory before the big day? And if, while she'd been vulnerable and alone, she'd developed feelings for someone else? Not only that, but the guy had capitalised on it, encouraged it? He didn't think he had words for the rage he imagined he'd feel. So, no . . . He wouldn't be making any moves.

Because in less than ten minutes, Alice would cease to exist. She'd become Lili again, firmly cemented back into her other life. And if her memories did come back all at once, like the doctor had warned they might, she'd forget every second of the time they'd spent together. 'Alice' would merely be an echo, reverberating in no one's ears but his own.

'Come on,' he said, treading softly as he started in the direction of the gate. 'It's time.'

CHAPTER FIFTY-ONE

Two weeks before the wedding.

I RAN OUT of the front door of the building, tears streaming down my face, and gulped back a sob as I saw what was left of my precious violin. The neck had snapped from the body. The strings were curled and broken. I knelt on the freezing paving slabs in my pyjamas and began scooping the bits of wood up.

Could it be fixed? I didn't even know. It would probably cost more than a new violin to put it right, and it might never sound the same, even if that were possible, but I couldn't bear the thought of giving up on Octavia. She'd been with me through everything.

Still crying, I made my way back inside into the elevator. The lights remained off when I got back inside the flat, and Justin was nowhere to be seen. I'd have been tempted to believe it had all been a horrible nightmare, but for the evidence gathered in my hands.

I carefully laid the pieces down on the kitchen counter, then ran back to the study to get the violin case. The only thing I could think of was protecting what was left of Octavia by placing it inside, but it felt as if I was laying her out in a coffin.

I hid the case in the cupboard in the hall, then I dithered

about what to do next. I didn't want to talk to Justin. To be honest, I wanted to run away into the night and never see him again, but I also knew I couldn't leave this until morning. I couldn't let him brush over it and pretend it hadn't happened, as he'd done with so many other situations.

I heaved a breath in and headed into our bedroom. He was lying in bed, his hands behind his head, staring up at the ceiling. He didn't look in my direction, although he must have heard me open the door. I stood at the threshold, heart thudding unevenly. 'How could you do that?' I asked, my voice raw with tears.

'I didn't do anything. It was you. You lunged for the thing and knocked it out of my hand. So, if you're looking for someone to blame—'

'No.' My whole torso was trembling. 'That's not what happened.' In my mind's eye, I could clearly see Justin's fingers releasing the neck of the violin a mere split-second before my hand closed over the air where it had just been.

'It all happened so fast,' he said. 'How can you tell?'

Because I knew. I *knew*!

I just stood there, shaking my head. 'You're right. I think we *should* call the wedding off.'

That got his attention. He sat up in bed and studied me, waiting to see what I was going to say or do next. After moment or so, he got out of bed and walked towards me. He tried to pull me into his arms, but I stepped back. I couldn't bear the thought of him touching me at that moment.

'Angel . . . Come on. Do you really think I'd do something like that on purpose?'

'But you did!'

'No, my darling. You know how unreliable your memory can be . . . How you space out and do strange things, think strange things. I was just making a point. Of course, I wouldn't destroy your violin. What kind of monster do you take me for?'

'I . . . I . . . '

He tilted his head, and his expression softened. All at once, all the love, the adoration was back in his eyes. 'I'm so sorry such an awful accident happened,' he said, his voice low and lulling. 'I know how devastated you must be.'

I blinked, trying to get my eyes to focus right. Had I . . . ? Was he . . . ? I felt like I had whiplash from sliding violently out of one reality and crashing into another. Oh, I was so confused. Of course, the Justin that I knew and loved wouldn't do something like that. He was passionate and temperamental, but he was never cruel. But the man who'd dropped my violin off the balcony hadn't seemed like Justin at all.

'Do you think it can be fixed?' he asked, stepping closer. 'If not, we can get you a new one, a better one . . . '

I wanted to say I didn't want a new violin. I wanted Octavia, not how she was now, broken and smashed, but how she'd been half an hour ago. However, I couldn't get the words to come out.

Had I been wrong about what happened on the balcony? Had I imagined what I'd seen? I got so much wrong these days, and Justin was right: my memory had been terrible in the last few months. I had the number of a psychiatrist he'd given me, but I'd been too scared to book an appointment.

Justin took advantage of my paralysis and scooped me

gently into his arms, pulling me against him with just enough pressure to make me feel warm and secure, but also lightly enough that I could push away if I wanted to. He nuzzled into my neck then peppered my hair with soft, reverent kisses.

'I love you more than anything in this world,' he whispered. 'You know that's why I sometimes behave the way I do. And you do have to admit, you did push me tonight. You knew I was going to be upset, and yet you still goaded me. But I forgive you, my angel. We can make this right. I know we can.'

He began to kiss me again, but this time it wasn't the butterfly kisses he'd pressed into my hair; they were more urgent, needy. His hand slid up my hip and under my pyjama top. 'Let me show you how much I love you. Let me leave you in no doubt.'

I stood there, not exactly frozen but not exactly able to move either. It was like I was disconnected from myself somehow. Not floating above, like some people say they do. It was like there was a 'me' that was there with Justin, letting him undress me, feeling the familiar tingle of desire even after all that had happened, but also another 'me', one who was more like a blank sheet of paper, standing looking on, inside of myself and outside of myself at the same time.

She was there the whole time Justin made love to me, watching me stare past his shoulder, a confused expression on my face. If Justin noticed that I wasn't as into it as he was, he didn't say or do anything to indicate it. He just kept going as he always did, until he'd given himself – and me – what he thought we both wanted.

Afterwards, when his breathing had softened and he'd rolled away from me, the two 'me's stared at each other. They didn't say anything. They didn't have to. And then, the blank me, the empty me, nodded, then turned and walked out the door.

CHAPTER FIFTY-TWO

Now.

ALICE PEEPED AROUND the edge of the yew hedge, survey-ing the main path from near the maze entrance. 'Coast's clear.' She and Ben began walking swiftly but silently towards the gift shop courtyard. It was made up of two-storey, mock-Tudor buildings, entered by wide arches on three of the four sides. They sheltered in the shadows of the one overlooking the lawn sloping down to the Tithe Barn, about two hundred metres away.

'I can see movement inside,' Alice whispered, gesturing towards the glass-fronted building, now glowing bright in the twilight. 'More people . . . But I'm not sure if it's rehearsal guests or staff getting ready for their arrival.'

'If we make a dash for it and it's just staff in there, they might call security again, and we'll be kicked out before we get a chance to talk to any of the guests. Best to hold off for now.'

'Okay,' she replied, with more than a wobble in her stom-ach. 'In that case, we should wait until the very last moment. Then at six-thirty on the dot, it's all stations go.'

Ben nodded. 'Agreed.'

It crossed her mind that they could wait there all night

in vain. Perhaps the wedding had been called off after all? However, just after six twenty-five, they heard voices further up the path and ducked further into the courtyard, tucking themselves behind the ice cream kiosk just inside the entrance. Moments later, a group of five or six people walked past the archway, talking amongst themselves. They were followed by a slightly larger group, and then a minute or so later, a couple of stragglers brought up the rear.

Just after they passed, Alice slipped out of her ice-cream stand hiding place and back into the shadowy nook of the archway, hoping to get a closer look. She sensed Ben join her as one of them said to his companion, 'Do you think they found her yet?'

The other guy shrugged. 'Dunno . . . My gut feeling is it's all going to be called off, but we had to turn up tonight anyway and show support.'

The first guy pointed towards the front of the barn. 'There's the poor bastard, standing outside.'

A lone figure had emerged and was standing just beyond the brightly lit entrance, little more than a silhouette. He shook hands with some guests and kissed the others on the cheek before ushering them inside.

Was that him? Was that the groom? *Her* groom? Alice edged a little closer to Ben.

Another small group of guests passed them, too intent on getting to their destination to spot two people skulking in the shadows, and then it was quiet again. When the man outside the Tithe Barn had finished greeting them, he stuffed his hands into his pockets, then began to walk away from the barn, head down. He looked lonely, Alice thought, maybe even a little bit sad.

This was her chance.

Her stomach quivered. She was at a threshold, she realised. In this moment, she was Alice, the woman who'd travelled with Ben for five hundred miles, who'd cried and laughed with him, who'd pelted him with snowballs. She'd slept in unfamiliar places, hitched lifts, raced for buses, even busked within a stone's throw of Kensington Palace.

She liked being Alice, or at least who she was starting to discover this person was. But that could end in a few moments. She'd be a different woman with a different name, a different life. The thought sent a shiver through her. It would be as if Alice had died. She looked at Ben and realised there was one last thing she needed to do here, in this life, before it became only a memory.

Raising herself onto her tiptoes, she placed her hands on either side of his face, brushing the soft hair above his ears with her thumbs. His skin was warm beneath her fingers, and she heard his breath catch. Before she could talk herself out of it, she kissed him, slowly and softly, and it was exactly as she imagined it would be. Maybe even the way a part of her remembered. If only she could remember the rest. She'd do anything to have that time in London with him back.

But that was why she was here, wasn't it? To get her memory back, so with great difficulty, she eased herself away from him and let her hands fall to his chest. When she had the courage to open her eyes, she found him staring back at her. This big, capable man who always seemed to know what to do in any given situation looked completely floored.

The air around them contracted and pulsed. She couldn't look away.

'Hey! What are you two doing here? I thought I told you to—'

She whipped her head round to see Mason, the humourless security guard, striding towards them across the courtyard.

Ben grabbed her by the shoulder, a look of desperation in his eyes. 'Run!' he said. 'I'll keep him busy.' And then he took off in the opposite direction to the barn, back through the courtyard towards the advancing security guard.

Mason was taken by surprise, almost losing his balance as Ben shot past him. He looked first at her and then at the tall man sprinting away from him. Alice knew if she stayed where she was a moment longer, the guard would head straight for her – she was definitely the easier target – so before he turned back again, she did exactly what Ben asked her to do. She ran. Away from Ben and towards the man she might very well be about to marry.

*

Ben moved as fast as his legs could carry him. He veered right to miss barrelling into the security guard, then ran towards the courtyard exit leading to the moat and castle. He had to keep Alice safe.

Glancing over his shoulder, he realised with relief that the burly security guard was keeping pace behind him rather than pursuing Alice. Now, if only he could get to the . . .

Uh-oh.

Mason's cries must have alerted another member of the security team patrolling nearby because now a lanky guy in uniform was running directly towards him.

Ben shot off to the right again, which probably wasn't the best decision because it would take him back around the outside of the courtyard buildings and not into open parkland, but it was the best he'd been able to manage under pressure. As he ran, he could see the Tithe Barn in the corner of his vision. He adjusted his course. Maybe, if he could get to where Alice was, give an explanation—

'Oof!'

Something heavy hit him with force and attached itself to his lower body, dragging him to the ground. He met it so hard, his shoulder bones jiggled. Nice rugby tackle. A few seconds later, a strong pair of hands gripped his arms, and, between them, the two guards wrestled him to a standing position. He didn't care. As long as their attention was on him and not on Alice. That was all that mattered. He was prepared to cause a fuss if necessary.

'Right,' Mason said, sounding like a rather pissed-off police officer.

'Listen, I know I shouldn't be here, but if you'd just let me explain . . . ' Ben tried to move in the direction of the Tithe Barn. Alice should almost be there by now. 'I need to get to—'

Mason let out a gruff laugh. 'Leave it out, mate. The only place you're going is the security office, where I will be calling the local nick.'

As they started to drag him back towards the courtyard, he looked over his shoulder, straining to keep Alice in view as the two men lumbered him along. *Where was she? Had she made it? Had someone caught her too?*

And then he saw her, running full speed to the guy standing outside the barn. Ben couldn't hear what was going on, but the man's head snapped around as if he'd heard someone call out to him, and then, in the next moment, he launched himself at Alice, wrapping his arms around her and pulling her into a fierce and possessive hug.

Ben stopped resisting the security guards at that point. They could take him anywhere they wanted – as long as it was away from there.

CHAPTER FIFTY-THREE

Now.

ALICE HAD ONLY just reached the man standing in front of the wedding venue when he took one look at her, let out a strange, slightly strangled noise, then threw his arms around her and hugged her so hard she thought she was going to pass out from lack of oxygen.

It was the moment she'd been waiting for, but it was nothing like how she'd imagined it would be. She thought she'd feel a sense of coming home, of slotting in like a missing puzzle piece. In the back of her naive mind, she'd thought that seeing someone she knew and who knew who she was might trigger a cascade of memories, but she felt . . . nothing. Unless you counted a sore shoulder from where he was crushing her.

He was repeating the same words over and over, 'Oh, my God . . . It's you! You're back!' and then, still hugging her and dragging her with him, he started moving towards the barn and began yelling for other people to come and see.

It was only when a crowd of people had gathered around Alice that she got her first really good look at his face, too overwhelmed to process it any earlier.

Nope. Not even a flicker of recognition.

And yet, this was the night of her wedding rehearsal. She was supposed to get married in two days. What on earth was she going to do? He looked like a nice guy – very put together, very smart – but she couldn't possibly marry him this weekend.

As more people poured out of the building, there were more hugs, more shouting, more questions. Where had she been? Why had she left? Why had she scared them all stupid? She felt like she was being grabbed at by a twenty-armed octopus, and she couldn't sort one voice from another in all the cacophony. After all the emptiness in her life, the holes and silence where the memories should have been, it was too much. Her ribs drew themselves tight, making it hard to breathe. She clamped a hand over her mouth and squeezed her eyes shut.

One voice rang out over the top of all the others. 'Back off! Just back off a second!' It wasn't the groom but a woman's voice, and a second later, slender fingers curled around her wrist, gently tugging her in the direction of the now-empty barn. 'Just give us some space! Can't you see she's completely overwhelmed!'

The roar of voices dropped to a murmur, but not of grumbling, of concern. Alice opened her eyes as she was led inside, vaguely aware of a slender figure in a shift dress leading her around a corner and behind a screen. The woman pulled out a chair for Alice to sit on, and she collapsed into it gratefully, heaving in some much-needed oxygen.

Her saviour crouched beside her, waiting patiently for her to regain her composure. 'Are you okay? Do I need to call a doctor?'

'No, I don't think so. Do you . . . Do you know who I am?'

The woman's eyes widened. 'Of course I do! You're my sister! What's going on, Lil? You've been missing for almost a week, and we've all been beside ourselves trying to find you!' Her voice lowered until it was almost a growl. 'I thought that bastard had done something to you . . . I've even been to the police . . . '

Alice's throat tightened further. 'Who . . . ? What bastard?'

The other woman stopped talking and frowned hard. Alice knew this must all be very confusing to her . . . her *sister*! She was still trying to get her head around it herself. There was something this woman needed to know, something important that would explain everything. But at that very second, Alice couldn't remember what that was.

They stared at each other for a few moments and Alice realised that she didn't know this woman's name, or how old she was, or what she did for a living, but she recognised the arch of her eyebrows, the way a dimple *almost* formed in her cheek when she spoke. Because she'd seen the very same things in the mirror. This really was her sister. She threw her arms around her and began to sob.

Her sister hugged her back tightly, allowed the tears to fall until Alice got to a place where could she could speak again. Her thoughts began to gather themselves as she calmed down, arranged themselves into a sensible order. She sniffed, pulled away and looked her sister in the eye. 'I've got amnesia,' she said. 'I can't remember anything, not past last Saturday morning . . . ' And then the whole garbled story fell out of her mouth, or at least, the main plot points, all the way from Invergarrig to this fairy-tale castle in the Kent countryside.

Her sister listened with a fierce expression, and when Alice had finished speaking, she said, 'Stuff the rehearsal! We're getting you to a doctor.'

She began to stand up, but Alice grabbed her arm. 'I can't get married on Saturday! Not when I don't even know who he is!'

Her sister blinked and stared at her, even more dumbfounded than she'd been a few seconds earlier. 'Oh, God! This is really bad, isn't it? This really is real . . . Olivia, it's not you getting married on Saturday. It's me! *I'm* the bride.'

Olivia? Was that her proper name?

'You're Elodie!' she said, fitting the pieces in her brain together.

A huge smile broke out across her sister's face. 'You remember me?'

Alice shook her head. 'Where's my . . . ?' She reached down into her bag, still slung across her body, and pulled out the wedding invitation with a shaking hand. She pointed to the names embossed in gold on the front. *Elodie and Isaac*. She turned it around and showed it to her sister.

Elodie took it from her, nodding gently. 'I see . . . Although you usually call me "Lo".' She smiled before adding, 'Even though I keep asking you not to.'

'I lost my phone and my purse – or they got stolen – but this was in my bag. It was the only clue we had . . . ' She pointed to the back of the invitation, showing the time and date of the rehearsal. 'I thought if I could just get here . . . ' Her voice started to crack, and she had to pause and swallow. 'If I could just get here, then I might find somebody who knew who I was.' Tears began to fall again.

Lo dropped the invitation and slid her arms around Alice . . . Olivia's . . . neck and hugged her gently.

'You found us,' she said, her voice similarly hoarse. 'Oh my God, Lili . . . I've been so worried about you. I wanted to call the wedding off, but Isaac said we should wait, see if the police managed to find you. If we hadn't had news by lunchtime tomorrow, I was pulling the plug on the whole thing.'

Lili. In comparison to Olivia, it felt warm and comforting. It was what Ben had called her once upon a time. She would have to tell him what her real name was, so there'd be no—

Oh, God . . . *Ben!*

In the midst of all the drama, she'd forgotten all about him. She quickly explained how Ben had helped her get back home, but also that he might need a hand because the last time she'd seen him, there had been a security guard in hot pursuit. Of course, there was a lot more to the story, but that would have to come later.

'Have you got a way of getting in contact with him?'

Alice reached into her pocket and pulled out her phone. 'His aunt gave it to me.' She tried dialling, but there was no answer, which worried her, but he might be hiding from security somewhere, unable to talk. She'd try again the next moment she got a chance.

Lo peeped round the screen hiding them from the rest of the room. Alice had been aware of noises – the door opening and closing, hushed voices – as they'd been talking and had assumed the rest of the rehearsal attendees had supped back inside to get away from the cold. 'Listen, Mum and Dad are hovering . . . I'd better go and explain things to them. And then we're getting you to a hospital.'

'I was checked over already. CT scans and everything.'

'Don't care. I won't be happy until I know for sure, and

neither will Mum and Dad. Do you think you're up to seeing them?'

'They're here?' For some reason, that made her feel incredibly emotional.

Lo nodded. 'They've been in bits, Lil. I know you might not remember them, but do you think you could say "hi"? I'll warn them not to crowd you.'

Alice nodded. 'Of course.'

'I'll go and fetch them.'

Alice sat up straight and tried to make herself look a little more presentable by smoothing down her hair. A few moments later, a couple in their late fifties appeared around the screen. The woman's eyes filled with tears, but she stayed where she was, hesitant about coming closer.

'It's okay,' Alice said. 'You can have a hug if you like. I'm okay.' She could only imagine how hard it must be for them, and she would have to get used to them sooner or later. This was her family.

They both rushed forward and gathered her up in their arms. It felt a little strange being hugged so passionately by complete strangers, but not as strange as she'd expected. There was warmth and comfort, and it felt nice to be known . . . that she had people who loved and cared for her.

'I'm so glad you're safe,' her mum said softly as she stroked her hair, and her father just let out a little sob and buried his face into her shoulder.

'I am,' she said. 'And I'm home.'

*

Ben sat on a sectional office sofa in the security suite of Hadsborough Castle. It was full of grey furniture, much like any other office. If he hadn't been able to see glimpses of the formal gardens outside the window, he'd never have known it belonged to a castle.

What did you expect, idiot? Suits of armour and torture devices?

He huffed softly to himself, causing Mason, who was standing against the opposite wall, arms folded across his considerable pecs, to glower at him more sternly. Ben looked away. The local police had been called. He wasn't looking forward to talking his way out of this one.

The office door crashed open. The lanky guard who'd chased him stood in the opening. He wasn't looking very pleased. 'You there,' he said, pointing at Ben, which was a bit redundant since he was the only 'prisoner' in the room. Ben braced himself.

'You're free to go,' he said, causing Mason's eyebrows to rise halfway up his smooth forehead. 'Bride called and said it's all been a mix-up, that you're supposed to be here – friend of a friend. Or something like that.'

Thank goodness for that. Being carted off to Maidstone police station would have eaten up the time he'd much rather spend checking on Alice. He stood up and gave the lanky guard an enquiring *What happens now?* kind of look. The man just shrugged and stepped aside so Ben could pass from the inner office, through the reception area and out a narrow door that led onto the courtyard. Before his feet hit the cobbles, he was already running in the direction of the barn.

When he got there, he pushed through the door and looked around, trying to work out who the best person to speak to was, but he couldn't see anyone who looked like they might be attending a wedding rehearsal, only a couple of staff in burgundy waistcoats with the castle's logo stitched on them. 'Where's the bridal party? I need to talk to the bride.'

'Gone to the hospital with her sister and the groom,' one of them replied. 'Rehearsal's cancelled.'

Ben swore softly under his breath. Still, it wasn't an impossible hurdle. Adrenaline began to flow in his blood again, and he realised instead of feeling drained from the drama of the evening, he was feeling pumped, ready to face anything. 'Which hospital have they gone to? Maidstone?' It was the nearest big town, so the logical choice.

The woman shook her head. 'I think they said somewhere in Bromley, the Princess something . . . '

'Thanks!' he said, then turned and jogged out the barn. He began running in the direction of the castle entrance, where the bus stop was situated, keeping up a gentle pace, but by the time he'd passed the stone bridge that led onto the castle island, jogging became striding, then he eventually slowed to a halt.

What are you doing?

Running on automatic like an idiot, that was what. He'd done what he'd set out to do. He'd brought her home. And he'd seen her run into the groom's arms with his own eyes. The fact the guy hadn't cancelled the rehearsal before now confirmed he hadn't given up hope she'd come back to him. And now she had.

With Ben's help.

He didn't know if he was a saint or an idiot.

But whatever he was, it was time to take a step back, let those who had a right to be with her in the hospital. He had to stop running around acting as if Lili belonged to him.

CHAPTER FIFTY-FOUR

The day of the wedding.

JUSTIN AND I got married in the long gallery of Hadsborough Castle on a dark and stormy afternoon. Inside it was warm, the space made magical by the glow of a hundred candles. We exchanged our vows in front of the fireplace as our closest friends and family looked on, and I put all thoughts of the turbulent months leading up to that day away. This was our fresh start. From now on, everything was going to be perfect.

The day passed in a blur of confetti, laughter and camera shutter clicks. Every single photograph taken that day, even the candid ones taken by friends and family, showed us smiling or touching each other, gazing adoringly into each other's eyes.

There'd been a complete transformation in Justin the morning after Octavia had her . . . accident . . . and fell from the balcony. He'd brought me breakfast in bed and had promised he'd find a way to restore my violin to her former glory. He even called her 'Octavia', which showed how devastated he was at how things had turned out.

The next two weeks had been idyllic. He'd showered me with gifts, romantic messages, more flowers than I knew what to do with. All those things were nice, but what really helped me heal from the trauma of that night was the way he spoke to me. All the criticism, the little digs and hints that I was doing things wrong or had let him down, had stopped. All he could tell me was how much he adored me. I was firmly back on my pedestal, and my poor thirsty heart sucked up every scrap of love and affection he threw my way.

He hadn't said as much, but I guessed it was his way of saying sorry for what happened that night, of showing me how hard he was going to try to be the perfect husband. It was one mistake, I reasoned to myself. Okay, a pretty big one, but I wasn't guiltless – I *had* stayed out too late, and I should have been firmer about the strippers.

My parents were bursting with pride as I walked down the aisle. I don't think Mum stopped dabbing the corner of her eyes with a tissue all day. And even Lo played nice, being polite to Justin. I appreciated that because I knew she was doing it for me, and I hoped any rift between us was now healed.

When the wedding breakfast was over, it was time for the speeches. Justin stood up, looking very dashing in his morning suit, and smiled at the sixty or so guests gathered in the gallery. 'I knew right from the very first moment I laid eyes on Olivia that she was the one,' he said, shooting an adoring glance my way. 'I knew she was special, like no one else I'd ever met, and I knew if I didn't do everything in my power to make her mine, I was the biggest idiot in the world.'

A flutter passed through the audience as every woman there sighed in unison. I looked up at Justin, and my heart swelled. I'd promised to love him, to cherish him, to care for him in every way possible, and when he looked at me the way he was looking at me right then, it made me want to live up to every word, to sacrifice everything for him, because that was what love was, wasn't it? Losing yourself in someone else until you couldn't see where you ended and they began.

We cut our gloriously lavish cake and danced our first dance to one of Justin's favourite songs by The Police, and when the end of the night finally came, the master of ceremonies gathered everyone together so I could throw my bouquet – which Lo caught, much to her surprise. Justin and I laughed and smiled as confetti showered over us and headed for a glossy limo. I hardly noticed the hollering and cheering as the car pulled away, glad at last to be alone with him, so we really could start our fairy tale together, just as he'd promised me.

When we arrived at a luxury hotel a short distance away, deep in the Kent countryside, we were treated like royalty. Staff bowed and scraped, met our every need in hushed tones, and finally, we were alone in the massive bridal suite, a bottle of champagne on ice and rose petals strewn about the floor and over the bed.

I turned to Justin, smiling. 'Shall I open it?'

I expected him to come over, wrap his arms around me and begin kissing my neck. However, he didn't answer me. He didn't smile or even look at me. Instead, he turned and headed into the bathroom, and seconds later, I heard the shower.

Okay . . .

I considered getting out of my wedding dress, which was now feeling a little tight, and the lace around my neck was chafing, but in the last couple of weeks, Justin and I had whispered late at night about our shared fantasy about how this night would go, how we'd slowly undress each other. I'd imagined him walking over to me, a sexy smile on his face, and then painstakingly undoing the covered buttons at the back of my dress, kissing my spine until he reached the curve of my back and slid it from my hips before I got to work on taking his tie off, undoing his shirt, and spreading my palms beneath the cotton.

I sat down on the end of the bed, crossing my legs to arrange my skirt pleasingly, leaning back a little so I could use my arms to keep myself from slumping onto the mattress. I was tired, but it wouldn't be long now. If our fantasy came true, it would be worth the wait.

So I sat there, and I waited, and I waited.

Just as I thought I was about to nod off, the bathroom door opened. I realised I'd wilted a little, so I pulled myself up straight, sucked my stomach in and smiled at him. Not a beaming, gushing kind of smile, more of a 'come over here and see what I've got for you' kind of smile.

He was wearing one of the hotel bathrobes, which gave me a bit of a start, but I reasoned it had been a long day, and he'd probably forgotten what we'd talked about. It didn't matter, I told myself. It would still be wonderful.

He walked towards me but didn't smile back. As he neared me, I stood up, offering myself up like a delectable present he could unwrap.

'I thought you'd have that thing off by now,' he said, looking me up and down. There was no hint of the sexy frisson in his tone I'd imagined would accompany any mention of getting naked this evening. And before I could reply, he turned and headed off to the well-stocked bar, bypassing the champagne bucket, and poured himself a large brandy. Then he looked back at me and saw me frozen to the spot, staring at him. 'What?'

A sliding sensation began in my stomach. I refused to acknowledge it. Not now. Not tonight. Everything was going to be perfect tonight. He'd promised! I'd married him, showed him how committed I was to him. He'd said it would make all the difference. What more did I have to do?

He nodded towards the bathroom. 'Your turn.' Then he walked into the living room of the suite and turned on the television.

I stood there for a moment, unsure of what to do. It was crucial I took the right approach. We were on a knife-edge, but I might still be able to rescue the evening if I played it right.

My first thought was to go out there, to lean over the back of the sofa, put my arms around him from behind and kiss his neck, but I discounted it. 'Your turn' might have sounded like a piece of useful information – bathroom's free! – but I knew it was a request. An expectation. And doing what Justin wanted when he was feeling tetchy always went better than following the script running inside my own head. When I came up with my own lines, he always got more upset. I'd been with him long enough now to know how to follow his stage directions, to say what he needed me to say to make everything nice again so, incorporating a few contortionist moves, I undid my own buttons with trembling fingers and had a quick shower.

When I emerged, the television was off, and Justin was in the bedroom, a single reading light illuminating the room from his side of the bed. My heart rate accelerated. It had worked. He was back with me . . . He was ready to start our honeymoon properly.

He glanced fleetingly at me, slipped off his robe and climbed between the sheets, then flicked the light switch, plunging the room into darkness.

I stood there for a moment, unsure of what to do, and then I peeled back the duvet, sat down on the edge of the mattress and started to get into bed.

'What do you think you're doing?' His voice wasn't low and sexy but hard and crisp, the same tone he used on the dancers in his company when they weren't getting things right.

I froze, one leg planted on the floor, one foot under the covers. 'I'm . . . I'm coming to bed.'

'I'm not sure I can cope with that tonight, Angel.'

I slid my leg in a little further, steadying myself with one hand as I prepared to scoot the rest of my body under the covers. 'It's okay . . . If you're too tired, we don't have to do anything but cuddle.' I kept my voice smooth and light and soothing, hiding my disappointment. 'There's always the morning, and we've got the rest of our lives to—'

'Don't play innocent with me. You know exactly how you ruined our wedding night.'

'I . . . No. Justin, what are you talking about?'

He let out a hard, barking laugh. 'You want me to spell it out for you? I saw you, Angel. I saw you talking to *him*. Laughing and smiling. You even touched him!'

Him? Oh . . .

'Do you mean Sam?' I vaguely remembered saying hello to him and the rest of his family. He'd leaned in to kiss me on the cheek, just as his brother and his parents had, and maybe

I'd placed my hand on his elbow as he did so, but I really couldn't remember.

'Of course I mean him! Or were there other men in the room you'd slept with too. Are you really that much of a slut?'

His words silenced me as effectively as a slap. My jaw tightened, and I glared at him in the darkness. 'I can't believe you just said that to me! On our wedding night!'

'I can't believe you flirted with another man on our wedding day!'

I sat there, mouth open. I'd wounded *him*? Well, he'd definitely got me back for that, and there was no way I was having sex with him tonight, not even if he got down on his knees and begged me.

I moved the leg that was dangling off the edge of the bed towards the floor and flumped down hard on the mattress beside him, turning away from him.

'No.' The word left an imprint in the silence that followed.

I ignored him.

I was just pulling the duvet up to tuck under my chin when he spoke again. 'No. You can't sleep here. I can't share a bed with you after the way you've made me feel.'

'But . . . ' I rolled over and looked at his back.

'You need to get out.' He said it so softly, so calmly, that at first I thought I must have misheard him. 'Now,' he added, and this time there was steel beneath his words. In my mind, I saw a flash of the man he'd become on the balcony two weeks earlier. The stranger.

I was so shocked that I did what he said. Before I'd even had time to analyse how to respond, I was on my feet, legs and arms suddenly cold.

What did I do now? I couldn't go down and ask hotel reception if they had another room – it would be too humiliating. Besides, I hadn't got a credit card or money to pay for one. Justin took care of all of that. 'But where will I—'

'There's a perfectly serviceable bathroom in this suite, but don't use the sofa – I have a feeling I won't be able to sleep much, so I might want to get up and watch TV.' His words were as empty and passionless as if he was ordering a coffee, less so, maybe, because he always charmed the baristas at his favourite cafés, especially the young, pretty, female ones.

I opened my mouth to protest, but he reached out to my side of the bed, grabbed a pillow and flung it in my direction. It dropped onto the floor beside me. I picked it up and stared at his silhouette in the darkness. My prince charming, the love of my life, my groom . . .

And then I hugged the pillow to myself, turned and walked towards the bathroom.

CHAPTER FIFTY-FIVE

Now.

IT WAS FAR too hot in the hospital, so Alice took her coat off and laid it on the trolley next to her. She still couldn't quite get used to thinking of herself as 'Lili', even if her sister kept calling her that. She and Lo were sitting inside a cubicle in the Accident and Emergency Department. Lo's fiancé and their parents were outside in the big waiting area near reception.

Lo had insisted they drive slightly farther to the Princess Royal University Hospital in Bromley, saying that if Alice was kept overnight, it was much closer to where their parents lived in Penge. It was a large, modern hospital with a dizzying amount of floors and corridors and so many people.

'You really ought to go and be with Isaac,' Alice told Lo. 'I'll be fine on my own, or someone else can sit with me.'

'No,' Lo said from where she was sitting on a hard plastic chair on the other side of the cubicle. 'I'm staying right here.'

'Okay.' From what Alice had gleaned on the car journey here, Lo had spearheaded the search for her, almost cancelling her wedding, so if her sister wanted to stay, she could stay. 'Can I ask you something?'

'Sure. Fire away.'

Alice frowned, gathering her thoughts. 'Back at the castle, you said you thought "the bastard" had done something to me. What did you mean?'

Lo sighed heavily and ran a hand through her wavy, high-lighted hair. 'I'd spare you this if I could, but it's probably better that you know. I wouldn't want him using this situation to reel you back in, especially not after recent events.'

Alice swallowed. This did not sound promising.

'You were married. And he wasn't a good guy.'

'I was married?' Just the idea of it made her stomach roll, reminding her of how she'd felt on the concourse of Glasgow station.

'But it's okay. You're doing better now. You're not with him any more.'

'I'm divorced?'

Lo nodded. 'You moved out more than a year ago.'

Her throat was dry, and it was getting hard to swallow. 'Why did I leave him? Or did he leave me?'

'You left him. After four years together. Three as his wife.'

Alice absorbed that, then asked, 'You mentioned that you thought he might have hurt me. Was he . . . Was he abusive?'

'Not in the physical sense but, like I said, he wasn't a good guy, and even though your divorce was made final a month ago, it hasn't prevented him from causing trouble. Recently, he—' Lo stopped herself, abandoned the hard plastic chair and came to sit on the trolley beside her. 'Listen . . . I know you said you've been checked over and everything, but the story of your marriage . . . Well, it's *a lot*. I'd really rather wait to say more about Justin until after we've seen the doctor. Does that make sense?'

Alice nodded. Unfortunately, it did.

Justin. She'd had a husband called Justin. And yet she had no memory of him. But from what Lo had said, maybe that wasn't a bad thing. 'Do you really think he has something to do with what happened to me?'

'We don't know what happened to make you leave. You'd filed for an injunction against him, which he definitely wouldn't have taken lying down, but you disappeared before I could ask you how he'd reacted to being served.' Lo paused, looking stricken. 'When you first went missing, I . . . I wondered if it was my fault.'

'Why would you think that?'

'Because of where Isaac and I decided to have our wedding.'

'The castle?'

Lo buried her face in her hands momentarily before looking back at Alice. 'Oh, God, Lil . . . I'm so sorry about this . . . How do I even say it?' She grimaced. 'You had your wedding there too. Well, not exactly in the same place – Justin could afford the banqueting hall inside the castle. But Isaac had his heart set on Hadsborough, and I asked if you minded, and you said no problem, go ahead. But I had this little niggle telling me it was a bad idea. I should have listened to it . . . But by the time I'd realised it was the wrong call, it was too late to back out.'

'It's okay . . . If I told you it was fine, there's no way you could have known it wasn't.'

Her sister looked so guilty that Alice reached across and covered her hand with her own. 'This was not your fault. I wish I could tell you what set me off, but until my memory returns, *if* it returns . . . I won't be able to shed any light on that.'

'You disappeared after my hen night. But nothing out of

the ordinary happened. We drank cocktails, we danced, and then went home. But then the next day, you didn't answer any of my calls or texts, so by the day after that, I'd begun to get worried. I've got a spare key to your place, so I went around and let myself in. Everything looked as it should be, but you weren't there, and no one at your work had seen you. That's when I called the police. They found some CCTV of you walking down Beckenham High Street about six o'clock on Friday morning. You had a jacket on, and you were wearing jeans and carrying that bag.'

As Lo said this, Alice saw a picture of herself digging her hands in her jacket pockets as she entered Beckenham station. This was quickly followed by another 'flash' – being on the Underground, hanging onto an overhead rail, letting the sway of the train lull her as it raced through the tunnels.

'I remember that! I've been having these images in my head sometimes. At first, I wasn't sure if they were memories, but I'm getting more and more convinced they are.'

Lo's eyes lit up. 'Do you think that means your memory is coming back?'

'I don't know, but . . . Oh, God, I hope so.'

At that moment, a young female doctor appeared around the curtain. 'Now,' she said, looking Alice up and down. 'Why don't you tell me what the problem is?'

*

Alice sat on the edge of the bed in a clean, bright room on one of the upper floors of the hospital, having just signed the paperwork so she could be discharged. Last night, she'd had another round of tests similar to those she had in Lochgilphead, and when the consultant psychologist arrived on her morning rounds, she'd referred Alice to the memory unit at Imperial College London and said that she was free to go home, although it would be good if she wasn't on her own for a few days. Her parents had very kindly said that she could stay with them. They seemed genuinely sweet people, but it was going to be very odd sharing a house with complete strangers.

At least now she'd been given a clean bill of health, Lo would stop talking about cancelling the wedding. She could manage being a bridesmaid, couldn't she? All she had to do was stand around and smile for bit, hold some flowers, eat a nice meal . . . She'd be fine tomorrow. Probably.

She wished Ben were here. He was always such a good sounding board, always made so much sense. Where was he? Back at Marco's hotel? She'd meant to call him last night, but she'd dropped instantly into a deep and dreamless sleep as soon as she'd been brought up to her room in the early hours of the morning.

She took her phone off the nightstand and dialled his number, but it went straight to voicemail. 'Hi,' she said when the beeps had finished. 'I'm at the hospital, but I'm getting ready to go home. It *was* my family, as security probably told you. My mum and dad were there. My sister, Lo – that's short for Elodie – insisted on taking me to get checked over, even though I'd already told her I'd been given a clean bill of health – well, except for the memory loss, that is.'

She was rambling, but it was just so nice to let it all spill out to someone who knew her, *really* knew her.

'I know my full name, Ben. I know who I am. I'm Olivia Jasmine Everett, and I live in Beckenham, but everyone calls me Lili. My family would love to meet you, to say thank you for coming all that way with me, for bringing me home to them. Lo has invited you to the evening reception tomorrow. If you can make it, of course.'

Her pulse quickened at the thought. There was nothing to stop her and Ben being together now. As far as she understood it, she was completely and utterly single. Hope began to float like a helium balloon inside her chest.

'Anyway, no worries about dressing up too much – Lo knows you've lost your wallet and didn't come prepared to go to a wedding, so, um . . . text me back, or call me and we'll sort out the details . . . '

She hung up, then stared at the blank magnolia wall of her hospital room. There was nothing to do now but wait for her parents to bring the car around to the front of the hospital.

Her phone was in her hand, so she opened up the camera roll and scrolled through all the photos and videos she'd taken over the last couple of days. It was only when she got to the most recent ones that she realised she hadn't made any entries in her travel journal since she and Ben had been hiding in the maze at Hadsborough Castle. A whole chunk of the story was missing.

She held the phone up, switched to video mode, stared at herself on the screen and began to record. 'Lili? Hi. This is you. The other you. There are a few things I need to tell you . . . '

CHAPTER FIFTY-SIX

Now.

BEN WOKE UP feeling as if he'd been hit by a truck. He blinked, rubbed his eyes and reached for his phone. Seeing the time on his lock screen woke him up pretty fast. Half-past ten? He never usually slept that late. However, yesterday had not been a very usual day, and it had been past four when he'd finally dozed off.

He'd just pushed himself up to rest against the headboard when his phone rang in his hand. FaceTime from Norina. 'Hey, there, sleepyhead,' she said, quickly taking in his dishevelled state. 'How'd it go?'

Ben hid a yawn with his hand. 'Yeah, sorry I didn't get back to you. It was a bit of a crazy—'

'Ben!' His aunt gave him a look he knew was not best to ignore.

'Sorry. The news is . . . Mission accomplished. Alice is reunited with her family, and I'll be heading home later today.'

Norina blinked. 'That's it?'

'What more do you want me to say? I mean, I can fill you in on all the details later when my brain's decided to remember what being awake is, but that's basically what happened.'

'You're not seeing her again before you come back?'

Urgh. This was one of the downsides of video calling. His face had probably already given him away. 'No. It's probably for the best if I don't.'

Norina frowned. 'I thought maybe you liked her.'

Ben shifted position and sighed. After a long while, he said, 'I do . . . But it turns out she's engaged to someone else. Not much I can do but let her go back to her life, and I'll go back to mine.'

'Och, that's too bad.'

'Yeah . . . '

'Uncle Ben!' A small face appeared on the screen, one with large glasses and an even bigger gap in her bottom front teeth than when he'd left. 'Look! My second tooth fell out!' She brandished the item in question so close to the screen that all Ben could see was a blurry white lump.

He grimaced. 'Wonderful!'

'That means the tooth fairy is going to come tonight! Do you think we can catch her? I'd really like to have a fairy of my own!'

He did his best to keep a straight face. There was something wonderful about Willow's unwavering optimism, given all she'd been through. Sometimes he thought he was certain to learn more from her as she grew up than she'd learn from him. 'I don't think we can. I mean, it wouldn't be fair to keep her locked up. And if you did, nobody gets visits from the tooth fairy any more. Not even you!'

'Good point,' Willow said seriously. 'I'm going to go and put this under my pillow right now, just to make sure everything's ready for tonight.' And she disappeared from view before he could yell, 'Bye . . . Love you . . . '

'That child,' Norina said, shaking her head. 'Anyway, I was going to say I'm sorry that things didn't work out with Alice. But this week has been good for you, so it wasn't all for nothing.'

'It has? How?'

'I've heard the "old" you on the phone since you left. Full of energy, enjoying life. I'd started to wonder where that guy had gone. It's been long enough now since your sister passed to maybe see a glimpse of him again. You know, you came home to Invergarrig to be Willow's guardian, but that doesn't mean you have to put your own life on hold. You have to find some way to stop punishing yourself for what happened to Cat.'

Ben exhaled. 'That's what Alice said to me.'

'Memory or no memory, that girl has her head screwed on right.'

'I know you're both right, but I can't get away from the fact that if I hadn't been absent so much, if I hadn't jumped ship and moved away at the first opportunity, things might have been different for Cat.'

Norina gave him a sympathetic look. 'It probably did have some impact, but you can't carry the burden of what happened to her all by yourself. I never did like my brother-in-law – warned my sister she shouldn't have married him – but he was the key player, the culprit, in this scenario. And although she stood up to him, did her best to protect the two of you, I never understood why your mum didn't leave him, so I suppose she had a part to play too. And Cat made her own choices. It wasn't you who put the needle in her arm, Ben.'

'No, but I feel like I set the stage so it was easy for her to do.'

'You only remember the fact that you left home at eighteen,

but you conveniently forget all the times you were home, all the times you made her clean up her act, or gave her money for rent and food, even making her do a will for Willow. I lost count of the girlfriends who got fed up and walked away because you always put Cat first. You were *always* helping your sister.'

'But not that last time, not when she really needed it, when it might have made all the difference.'

'We'd tried for years to help her, and you know that *not* setting boundaries only did more harm than good. Even if you had given her that money, it wouldn't have changed anything. It just would have delayed it.'

He looked at his aunt bleakly. 'That night, when she came to see me to ask for the cash, she got so angry. It was the last time I saw her.' His throat tightened. 'She told me I was just like *him* . . . my father.' He refused to call that man 'Dad'.

'I want you to get that out of your head, you hear me? You are nothing like that waste of space! Ben Robertson, you are a good and kind and loyal man. Willow is lucky to have you as her stand-in father.'

Ben looked away, aware that his eyes were stinging. He trusted Norina's opinion and hearing her confirm what Alice had told him made something break free inside him.

'We all feel responsible for Cat,' Norina said huskily. 'We all wish we could have done more, but in the end, the choice to change was in her power, not ours.'

'I know,' Ben whispered, and for the first time, he felt the truth in those words, rather than just telling himself they were right.

'And as for Willow . . . You can see for yourself how much

that little girl adores you. If there's one thing I'm certain of, it's that you're never going to let her down.'

'Thanks,' he said, swallowing a lump in his throat, and then, because it was getting all too emotional for him, he added, 'Anyway . . . I'd better go and find out about train times. I'll call you again when I've got more details.'

'Aye, you'd better,' his aunt said, her expression more playful than her tone. 'My car is still stuck in Glasgow, and I'd really like to know when I can have it back!'

Oh, God . . . He'd forgotten all about that. 'I am *so* sorry.' Thank goodness, he'd left it in a little side street with no meters. 'I'll be back – with the car – on Sunday.'

He said his goodbyes and rang off, meaning to jump out of bed and get properly dressed, but as he went to lay his phone back on the bedside table, he noticed he had a voicemail waiting for him.

He pressed the right series of buttons to listen to the message, and the sound of Alice's voice hit him like a punch in the gut. She sounded sweet and happy and excited.

'I'm at the hospital, but I'm getting ready to go home. It was my family, as security probably told you. My mum and dad were there. My sister, Lo – that's short for Elodie – insisted on taking me to get checked over . . .'

Elodie. The name snagged Ben's attention as the message ran on. There was something important about that. A second later, he was jumping out of bed. 'She's not Elodie!' he shouted to nobody in particular.

That had been the name on the invitation! Elodie and Isaac . . . Alice's *sister* was the bride! It took all he had not to run out of the room in his T-shirt and boxers, grab the first person he saw and tell them the good news. With shaking fingers, he dialled Alice's number. 'Hi,' he said when she picked up. 'How're you doing?'

'Better now you've called.' He could hear the smile in her voice, and it put one on his face too.

'You're not Elodie,' he said because those seemed to be the only words in his head at that moment.

She laughed gently. 'No, I'm not. And I'm definitely not getting married any time soon. I'm disgustingly single.'

Not for long if I have anything to do about it.

'When can I see you? Can I come today?'

Alice sighed. 'I would love that so much, but because my sister's maid of honour did a disappearing act, the bride is a bit behind with wedding prep. The least I can do is pitch in this afternoon. But you can come tomorrow evening. Did you hear my message?'

'I did. And I'll be there. I promise.'

The same words he'd said the last time they'd arranged to meet. And this time, she'd be there too.

PART III

CHAPTER FIFTY-SEVEN

Two years since the wedding.

I OPENED THE front door to the flat, only narrowly avoiding dropping the huge arrangement of flowers I'd just picked up from the florist. I hurried down the hall to the kitchen, where I put the floral display on the counter, shrugged my coat off and replaced it with an apron. Justin had invited a select group of arty friends for a dinner party that evening, and although it was only early afternoon, I wanted to get the boeuf bourguignon underway.

I'd just got around to braising the baby onions when I heard the front door open, and I held my breath. I could never tell what kind of mood Justin was going to be in when he got home, which always left me unsure which version of myself I should be. Some days, he'd surprise me, being the man I fell in love with: charming, sexy, attentive . . . but those days were getting fewer and fewer. More often, he was moody, spoiling for a fight before his key hit the lock. As I heard his footsteps getting closer, I pasted on the serene smile and tried to look both happy and non-threatening.

'Good morning?' I asked as he came up behind me and looked over my shoulder.

'Where have you been?'

His tone wasn't harsh, but it wasn't exactly happy either. Sometimes, I wondered if it wasn't easier when he shouted and screamed right from the get-go. At least I knew where I stood then.

I twisted my head to meet his gaze. 'Right here, getting the dinner underway.'

'I meant before that.'

'I went to get the flowers.' I pointed to the vase sitting on the counter. He'd specified white lilies, and they were definitely white lilies – I hadn't got it wrong, had I? Although I'd written it down the moment he'd said it, suddenly I was second-guessing myself.

He flicked a glance in their direction and then looked back at me. 'The florist is two-point-three miles away. That's a round trip of four-point-six miles. The mileometer on your car says you drove five-point-three miles today. Where else did you go?'

I stared back at him with wide eyes and lied. 'N-nowhere.'

Even though there were some really fabulous florists in Kensington, Justin always insisted on using a place in Mayfair on the other side of Hyde Park. I knew he used my phone's location details to check where I was sometimes, so when I'd picked up the flowers, I'd slipped into the café next door to have a macchiato, even though I hadn't asked his permission to do so. I'd hoped that would be close enough to make it seem I was still at the florist and it definitely wouldn't have affected the mileometer. 'Roadworks along Park Lane meant I had to take a detour.' I felt guilty even though I was telling the truth. Traffic had been awful on the way back. 'I ended up circling north of the park instead of south.'

He made an acknowledging grunt. 'I think my taxi ran into the same jam. You'd have been better off cutting through the park rather than going all the way around.'

There was no point in telling him that there'd been a huge queue of cars trying to do just that; his suggested route had been just as busy. That would be seen as arguing back. I smiled back at him. 'Of course . . . I should have thought of that.'

But my words did nothing to soothe him. If anything, I could see his hackles rise further. He was in the mood to find fault and I'd spoiled a promising opportunity with a perfectly reasonable traffic jam.

He glanced around the kitchen. I could tell he was scanning for an outlet for his frustration and I held my breath as he momentarily studied the flowers then moved on. Phew. Eventually, his gaze landed back on me. Cooking always made me hot, and I could see him taking in the wisps of hair that had started to curl in the heat, the slight sheen to my skin. 'Do you have to wear *that*?'

I flinched inwardly but took care not to let it show. 'I'll take the pinny off when I'm finished cooking.' He hated that I wore one, but he hated it even more if I got drips and splashes on any of my beautiful clothes. But then I realised he wasn't staring at my attire but at the little silver bee dangling just above the top of my apron.

'I don't even know why you hang onto it. It's ugly. You have much nicer pieces.'

I suppose I did. All things he'd bought me. Apart from this pendant, nearly every other bit of jewellery I'd owned before we'd got married had gone. Justin had quite a thing about ownership.

'I'm going to change before dinner anyway. I was thinking I'd wear the necklace you got me for Christmas,' I said smoothly. 'It's stunning, and it'll go well with the dress.' White chiffon. Also new. Also picked by Justin.

He nodded, but his eyes remained trained on the silver necklace. 'Who gave that to you?' It wasn't the first time he'd asked.

I glanced away. 'I already told you. Lo gave it to me.'

'Oh, Angel . . . ' His tone was light, almost teasing. He waited for me to look back at him. 'I can always tell when you're lying. It means something to you. You'd have disposed of it by now if it didn't. And that can only mean one thing – another man gave it to you.'

I shook my head gently.

'And not just any man, but a lover.'

I swallowed.

'It was him, wasn't it? That boy . . . '

I still couldn't believe he was going on about my old next-door neighbour almost two years after our wedding. I hadn't seen Sam, hadn't even *thought* about him since that day, but it didn't seem to make a difference. 'No. Sam never gave me anything.'

I wasn't going to admit there was another man in my past. It would only give him twice the amount of ammunition. But Justin was right about one thing – this pendant did mean something to me. And it wasn't about the man who had given it to me. I'd kept it because it reminded me of who I'd once been, someone I seemed to have lost.

When we'd parted, Ben had said the charm would help me find my way back to him, but when I'd thought back to what he'd actually said about bees, I'd realised he'd said they could always find their way home, and I'd decided it meant I'd find my way back to *me*, the girl Justin had fallen in love with, the one who'd been full of potential and possibility.

I hadn't picked up a violin since before our wedding and losing my music had meant more than losing a career. Who was Lili? I didn't even know any more. So, on days when I felt my identity blurring around the edges, I slipped this necklace on as a tangible reminder that I had once been more than I was now.

'It was a present from Lo,' I repeated.

Justin shook his head. 'I just told you I can tell when you're not being honest with me.' His hand shot out and closed around the pendant, tugging at it hard. 'Do you think I'm going to let you laugh in my face like this! Take it off! Take it off now.'

The fine chain dug into the back of my neck as we struggled for possession. 'Justin! You're hurting me!'

'You're hurting yourself, Angel. If you'd just let go, this would all be over.' And then, with one swift twist of his hand, he yanked and the skin at the back of my neck stung as the clasp dug in then gave way.

Justin backed away, the necklace in his hand, a triumphant expression on his face. 'I'm putting this cheap tat where it belongs,' he said, dropping the necklace inside the kitchen bin.

'No!' I shrieked, running forwards, but he moved to block my way.

'Don't even think about it.'

I froze, eyeing him carefully. I knew better than to ignore that smooth tone.

'After this little display, I'm not so sure I believe you about going to the florist's. Another lie, probably.'

'But the flowers are right there. I—'

'And you know what it means when you go out without permission . . . '

I stood there, shaking my head. *Please, no,* I begged silently as he turned and walked towards the front door.

'Our dinner party is ruined,' he said over his shoulder, 'and I'm going out. I don't even want to look at you at the moment. And while I'm gone, you can call our guests and tell them not to come.'

I ran after him, hoping to reach the front door before it could slam behind him, but I couldn't match his stride. My fingers closed around the handle as I heard the lock turn a second time. 'No!' I shouted, beating my palm against the door. 'Justin . . . you don't have to do this! You don't have to lock me in!'

His muffled voice came from behind the door. 'Unfortunately, I do, Angel. You've proved once again that you can't be trusted.'

*

My feet were cold. And wet.

I looked down and saw that the heels of my stilettos were half-submerged in dank, brown mud. Murky water lapped at my toes.

Where was I?

I shivered and wrapped my arms around myself. The sky was the colour of brushed steel and a fine mist hung in the air over the river. I could see the dome of St Paul's above the rooftops on the opposite shore, which meant I was . . . on the *south* side of the river? I turned to find myself at the edge of a muddy and rocky beach, nestled beneath the unmistakable concrete and glass of the South Bank Centre.

I didn't remember leaving the flat, let alone how I'd got there.

I patted myself down, checking for injuries, taking inventory. I was wearing the same clothes, minus the apron. No coat. My hand flew to my chest and I found a comforting lump of bee-shaped metal there. I raised my hand and rubbed the raw skin at the back of my neck. I must have pulled the pendant out of the bin after Justin had left. As I explored the chain with my fingers, I realised it was another one from my jewellery box, longer and finer than the original.

I didn't remember doing any of that that either.

My stomach hollowed out and I feared I would vomit.

It had happened again, hadn't it?

I carried on my self-check and found my phone in my right trouser pocket and a small silver key in my left. Well, that explained how I'd got out.

For at least six months, Justin had taken to locking me in the flat if I did something he didn't like, or if he even *suspected* I might. Given the level of his paranoia, it was becoming a pretty frequent occurrence.

But yesterday the cleaner had left her key on the kitchen counter. I'd been about to call after her, but then I'd stopped and stashed it quickly and silently in my pocket. It was the miracle I'd been waiting for – freedom, a means of escape.

The momentary warmth caused by finding the key evaporated. Standing there, shivering beside the Thames, I was scared. What if I had a brain tumour? What if there was something seriously wrong with me? Normal people didn't do this kind of thing, did they?

As if to add weight to the suspicion, a voice called out from the concrete embankment beyond the beach. 'You all right, love?'

I turned to see a middle-aged couple, foreheads creased in concern, leaning over the railing. I stared back at them, jaw frozen shut, unable to answer even that simple question. The woman headed down the steps leading to the beach. I watched her get closer and closer, my toes feeling the cold lap of river water. I still hadn't moved.

'Looks like the tide's coming in,' she said nervously when she got close. 'We saw you standing there and, well, we thought you were about to . . . um . . . that you might need a bit of help.' In that very British way, she'd said both nothing and everything. She must have thought I was about to walk into the dirty waves, ready to blot everything out.

I should have been horrified at that realisation, but the idea didn't shock me. Quite the reverse. I realised how simple the plan seemed, how beautifully efficient.

That wasn't normal either, was it?

'Are you okay?' she asked again, her voice soft with concern.

'No,' I croaked back. 'I don't think I am.'

'Do you need . . . ? I mean . . . ' She glanced at her husband. 'Is there someone we can call for you?'

'No,' I said shakily. 'I've got my . . . ' My phone. I had my phone with me.

I clamped my hand over my mouth. How could I have been so stupid? I slid my hand inside my pocket and pressed the button to turn it off, hoping Justin hadn't checked my location as he often liked to do. If he found out I'd left the flat, he'd want to know how I got out, and then what was I going to do? He'd make me tell him about the key and any hope I had of escaping, living a normal life, would be gone! I began to shake, my ribs squeezing inwards, preventing me from drawing a full breath.

I realised I was on the verge of having a panic attack, but instead of letting the terror consume me, I began to get that floaty feeling again, the one that allowed me to stand outside myself. I watched myself gulping in breaths, the concerned look of the other couple exchanging glances, unsure of what to do, and in that instant, I knew without a shadow of a doubt that even with a 'miracle' key in my possession, this was not 'normal life' at all. It wasn't even close.

Like a rubber band pulled too tight, I snapped back into myself. 'Do you think I could borrow your phone?' I asked the woman, not wanting to risk turning mine back on.

She nodded warily but passed it over to me.

'Thank you,' I said, my heart full of gratitude and relief as I dialled Lo's number, even though she was probably at work and might not pick up. I almost cried when she did, even though we hadn't spoken in almost eight months. 'It's me . . . '

'Lil?' she said warily.

'Yes . . . ' I broke off and choked back a sob.

'What's wrong?'

Hot tears fell down my face. She didn't sound angry with me at all, just concerned. 'Can I . . . Can I come and stay with you?' She'd moved into a lovely flat in Bromley a year ago and had told me I had first dibs on her spare bedroom if ever I needed it.

'Of course.' There was a softness in her tone and not even a hint of *I told you so*. I wanted to hug her so badly it hurt. 'I'm taking a half-day and going home right this second.' I could hear keys jangling. 'I'll be in when you get here. And Lili?'

'Yes?'

'You're going to be safe with me, I promise.'

CHAPTER FIFTY-EIGHT

Now.

ALICE CLUTCHED A bouquet of white roses interspersed with delicate green ferns and heather and tried to look as if she was relaxed and comfortable and happy. Lo and Isaac's wedding ceremony had gone ahead as planned. She looked at her sister, radiant in her gorgeous gown, as guests threw confetti over the pair of them, and the photographer snapped away, catching every moment.

People kept coming up to her – strangers – and kissing her affectionately on the cheek, saying how well she looked but, thankfully, there'd been too much hustle and bustle for a proper conversation with anyone. Close family knew about her disappearance and amnesia, but no one else. She kept trailing around, doing her best to play the part of an ecstatic sister, but she couldn't help feeling like a fraud, like she was the understudy who'd been rolled in because the real maid of honour couldn't make it.

Bit by bit, her memories were coming back, the 'flashes' occurring with growing frequency. A sound or a smell, a place, or a turn of phrase could set one off. Sometimes they arrived with no obvious trigger. While she was pleased she was making progress, she also couldn't wait for the process to be over so that she could feel like a whole person again.

Her bridesmaid's dress was dark-green velvet, with a V-neck, long sleeves and a sweeping skirt, but the best thing about it was that it had pockets. She slid her fingers between the folds of the fabric and closed them around her phone, just to make sure it was still there and she hadn't lost it. Not the mobile belonging to Lili Everett, but the one Norina had given her.

This phone held her life as she knew it. She'd added to her video diary, talking herself through the different photographs and the events of the previous week, recording every little detail she could remember about Ben. Just in case.

While the photographer took a couple of shots where Alice wasn't needed, she took the opportunity to check for new messages. There was just one: *Only four hours now.*

I can't wait, she texted back, grinning, but then had to quickly put her phone back in her pocket because she was being called back for more formal group shots, but as she stood beside Lo and Isaac, different groups of family and friends coming and going, she let her mind drift.

Lo had mentioned that she'd had her own wedding here, in this very castle. She wondered if she'd stood in this very spot, if she'd been the one wearing the wedding dress, smiling blissfully at her groom.

No, not here.

The information arrived in her head silently and easily, as if it had always been there rather than locked away and missing for the past week.

It had rained that day, making the skies dark and gloomy.

She and Justin had posed for their photographs in front of the ornate fireplace in the banqueting hall inside the castle, surrounded by extravagant flowers and a million candles.

She grabbed onto the sleeve of the person next to her.

'You okay, hun?' her cousin Kerry asked. 'You've gone as white as a sheet.'

No, she wasn't. She wasn't okay in the slightest because that one concrete memory had started a chain reaction. On the outside, she was perfectly still, but on the inside, everything was churning.

Her current memories were new and fresh, like writing in wet sand, and the tide of her old ones surged in like a tsunami. And when the giant wave of knowledge retreated, the shore beneath was smooth and flat, scrubbed clean of anything that had been there before.

CHAPTER FIFTY-NINE

One year after the separation.

EVEN WITH THE bass beat thudding through my body, I could feel the buzz of my phone in my pocket. A missed call. I'd already had more than twenty this evening. I tried to pretend it hadn't happened, tried to move my body to the music on the nightclub dance floor. I was there with Lo and a gaggle of her friends, celebrating her last night of freedom.

Marriage doesn't mean freedom. I thought sourly. *Anything but. And that doesn't even change when the marriage is over.* I had the buzzing of my phone in the back pocket of my jeans to remind me of that.

I knew it was Justin without even checking. Our divorce had been made final only a few short weeks ago, and I'd hoped that would mean he'd give up, stop contacting me, stop either trying to win me back or berating me for being an ungrateful, back-stabbing bitch. For a few blessed weeks, everything had gone silent. But this morning someone had sent me a link to an online news article about Justin – about his Arts Foundation funding being withdrawn – and I knew, just knew, I wasn't going to be that lucky.

The reason for tonight's barrage of phone calls had its

seeds back last summer. I'd been seeing a therapist since I'd left Justin, but after an initial burst of progress, I felt as if I'd got stuck, circling round and round the same issues. She'd suggested a journal, a way to process what I was feeling and thinking. I'd gone out and bought myself a nice notebook for the purpose, but it still lay unmarked in the top drawer of my bedside table. For some reason, it felt more natural to say these things out loud than to write them down, so I'd picked up my phone and had begun to record, keeping the camera turned away from myself, not ready yet to see in my own eyes all I'd allowed Justin to do to me.

After a while, I'd begun to post short videos on social media, always keeping the camera trained on a bookcase or a pot plant, always using a filter to alter my voice. The anonymity had been freeing. And it turned out my posts resonated with other women too, many who didn't know – as I hadn't – that they were being emotionally abused. Hadn't I laughed when Lo had suggested it after my own hen night? I'd been so deluded. And if I could highlight some of the red flags, save just one woman from being sucked deeper in by a man like Justin, it was worth the discomfort of sharing what I'd been through.

But it turned out I hadn't been able to keep my identity *completely* hidden.

Just before Christmas, Justin's first ex-wife had found my account, put two and two together and slid into my DMs. For years I'd believed she was the evil witch who'd broken Justin's heart, made him who he was today, but when I met up with Paulina, I'd discovered he'd treated her exactly the same way he'd treated me. It had been cathartic to talk with her, to share stories and realise that I wasn't crazy or overdramatic. That had done more for me than months of journaling could have accomplished. I'd begun to feel as if I was at least *starting* to move on.

Unfortunately, instead of finding peace from digging through our shared experiences, Paulina had found rage – perfectly understandable, justifiable rage, in my opinion – but it had consequences. For both of us.

She'd sold her story to the papers and the article had gained more traction in the slow news period after Christmas than it might have done at another time of year. Then more women had added their voices, either in interviews or on social media – dancers who Justin had bullied in the rehearsal room, ex-girlfriends he'd terrified and controlled. The dance world's golden boy had begun to look a little tarnished, to say the least.

That's when the phone calls had started again. Never texts, never voicemails. Never anything I could save as concrete evidence – because it would always be my word against his as to what had been said, and he wasn't the one who'd had to see a therapist for emotional instability, for anxiety and 'spacing out', was he? And even if I changed my number, he always seemed to be able to find the new one, probably by charming someone in my wider family who didn't know what he was really like – I hadn't really wanted to share the details of our marriage with anyone but my immediate family. I was too ashamed.

I'd logged it all as my therapist advised me to and then had refused to answer any more of his calls. They'd doubled in frequency after that, and I'd started jumping every time my phone made a noise, even if I had it on silent. Then, two weeks ago, I'd seen his car parked in the road where my new studio flat was. And then again the next day. It had freaked me out. I knew what he was doing. *We might be divorced now,* I could hear him whispering smoothly in my ear, *but I'm in your life still. You'll never truly get rid of me.*

The only way I could think to counteract the gathering sense of panic and helplessness was to collect the evidence I'd been keeping on him ever since we'd separated and file an application for a non-molestation order. Justin had been served with notice of it yesterday, so he could prepare for the court hearing that would decide if it was granted or not.

Which would make it stupid of him to phone me once, of course, let alone twenty-four times. At least, it would have been stupid if he hadn't thought to get himself a burner phone. I'd been distracted getting ready for Lo's hen night when I'd picked up the first call, even though I was usually wary of numbers I didn't recognise. The screaming at the other end of the line had made my eardrums ache: how I'd better not 'tell tales' as all the other lying bitches had done. How he'd make me sorry if I did. My stomach had rolled as my shaky fingers had fought to end the call, to make him go away.

Because I had 'told tales' already, hadn't I? Only Justin didn't know I had. Not yet. But I was kidding myself if I didn't think that moment was just over the edge of the horizon. Every time I thought of what he might do if he found out, I felt sick.

A hand fell heavily on my shoulder and I almost jumped out of my skin. A moment later, I felt Lo's tequila-soaked breath on my neck. 'You okay, sis? You're looking a bit queasy.'

I stretched my lips into the widest smile I could manage. 'I'm fine – probably shouldn't have had that last cocktail.'

Lo pressed a wet kiss to my cheek and grabbed my hands to pull me into the circle of dancing women nearby. I played along, bumping hips with Lo, waving my arms in the air along with everyone else. Even though I'd turned my phone off before putting it back in my pocket, I could feel the heat of all the missed calls. I wouldn't tell her about it tonight. Maybe after she came back from honeymoon. She'd put her own life aside too much for me since I'd left Justin, letting me live with her and Isaac for a few months until I found a job and a place of my own. I wasn't about to ruin her hen night – or her wedding. She was so happy with Isaac, and I was so pleased for her, even though it had been hard to watch their relationship bloom as my marriage had deteriorated into something dark and toxic.

But playing the part of the upbeat maid of honour was exhausting. All I wanted to do was go home, crash into my bed and pretend this night had never existed. I managed to dance my way out of the centre of the circle, letting Lo's friend Annie take my place, and hovered on the fringes of the group, turning my phone back on so I could check the time. Surely it couldn't be too much longer until they all got tired and started making noises about ordering cabs?

What I saw on my phone screen stopped me in my tracks. I opened the picture message up without thinking, my fingers tapping on the screen before my brain could shout 'No!' at me.

It was a picture of me, slightly blurry, taken from a distance. In it, I was wearing the sparkly (and rather revealing) top Lo had lent me for this evening. My stomach turned to cold, hard stone. It had come from Justin's burner phone.

Where had this been taken? When? I forced myself to scour the background of the photo for more information and realised it had been taken outside the restaurant we'd had dinner at earlier on. He'd been there? Watching me?

I spun around, trying to see into the shadowy corners of the club, my heart clenching hard with each rapid beat. I couldn't see him, but that didn't mean he wasn't there.

*

Lo waved from the back seat of the cab as it pulled away, blowing me drunken kisses. I stood at the garden gate of a large Victorian house split into six small flats, smiling and waving. Once the car had disappeared around the corner, my arm fell heavy by my side and I turned and walked swiftly up the path, feeling all the while as if unseen eyes were watching me from the bushes. I wasn't going to feel safe until my flat door was bolted and triple-locked behind me.

Because Justin clearly wasn't done with me yet. Not by a long shot. Punishment for filing the injunction against him, I guessed.

Another picture message had arrived twenty minutes after the first, a snap of the entrance of the club we'd been in. I'd almost lost it at that point. I'd had to go to the ladies' and lock myself in a cubicle until I'd stopped hyperventilating. I hadn't stopped shaking since. It was just as well my sister was too squiffy to notice I was behaving oddly.

While the building my flat was in was old, it had a very modern entry system, and I held the electronic key fob in my hand as I walked down the path, and I'd just begun to lift my arm, ready to wave it against the sensor beside the hefty black front door, when there was a shift in the shadows of the porch. A figure stepped out of the darkness and blocked my way to safety. I froze.

'Ju-Justin,' I stammered, trying to sound calm and in control and failing completely. 'What . . . What are you doing there?'

'Waiting for you, Angel,' he said in that silky voice that made my skin crawl. 'Nice night out?'

My attempt at composure crumbled at that point. I tried to dodge past him, waving my key fob madly in the direction of the lock, and I caught the side of his face with the back of my hand. Almost instantly, his fingers closed around my wrist and he pulled both my hand and the key out of reach of the door.

'Don't you dare lay a finger on me,' he barked at me, any pretence of civility slipping quickly away. 'Not after what you did. It's all your fault!'

I held my breath. Did he know? Because it kind of *was* my fault. My videos had been the catalyst for everything that had happened since.

His fingers dug into the skin of my wrist, burning with friction. 'If you hadn't left me, things would be different. I'd have had someone by my side when Paulina made all those wild allegations, someone to tell the world it wasn't true. But instead of helping me, the way a wife is *supposed* to do, you left me to struggle with it all on my own, and then *this* . . . ' He pulled a crumpled wad of paper from his pocket. 'A non-molestation order? I never laid a hand on you, you know that! You've got to drop this, tell them it's all lies!' He threw the papers on the ground, and they lay in the flower bed, soaking up the beginnings of a hefty dew.

I knew I should tell him calmly that it wasn't lies, that he needed to let me go and leave, but my heart was pounding so hard I thought I was going to faint and I could feel a giant wave of terror hovering over me, threatening to obliterate me in its wake.

That's when the floaty feeling began. The sense that reality was too much, that I needed to slide through a secret door and protect myself from it.

No. I'm staying here this time. I'm staying in this moment. I'm not letting him have that power over me any more.

Of course, this kind of thing had been easy to recite in a therapy session, but it was a lot harder when Justin's fingers burned on my wrist, when his breath was sour and angry in my face.

He was still ranting, I realised, about his funding and how the company was probably going to close, but then he started on a subject that caused me to go still and invisible, to try and make him believe I wasn't standing right next to him.

'If I find out who that vicious bitch is, I'll make her life a living hell,' he was saying. 'I combed through Paulina's account for days, seeing what she liked and commented on, and it was this lying tart's videos that started her off . . . '

The sound began to blur again then. It was like watching the television with the volume down. I could see his mouth moving, even make sense of the words, but all I could hear was a violent rushing in my own ears. I knew it was just my imagination playing tricks on me, but his face began to seem like a mask, twisting into more and more grotesque shapes. It was all I could pay attention to, even though I knew I needed to do something, that this wasn't going to end well if I stood there like a rabbit frozen in the headlights.

But then the mask froze; his eyes became glassy, widening

in realisation. For a moment, we were suspended in time, and then his eyeballs swivelled and he looked at me, seemingly into my soul. 'It was you . . .' he whispered, too shocked in that second even to be angry.

It probably should have been an insult that he hadn't considered me capable of making those videos before, but I was too scared to be offended. I don't know how he'd worked it out but he had. Probably because he'd had this weird sixth sense when it came to me, as if I was made of glass and he could see straight inside me, no matter how hard I tried to hide what I was thinking and feeling. Probably what made me such an attractive target in the first place.

I had a millisecond of shocked stillness to act, and I made the most of it, wrenching my hand out of his grasp, just catching a glimpse of his expression as it changed from astonishment to something darker and much more murderous. I thought I'd seen the worst Justin had to offer – but I'd never seen him like this. He was right; he'd never laid a finger on me while we'd been married, but now every nerve and muscle in his body seemed primed to strike.

Somehow I put some distance between us, heard the beep of the lock as my fob waved over it, and I managed to slide inside and throw my weight against the door. Justin did the same from the other side and for a horrifying second I thought all was lost, but I'd started pushing first, and the momentum was enough to hear the lock click into place. I saw Justin's face through the glass as he shouted obscenities at me, and then I turned and ran, taking two stairs at a time as I fled for my first-floor flat.

I didn't stop at locking and triple-bolting the door, especially as I could still hear the enraged banging from downstairs.

I dropped my bag, kicked off my heels, and sprinted for my bathroom. Once inside, I locked the door then sat huddled, my knees pulled into my chest, against the bath. I squeezed my eyes shut and tried to block out the noise coming from the garden below.

I knew I needed to call the police, that I needed to get myself somewhere safe, but my phone was in my bag, sitting by the front door. Stupid, stupid, stupid . . . So I just sat there, shivering.

I don't know how much time passed. I heard other noises in the building. Voices shouting, both male and female. And then, eventually, everything went quiet.

Still, I didn't move.

Justin was clever. It was how he'd got away with what he had for so long. And he knew how to be patient. Just because it was quiet, it didn't mean he wasn't still there somewhere in the shadows, watching . . . waiting . . .

In that moment, I wished I *could* float outside myself again, that I could drift above the garden, waiting for the dawn, checking every bush and shadowy corner. I could make sure Justin really had gone away.

And then, somehow, I was doing it.

I was standing by the bathroom door, staring at the pathetic creature curled up against the bath, somehow outside and inside myself at once.

No. I know I said I wanted this, but I don't, I really don't. Not again. Not after all this time . . .

It's the only way to keep you safe. The thought travelled from the version of myself standing at the bathroom door to the other me sitting on the floor. *You know that, don't you?*

I wanted to argue. I wanted to tell her to stay, to fight Justin, not to run away yet again, but I couldn't. For a long time, I didn't say anything, but finally I nodded. 'Go . . . ' I whispered, and then I closed my eyes and let the blessed blackness envelop me.

CHAPTER SIXTY

Now.

LILI SAT ON the flapped-down toilet lid, shaking, her head in her hands. She'd come in here to have some time alone because Lo was hovering when she should be enjoying her wedding day, and neither of her parents wanted to let her out of their sight. Hardly surprising, given that she'd caused a bit of a scene when the wedding photos were being taken.

The last thing she remembered before that moment was huddling in her bathroom after the hen night, the echoes of Justin's pounding on the front door echoing through her head. She'd never been so terrified in her whole life – and after three years with Justin, that was saying something. It was as if she'd been teleported from the darkest moment she'd ever experienced right into the middle of her sister's wedding. Who *wouldn't* freak out if that happened to them?

Her dad had taken her aside and explained the memory loss to her, but she still couldn't get her head around it. She'd disappeared and ended up in *Scotland*? It just didn't sound real.

And being back at Hadsborough Castle wasn't helping. Why hadn't she told Lo it really *was* a big deal when Isaac had set his heart on this venue? Probably because, last summer, she'd been in denial, telling herself Justin was part of her past and not her future. If she'd been aware of how bad he was going to get, she'd never have brushed her misgivings under the carpet.

A soft knock on the cubicle door made her jump up as if she'd been electrocuted. 'Lil? Are you in there? Are you okay?'

Lili placed a palm against her thudding breastbone, swiped at her tear-stained cheeks and opened the door.

'Oh, sis . . . ' Lo said when she saw her and drew her into a hug. 'I am so, so glad that you remember us all again, but I know this must be really hard for you.' She pulled back to look at her. 'Do you want me to cut the reception short so we can take you to a doctor? We can have a big party another time. You know, like people do when they get married abroad.'

'No, please don't do that,' Lili said huskily. 'I've ruined enough of your wedding day as it is.'

'Okay, but once we've cut the cake and had the first dance, I'm asking Kerry to take you back to Mum and Dad's. To be honest, you'll be doing me a favour if you get her out of here. Do you remember that birthday party where she did the "Thriller" dance, zombie shuffled a bit too convincingly and fell over, taking out a whole table?'

Lili couldn't help smiling. She did remember that, and the fact she was able to made her want to cry again.

'And then tomorrow we'll take you back to the hospital, just to be sure.' Lo hugged her again. 'I know I've said this before, but I'm so sorry I didn't understand the full depth of how Justin treated you until it was too late, and I'm sorry that I allowed him to drive a wedge between us.'

Lili squeezed her back. 'It wasn't your fault. Isn't that what you tell me when I start beating myself up about being with him? We all know how good he was at manipulating people, and he fooled the lot of us.' Her dad had been livid when he'd found out the truth about the knight in shining armour who'd supposedly saved his daughter. And she reckoned her normally placid mum would still punch him in the face if she got the chance.

'I'm telling you now, sis, I've got your back – one hundred per cent. I'm going to make sure that nothing ever happens to make you lose yourself that way again.' Lo hugged her again then took her hand. 'Now, come on . . . Us against the world. The evening reception's about to start and I need my maid of honour by my side.'

*

It was just after seven o'clock when Ben arrived at Hadsborough Castle. He walked through the grounds to the Tithe Barn, his pulse trotting. He'd managed to buy a plain shirt and a pair of trousers, and he'd borrowed a tie from Marco, which he now realised was a mistake. For some reason, it just wouldn't sit right, no matter how he tied it.

It felt like he was going on a first date, and he was a jumble of nerves, even though he and Lili had been calling and texting as much as possible over the last twenty-four hours. It was strange, although he'd first known her by that name, he was struggling to stop thinking of her as Alice. He sighed. It would come.

He gave his name to an usher at the door, who nodded and

scurried away, then moved further into the function room. By the looks of things, he'd arrived at the barn just in time for the cutting of the cake. He scooted to the back of the crowd, scanning it for any sign of a wavy, blonde bob. When the bride and groom arrived at the podium to plunge a knife into the three-tiered wonder, he spotted a group of bridesmaids, all in floor-length green velvet, and – yes! – there she was, standing at the back, holding a half-full glass of champagne.

He kept his eyes on her, willing her to look his way, but her gaze was trained on her sister and new brother-in-law. When the bridal party scattered in different directions, Ben made a beeline for the maid of honour. 'Hi,' he said, smiling – well, *grinning* – at her. The moment he'd been waiting for, not just for forty-eight hours but for five-and-a-half years, had finally come.

She'd been talking to one of the other bridesmaids and she turned to look at him. 'Hi,' she said back, and she smiled too, but it seemed a watered-down version of the ones he'd seen on FaceTime earlier that day. Her reaction seemed a little . . . not wrong, just . . . not right, either.

But then her smile solidified into a frown. 'You . . . !' she said. 'You're Ben the Photographer!'

Yes, he was, although that seemed an odd way to say hello, but . . . whatever. He stepped forwards to kiss her cheek, but she backed away from him. 'What the hell do you think you're doing?'

Ben froze. 'Alice . . . What's wrong?'

She looked back at him in bemusement, then let out a short, hard laugh. 'You're incredible . . . Five and a half years, Ben!

Five and a half years of silence, and then you just turn up at my sister's wedding reception and behave like nothing happened.'

Ben wanted to remind her she'd been the one to invite him, but his brain didn't seem to be in a hurry to send the signal to his mouth.

'And to make matters worse, you couldn't even get my name right! My name's Lili, not *Alice*!' And then she threw the contents of her glass of champagne over him, which hit him square in the face and then dripped downwards onto Marco's tie.

What . . . ? How . . . ?

And then the penny dropped. Only, it wasn't as something as light and inconsequential as a coin; a whacking great boulder of ice crashed from his brain down to his gut and lay there, freezing his innards.

Lili's memories were back, and Alice's . . . ?

Well, they were gone.

CHAPTER SIXTY-ONE

Now.

BEN STOOD THERE, his face damp with champagne, and stared at the space where Alice . . . no, Lili had just been standing. He could do with a drink. Or, more accurately, *another* drink. One he wasn't actually wearing. Still dazed, he wandered to the bar and ordered himself a double Scotch, knocking it back in less time than it took to pour it.

What was he going to do now? It hurt his head to try to work out all the implications of what had just happened. Before he could even start, he felt a tap on his shoulder. He turned to find the usher he'd given his name to earlier standing there with the bride. For some reason, she didn't look very pleased to see him.

'Ben Robertson?'

'Yes.'

'Thanks, Tayo,' she said to the usher. 'I'll take it from here.' She stared at Ben for a moment. 'You look familiar . . . We haven't met before, have we?'

He shook his head. Lili had talked a lot about her sister when they'd been in London together, but he didn't even remember seeing a photo of her.

He was about to say as much when she added, 'I need to have a word with you. Outside.' And she hooked her hand in Ben's elbow and steered back through the double doors he'd only just come through and kept going until they were a short distance from the barn. 'Have you seen Lili yet?'

'Yes,' he replied, even though that solitary word did nothing to encompass the jaw-dropping experience of their last encounter.

Elodie swore. 'I was hoping to head you off before she saw you.'

'I said hello and she threw her drink over me.'

'She did?' Elodie's frown deepened. 'I knew she might be off-kilter because . . . but that doesn't seem very . . . I mean, I don't know why she would . . . '

There was a whole load more to this story than her sister knew, obviously. 'I'm guessing her memories came back,' he said flatly, thinking it wouldn't be a bad idea if they both filled each other in on what they knew.

'Yes,' Elodie replied, shoving her confusion to one side and picking up his thread. 'A couple of hours ago.'

'And her memories of the time she was away with me are . . . ?'

'Gone. Yes.'

Ben took a moment to absorb this, dully aware of something akin to a landslide happening inside. He'd known this was a possibility, of course. But now he realised he'd been too blinded by hope to really believe it would happen. It just seemed too cruel when he'd only just found her again.

'I was hoping to get to you first, warn you she might not recognise you, but I didn't realise she'd be so rattled by seeing you that she would . . . ' She drifted off, looking confused again, but then her expression became more determined. 'I suppose that makes what I'm going to say a bit easier.'

She sighed heavily, then carried on. 'Listen, my family are really grateful for everything you did for my sister, but I want to know if you're willing to do me a favour . . . Well, not for me really – for Lili.'

'Of course.' He'd do just about anything for her.

'I'm sure you're a really nice guy, and this will probably seem really unfair, but I'm asking because it's what she needs.' Her eyes became shiny, and her voice roughened. 'My sister was in so much mental turmoil last week that her brain just seemed to . . . I don't know . . . switch a part of itself off. And you are intimately connected to that experience. I'm worried that if she sees you, it might take her back to that dark place, that it might even trigger the same thing happening again. Do you understand?'

He nodded. He didn't like it, but he did.

'She doesn't remember being the person you spent the last week with. She has no idea who "Alice" is – or who you are – and I'm asking you to let it stay that way. I'm asking you to go back to wherever you've come from and not contact her again.'

Ben opened his mouth but Elodie got in first.

'She's been through so much over the last few years, even without this recent disappearing act. She needs some peace and stability in her life at the moment – and you can give that to her by doing this. *Please*, Ben?'

It was the desperation in her voice that got him. She was right – he could do this for Lili. Even though he didn't want to.

Even though it felt like giving up. But what else could he do? He wanted to make her happy but look at how she'd reacted when she'd seen him. Without the memories of the previous week, he would only ever be the loser who'd ghosted her all those years ago.

The bride looked at him, eyes full of hope. 'Do you think this is something you can do? For Lili?'

Ben stared back at her, so much like her sister. He could tell she loved Lili fiercely, and this was what Lili needed right now, wasn't it, to be with people who could love and protect her? It was what he'd promised he'd do for her. Whether he liked it or not, his job here was done.

He nodded, ignoring the crushing sensation in his chest. 'Yes. That's something I can do.'

*

The day had already been the strangest day of Lili's life and then *he'd* turned up. What was he doing here at Lo and Isaac's wedding? Didn't she have enough to deal with already?

And the way he'd rocked up, all smiles and sexy long legs, saying 'Hi' – as if they were old friends, as if he hadn't disappeared into the mist, never to be seen again. When he'd got her name wrong, she'd lost it.

She didn't know what she was more upset about, the fact she'd thrown her drink over him, creating yet *another* moment of drama, or that a tiny pathetic part of herself had leapt up and sung for joy when she'd seen him.

She strode out of the main function room and down the corridor that led to both the toilets and fire exit. The look on his face when she'd chucked her champagne all over him had been priceless. She'd laugh if she wasn't so stupidly close to tears.

She ducked into the safety of the ladies' once more – they were going to have to name one of these cubicles after her soon – but finding both the stalls occupied, she walked right back out again and followed the corridor to the fire exit. When she stepped outside, she found her cousin Kerry having a sneaky fag.

Kerry lifted an eyebrow and held out the pack. Lili shook her head, but joined her cousin in staring silently into the darkness. A short while later, Lo crashed through the fire exit looking more than a little ruffled. 'There you are! I was getting worried. I couldn't see you anywhere.'

Lili sighed. 'Just needed some fresh air.'

Lo scowled at Kerry, who shrugged, stubbed her cigarette out on the ground, then made herself scarce. When she was gone, Lo collapsed back against the wall. 'What a day . . . '

'Sorry,' Lili muttered, staring down at her dress.

'Don't you do that,' Lo said. 'None of this is your fault. Got it?'

'Okay.'

Lo smiled. 'You could sound more convincing, but that'll do for now.'

They stood there in silence for a few minutes, enjoying the cool air after the heat of the reception room. Somewhere in the distance, an owl hooted. 'Can I ask you something?' Lili said.

'Fire away.'

'How on earth did you end up inviting Ben the Photographer to your wedding?'

'Ben the *Bloody* Photographer,' Lo reminded her, resurrecting the name she'd given him in a show of sisterly solidarity. 'And I didn't invite him. I've never even met him. What are you talking about?'

'Well, somebody did. Because he was just here!'

Lo started to chuckle. 'That's impossible! There's no way I'd ever invite Ben the . . . ' she trailed off, looking both confused and concerned at the same time.

'Lo?' Lili asked, leaning forward to get a better look at her sister's face. 'You okay?'

Lo seemed frozen in space. 'Um . . . ' she said, looking most distressed.

And then Lili felt terrible for bringing it up at all. She'd already hijacked significant parts of her sister's big day. She did not need to make a mountain out of *that* molehill. That was done and dusted, more than five years in the past. There had to be a safer subject she could steer the conversation on to. 'You said you'd invited the guy who helped me get from Scotland back to London,' she began. 'Any sign of him yet?'

But, if anything, Lo's face grew even more pinched. She stared back at Lili, and then, very slowly, shook her head. 'He . . . He couldn't make it after all.'

'That's a pity. I wanted to thank him. There's no telling where I'd have ended up without his help.'

Lo seemed to recover herself, pushing away from the wall and pulling open the fire door that hadn't quite properly slammed shut behind Kerry. 'Maybe it's for the best,' she said, as she stepped across the threshold and beckoned Lili to follow her. 'You've got a great new future to look forward to. Let's leave the past in the past.'

PART IV

One Month Later

CHAPTER SIXTY-TWO

Now.

BEN FOUND HIS aunt sitting in Fernpoint's garden, taking a break with a large cup of coffee and enjoying the March sun, as she sat on a bench and watched Willow desperately attempting to turn a skipping rope more than twice before she tripped herself up and landed flat on the grass. It didn't stop her trying, though.

He showed Norina a large A4 envelope. 'Those papers I've been waiting on arrived.'

'You're really going to do it?' She lowered her voice so Willow couldn't hear. 'You're going to notify the council you'd like to adopt her?'

Ben nodded. When he'd got back from England, close to a month ago, he'd resumed his search for the man named on Willow's birth certificate. A stroke of luck in finding one of Cat's friends had given him the lead he needed and he'd gone down to Glasgow to meet the guy. He hadn't been interested, had told Ben in no uncertain terms he wanted nothing to do with the kid, that he wasn't even sure it was his and had seemed quite relieved when Ben had asked if he'd consider giving up his parental rights. Even though Ben's heart had broken once again for Willow, he was pleased the matter was going to be settled once and for all.

Willow spotted him, dropped her skipping rope and ran towards him. 'Uncle Ben! Are we going on our fairy walk now? You promised!'

'That we are. Go and get your coat.'

Ben walked behind his niece when they reached the castle grounds, keeping an eye on her as she ran along the wide path, over the bridge and into the woodland beyond. There was a strange feeling of lightness in his chest, despite the disappointments of recent weeks. Part of it was that he was excited to begin the adventure of watching Willow grow up, of being the best father he could be to her, but there was something else . . .

'Look!' Willow called, running into a small clearing in the woodland. 'Can you see it? Can you? I think it's a fairy, I really do!'

Ben looked to where she was pointing. He could see something glinting high up in the breeze, the sun catching it from behind, and it twirled and floated up between the trees. If it were later in the year, he'd have said it was a dandelion head lit up by the long rays of the afternoon sun, but it couldn't be that, and a wisp of sheep's wool caught in the wind would probably be too heavy to float that high. 'I think you might be right, Willow. I really do.'

She ran over and jumped into his arms, squeezed him tight and said in a breathless voice, 'Oh, Uncle Ben! I'm so happy I could burst!'

He hugged her back, revelling in the feel of her warm little body against his. 'Willow?'

She looked up at him, eyes bright and trusting.

'How would you feel about calling me "Daddy"?'

Her little eyebrows shot up. 'Really?'

'Yes, really.'

She let out a squeal so piercing he was sure his eardrums must be bleeding. 'I got a fairy *and* a daddy in the same day? Just wait until I tell Auntie Nee-nee!' And then she ran off in the direction of the exit, all thoughts of further fairy hunting forgotten.

Ben walked behind her, calling out now and again to make sure she didn't get too far ahead, and as he walked he took in the weathered peaks of the mountains, the dense green of the pine trees. He could see the grey stone and slate of the majestic castle turrets rising before him and smell a hint of salt on the air as it blew in from the loch, and he realised what else was making him feel light inside: for the first time in his life, maybe, he was happy to be home.

CHAPTER SIXTY-THREE

Now.

'YOU WERE AMAZING in there!'

Lili turned to see her sister striding down the courthouse corridor towards her and gave Lo a weak smile. They should have attended a hearing regarding her application for the non-molestation order against Justin while she'd been missing, but her solicitor had managed to explain her unexpected absence and reschedule. Today had been the day.

'I mean, you were calm, clear . . . *very* convincing.' Lo wrapped her arms around Lili and squeezed tight.

'I didn't feel very calm and clear,' she mumbled against her sister's shoulder.

'But the judge granted the order. She believed you. Justin can't come near you again, or he'll be arrested.'

Some of the tension Lili had been feeling all day ebbed away. It was wonderful to hear someone say those words out loud. 'It's just the beginning, though,' she said. 'I've decided I'm going to join some of the other women who've come forward and press charges. For the stalking and harassment since we separated for sure. The coercive control while we were married . . . ? Well, even though the laws have changed, it might not fly.'

'It doesn't matter,' Lo said, releasing her. 'I'm proud of you for even trying. It's like I've come back from honeymoon to find a whole new you!'

They began to walk towards the exit. 'I think the intensive therapy has been helping, but . . . I don't know . . . it's not just that. I know I can't remember anything from the time I was missing, and I have no idea what I did, but I feel different. It feels like something has shaken free, Lo. It's as if part of me remembers it even if I don't.'

Lo gave her a strange look. 'I know it's early, but I think you deserve a cocktail – my treat!'

'Where on earth are we going to get a cocktail down Bromley High Street on a Thursday afternoon?'

But Lo being Lo, they found somewhere, a hip little bar tucked away down a side street that did food as well. When they'd worked their way through one espresso martini each and most of a plate of nachos, Lo said. 'Are you serious about wanting to know what happened while you were away?'

Lili scooped up the last remaining bit of guacamole with the corner of a tortilla chip. 'Of course. It's most unsettling to feel as if there's a great black hole in my brain where some of my memories should be. Every day I wake up and I get this vague sense that something's missing, like my brain is trying to tell me there's something important I need to know, and I wonder if those missing days are the key.'

Lo nodded seriously, and then she reached into her handbag and produced an old iPhone. 'This was found in the ladies' toilet at the wedding venue. They sent it on. It arrived while I was away.'

Lili glanced at the phone. 'So?'

'It's yours.'

Lili laughed nervously. 'No, it isn't. I just got a new one, actually, to replace the one I lost on the way to Scotland.'

'It's definitely yours,' Lo said, holding it out. 'I saw you with it when you came back. Someone gave it to you to use when you were missing.'

Lili took the phone from her sister. 'But you've been back from honeymoon for almost two weeks. Why didn't you say anything sooner?'

'To be honest, I wasn't sure if I should give it to you. I was tempted just to hide it and never say anything. I've been in full-on Mamma Bear mode since we found you again, if you hadn't noticed.'

Lili gave her sister's arm a rub and chuckled. Yes, she had noticed, but this was why she loved Lo.

'Anyway,' Lo continued, looking down into her lap, 'when your memories came back, I made a decision that I'm now second-guessing. I wonder if maybe I was being overprotective, even a bit controlling – and that's the *last* thing you need after Justin. And then I saw how strong you were today and I realised I wasn't giving you enough credit.'

'Wh-what's on it?' Now her wish had been granted, she realised she was nervous and curious in equal parts.

'Everything. You did a really comprehensive job of documenting it all. Open the camera roll and go back a bit.'

Lili did what she was told, scrolling back to images dating from just after she'd disappeared. There were a few pictures of pine-clad mountains and then one of a little girl with pigtails and an irresistible gap-toothed grin. 'Who's this?'

Lo shrugged. 'Absolutely no idea.'

There was a video of the same little girl, spinning around in a grassy clearing, and then a picture of a road sign: *Welcome to Invergarrig.* Lili frowned. That name was familiar for some reason. 'This is where I ended up?'

Her parents had told her she'd turned up in a small Scottish town, but hadn't mentioned which one. Maybe they hadn't known the name. In fact, now she thought about it, they'd been quite tight-lipped about details of her disappearance, saying she hadn't had much time to fill them in before her memories had come flooding back and she'd forgotten everything herself.

Lili continued flipping through the images. There were stations and departures boards, but then she came to a video taken on board a train, a guy with wavy dark hair who used his hands a lot while he explained the route they'd taken. Lili stared at it, even more confused than when she'd started watching.

Her mum had mentioned there'd been a man who'd helped her get home, but Lili had assumed the guy had merely assisted with looking up train times and routes. She'd also assumed the guy was a stranger.

But this was Ben Robertson, the guy she'd met in London who'd then ghosted her. Yet here he was in the flesh, not just helping her find the right platform but travelling with her, making sure she was safe. And the way he looked at her when she was behind the camera . . .

Lo took a sip of her cocktail and then answered the question Lili hadn't yet asked. 'Yes . . . He was the one who travelled five hundred miles with you. It was Ben the Bloody Photographer.'

'I don't understand . . . Oh! Invergarrig. That's where Ben

said he came from. Did I . . . Do you think I went there to find him?'

Lo gave her a look that said, *the hell if I know.*

'Oh, my god! That's why he was at the wedding! You invited him to say thank you! But . . . ' Lili's eyes narrowed. 'But why didn't you tell me? When I asked you where the guy was, you said he couldn't make it.'

Lo looked down at the table. 'Well, I lied about that – at first because I thought it was better you didn't get confused by seeing someone you'd met while your memory had been messed up, and later because I realised Ben-who-helped-you-get-home and Ben-who-you-met-five-years-ago were one and the same person.' She met Lili's gaze. 'He hurt you so much last time you got tangled up with him. I thought maybe it was better to let things be.'

Lili stared at the phone again, not quite able to process all this new information. 'If this is true, why hasn't he got in touch since I've been home? Had he ghosted me – *again*?'

'Ah, well . . . That might be my fault.'

Lili raised her eyebrows and waited for her sister to continue.

'You've got to understand, Lil. It was very confusing for you when you got your memories back. None of us had any idea how to handle it, and the doctors had suggested you not get too stressed. I was worried you might slip away, forget you were Lili and become this "Alice" person again. Maybe forever. Then we'd never get you back. So I . . . '

'Lo? What did you do?'

Lo sighed, looking pained. 'I told him to go home and leave you alone, that he'd only be making things worse for you if

412

he kept in contact. I thought it was for the best. I'm so sorry. But now I see how well you're doing, I realise that maybe it wasn't my choice to make whether he was still in your life.'

Lili wanted to be angry but she saw the guilt and remorse in Lo's eyes and couldn't stoke that fire. Lo had been stressed beyond belief when she'd gone missing. That had to have been bad enough on its own, but it had also been the week running up to her wedding. No wonder she'd got a bit overemotional. She could even imagine herself doing the same for Lo if their situations were reversed.

'Why did he travel with me? And why did he disappear all those years ago?'

Lo nodded to the phone in Lili's hand. 'Everything you want or need to know is in there, in those photos and videos.'

CHAPTER SIXTY-FOUR

Now.

LILI DIDN'T LOOK through the strange iPhone Lo had given her straight away. It was all too weird to think about. This was concrete evidence of her brain's complete malfunction, wasn't it? Images of places she'd never been to and people she'd never met. Except . . . she had.

She went to bed having stowed the phone in one of her kitchen drawers, but at two-thirty in the morning, unable to stop tossing and turning, she got up again, grabbing a soft, warm cardigan to throw over the top of her pyjamas. After putting the kettle on for a cup of tea, she pulled the unfamiliar phone out of the drawer and went and sat down on her sofa. Taking a deep breath, she opened up the camera roll.

First, she watched the most recent videos, ones of herself sitting in a hospital room explaining everything that had gone on both in that missing week, and why Ben had never got in contact all those years ago. Once she'd watched those, she went back to the beginning again, taking a bit more time over each photograph, even if it was a blurry departures board or a station platform.

When she reached the train video, the one she'd watched

with Lo in the bar with Ben introducing himself, her insides fluttered exactly the same way they had when she'd met him in London. If only she'd known about his lost phone back then . . . She could have turned up at the garden the next summer as planned. Or even if she'd just given him the benefit of the doubt instead of assuming the worst. They could have been together all this time. Maybe.

She shook her head, silently admonishing herself. There was no point in going down that route. What had happened, had happened. And then Justin had swooped into her life. By the twelfth of July the following year she'd been living with him. Besides, you couldn't second-guess your own life, only deal with the choices you'd made. There were no do-overs.

And Justin was the choice she'd made. Yes, he'd brainwashed her, manipulated her, gaslighted her, but she'd chosen to ignore the red flags so many times, wanting to believe him when he said he'd change, that he'd try harder. She'd even chosen to go back – three times! – even when he'd been appalling to her. Looking back now, she could see it was a miracle she'd left at all.

To distract herself from those thoughts, she went back to the phone. After the train video were images of a generic-looking hotel, the outside of Penrith station, where there was also another video – her, this time, being a bit goofy and messing her words up.

Lili watched herself with wonder. In this video, she looked younger . . . No, that wasn't it. It was that this version of herself didn't look weighed down. She looked light and free. Happy. And even though she did a *terrible* job of summarising the travel situation, this woman wasn't petrified she'd make a mistake, or that if she did, she'd be punished for it.

There followed some beautiful photos of a ruined castle in the snow. The next video she came to was of a snowball fight between herself and Ben. They were laughing and chucking lumps of snow at each other. It made her smile to watch it at first, but then she hiccupped a sob and tears began to flow.

Who was this woman who knew how to find joy in life?

There were two more videos after the snowball fight, the first, a sweeping shot of the scenery. She almost deleted the second one without looking at it, because the thumbnail showed a rather unflattering view of the underside of her chin, but when she pressed play she heard Ben talking, so she laid it down on the coffee table and listened.

What ensued was a ten-minute conversation. The visuals were terrible – it was obvious she'd hit the record button by accident after taking the previous video – but the conversation was gripping.

He was talking about why he'd given up photography, how he'd come back home to look after his niece . . . and then the whole story came out. His sister's death. His guilt. It was heart-wrenching. Lili wanted to climb inside the phone and give him a hug.

And it was clear the Lili who'd been there at the time had felt the same way, because the scene went dark and the words become muffled. Lili guessed she'd slipped the phone into her pocket. His voice became louder, even though his was talking more softly, giving her the sense that the two of them had got closer. A lot closer.

'Don't . . . ' she heard herself say, and there was so much tenderness, so much intimacy in that single word.

And then there was silence for a few moments, and his voice come out, hushed and ragged, 'This is a bad idea.'

Lili's stomach swooped. She had a gut feeling of what was going on, but it almost felt too intimate to be listening in, as if she was snooping on someone else.

'I know . . . but can we just . . . you know, stay like this for a moment?' And then there was only breathing, soft and shallow, until the video ended.

Lili closed her eyes. Oh, she didn't know if it had been a good idea to watch these. It felt as if she were seeing herself in a parallel life, but one she would never be able to find her way back to, one she would never be able to inhabit. Even so, she couldn't stop scrolling through, exploring that forbidden landscape.

There were coaches, two girls and a guy with a car she didn't recognise, a motorway service station. A cluster of pictures of musical instruments in what looked like someone's study, but might have been inside the same hotel featured a few shots earlier. And then she came to another video.

It was the sound that grabbed her, right from the first split-second she heard it – music. But not just any music, a lone violin, and she recognised it . . . Lili covered her mouth with one hand, her body juddering with silent sobs.

It was her!

She was playing the violin! In the bandstand in Kensington Gardens, literally just a few hundred metres away from Justin's flat. And she was playing with as much love and joy as she had done before she'd ever set foot in that blasted music school. The sound made her insides soar but also tore her to shreds with each pull of the bow.

How had she done that? She'd never played again after he'd dropped Octavia off the balcony of his flat, even though he'd paid to have her repaired and restored.

Every time she'd looked at the violin after that, she'd only been able to think of the way he'd looked at her that night. The stranger, she'd called him. A visitor who'd appeared more and more often after they'd tied the knot, even on their honeymoon. But it still took her years to work out he wasn't a stranger at all, that it was the *real* Justin. It was the one who charmed and love bombed and made everyone adore him who was the decoy.

In the very last seconds of the very last video, the other her – Alice, as Lo had told her she'd named herself – looked Lili in the eye, very seriously, and spoke to her future self. 'I've got one last thing to say before I finish this video diary and begin to rebuild my life, and it's this . . . Don't walk away from him again. Don't forget Ben.' Her face crumpled with emotion, then she took a breath and carried on. 'He's the sweetest, kindest, most loyal man you will ever meet. You messed up once not trusting him. Don't make the same mistake again.'

Lili sat there, stunned, her heart aching. When she thought about the man in the videos, she didn't doubt what she'd told herself one bit. But that was only half the equation wasn't it? Ben might be Ben, and he might be all the wonderful things she'd said he was, but she wasn't Alice. She wasn't the woman he'd spent the last week with. She wasn't even sure she was a shadow of that person.

After sitting there thoughtfully, the mug of tea going cold in her hands, Lili put it down, stood up and went into her bedroom, where she pulled some things from the bottom of the wardrobe until a hard, shiny case was revealed.

Octavia. Or as much of Octavia which had been able to be salvaged and rebuilt, which wasn't much. She placed it on the bed and then, with shaking fingers, opened the catches and let the lid fall back onto the duvet. She almost closed it back up again, but then she heard the strains of music in her head, the music she'd heard on the video of her busking in Kensington Gardens.

It was quarter to four, so she picked up the violin and headed for her tiny bathroom in the centre of the flat, the only room without a window and probably the most soundproof. Once the door was firmly closed behind her, she drew a breath, not allowing herself to think too hard about what she was about to do, closed her eyes, and lifted the violin to her chin.

The first note was shaky. As was the second. But it was bearable. It was *doable*.

Faster and faster her bow arm began to move, falling into familiar patterns and rhythms, and then her whole body began to join in, swaying and dipping as she gave herself over to the sound. The notes hit the tiled surfaces and bounced back, reverberating through her, until all that was left was her and Octavia and the music they were creating together, filling every atom of her body and soul.

CHAPTER SIXTY-FIVE

Now.

BEN STOOD AT the back of Invergarrig's one and only art gallery, a softly fizzing glass of champagne in his hand. Only last year this space had been yet another of the town's gift shops, stuffed to the rafters with tartan, shortbread, and 'Nessie' soft toys, but now it housed paintings, pottery and various crafts by artists from all over western Scotland. And tonight was the first night of an exhibition by a local photographer – him.

Both Norina and Alice . . . Lili . . . had talked to him about not turning his back on something he loved, and he'd taken it to heart. He'd thought it was travel that brought him alive, the rush of the adventure, but now he realised it wasn't the trains and buses and hotels that had brought him excitement. Doing it with Lili had been the adventure, doing it with someone he cared about.

All he'd ever really been doing all those years he'd skipped around the globe was running away. Cat had accused him of that and she'd been right all along. He'd let his father drive him from his home, and guilt about Cat had kept him running. But Lili had shown him what it was like to be brave, to run towards one's life, even if you weren't sure what the future held. And so he'd dug his camera out of the bottom of his wardrobe and had started taking pictures of his hometown, of the surrounding mountains and glens.

The best of his efforts, both recent and over his years of travel, were now proudly displayed on the bare white walls of the gallery. In pride of place was a large print of a young woman in a ruined church. Ben walked towards it, his heart heavy. He'd dithered about including the photo of Lili in the exhibition, but it had been one of his best. He'd avoided looking at it properly while they'd been setting up, but now he made himself stand right in front of it and study every play of the light, every shape and angle.

It transported him back to the moment it was taken. His memories of that day were so vivid that he could almost feel the humid July air on his skin, hear the soft trickle of the fountain nearby. And Lili . . . It was almost as if he could feel her in the room with him.

'Nice photo,' someone said behind him. A woman's voice.

Ben stopped breathing.

He turned and found the subject of the photo standing no more than a couple of feet from him. 'You're . . . You're here.'

She laughed and nodded again. 'Yes, I am.'

'And you remember me?'

'I remember meeting you in London, spending a wonderful time together before we said goodbye, but those are the last and only memories I have of you.' She stared at him for a moment, eyes full of regret. 'Sorry, Ben. I don't remember travelling from here to London and beyond. That's all still lost.'

'But . . . What . . . ? How . . . ?'

'Why am I here?' she finished for him, then looked around. 'It's quite crowded in here. Is there somewhere else we can talk? You look like you could do with some fresh air.'

He nodded and led her through the crowd to the back of the gallery and stepped into the passageway, but it was dingy and damp there, so he kept going towards the loch, to the railings outside his cottages. Not many people used this as a shortcut.

'The first reason I'm here is that I needed to see you to say thank you for everything you did to get me home again. I . . . became aware . . . that you were having this exhibition, that you'd be here on opening night, and I thought it was the perfect opportunity.'

He could still hardly believe she was standing there. 'You didn't have to come five hundred miles to say thank you. You could have done it over the phone.'

'I know.' She smiled that smile at him again, the one that made him think of loosely packed snowballs, ruined castles, their two foreheads pressing together as they sheltered from falling flakes of ice. 'But I wanted to do more than that. I wanted to see if you'd like to go out to dinner with me . . . Or stay in. I didn't know it last time I saw you, but I'm a shockingly good cook.' She raised her eyebrows, waiting for his answer.

All her words were making sense to him – he could understand them on a linguistic level – but at the same time, he had absolutely no idea what was going on. 'You want to go on a date with me?'

Her head bobbed up and down and she started to look a little less confident. 'Yes . . . If you want to?'

The rush of emotion he felt almost propelled him towards her, but he held back. 'I do. More than anything. But what is this – just a dinner and then goodbye again?' As tempting as it was, he wasn't sure he could handle that.

'I have no idea.'

'But you live in London,' he said. 'And I live here. How on earth is this going to work?'

She shrugged and looked helplessly at him, then let out a soft laugh. 'To be honest, Ben. I have no idea what I'm doing here. I have absolutely no idea how all of this can work. But I do know one thing . . . ' She stepped closer and took hold of one of his hands. 'I don't want to be the pathetic, timid creature I was before I came here last time. I don't want to be hiding, too scared to live in case I make another mistake. I want to be the version of myself I saw in those videos when I was with you. Do you think we could get to know each other? Again?'

He brought his other hand to wrap around hers, as he looked down at her, held it tightly. 'I can't think of anything I want more.'

And then she rose onto her tiptoes, and pressed her lips against his, just the way she had before they'd been separated at the castle. His arms came around her and he drew her close, deepening the kiss the way he'd wanted to but had never had the chance. This time there was nothing to stop them. No phantom groom, no burly security guard.

It was only when they broke apart again he spotted two spectators at his bedroom window. Norina smiled and Willow was making him fervent 'thumbs up' signs, which only made him snort, and then Lili turned around and spotted them as well.

'Sorry,' she said, looking a little guilty. 'I needed help with travel and a place to stay, so I might have roped them in and sworn them to secrecy.' She blew Willow a kiss, which Willow caught and slapped onto her own cheek before pretending to faint, which only made them both laugh again. Giving him a wink, Norina closed the blind and their audience was gone.

She reached for the delicate silver chain around her neck and pulled her bee pendant free from under the neck of her chunky-knit jumper. 'This has been my lucky charm for years, even when I didn't realise it was.' She gave him a lop-sided smile. 'I mean, I know we're about five hundred miles away from where we'd originally planned to meet, and well over five years late, but I suppose you could say it worked.'

'I suppose you could.'

She sighed. 'I wish I could remember the time I spent here and travelling with you. It bugs me that I can't. I mean, I've seen the pictures, watched the videos, but it's not the same.'

'No,' he said, brushing the hair from her face and taking in every last detail, imprinting this moment on his own memory so firmly it would never be lost. 'But maybe it doesn't matter, because we can make new ones. Together.'

ACKNOWLEDGEMENTS

First and foremost, I would like to thank my family for their support in my career, unpredictable and wonderful as it is – especially my aunt Norina. She was always one of my biggest cheerleaders and as I started to pull the ideas for *Never Forget You* together, I knew I wanted to set it in a fictional version of her home – Inveraray – and when I needed to flesh out Ben's family, I thought I'd give him an aunt who ran a Bed and Breakfast, just as mine did. At this point, I decided to ask my one-of-a-kind aunt if I could base a character on her, because I thought she'd get a kick out of it. However, we were never able to have that conversation, as she fell ill and passed away shortly afterwards. After a lot of thought, I went forward with naming my character 'Norina' in her memory. Ben's aunt in the book is not completely the same as my cheerful, resourceful, no-nonsense aunt, but certainly shares a lot of her qualities and quirks. I hope *my* Norina would think of it as a fun and fitting legacy.

I would also like to thank the people who helped me dig in and do some of the mountain of research needed to write this book – any mistakes are mine and certainly not down to the wisdom and knowledge of those I interviewed!

Many thanks to Vincent Greene, who chatted at length with me of his experiences of being a professional violinist and experiences of music college. I am also very grateful to Nick Heinimann, travel photographer extraordinaire, for talking to me extensively about his career. Check out @roamwithnick on Instagram if you'd like to see some of the shots that inspired Ben's portfolio of work in the book. I would also like to thank Mid Argyll police, especially Community Sergeant Iain MacNicol, for answering my queries about how a missing persons investigation might be handled in their area, and for the very lovely Dr Carol Cooper for filling in the gaps of how a community hospital might handle a very unusual case of amnesia!

As always, I give massive thanks (along with cheering and much flag waving) to the amazing team of people around me who help me take my idea and bring it both to life and onto the bookshop shelves. To Amanda Preston, my agent, for your unfaltering positivity and enthusiasm, and your wisdom and experience. To the team at HQ, who are passionate and knowledgeable, I am so very pleased to be one of your authors. To my editors for this book, Katie Seaman and Emily Kitchin, thank you for helping me take my fledgling idea and polishing and shaping it into something so much more than I ever thought it could be. I am also in awe of the brilliance of the HQ marketing and PR teams, especially Joe Thomas. Thank you so much for all you do to get my books out into the world and into the hands of readers who will love them.

Last but definitely not least, I'd like to thank the friends who've been my support system as I wrote this book in a very trying time, both globally and personally. Thank you to my fellow authors who understand the ups and downs of this life like no one else – Susan Wilson, Heidi Rice, Daisy Cummins, Iona Grey and Sheila McClure. I needed the laughs, pep talks and hugs (virtual and actual) you gave more than you realise. I'd also like to thank Phil and Caroline Allen for being such a wonderfully warm, wise and grounding presence in my life in the last year, refreshing the spiritual side of me when I felt that well was dry and reminding me why I do all of this in the first place. Which leads me to my final thank you – to the One who gives me strength, love and inspiration, day to day. I know I could not do this without You.

Reading group questions

1) Lili's attempts to grapple with her amnesia and recover her memories form the crux of the novel. How important do you think memories are in identity formation? What do you think your own core memories are, and how do you think you would react in Lili's situation?

2) How do you think the novel's structure, and its switches between past and present, impacted your reading experience? Why do you think the author chose to divide the chapters in this way?

3) Justin's behaviour towards Lili slowly escalates in severity over the course of the novel. How did you respond to Justin as a character? Did you notice any early red flags?

4) Ben and Lili don't manage to reunite at the church due to bad luck. How key a role do you think that luck and circumstance played in the novel? Do you believe in coincidence?

5) Music is an important part of Lili's identity, as is photography for Ben's. Do you have a passion in your life? How would you feel if you could no longer access it?

6) The smashing of Octavia is a key turning point in Justin and Lili's relationship. To what extent do you think Octavia functioned as another character in the novel? Why do you think the author chose to name the violin?

7) 'The high of heading off to new places, only half a plan in his head, had kicked in.' Travel is a major theme in the novel. Have you been traveling? If so, how did your experiences shape you? If not, would you one day like to?

8) How did you respond to the author's portrayal of Ben's grief? How important to his grieving process do you think his decision to adopt Willow is?

9) Lili has a variety of different names and nicknames, bestowed upon her by various characters throughout the novel. Do you have any nicknames? How do these shape your relationships with the people who use them?

10) Ben encourages Lili to keep a travel diary, to document her adventures as Alice. Do you keep a diary? How important do you think it is to keep a record of your life, and how has technology enabled us to do this?

11) Justin is older, and significantly wealthier, than Lili. Do you think Lili would have been more immune to Justin's charms had she been from a more middle-class background herself?

12) 'In that moment, Charlie Banister was right there, watching me, taunting me.' Lili's initial confidence at music school is crushed by bullying. Discuss the wider impact bullying can have on a person's life. Do you think it is taken seriously as a problem in society?

If you have been affected by these issues, help and support is available from the below services across the UK. If you are in need of immediate assistance, please contact the emergency services.

- **Refuge** (England): https://www.refuge.org.uk/
- **The Domestic and Sexual Abuse Helpline** (Northern Ireland): https://dsahelpline.org/about-us
- **Domestic Abuse and Forced Marriage Helpline** (Scotland): https://www.sdafmh.org.uk/en/
- **Live Fear Free** (Wales): https://gov.wales/live-fear-free
- **Men's Advice Line** (UK-wide): https://mensadviceline.org.uk/about-us/

For countries outside the UK, an international directory of sexual and domestic violence agencies is available here: https://www.hotpeachpages.net/index.html

Loved *Never Forget You*? Don't miss another emotional and heart-warming romance from Fiona Lucas, available now

Anna's world was shattered three years ago when her husband Spencer was killed in a tragic accident. Her friends and family think it's time she moved on, but how can she when she's lost her soulmate?

On New Year's Eve, Anna calls Spencer's old phone just to hear his voicemail greeting. But to her surprise someone picks up. Brody answers and is the first person who truly understands what Anna is going through. As they begin to speak regularly, Anna finds herself opening up and slowly she discovers how to smile again, how to laugh, even how to hope.

But Brody hasn't been entirely honest with Anna. Will his secret threaten everything, just as it seems she might find the courage to love again?

ONE PLACE. MANY STORIES

Bold, innovative and
empowering publishing.

FOLLOW US ON:

@HQStories